PRAISE FOR DAWN

"Fantasy with a sci-fi bent. The author has created a uniquely original world, full of intrigue and terrors that rival *GOT*."

— Reader Review

"A delightful surprise … hooked me in straight away."

— Reader Review

"Reminded me of *Game of Thrones* except that it also included witchcraft elements. Having recently developed an interest in all things Wicca and witchcraft related, this was a delightful surprise. I have rarely stumbled upon books that contain divination tools etc. as an important part of the story so it hooked me in straight away. The author has created a completely new fantasy world unlike any other."

— Celine's Book Corner

DAWN

MORGAN SYLVIA

PRELUDE

Lightfest; a day of celebration that led to a night of abandon. The people of Aris greeted the sacred day in masks of feather and bone or clay, and laughed and clapped and cheered as they watched the athletic games and pole dancers. They met the night with music and feasts, with wine and laughter and camaraderie. Great bonfires blazed in forest and city, in field and courtyard, on the sandy shores of the Oburion and on the banks of the great Gherot River. Drums called a sylvan, primal heartbeat into the air and into their flesh, and dancers spun and swayed. The year's first faire sprang up overnight outside the city walls, dotting the landscape with brightly colored tents and wagons that unfolded into makeshift stages. Buskers, fire dancers, and vendors wandered the crowds, competing for both coin and attention. In pallid moonlight, Reonih bards sang their magics to the flames and to the moons, as the gates to the Otherworld opened and the Zhur veered close. In the sacred grove, the sages slit the throats of a white hart and drank its blood beneath three full moons. They threw some of the Elders' artifacts onto the fires along with the sacred herbs when they roasted the beast. And the people of Aris, masked, faces painted, flowers in their hair, cups and horns in hand, listened as the Reonih bards sang of fallen gods and the world they had fled generations ago, and the need to make this world theirs. As the drums and lyres reminded them of who they used to be, they looked up at the sky, which was lost to them now, and reminded themselves that they were alive, if only for a short time. Alive, vital, and human. They danced as though there were no tomorrow. They drank as though there were no yesterdays, for on Lightfest, there were no rules. Aris was a strict society every other day; only on Lightfest, when all its citizens—srih and peasant, merchant and fisherman, farmer and crafter, Reonih and Selin—celebrated as one, did it truly know release.

As the night grew long, the young slipped into the shadows, masked and anonymous, and fell into tangles of limbs. The drumbeats slowed as the fires burned low and the crowds thinned out. Eventually the revelers went home, or passed out in fields or in parks, or, in some cases, on the beaches. In the small hours, out in the wood, out in the night, there was only silence, and the occasional trailing sound of a distant drum or lyre. The forest creatures stilled, as though the night belonged to the gods. The last distant strains of music fell from the sky and the forest stilled until it lay silent. Too silent.

Death rode the winds.

The bard felt its presence in the night as keenly as he felt the manacles that bound him to the ancient stone altar. Far above, the moons seemed to brighten, painting the forest with tints of richer color. Only Octavian, the moon of war, was full, and shone a dark dull red against a spattering of brighter stars. He noted the irony of the situation: that he, who had been sworn to peace, would die beneath the warriors' moon.

He scanned the night-blackened sky above him, watching and waiting. Soon enough, he found what he sought. A winged shadow crossed the second moon, a silhouette too large to be a bird, bat, or erlit. His heartbeat quickened, and he felt the blood rushing through his head. His tongue was thick and sluggish with thirst, his throat scratchy and sore, and his stomach twisted with nausea. His aching muscles cramped into agonizing spasms, protesting the forced immobility. They had offered him a draught, to soothe the pain and fear. He had refused it. Knowing it was the last thing he would feel, he wanted to experience all of it: every emotion, every sight, every sight and sound, every sensation. Even the pain.

Again, the shadow danced against the moonlight. It crossed the third moon this time, red Octavian, moon of war. The tiny portion of his mind that was still rational noted the irony of that; the rest of his thoughts focused keenly on his imminent death. Time played games with him, seeming to speed up and slow down at once. Goosebumps shivered over his flesh.

A flock of birds took to wing, perhaps sensing that a larger predator hunted the skies.

The forest grew silent. He shut his eyes, allowing himself to savor the memories that played furiously across his thoughts. Images burst into his consciousness, razor sharp and vibrantly colored. Memories rushed through his thoughts at breakneck speed, tinted in gold and sorrow, taking on a clarity that made them even more bittersweet. Memories of song and sunlight. Memories of life in a noble House, in a peaceful forest glade, and in a court of poisoned intrigue.

Memories of her.

His thought processes sped up. His awareness grew, and he felt for one final time the deep pulse of life in the world around him. Colors, scents, and sounds that had seemed minute before suddenly became overwhelmingly vivid. He was, in that instant, more alive than he ever had been.

There was movement in the night-dark sky above him, a flash of wings in the starlight. Then the demigod dove for him, driving down out of the night sky. The Zhurlord bore down on him with an impossible speed. Its human face, chillingly perfect, fixed its gaze on him, watching him through emotionless eyes as it drew closer. Huge ebony wings eclipsed his vision, blocking the rest of the world from view.

In the next moment, the Zhurlord closed in on him, its features changing, shifting, even as it dove. He saw steel flash in the starlight, felt a sharp searing pain as the blade opened his flesh. Despite his determination not to, he screamed as warm liquid seeped over his skin. He knew a searing pain, which was in truth easier to bear than the choking fear that welled up within him. Air and blood escaped his lungs at once. His senses went berserk as his brain realized that something was seriously wrong, and his body fought desperately for survival, every cell of his being struggling to stay alive.

It was a fight he could not win. Blood reddened his vision. The world went dark.

Death came quickly. He felt nothing as flesh released his soul, but his awareness changed. He found himself suddenly floating up into the air, then looked down and saw his body, torn and bloodied, still bound to the ancient stone altar. The sight should have frightened him, but it did not. Instead, he watched with a surreal sense of detachment as he rose ever higher into the sky.

The other Reonih had told him that this would happen, that he would rise up out of his flesh. If they had been right about that, it seemed only logical that they would be right about the rest of it. The last remnants of his fear dissolved. He looked back one last time at his corpse, and then it was lost to view as he rose even higher into the sky. For a brief, eternal instant, he knew true freedom.

Then, slowly he became aware of the others.

Once he realized what he had become, the real terror set in.

CHAPTER 1

Dawn brought the nightwing to Stiva's window, where she stood watching night bleed into day, watching Aris stir from its slumber, watching the rising sun cast a cold black shadow on her life. Knowing that she would not be able to sleep, Stiva had not even tried, but had instead spent the better part of the night staring numbly out her window, waiting for daylight.

The day met her with a stunning sunrise. The sky slowly shed its darkness for an apricot haze, bathing castle and city in a warm glow as the blood-red sun rose over the Oburion Ocean, painting the sky with vivid color. Moons glittered like jewels caught in a web of gold-veined clouds.

A black dawn it was, for all its breathtaking vitality.

In the midst of it, the ebony-winged phantasm appeared, rising like a phoenix from the pool of light gathering on the amethyst waves, a shadow taking form against a blazing sun. A creature from the realm beyond death, the nightwing was one of the mystical harbingers of serious omen. The Reonih said they only ventured forth from the netherworlds when something terrible was about to happen. That it had chosen this particular day to make that journey verified the accuracy of such beliefs, and the validity of other omens Stiva had seen.

Long years she had dreaded this day, this dawn, and her dreams had not been silent on the subject. It was almost a relief to know her fears had not come entirely from her own mind.

The wraith drew closer, then closer still, until it hovered in the wind before her. A dream-wrapped thing, it was, a creature of silken trailing wings and glittering jet eyes, brandishing ebony talons the length of her forearms. Death clung to it like a shroud of smoke, drenching its movements with the essence of the grave. Illusions shimmered like mist in the air around it, radiating a cold that chilled her even through the blanket she had wrapped around her shoulders. The window, a delicate construct of tinted crystal panes in a seashell-embellished thi-wood frame, slammed back and shattered against the castle wall as it approached.

She dared, foolishly, to look into its lifeless eyes, seeking knowledge, or perhaps some baneful truth. Her vision at once succumbed to the Sight, and a blurred, nightmarish jumble of senseless images assaulted her inner eye.

Rocky cliffs, winged shadows, moonlight. Blood.

Dreams that had haunted her through childhood returned with a power and a clarity that had no business in a nightvision. The images hit with physical force. Pain struck red stars against her skull and she reeled, grasping the wall for support.

When her vision cleared, the nightwing was gone. Morning had reached the castle, and Aris was rousing itself. Below her, castle, city, and harbor gained slow illumination from the pallid sky. Somewhere nearby, one of the Reonih bards began to sing for the new day; both morning and mourning, this dawn. One by one, others joined him, lifting their voices to the sunrise, which they had done on every morning she could remember. But this was not the usual song. This dirge had not been heard since the death of her grandfather, long seasons past.

They sang the death of a king.

And perhaps, Stiva thought, the death of a kingdom.

As the song ended, the clanging of weapons and armor that followed as the night watch was relieved roused the rest of the castle. Servants, cooks, and grooms rose from pallets and cupboards to begin their chores, the laundresses and bakers went to work, and handmaids flocked to the kitchens to fetch breakfast for their masters. Usually, a rising clamor of voices, footsteps, and thuds accompanied all this activity. Not today. Servants, pages, and squires crossed the courtyard quickly and silently. Tension lay draped over the castle like a blanket.

Or a funeral shroud.

It was the dawn of a new world. A new age.

Came the sound of the door to her bedchamber opening, the faint sound of soft footsteps crossing silken rugs. A voice cut through her thoughts, calling her name, young, feminine, and familiar. This was Twyla, Stiva's maid and companion, friend and kin, confidante and chaperone. She had, Stiva knew, had spent a good deal of the previous night fending others away so Stiva could be alone.

Twyla stepped into the room, alone, clad in black. Normally, she would have been followed by Stiva's other maids, Adele and Mina, who would be carrying her breakfast on silver trays; yrehn and fruit, perhaps, or rose water and pastries. Not today, though. None of the royal family would eat today.

"Stiva? What happened? I heard glass breaking."

Twyla trailed off, warily eyeing Stiva and the shattered window in turn, her usually clear green eyes clouded with concern.

"The window," Stiva murmured. "The wind."

"There is no wind." Twyla's voice, like her face, was full of concern. She had the accent of the nobility, though she owned no former title, no rank but that of lady's maid. "Are you alright?"

She shut her eyes, trying to drive the visions away. She felt disembodied, displaced from herself, drained of both strength and emotion. The strange, chaotic mix of feelings that should have enveloped her over the last days—terror, grief, worry, fear, sorrow—remained locked into a tiny corner of her mind, out of reach. She was numb, dazed; her heart, overwhelmed, had purged itself of all sentiment. It was, accordingly, a numb, dazed look she turned on Twyla, who absorbed it with a deepening frown.

Twyla swallowed, speaking quietly. "It's time to get ready." She laid a slender hand lightly on Stiva's shoulder. "Be strong, today, Stiva."

Stiva's eyes snapped to Twyla's face, an unjustified retort rising in her throat. But her anger quieted immediately when she saw the worry in Twyla's eyes. Unable to bring herself to speak of what she had seen, even to Twyla, Stiva simply nodded, then turned and went into her dressing room, still trembling. Twyla followed silently.

Her thoughts still taken by the wraith, Stiva took her seat at the vanity as Twyla gathered up various pieces of clothing and jewelry. She stared out the window, watching the chrysalis of sunlight born from a painted sky, her thoughts all the while descending into blackest midnight.

The day itself soon followed suit; the clouds drew in again, thickening, until the sky was a drab, cold brown that promised rain for days to come. The sea released a chilly, damp wind, and the last traces of color faded from the sky only moments before the rain began.

Stiva remained silent as Twyla brushed out her coppery mass of long, loose curls and pinned it up into an elaborate coiffure, painted her face, helped her don the requisite black gown and ceremonial veiled headdress, and then carefully hennaed her slender hands with the proper runic markings. The dazed state of mind she had been in for days was just beginning to disintegrate as she belted on the ornate formal dagger, but the moment she left the elegant, familiar comfort of her private suite, clarity returned, and she strode out into the hall with determined, purposeful strides.

Delaying would accomplish nothing.

The two Selin guards posted outside Stiva's door fell into step behind her automatically, having the courtesy to keep more distance than usual. They had long been her shadows, had Delis and Jarvor, yet she gave them little more thought than she did her true shade. They would lay their lives down for hers without hesitation, but this was to be expected. They were Selin, elite warriors born, bred, and bled to that duty. They wore the sigil of the Black Boot, the Selin caste that comprised her own personal guard. They would not sacrifice their own honor by shaming that badge.

There was more to being Selin than wearing a uniform. It was a way of life, one dictated by both birthright and a code of honor. One saw a man in Selin red, and one saw a warrior who would bleed his veins dry before showing the palest hint of fear, a man who would bear starvation, torment, or injury without complaint or compunction, a soldier who knew his comrades far better than his own blood kin. The Selin were a breed unto their own, utterly unlike the jeweled srih nobles they guarded. To be srih was to be of the nobility, the warrior aristocracy that belonged equally to court and field. To be in the Selin was to be of the Selin, proud, harsh, disciplined, and deadly. Nothing more, nothing less.

Thus accompanied, Stiva entered the outer hall, which wound around the castle's exterior. With its great arched windows that overlooked the city, harbor, and surrounding hillsides, the hall provided a view that was usually magnificent. Today, however, the vista was bleak. Instead of the brightly colored standards of srih Houses, merchants' symbols, and trade halls, black flags fluttered on poles and atop the pointed roofs. The harbor was eerily empty, the white-capped waves undecorated by ship or sail. Fishing and merchant fleets would both stay in port today, and the soukh, Aris' great market, would remain closed.

A familiar figure emerged from the shadows of a lesser hall as Stiva passed, and fell wordlessly into step beside her. They walked in silence, expertly maneuvering the long black trains that trailed behind them like smoke. Formal funeral wear, however uncomfortable, was not new to either of them.

"He's back, you know," Talia said, forbearing greeting. "He arrived last night by vlorship."

"I know. I sensed his return. I would have known he was here even if the bells *hadn't* announced his arrival loud enough to be heard in the Arriks." Stiva answered her aunt without looking at her, her face and her voice, like Talia's, carefully composed. She kept her green eyes firmly fixed straight ahead as she walked, chin raised, steps precisely measured. Such were the airs assumed by royalty, the bearing produced by a lifetime of training. Usually Stiva chafed beneath the poise her bloodline required her to show, but today she wore it like a mask, finding safe haven behind the impassive expression.

"Then you realize you have no excuse for not being there," Talia said curtly. Beneath the black lace veil, her delicate features frowned in disapproval as she continued in a sterner tone. "You should have gone down to greet him when he arrived. It was expected, as a courtesy at least. You are srih, Stiva. The warrior aristocracy disrespects childlike sulking, especially among its own. You know that as well as I do." Talia glanced at Stiva from the corner of her eyes. "Today won't be easy for him either, you know. You should present a united front for the people. They will wonder, if you don't show your support."

"Then let them wonder," Stiva said darkly.

The remark earned her another sharp look. "Have you had any word from him?" Talia asked. "Or sent a page with a greeting, at least?"

"No. Not yet." Stiva replied flatly. "But Twyla told me he brought a new steed back from Vrehn. A vota cat. Twelve hands high." She hesitated, and then added sourly: "He's taken Lhin's cage."

"Good," Talia said curtly, unsympathetic. "We needed new feline stock, and the votas are an excellent breed. Chandris has every right to the largest cage. All my heart goes out to you today, Stiva, but not a bit of it is on Lhin's accord. That cat's spoiled, anyway."

"I wasn't asking for sympathy," Stiva said coldly.

Another may have missed the anger underlying Stiva's voice. But nothing escaped Talia. No nuance of expression or tone, however faint, evaded her observation. Ironically, Talia herself was almost impossible to read. Her demeanor invariably stayed within the borders of detached aristocratic poise and aloof composure. Stiva felt her aunt's eyes boring into her, intense, searching, more than a little intrusive. Though she had married into Aris, Talia had been born into the House of Fahrin, and that was a family notoriously well enamored of sharp wits, sharp tongues, and sharp weapons. Talia was no exception.

Brown stone surrounded them as they left the outer hall for an interior one, the Hall of Ancestors. This corridor was long, arched, and cavernous. They crossed over intricately woven Shadrian carpets, shadows in trailing black silk, gliding through alternating regions of shadow and pale, flickering torchlight. Sunlight never touched this hall, which bisected the center of the castle, but it was always well lit. The lanterns and torches that illuminated walls hung with the arms and relics of ancient battles were never allowed to dwindle. This was not an issue of convenience or comfort, but rather one of pride. The weapons, paintings, and fading tapestries stood as legacy to countless generations of Aris' bloodstained kings. They were too sacred to dishonor with darkness.

The people of Aris had always been warriors.

Talia again broke the silence. "I don't understand you, Stiva. You knew he would return eventually."

"Of course," Stiva said quietly. "In some ways, it's like he never left."

Beneath the veil, Talia's dark eyes became inquisitive.

"We share dreams, even now," Stiva continued. "Almost four cycles he's been gone, and in the night sometimes I see places he has been, distant places, exotic places ... places I have never seen. The seven

Towers of Jara, the boiling streams and fire-bleeding mountains of Turrel, the water mazes of Vrehn, the deserts of Zors, even the stepped fountain gardens and ruined steel cities of Orake. These places my dreams—his dreams—have taken me to. I have ridden dolphins in the green Yeverad sea, raced vota cats through the jungles of the southlands, seen the painted faces of Trianic dancing girls, and heard the wisdom of the sages in the seventh Jaran Tower. When he rages, I feel it. When he's ill, I feel it. When he is exhilarated, I feel it. Somehow we are never so far apart as when we are together."

This last was an afterthought, spoken more to herself than to her aunt.

"Was a time you could not be separated," Talia pointed out.

As if Stiva could forget.

Stiva shook her head, distress creeping into her manner. She fought it down, reaching once more for the cool composure her House dictated she wear. It escaped her entirely. Her throat tightened with a lump of unspilled tears, and her next words emerged in a broken whisper. "His dreams are mine, and they frighten me. All of him is hunger, like a yawning abyss. I fear he will drown the land in blood. I fear his greed will swallow Aris whole."

"Nonsense," Talia scoffed. "Chandris has a sound head on his shoulders. You're the restless one." She stopped walking, and put a hand on Stiva's arm, stopping her too. "Stiva, you have circles beneath your eyes, as though you haven't slept in days. And Mina told me your bed has hardly been touched all week. It's only to be expected, I suppose, but sheer exhaustion should have dropped you by now." A knowing tone invaded Talia's voice. "Are you having nightmares again?"

At Stiva's reluctant nod, Talia sighed. "You should have one of the Reonih bring you an amulet to keep your dreams peaceful. Or have your friend Marcelle spend a few nights in your suite."

Stiva doubted that even an amulet from the Reonih high priest himself would keep the dark visions from her dreams, but to appease Talia, she nodded. "Perhaps."

Stiva walked forward again. Talia followed suit, but persisted. "I do not think it is today's ceremony, has you worried. Sorrow demands extra sleep, not a lack of it. It is anxiety, makes for wakeful nights."

Their voices echoed eerily off stone walls hung with tapestries and weapons, bisected by series of sculpted arches. The halls of Aris were long, straight, and cool, as were its people.

Stiva shot her aunt a sidelong glance, annoyed.

Talia sighed. She wrung her hands, a nervous habit, one of the few she allowed herself. Her voice lost a fraction of its inherent snobbery, quieting now, becoming almost benevolent. "I don't mean to fret, Stiva. I'm just worried about you. For this all to happen at once, so unexpectedly … these days have been hard on you, I know. These times test us more than any war." Her voice sharpened again, as though it could not bear to produce gentleness for long. "But I expect that you will conduct yourself properly today, and present a noble, serene image, as is fitting. You are nineteen cycles old now, old enough to know what you are and what it means."

"Keep your grief behind closed doors," Stiva said bitterly. "Is that what you are trying to tell me, Talia?" She tilted her head, hearing the edge return to her voice. "Or is it my anger you want me to hide?"

"Both, perhaps," Talia admitted, speaking more frankly than Stiva had ever heard her. "There is a thin line between showing emotion and showing weakness. We all learn to walk that line, even the Reonih. I fear for you, Stiva, because when you bury her today, you will bury the anchor that has always kept you within reason."

Talia reached out to grasp Stiva's arm, bringing her to a sudden halt. Stiva found herself faced both by her aunt and the intense, almost desperate expression Talia wore. It unnerved her. Of all the things she had known she must face today, she had never expected Talia to be one of them.

"I'll be honest, Stiva," Talia said, voice and eyes intent. "Kele asked me to speak with you. He and I, on behalf of all Aris, are asking you to reconcile with Chandris. He has enough to deal with now, without this incessant feuding between you to add to it all. This land has known five hundred years of war, but Aris has not tasted true defeat for centuries. Our enemies are like wolves at the gate, smelling fresh meat. You know as well as I do there will be blood spilled this summer. Chandris will have to prove himself in battle and in state, if he is to hold Aris together. He needs his attention on matters at hand, not on you. Stiva, I am begging you, for the sake of everyone that lives within these borders, not to trouble him anew, not to distract him." Talia swallowed, hesitating briefly. "And on my own behalf, I ask forgiveness. I admit it was my hand stirred the trouble between you. I bitterly regret that."

From far down the hall, the echoes of someone's grief drifted towards them, a wailing, tearful sound. Stiva, thrown off balance by Talia's words, fought to find her own voice, which suddenly seemed choked. She found words hiding in her stomach, and forced them out. "It wasn't your fault, Talia. You suffered as much as we did, if not more. The blame was never yours."

"Chandris saw it differently," Talia told her grimly. "Stiva, I have never asked you for anything. I'm asking you now. Let it go."

Uncomfortable at being put on the spot, Stiva looked away from Talia's eyes to the first thing she found capable of visual distraction; a painting, one that had often caught her attention in childhood but had not drawn her eye in some time, though she passed it almost daily. The work of some obscure artist—-a student of the Jaran Tower, as evidenced by the crude obelisk shape scrawled beside his runic signature—it depicted shadowy, winged figures crossing three full, bright moons on a cloudy night. Anatomically, the perfectly shaped forms looked human ... except for the wings that both bore them and identified them as Skyborne, one of the other races, the Zhur.

Some said the Zhur were gods. Others called them demon. Most legends painted them as bloodthirsty beings, but some stories and ballads described them as owning a more benevolent nature. Earthborne, Seaborne, Fireborne, Skyborne, the Zhur walked between worlds. They killed, though whether they did so for pleasure or release, sustenance or vengeance, no one could say. The rest was legend, myth, clouded by time. The Reonih knew more, but the Reonih kept that knowledge, along with many others, to themselves.

Stiva felt herself drawn, as though enchanted, to the portrait. Once more, the images sent by the nightwing flashed through her mind, matched by the visions she had seen in dreams.

Rocky cliffs, black wings, blood on stone beneath a silver moon.

Chills caressed her skin, tickling the hairs on her neck.

"Put it behind you," Talia was saying. "Put it to rest with Cronn and Lara. Chandris never wanted you hurt."

Stiva wasn't listening. Her attention was still fixed firmly on the painting. Talia, puzzled, followed Stiva's gaze to see what held her so spellbound. Having found it, she looked back at her niece, frowning. "Have you even heard a word I've said?"

Stiva looked blankly at her aunt.

It hit her full force then. The ramifications of what had happened — what *was* happening — struck hard, and she felt the numbing blanket of shock disintegrate. All the emotions she'd held at bay came rushing back at once. Sorrow washed over her, and she felt at last the full force of the grief and pain of her loss, along with the staggering impact this day would have on her life, on all their lives. Silent tears coursed down her face. Her shoulders shook. She wept.

Talia surveyed her niece coolly for a moment. Then she raised a perfectly manicured, rune-painted hand and delivered a sharp, ringing slap to Stiva's cheek.

"Pull yourself together," Talia snapped, as Stiva, stunned, raised her eyes to Talia's face. "Do you intend to stand there slobbering and bawling as your parents are put to rest? To shame a king at his funeral?"

Stiva's eyes narrowed. She glared at her aunt, livid. But Talia looked back calmly, and Stiva's own rage faded quickly, replaced by the composure Talia had sought to pound into place.

"It isn't just the dead I weep for, Talia," she said quietly. "Lara will cross today into the Otherworld. I do not mourn that venture without knowing that she has, in a way, always belonged there. And I do not mourn Cronn, for he was lost to me years ago. It is the living I sorrow for, for I do not know what will become of us now. Fear chokes me, and I cannot even whisper to anyone that I think, or feel, or grieve. Instead, I must be a statue, a doll ... another emotionless srih figurehead."

Another sob echoed down the long passageway. It was a ghostly sound, surreal and somewhat unnerving. The castle was haunted, some said. Countless stories, passed down over centuries, fed the gossip. Generations of restless dead hovered in the darker corners, voices whispered on night winds, and cool breezes were wont to appear out of nowhere on the hottest days, without cause, without reason. In a way, it was almost logical. Aris was much more familiar with violent, untimely deaths than with quiet, natural passings. Sometimes at night, Stiva thought she could hear them calling from beyond the gate to the

Otherworld, whispering the creed of Aris, the code that had been pounded into all of them since birth.

Honor. Courage. Serenity.

Two more souls would join the ranks of the unseen that day.

Talia drew a deep breath, and spoke frankly. "You've had your freedom these years, Stiva, and you've indulged your Reonih blood, more than your mother ever did. Don't get me wrong; I think the Reonih are a beautiful people, and I am glad to have them nearby, glad for their wisdom and guidance. But you were born to the halls of Aris, not to a Reonih forest dwelling, and you have known for years that you will never wear Reonih robes. It is time for you to put that part of your life aside. Aris needs you. The Reonih do not."

"You don't need to remind me of that, Talia," Stiva said bitterly. "I've never forgotten."

"Perhaps you should."

Anger Stiva had thought buried resurfaced, a sour pool of rage roiling at the center of her heart. She fought it back, hid it, because she was of the House of Aris, and that meant she must.

But her eyes, almost of their own accord, went back to the painting.

"What is it about that painting?" Talia snapped.

"It reminds me of something," Stiva murmured vaguely. "A dream I had recently."

"There goes your Reonih half again." Talia sighed. This time her rebuke was gentle, uncharacteristically so. "Best, I think, that it releases itself in dreams, and in your voice when you sing. You've a good head on your shoulders, despite it."

Stiva started to reply, but was interrupted by the sudden swoop of an erlit. The creature dove, passed between them, and was gone, torchlight glinting briefly off its tiny, jeweled scales and reptilian head. The castle was hopelessly infested with the tiny dragons. While they kept the place free of insects and rodents, they were for the most part a nuisance.

"Damn pests," Stiva muttered, brushing a scale off her sleeve.

"Death always excites them," Talia said.

They continued on. Nothing more was said between them, for at the next arch two more crimson-clad guards fell in beside them, and Jarvor and Delis moved closer in.

They descended a wide, winding staircase, thereby reaching the rotunda at the main entrance to the castle, where a quiet cluster of soldiers, servants, and nobles were waiting. Normally, there was a great deal of traffic in the rotunda. With pages and squires running to and fro, servants going noisily about their business, heralds loudly announcing important arrivals, and soldiers, diplomats, Reonih, merchants and srih constantly entering and exiting, the rotunda usually tended towards the noisy side, at times bordering on chaotic.

Not today.

Death had touched Aris, and hung like a cloud above its very stones. A deep chill had crept into the hearts of its people, and true grief ran deep within its shadowed hallways, cloaked in silence. The gathering was sober, draped in formal funeral wear. The tearstained eyes that went to Stiva and Talia as they entered were shaded both in sorrow and fear. The sorrow was for the past, for what had been lost to them forever. The fear was for the future, which rested precariously on the shoulders of the one who stood at their center, the tall straight youth whose shining red-gold hair and clean features were branded eternally into Stiva's heart, mind, and soul, for they were the masculine echo of her own.

Chandris turned slowly, his polished armor reflecting the torchlight.

For the first time in almost four cycles, Stiva met the eyes of her twin.

CHAPTER 2

The funeral procession, wrapped in mist and cold droplets of rain, wound its way slowly up the rocky trail, banners hanging limp in the soggy air. Aside from the marching time dictated by a single drummer, only the crunch of gravel crushed underfoot and the cries of occasional seabirds broke the silence. Inside the gleaming carriage, dark thi-wood creaked and the silken cushions were damp. The embroidered curtains were pulled shut over the side windows.

Stiva rode quietly beside her brother, in darkness.

She reached a pale finger to the window cloth, adjusting it just enough so that she could see out. Deprived of sound, the world also lacked color that day. It was a world painted grey they passed through. Dark, gloomy clouds filled the sky, obscuring the sun. The light season, in passing, had taken its vibrancy with it, leaving the land with a drained, listless complexion. Earth, sea, and sky all wore drab, bleary tones; only bleak browns and greys covered hills that had until recently been a vivid pallet of gold, red, and green. Even the commoners gathered along the roadside were pale, hushed, and colorless, their clothing perfectly matching the duller shadings of the land around them.

It was the first day of the dark season.

Thick fog hid the ocean from view. It made her uneasy, remembering another occasion, when the mists had concealed more than cold wind and turbulent water, remembering warships taking shape slowly within the haze, black as death, horrid, menacing shapes floating on a silent purple sea.

She wished her father had died that day.

But the king of Aris had not died in battle.

Cronn had always wanted a noble death, perhaps a bloody one. It seemed fitting, for he had lived a noble, if bloody life, and had managed to hold Aris for over forty cycles. Cronn had earned a better death than the one that had claimed him, which was the way he'd always dreaded ending his life: keeling over in the banquet hall in the middle of supper, in a crowded room filled with intimate strangers.

His heart, Cerrow had said.

Stiva's eyes sought out the Reonih assemblage near the head of the procession, searching the multitude of robed figures for Cerrow's thin form. Annual convocations aside, it was a rare occasion that saw such a huge gathering of Reonih. The death of a king, however, was sufficient cause to muster them from near and far. The white-robed sages seemed to float over the earth, mystic and graceful, utterly absorbed in their function, which today was to lead the dead king to the gates of the Otherworld. Behind them, clad in green, went the healers, while the bards, in blue, went last, their instruments and voices silent.

As though sensing her stare, Cerrow turned a bit as he walked, his white robes whipping in a sudden gust of wind. She felt his gaze on her, and shivered.

They rounded a corner, and the castle came back into view, a fat, corkscrew spiral that sat atop a hill overlooking city and harbor. The original construct was conical, almost a rounded pyramid, wrapped in defensive walls and towers as well as fragrant gardens and delicate reaching spires. Over the centuries, numerous additions had enveloped the main structure in an elaborate complex of wings, courtyards, and outbuildings, but the main building dwarfed all of the additions. From certain vantages, it looked vaguely reptilian, for it had been reinforced with shellscale that protected the stone like armor. The shellscale was chipped and worn now, but on sunny days, one could still see traces of its iridescent hues, rainbow swirls of colors shimmering through the amber-gold of the shells' tough outer casings.

Though the castle was a breathtaking sight, Stiva had stopped taking pleasure in its beauty long ago. Like everything else it held, Aris had paid a high blood price for that shellscale. Four hundred divers had drowned plucking the great shells from the Oburion; claimed by the Waterborne, some said, in reparation for the harvest. Since the first time

Stiva had heard one of the bards sing that tale, she had never been able to look at her home in the same way.

She let the curtain go. It slid into place with a whisper of thick velvet, a silent scream.

Her thoughts turned to the fallen. Cronn had, at best, kept fatherly emotions at a distance. At worst, he had despised her. The familiar medium was that mostly he had ignored her. If Chandris had been the apple of Cronn's eye, then Stiva was the worm in the center of the apple. Only when she sang did he look at her as though she were worth something. All the same, she mourned his loss bitterly. Cronn, at least, had known the necessity of limits. He had never acted rashly, or without counsel and long, deliberated thought. He had never pushed his men or his subjects beyond the limits of endurance or reason. Politically strong, Cronn had been known for silent, keen observation, concise reckoning, and carefully planned action.

His successor had inherited none of those traits.

Thunder rolled in the sky.

Omen.

A roar of feline rage cut the air, followed shortly by the sound of a whip. The cats, sensing death, were restless. Their uneasiness carried to the birds and horses; the carriage jolted suddenly as a result, and Stiva grabbed the handrail for balance. From further back in the line, squeals of equine and feline irritation carried up as the riders fought a contagion of skittishness.

In some weird way, the jarring motion broke the tense silence in the coach. The occupants blinked, as though waking from a dream, and surveyed each other warily.

"Are you going to sing at the ritual?" Chandris asked suddenly, startling her. "We're almost to the House of the Dead."

"No." Stiva shook her head, refusing to look at him. "Better if Reide does it, or Kira. It should be a robed bard, today, a true Reonih. I'm just an apprentice."

Those were the first words spoken between them in years.

Maren, their younger brother, piped up instantly. "Why? It would be awful if someone else sang Father's death-song. No one else sings like you, Stiva, not even Kira. You have to sing. You just *have* to."

"You know the death-song well enough," Chandris commented.

Stiva gritted her teeth, fighting the urge to rake her nails across his face. "Hush, Maren," she said dully, instead. "You know we aren't supposed to speak yet."

"I won't be quiet until you say you will." Maren said, his voice and words brimming with the untempered stubbornness of youth.

"She will," Chandris said coolly.

Stiva glared at her twin, and a retort rose almost instantly to her lips. But she bit it back, looking her rage out the curtained window instead of into his eyes. It was dishonorable to argue or cause problems at a funeral. Beyond that, it went into more complicated matters. Today, and every day from now on, Chandris was rightfully able to give her orders. Their parents' funeral was not the place to argue that.

"Mother must be cold." Shira, their younger sister, spoke calmly, in the neutral tone they all knew so well, the soft, soothing voice meant to still arguments. Shira was a born peacemaker, tending to avoid and prevent conflict whenever possible. Had she been male, Shira would have been destined for a life of diplomacy, securing treaties and alliances in foreign courts. Instead, she was left to easing family tensions, which was no easy feat in the best of times.

Chandris looked at Shira. "The dead do not feel cold, Shira, but maybe in their dreams."

Maren's eyes grew suddenly wide, and he stared at Chandris. "But she isn't dead!"

"To us, she is," Chandris said quietly. "To the rest of the world … soon enough." He looked briefly out the window to the open carriage their mother rode in, just ahead of them. Dead, to them, yet her flesh was still warm, her blood still ran, and her breath made clouds on the chill air. Some in the crowd mourned her, but many would not. Lara had never been a popular queen, though she had done Aris no wrong and had, in fact, worked quite a bit of good. Born, bred, and raised Reonih, Lara was a princess from a powerful tribe in distant Shadri. Pahnryn, her father, was the high priest of Shadri, a well-respected elder. She had distanced herself from him—and from the rest of her people—by marrying into Aris' warrior aristocracy, even though Aris' srih had distrusted her motives from the start. While Lara had never been truly hated, she had never really won her subjects over either. They saved their adoration for Chandris, their loyalty for Cronn, and their hatred for the enemies lining Aris' blood-soaked borders.

Lara had followed her king west, away from her home, against Pahnryn's wishes and counsel. And now she followed him into death.

Little said, but it was enough to upset Maren, who at five cycles was too young to understand such things. His green eyes clouded instantly, and a note of panic crept into his voice. "Mama isn't dead. Father's dead, not Mama."

Shira quickly put an arm around the little boy, trying to soothe him with a gentle tone. "Maren, Mama chose to go into the House of the Dead with Father, so that they can always be together. They're going to go into the Otherworld together, and someday, when they're reborn, they'll be together again. It's the greatest honor she can do him."

"No," Maren said firmly. Clearly beginning to panic, he shook his head vehemently. "No!"

Tension rose sharply. They all recognized the signs of an impending tantrum. Shira tried her best to prevent it. She bent over so that she could speak to him at his level, maintaining a soothing tone as she spoke. "It was her choice, Maren."

"No!" Maren insisted, his voice rising feverishly. He turned to Chandris, eyes wide and brimming with tears. "You won't let her, will you, Chan'ris? You're king now, you can make her stay."

"Uncle Kele is regent now. I won't be king until tomorrow," Chandris told him flatly. "Besides, that wouldn't be honorable. She made her choice, and we have to respect it."

"No!" Maren screamed. "Kele isn't the real king; you are!"

"Damn it," Chandris growled furiously. "Didn't anyone even try to explain this to him?"

"Yes, but he's still too young to understand," Shira told him. "Ghodrik only started tutoring him last season." She pulled Maren onto her lap, but her efforts to placate the little boy only drove him to a frenzy of choked sobs and loud shrieks.

"Keep him quiet!" Chandris snapped.

Shira rocked and patted and hushed, but Maren only wailed louder.

Chandris cursed under his breath, then leaned over and seized Maren's little arm roughly. "You will stop that noise right now, young man!"

They all jumped. Chandris had certainly inherited Cronn's heart-stopping bellow of authority.

Maren, terrified, fell silent.

"You are a prince of Aris and you will behave like one," Chandris continued harshly. "Cry later, in your bed, or not at all, but if you continue this whining, I will lock you up in the dungeon until you're ready to behave properly. Do you understand me?"

Maren put his fist in his mouth, hiccupping, and climbed further up on Shira's lap, terrified.

Stiva was horrified. "Chandris, he's only a baby."

"He's old enough to start learning who he is, what it is to be of Aris," Chandris snapped.

Stiva settled into the cushions, biting back a venomous reply. But she couldn't resist one last barb. "He already knows what treachery is."

Chandris glared at her.

They rode the rest of the way in silence.

It was not long before they crested a low hill and stopped, the carriages coming to a halt on the rim of a long, shallow valley. The mound in the center of it had, countless centuries ago, been leveled into a plateau, upon which stood a ring of standing stones. Grass did not grow there. It was only stones and bones and ghosts that place held. The valley was empty, save the circle of monoliths and the great underground tomb that was the burial place for generations of Aris' dead royalty. A hundred kings slept there, far below the ring of standing stones, deep in the bowels of the earth. House of the Dead, it was named, that great catacomb. It was not a place lightly spoken of. To disrespect it was to ask for early entrance, some said, and a restless tenancy.

Stiva felt something, a tension in the air, an unnatural presence which set the hairs on the back of her neck prickling. It wasn't the tomb itself that unnerved her, but the circle of standing stones before it. Ancient beyond reckoning, the monoliths had multiple uses and, it was said, multiple powers. They tracked the passage of time, marking the seasons. They told a tale that crossed stars, that of the ancients who had braved the sky itself to find this world, for the history of the Elders was scratched onto their surfaces, etched deeply into the stone in a runic scrawl only Reonih could read. They were a lexicon, deciphering the dance of distant stars; annually, on Lightfest Eve, one could see

Denebola, the Elders' home star, poised atop the central pylon. Most importantly, the stones tapped a vein of mystical energy, a ley-line that ran beneath the earth's surface, encompassing a reservoir of power the Reonih utilized on occasion. The energy channeled by the stones was capable of opening a gateway to the Otherworld ... it was rumored that the stone circles were gates themselves, the doors through which the Zhur passed when they moved between worlds.

Though raised by Reonih, the stone circles were one of the more tangible legacies of the Elders, who had colonized this world, conquered it ... and almost been conquered by it. Their knowledge, now lost, had nearly made them into gods, but their arrogance, their greed, and—perhaps most of all—their carelessness, had poisoned their homeworld. They had fled across the universe in search of other planets to ravage and rule, and then seeded those new worlds with beautiful hells and shining cities. But the Elders' descendants did not have sole claim to this world. They had found a sparse, yet thriving population of indigenous people, who had, the Reonih claimed, only recently begun to recover their numbers from some cataclysmic event upon the arrival of the Elders. The already fragile native populations had shrunk to small pockets within just a few years of the Elders' arrival. This was not due to war, but biology. The Sijhani, though healthy and strong overall, had been unable to fend off the diseases the colonists had brought. The colonists themselves were immune to the viruses, but the natives had no resistance to them.

The results had been tragic.

Wave after wave of plague had decimated the native populations. Then, even as the Elders built up their cities, the Zhur began to attack. The Sijhani retreated into the wild and raised a network of thornwalls. They had never fought the Elders, choosing instead to slip further into primal lands, terrain that offered game, shelter, and privacy, while colonists cleared and settled coastal areas, plains, and the outer reaches of forest. The Sijhani—and their eastern counterparts, the Djaki—to this day lived beyond the borders of Aursa, their territory marked by thornwalls in the north, as well as the Deloran mountains to the west and the Arriks to the east. Though the occasional Sijhani straggler, exile, or outcast took up residence in Aursa, either as a craftsman or a laborer, the majority of them kept to their own lands. They traded with Aris, usually via the Reonih, but wanted little to do with Aursa, otherwise. They had kept their distance, even as the Elders had built their cities with technology this world had never known, and introduced new crops and cattle.

Sown the hatred of the Zhur, the Other-races, who had proven far harder to tame than the planet itself.

The Elders had discovered things here that even their science could not best. The primordial gods of this world still lived, and they walked it with fangs and claws and a taste for human blood. Elemental deities, the Zhur had tangible control of forces even the Elders could not enslave; wind and weather, fire and rain.

Angered, they had brought the Elders' civilization to its knees. Wave after wave of destruction had plagued the budding civilization. Earthquakes, floods, fires, mudslide, hurricanes, cyclones: the Zhur had leveled cities that were not even a hundred years old. In Shadri, entire cities had fallen into the sea. Drought and famine had followed, until, in the end, only a handful of colonists had survived. There was no choice by then, but to broker an uneasy peace. Many of the survivors had fled into Sijhani lands, seeking sanctuary.

The first Reonih had walked out of the ashes of that destruction. Formed alliances with the Sijhani, essentially trading knowledge for peace. Ultimately, the survivors—both Reonih and civilian—had forged a new order, one based not on Elders' technology, but on the resources and ways of their adopted world. Today, the Reonih were lawmakers and philosophers, healers and sages and historians, but their true power lay in the realms of the unseen. They alone dealt with the supernatural forces that walked—and, some said, ruled—this world.

As they would today.

The procession drew to a halt. Stiva, overtaken by a wave of vertigo, had to grasp her brother's arm as they climbed out of the carriage. He gave her a worried look and then squeezed her hand reassuringly.

It was the first sign of peace between them in years.

At fifteen, Stiva had fallen in love. Trin was the youngest son of the House of Barls, srih by birth, Reonih by choice, free, reckless and full of laughter, living the dream she held for herself, that of a bard's life. They would have been a perfect match, had Chandris not thought him beneath her. Eventually, he had outright forbidden her to see him. It was the first time he had ever pulled rank on her. Stiva had ignored the order. That ignorance had cost Trin his life.

Chandris, enraged, had given his first formal challenge. But an ill-timed broken arm had prevented Chandris from the fight. Their cousin Mykhal had stood for him, had *insisted* on standing for him. None of them had thought Trin, a bard, would best him. But Barls was a srih house, part of the warrior aristocracy. They had all underestimated Barls' thoroughness in training even lesser sons. The duel was not supposed to be a death match. Trin, too well trained and too long out of practice, had reacted instinctively, and had sunk his blade into Mykhal's gut, delivering a slow, painful death that even the best Reonih healers could not circumvent.

The twins, once inseparable, had erupted into bitter feuding. Open hostility had raged between them, curses flying back and forth and blows struck, until the Selin who guarded them were roused and uneasy, until the rift threatened to divide Aris, until Kele and Talia's incessant quarreling had seemed petty in comparison. Eventually Lara, desperate, had gone to the Reonih Council for help, seeking intervention and guidance. She'd even sought Pahnryn's advice, despite their chilly relationship, asking his feedback through messages, fearing the discord would put a hex on the royal clan forever.

At fifteen, Stiva had watched Trin taken away to die on the Reonih altar, an offering given to appease the gods. Such had been Mohr's interpretation of the divinations he had cast. *Blood for blood*, Mohr had said. *Barls has spilled royal blood, which is sacred. The House of Barls must bleed as well.*

Blood sacrifice was rare, now, though not entirely eradicated. It was mostly rapists and murderers the Reonih gave to the Zhur, these days, along with the occasional traitor. The sacrifice of a srih or bard was nearly unheard of. But Cronn had allowed it, knowing that to refuse Mohr's judgment in the matter would only escalate the tension. With half of Aris screaming for Trin's head, Cronn had decided to acquiesce, rather than risk rebellion.

Trin had gone bravely to his death, without protest. The tension had only escalated. Barls, seeking vengeance for Trin's death, had openly rebelled, seeking to overthrow Cronn. Aris rose in arms, and civil war threatened. Barls received bloodgold from Cronn himself. With that,

Trin's death was bought and paid for. That was the way of the srih, to acknowledge an unfortunate death with red gold. Once the coins were accepted, it would have constituted a breach of honor on Barls' part to pursue matters further.

Though Aris had lost men in each generation to warfare and intrigue, something about Mykhal's death had shaken the srih house to its core. None of them had ever been the same since.

It seemed like it had happened a million cycles ago. It seemed like yesterday.

Chandris had gone abroad, as all princes did, sent to learn the ways of the world before taking on his duties as heir apparent. Barls settled, brought to heel, and a civil war went narrowly averted. And Stiva had found herself unofficially disowned by her father.

Such were the results of royal honor.

Death had separated the twins. Death brought them together once more.

Ceremony dictated the sequence of movements that came next. The Reonih moved as one, positioning themselves in a circle within the ring of stones. The pallbearers drew Cronn's funeral wagon into the center of circle, while Cronn's kin and comrades—the srih, Selin, merchant princes, vassals, and advisors that had comprised his inner circle— gathered around their fallen king. The onlookers formed a third, larger ring.

The moment grew surreal. Stiva looked around at the faces that decorated her life. Lara stood beside the sarcophagus, pale and seemingly oblivious to the rest of the world. Talia's husband Kele, Cronn's only surviving brother, stood silently beside his wife, stone-faced. Their surviving son, Aret, stood apart from them, among the Selin. Little Maren clung silently to Shira's hand. Twyla was again a silent comfort behind Stiva. Their closest friends, Reide and Marcelle, stood nearby. Across from Cerrow, Lyle, the commander of the Selin, stood at attention one final time before his king.

Chandris stood among them once more, a dark sun blazing in their midst.

Stiva did not hear the next part of the ritual. The words, gestures, and movements of Mohr, the Reonih high priest, were nothing more than words, gestures, and movements. Though usually she found Mohr fascinating, today she barely heard a word he said, and she missed a good deal of his speech, only regaining focus when he lit the incense. His voice seemed a part of the very wind, the world around them, the valley and the stones and the mountains in the distance. "There are nine realms in the Otherworld, and the path through them is perilous and long. You will face the Zhur. You will be judged by the gods, and sent to the lands of the unborn. If you carry honor with you, you will be blessed in your next life. If you prove unworthy, you will be reborn into misery."

Came time for them to speak their farewells, to wish Cronn well on his voyage into the Otherworld. Stiva emerged from her daze to see Chandris step forward. His voice rang out clearly against a sudden blast of frigid wind.

"Father, you gave me life. You gave me honor. You carried your sword bravely, and your crown wisely. You may leave this world knowing that your legacy will carry on, and your name will be well-spoken of in the ages to come. May the things that have separated Aris in the past pass with you. I will uphold the way of Aris, which is just and brave. I will honor you in every way, and act with your wisdom and bravery in mind. I, your firstborn, your heir, bid you farewell."

It was a simple eulogy.

It was a lie.

Stiva went white. Rage darkened her world, darkened her thoughts, darkened her eyes, so that she could barely see straight. Tears rose to her eyes; forcing them back, she found Chandris looking at her calmly. Not the faintest trace of turbulence showed in his green eyes, only coldness and a muted look of triumph. Only the barest thread of discipline kept her from leaping for his throat right then and there.

Another shared her rage. Lara's eyes bored into Chandris' face, from where she stood beside her fallen husband. She too had noticed his arrogance. And she spoke against it, though she was—officially, at least—dead.

"You were not," Lara said. "You were not the firstborn."

Her whisper carried like a shout.

The wind gusted up suddenly. That was not unusual, so near the sea, but many shivered and grasped amulets.

Aris was nothing if not superstitious.

"You were not firstborn," Lara said again, louder. "Stiva was."

Chandris looked her in the eye. Looked through her, with no sign of reaction. No one said anything. The living dead went unheeded, unheard. It was Arisian tradition.

Lara was from Shadri.

"I curse you," Lara said, as Chandris spoke her name in start of her eulogy.

The sky darkened, as if in agreement.

Chandris persisted, and spoke a few brief ambivalent lines about Lara. Then he stepped back, and Stiva realized it was her turn. For a moment, she could not move; she stood frozen in place, rooted to the spot, as immobile as the great stone monoliths. Somehow, she found the strength and stepped forward, searching her soul for words that could express the volumes of emotions she felt. Her delay was long enough to cause a bit of restless shuffling within the gathering.

Finally, the words came, and she spoke clearly. "Cronn, my father, my king, I bid you farewell. Leave this world with the knowledge that you were a strong king. You have earned the right to enjoy a long period of rest and glory at the hands of the gods in the Otherworld before you return to this one." She hesitated again. Then, careless of tradition, she looked her mother in the eye, though tears blurred her vision. "Lara, you are a gentle soul, as warm and loving as a mother could be. Freedom for you. May you ride the wind and sea at Cronn's side in the Otherworld. I have every belief that when you find your way back to us, to this world, you will return in the shape of something as free and beautiful as the mother I have known and loved. I hope that you will know peace, always, in every form you wear." Her voice dropped to a whisper. "Freedom for you."

Lara's eyes glistened with tears. Stiva saw her lips turn up, ever so slightly, but her mother did not again break tradition. It was a curse, if a dead woman smiled. As it was if she spoke, but that was done already, and though the wind seemed colder and fiercer for it, and if the rain bit more sharply … it was still Chandris' moment. All eyes remained glued on him, including Stiva's narrowed, feminine versions of his own.

Kele stepped forward, lurching a little as he moved. It was no surprise to Stiva that her uncle was drunk already. Nor did the scathing look Talia shot her husband as he staggered forward particularly startle her. Stiva had no idea what he said. Kele's words, and the words of the others who had sufficient rank to speak, blended together into a muddled stream of words and phrases. Later, she would recall only vague bits and pieces of the praise heaped like gold upon a dead king, words of severance, meant both to glorify him and prevent him wanting to linger on the earth.

It began to rain harder.

The Reonih performed another section of the rite, encouraging Cronn to face the next world without regret. Then it was time for the death song. Kira, the Reonih master bard, and Reide, Aris' resident bard, both moved into position, instruments in hand. Their eyes urged Stiva to join them as the haunting melody filled the air. So she stepped forward and sang, too emotionally numb to even be nervous. Somewhere in the back of her mind, she feared she would falter, but her voice rang out clear and strong, and many wept.

Her voice, unlike so many other things, had never betrayed her.

Mohr performed the final part of the ceremony, which dealt with enticing the gods to open the gates and take Cronn through to the Otherworld. As Mohr finished the ritual, the doors to the House of the Dead swung silently open, right on cue. Though many, Chandris included, believed that some hidden latch controlled the doors, Stiva could see no sign of such manipulation, though she watched closely.

The funeral carriage pulled up to the doors of the tomb, and the pallbearers began unloading it. Into Cronn's tomb went a fortune in gold and jewels, casks of wine and barrels of grain, oil and incense and weapons, the cremated remains of several mistresses, his animals, and other fitting gifts. Unable to face looking at the tomb itself, Stiva stared at items she herself had selected as funeral gifts. Then the servants carried Cronn's sarcophagus into the blackness, and all that remained was for Lara to follow him into eternal night.

Lingering one last moment in the pale, murky light of the day, Lara looked at each of her children, regal and proud even to her last day. Then she turned and walked behind him into the darkness, her head held high, the vial of poison in her hand shining dully.

The doors shut once more. Forever.

Stiva wanted to scream, to collapse, to throw her down on the ground and wail, to pry that huge stone away with her bare hands and shake her father awake just to shout at him. *You never said goodbye. Never told me you loved me, until the night you fell over at the dinner table and I knelt at your side and felt you fading away. Even then, it was Lara you saw, not me. And now you've taken her from me.*

A hand fell on her shoulder. "Come on," Reide said gently. "It's time to go back."

The Grey Storm, the caste of Selin who had served as Cronn's personal guards, remained behind, to protect the tomb. No longer the King's guard, they would still serve his castle, but with his death, they were now retired to lighter, reserve duty. They would guard this place in shifts, protecting against grave robbers.

As they rode back, Stiva watched the darkening sky with searching eyes, scanning the clouds for some image of her father. For Lara, it was too soon; the poison she had taken with her would not have affected her yet.

Something twisted in the sky, a figure too large to be a bird.

Omen.

CHAPTER 3

The voices began again that night. Soft, whispering murmurs, they were, elusive and fragmented, always hovering on the other side of clarity. Disembodied, floating sounds danced around images that never quite made sense: surreal visions of fluttering black wings and black curtains, black winds and black water, chained together by strands of smoke and mist. The nightvisions chased each other through Stiva's turbulent dreams, spinning and blurring together, moving faster and faster into one another. Lara's voice joined the others calling from the netherworlds only as they faded, slipping away with her slumber, which had been a brief, uneasy sleep at best.

Long, long, her dreams had been distorted, but these were vivid in their chaos, more urgent than they had once been. It meant something. Stiva knew that even as she opened her eyes onto a rain-soaked midnight. The message's exact meaning refused to crystallize in her thoughts. She turned it over and over in her mind, but could make no sense of it.

Nothing made sense anymore.

Stiva stirred, freed herself from a tangle of silken sheets, then rose and crossed the room to her hastily-repaired window, which she threw open to the night. Something moved in the indigo clouds; a shape danced around the seventh moon, then slid deeper into the sky, disappearing from view even as her gaze found it. Like the tiny sprites that inhabited the forests and the nymphs that lived in streams, it was only visible for an instant.

Skyborne, receding dreams whispered.

I have to talk to Mohr, Stiva thought. *He'll know what it all means. The nightwing, the dreams, the omens at the funeral. Maybe it has nothing to do with me, or with Chandris. Maybe there is a Zhurlord hunting in Aris, and that is rousing the Otherworld. The Reonih will deal with it.*

The watchtowers remained dark, black cylinders tracing themselves against a net of stars. Darkness on those hills meant peace and quiet. It meant that all was as it should be. It was when the watchtower flames flared up that one needed to worry, for that signaled trouble—usually, at least as of late—a night raid. And that meant riders out the gate, men going to war in the dead of night, armor and weapons clanking. A song of death, come the dawn.

Occasionally, the towers were lit for a shipwreck, which announced another type of chaos altogether, as the perilous reefs surrounding Aris' rocky harbor claimed another galleon. Aris had the only deep-water port west of Trian, which made it a crucial stop for the merchant fleets that sailed from Vrehn, Turrel, Orake, Zors, and ports even more distant. But the merchant princes had learned to take the good with the bad, for the waters of Aris, like those of Shadri, were notoriously dangerous. The waves of the Oburion—or, some said, the Seaborne—claimed their share of the wealth that crossed them. When that happened, the harbors would come to life, as less scrupulous sailors and divers scrambled to salvage what cargo they could. More often than not, it was looting and theft, rather than rescue, much to the dismay of newly shipwrecked captains. A sizable portion of Aris' wealth had been snatched from the grip of the Oburion, stolen from the hands of the gods … or from the Zhur who ruled the deep and who, it was said, fancied silver over gold. More than one sailor fortunate enough to survive a wreck in Aris' harbor turned up at the feet of a Reonih high priest the next day, half-mad, brimming with fantastic tales of things he had seen beneath the waves, claiming redemption, claiming to have been changed, and begging the right to wear the apprentice's robes.

Most were turned away.

Stiva settled into her window seat, sinking into a rainbow of embroidered silk cushions. Cool breezes caressed her skin, perfumed with the musky, earthy scent of the forest. The wind was a soothing balm against troubled thoughts. The terror of her black dreams soon faded away, leaving her in a more contemplative frame of mind.

Since childhood, this window had been her special haven. She would sit for hours watching sea and sky, half of her wrapped in smoky, orange firelight, the fragrances of potpourri and incense, and the dusky grandeur and stone security of Aris, the other half exposed to starlight or sunlight, fresh air, and the sounds and smells of ocean and forest. She often felt that she was poised on the edge of one world, gazing down into another. The rugged, unknown beauty of the wild, mysterious world outside the walls of Aris called her soul, an enticing song of freedom. Sometimes she imagined she only had to open her arms and jump, and she could fly away, freeing herself forever from the bloody wars, sinuous politics, and suffocating codes of Aris.

In her lifetime, more than one despairing soul had proven otherwise. There was no shortage of suicides in Aris' haunted past.

A cool ocean breeze stirred the curtains. Shivering, Stiva wrapped a silk shawl around her shoulders. Her skin warmed quickly, but the cold in her soul was not so easily dealt with. As her thoughts tumbled over the day's events, she searched starfields and clouds, at once hoping for and fearing a second glimpse of the winged creature. But it did not return, and eventually her gaze went elsewhere. Below her, the city was a collection of glittering lights and torches shining like tiny stars against night's velvet darkness. The sea was unusually calm, shattering pastel moonlight on its surface. Near shore, pulses of vividly colored light flashed in the sea, rainbow hues distorted by the water, marking the presence of hunting lightfish. Further out, a silver, sinuous form twisted and roiled in the froth of a breaking wave. Stiva frowned. Sea dragons did not often come so close to shore, though it was not unheard of. Rumor had it they either protected the Seaborne or were protected by them. No one knew for certain.

The wind tasted of freedom. Never had the longing to escape Aris been so sharp, so strong as it was now. Every cell of Stiva's being screamed at her to run, to leave Aris and its bloody politics behind. The forest called her soul, a song of forbidden longing, its mystical beauty tempered with horror. Aursa's deepest woods were forbidden to all but the Reonih, though that law was frequently broken. The forest was a spellbound place, some said, wrought with perilous magics. Songs, myths, and stories all said that wild beasts and Zhurlords dwelt in the shadows: predators alike, though they hunted in different ways.

Animals were only interested in the flesh … but the Zhur craved blood and souls, and those who fell prey to them were denied freedom even in death, soulbound to dark, primordial gods.

Or so the stories went.

Stiva's hand went to her throat, feeling the smooth weight of her mother's amulet. She had found it on her pillow the night before the funeral, and knew that Lara had left her a gift more precious than any jewel. Lara had received the amulet from her native tribe, the Reonih of Shadri, when she had gained the blue robes of the bard's order. The amulet guaranteed right of passage in Shadri—particularly in the mushroom forests Lara's tribe originated from—and offered its bearer the right to claim sanctuary there. But, more importantly, it was something of Lara's, a tie to kin she had never met. Lara had often promised to bring Stiva to her homeland; that was another dream shared in quiet, private moments over the years. She had always wanted to meet her grandfather, Pahnryn. That seemed even less likely, now.

Lara was from the primeval mushroom forests of distant Shadri, which stood in the shadows of an even more formidable landscape … the Arriks. Towering masses of stone, the Arriks dwarfed the mountain chain west of Aris in size, scope, and power. Some said they were the realm of the Skyborne, rising even above the clouds. Many a winter night had passed that Lara had sat by the fire and sang the legends of her homeland, and the Zhur who walked it still. The songs had captivated Stiva since childhood, though Chandris found them boring. The ancient ballads were perhaps the kindest legacy the Zhur had given them. The rest was sheer terror, strengthened by nightmarish accounts of a time when no man could safely walk the earth without fear of an inhuman hunter appearing out of forest, sky, sea, or fire.

Some—Chandris included—brushed the stories off, cynical.

Stiva knew better.

Sighing, Stiva reached beneath one of the cushions and retrieved a small pouch. It was some time before she found the strength to withdraw the runesticks, as they awakened memories of Lara, memories that were still too painful to linger upon. The designs etched into the smooth, polished wood of the runesticks had always had a mesmerizing effect on Stiva, as though she could see the energy flowing through them. She stared at the sticks for some time, tracing the runes with a forefinger, before casting the sticks abruptly onto the floor before her.

The patterns were hardly comforting. They spoke, as far as she could discern, of warnings, change, and betrayal, of death and war and supernatural presence. She wasn't surprised.

Stiva sat at the window seat, staring into the night.

It was thus that Chandris found her.

He made no attempt to enter her suite quietly; the heavy, gilded, thi-wood door creaked while it opened, creaked again as it shut, and finally fell into place with a dull thud. Stiva did not turn as the sound of footsteps marked his progress through her rooms, until they reached the center of her bedroom, whereupon both the sound and its source stopped.

It was arrogant, even for a king, to enter a woman's chambers without knocking.

Chandris had always been arrogant.

So, for that matter, was Stiva. She refused, for some time, to acknowledge his presence, to speak, to even look at him.

Came a voice out of her soul, out of her past, out of the world at her back.

"A black sea, in a world of mist and shadow. Winged figures dancing in the wind. Rocky cliffs, reaching for a pale, cloudswept moon. Shadows calling. A pale star, bleeding, where shadow and sunlight entwine." Chandris spoke quietly. "I still see your dreams when I close my eyes. Were I to spend a thousand years in a place a thousand years away from you, I still would. When we are dead, Stiva, when we are bones and dust, we will still share visions. So it does you no good to refuse to speak to me. I can see inside your mind."

Stiva looked at him sharply. Firelight planed his face, turning half of it red, masking the other half in shadow. He took it upon himself to light some candles. Fragrant smoke filled the air as the muted colors of finely woven silk rugs and tapestries grew visible, and the details of her oil paintings, wood carvings, pottery, and other furnishings became clearer. Here and there, precious metal or pieces of jewelry caught the light and reflected it like tiny stars.

Stiva stood up and went to blow out a few of the candles. "These are my chambers, Chandris. I prefer the darkness."

"Then wallow in it once I've left," Chandris returned smoothly. "I came here to talk, and I like to see who I'm talking to. Sit down, Stiva. We have a few things to discuss."

She certainly didn't need his invitation to sit, especially here, in her own apartment. But she let the matter slide, not wanting to waste energy on a pointless argument when it would likely soon be needed for more serious issues.

She had never quite been able to determine which one of them was the dark twin and which was the light. Only that Chandris took after Cronn, and Stiva took after Lara, and that the elements and characteristics that had made their parents fall so deeply in love, as well as the ones that had driven them to raging discord, at times nearly to each other's throats, had been duplicated, eerily so, in their eldest children.

Twins. If they had been of a lower caste, or of the same sex, one of them would have been drowned at birth, an offering to the Seaborne. Twins were bad luck, folklore said.

Stiva was inclined to agree.

She went back to the window seat and directed her stare outwards once more, to sea and starfields. "You have no leave to be here."

"I go where I please." Chandris said. "I am king here now. I no longer need your permission."

She looked at him coolly. "Then you no longer need my respect. You disobey courtesy, if not law."

"So be it." Chandris shrugged. "You're hardly a model for it yourself. No less than a blatant insult, your refusal to greet me when I arrived last night. We aren't children anymore. You, at least until I marry, are the matriarch of the House of Aris. Act it."

Here it was, already. Sometimes the politics of simply breathing air into noble lungs could get tricky. Protocol dictated every nuance of their interactions. Even the littlest thing must be approached with poise and manners, even if only servants were present.

But behind closed doors was a different thing entirely. "There was no breach of etiquette there," Stiva told him sharply. "Officially, I'm still in mourning. I'm not formally required to greet anyone yet, and won't be for another moon cycle."

Chandris could not argue that point, so he didn't try, though his eyes narrowed.

"Unofficially," Stiva continued coldly, "I didn't want to see you. I still don't. Oh, don't worry. I won't make it formal. But I save my acting for public."

"Stiva—"

"I hate you," Stiva whispered.

"Then you hate yourself," Chandris said quietly. "And I am sorry for that, for half of me is lost to that hatred."

The words fell into oblivion. So did her energy, the strength of her heart that had learned to go on without half of herself. She looked at her feet, at the tiny, iridescent shells on her toe ring, suddenly drained, exhausted. Her voice was tired and cracked when she spoke. "Why have you come here, Chandris? What do you want?"

"Officially," Chandris said, "I've come here to receive the proper respect due a returning monarch. You have not yet acknowledged me as your king."

"You haven't been crowned yet," Stiva said flatly. She refused to look at him again, knowing already what she would see, the one thing she had always despised about him; the gleam of smug satisfaction in his eyes. "You'll get my vows of loyalty at the coronation tomorrow, along with everyone else's. Now please leave me alone."

"Not so easily, Stiva."

She looked at him then, and found not triumph in his eyes, but sorrow.

"Unofficially," Chandris said quietly, "I want my sister back. I miss her. I love her. I am not whole without her."

It shocked her so completely, to hear him actually admit to emotion, that her poise disintegrated. Pain bubbled to the surface of the deep lake of her emotions. Tears rose in her eyes. She had felt the trauma of separation from him to the core of her soul. She had learned to deny it and to deal with it only by hating him, and had built an outer shell of strength to protect herself from emotional meltdown. Questioning that hatred now, even for a moment, stripped her of everything she had become since he'd gone, and brought her back to the child he had left behind.

And that child stared at him as she had then, hurt and betrayed to the innermost cell of her being.

"You cannot," Chandris said, "avoid me forever. You cannot cut the tie that binds us, Stiva. You are bound to me by the blood in your veins, the flesh on your bones. And you can never break that chain, though if you go on like this, it will strangle you."

It was the first time they had been alone together for nearly four years. That time had brought them from the final stages of adolescence into true adulthood. There were changes in both of them. They were strangers now, though they had shared a womb and a birthing day ... and, it was said of twins, a soul.

"You would have stayed away forever," Stiva said flatly, "if Cronn hadn't died."

"Half of me never left," Chandris murmured. "My better half. I will admit that much."

Stiva gave a bitter laugh. "We were born in a storm, under the darkest moon, at the height of the strongest tide, a mixture of Aris and Reonih. Face it, Chandris. We were cursed from the moment we were born, from the first breath we took. Better we just avoid each other. Better for us, and for everyone else."

"Oh?" Anger colored Chandris' voice. "Better, perhaps, for gossip-mongers and our enemies, for it gives them fuel to heighten our discord, something to use against me, leverage with which they could divide Aris. But is it better for Aret, always caught between us? Or for Shira, who's already a nervous wreck trying to keep us civil? Is it better for Maren, never to see us in the same room but on formal occasions, never see our eyes meet when we chance upon each other in the halls or at court?"

"Don't try to tell me what's best for Maren!" Stiva's temper flared up, and her voice rose with it. "Not after what you did to him today."

"I shouldn't have had to deal with him like that in the first place!" Chandris retorted, mirroring her rage. "But he obviously needs a strong dose of reality. I can see Reonih influence on him already, Stiva. He is dreamy-eyed, being raised songs and stories. Will come a day I need to rely on him, and trust him with my life and the lives of my men, and I do not want his head filled with fantasy between now and then. He should be throwing spears at targets, not tossing silver chalices to nymphs and naiads."

"He's a child, Chandris. There will be plenty of time for war when he is grown. He will know blood and battle soon enough. Let him enjoy his youth for a little while."

"Why? I never could." Chandris' voice quieted. She knew it for respite, the eye of the storm. There was still furor building behind it, though he finished softly. "I do not want him to grow up surrounded by hatred. There is enough of it outside these walls, and Kele and Talia alone argue enough for the entire family."

"There is a person missing from this place," Stiva said, speaking in a low, quivering tone, "who will never return, never again see the sun, for our discord. I cannot just forget that."

"I never asked you to forget. I miss Mykhal too, you know. He was my best friend." Agony flickered in his eyes, mirrored in hers. "But it is done and over with. You cannot hold onto your rage forever. If anyone has the right to hate me for his death, it is Kele and Talia, and they have forgiven it."

"Are you so sure of that?"

"They blame the will of the gods."

"You blame the Reonih, who serve that will. And I blame you." Her gaze fastened on him, but what she saw was the past, vivid memory brought painfully back to life.

"We've been through all of this before." Chandris sighed. "I don't think we really need to have this argument again."

"Neither do I." Stiva agreed coldly. "It won't bring Mykhal back. It won't bring Trin back, and it won't bring our parents back. Why did you come here, Chandris? To throw this all in my face, and remind me that I will never have the freedom even to love who I want? To taunt me with your power, your freedom, the fact that you control Aris and I cannot even choose whom I take for a lover?"

"Not if you make such foolish decisions as that!" Chandris shouted. "A lesser son of the House of Barls, Stiva? A man content to spend his time writing music and poems?"

"He was a Reonih bard, not some street minstrel. *He had talent, until your sword separated him from it!*" Stiva lost her composure and screamed at him, her voice resonating with fury. "And the fact that he was a lesser son did not make him a lesser man. Do you think Maren is so far beneath you? Is Aret so different than Mykhal was?"

Any pretense at a civil reunion dissipated as the old tensions exploded and anger resurfaced, bringing them both back to the strife that had torn them apart.

"Talent?" Chandris snorted. "Stiva, you have the title and heritage of a queen. If you choose to take minstrels as lovers after you're married, that is one thing. But you have known since we were Maren's age that Aris' needs must always come first, and what Aris needs from you is alliance, the kind of alliance we will gain if you marry a king or crown prince. It's your duty, and you know it. You've always known it. Why would you risk losing that opportunity for us all by blackening your name with scandal, never mind risking pregnancy?"

"He made me feel free." Stiva said in a choked voice. Tears threatened; she fought them back. "Why have you never understood that, Chandris? Since the day we were born, our whole lives have been dictated to us; what to wear, how to act, whom to speak to, where to go … everything. And don't even try to tell me it didn't get to you sometimes too, because there were times it bothered you more than it did me. I had one tiny corner of my life that was my own, and you took that from me. You didn't kill him to protect me, or to protect Aris. You did it because of your obsession to control everyone."

"Obsession?" Chandris repeated the word incredulously, as though he could not believe she had said it. "We were fourteen when Cronn made me your guardian. At any given moment since then, I could have ordered you married, sent away, put in chains … it would have been done. You knew it then, and you know it now. I told you not to see him. You defied me, and he defied me. That left me no choice. How am I supposed to rule Aris if my own sister openly disobeys me?"

"What good did it do your precious crown?" Stiva glared at him. "Do you think the house of Barls is more loyal for it? Do you think losing Mykhal made us any stronger?"

Chandris face darkened, and his hands clenched into fists. For a moment, she thought he was going to hit her. He didn't. Instead, he paced a tight circle, ran his hands through his hair, and took a deep breath. Through her anger, Stiva was impressed. Something, or someone, had taught him the one thing he had always lacked before. Self-control.

"I came here," he said, his quiet tone produced by visible effort, "To make peace. Not to argue. Not to fight. Stiva, I know I have not always done the right thing by you. I was thinking of Aris; always, always, I must think of Aris, whatever I say or do. And I was thinking of you; I didn't want you disowned and left penniless. That was what Cronn wanted to do."

"You were thinking of yourself," Stiva said bitterly. "If Cronn had disowned me, it would have freed me to live the life I want; to be Reonih."

"Really?" Chandris demanded hotly, once more on the verge of losing his temper. "Do you think I enjoyed watching him die? Do you think I liked the look on your face?"

"Actually, yes, I do!" Stiva yelled.

He looked at her as though she had stabbed him. "You were wrong," he said quietly. "You'll never be so wrong again."

He drew a breath before continuing. "We're srih; we live in a bloody, cold world. Maybe someday I can change that. But I can't do it alone."

She looked at him, really looked at him, long and hard, taking in dozens of minuscule changes that had transformed him. His hair, like hers, had darkened from the corn-silk color of childhood into a deeper, dark gold traced with red; hers was more red, traced with gold. His face had matured; it had more angles now, more definition. He had muscles now, instead of the gangly, skinny limbs she recalled. His eyes had traded boyish candor for serenity. The last traces of the boy she remembered had washed away, vanished forever into manhood, into a stranger that stood looking at her with a face frighteningly like her own.

She realized suddenly that the rift between them would probably never heal if it was not done tonight. She knew what it had taken for him to come here and take the first step. After Cronn, Chandris was proud beyond arrogance, always keeping his emotions buried behind a king's composure. He would not again come to her seeking absolution, and he would never directly ask her forgiveness. Tomorrow the crown of Aris would rest on his head, and with it the weight of a people's problems, the troubled fate of a troubled city-state. Stiva felt her anger washing away, though she tried to hold on to it, if only for her own selfish pride.

Pride, and the fact that her rage was the only protection she had against the sickening feeling of guilt that threatened to replace it.

Chandris. The shadow that had never cleared, the other, lost, half of her soul. He had always been her king, however often, however bitterly she had despised the fact.

"We aren't children anymore." Chandris' voice reached her on a wisp of fragrant smoke. "Our parents are dead. I do not think they wanted to die without seeing us reconcile. When Aris rose to regency, it was strength that kept our line alive. Strength, and wisdom. I have to protect Aris first, before anything else, even you. Cronn and Lara left us more of a legacy than bitterness and anger. They left us a city-state to hold, and that is no easy feat. I will not be the last king of Aris. I refuse to let that happen. I refuse to let your rage distract me, and I refuse to let an old feud get in my way. It is time to end this little war of ours, here and now, before any more lives are lost. Enough harm has been done. Enough blood has been spilled."

"You think it so easy," Stiva said bitterly. Her voice was as thin and weak as a child's. "Chandris, it has been years since we stood in the same room without fighting."

"It has been years since we stood in the same room, period," Chandris told her dryly.

Silence stretched long.

"Lara knew it was coming," Stiva said suddenly, staring once more out the window. She did not look at him as she spoke. "She'd been having dreams for weeks before it happened. She tried to warn Cronn, but he wouldn't listen to her. Or to me."

"Is that such a wonder?" Chandris asked, musing. "All she ever spoke of were dreams and mystical Reonih nonsense about gods and nature and the Zhur. Her words were like the wind; insubstantial, even at their strongest."

Stiva looked at him bitterly. "You didn't always think so."

"I grew up." Chandris replied, adding, "I was hoping you had too, but you are too much like her; entranced by wind and rain, completely spellbound by Reonih mysticism."

Stiva took that as a compliment, even knowing it probably hadn't been meant as one.

"You haven't changed a bit," Chandris said.

Stiva resented that, and told him so. "Chandris, you act as though I were blind and deaf to everything but my own daydreams. In truth, I know everything that goes on within these walls, and a good deal of what happens outside them. So did Lara."

"She taught you her ways, didn't she?"

Stiva, hearing something in his tone she did not like, narrowed her eyes. "What?"

"There are rumors about you," Chandris told her. "I have already heard some of them. They say you are fey, that you practice the blacker magics of the Reonih, and summon the Zhur to you in the forest. They say you have learned not just music, but song-magic." He hesitated. "Some have even said you were responsible for Cronn's death."

There was no reason at all for that to come as a shock. It was no secret that Stiva and Cronn had never gotten along. But at the end of it, the separation and the silence between them had been much less hostile than at its beginning, more like an unspoken truce than stewing anger. It had, at least by Stiva's reasoning, simply been that way for so long that neither of them had known how to change it, or what to change it to, and so neither had tried. It had never occurred to her that the rest of Aris might see it differently, that they might not understand that. Thus, the revelation of this latest rumor came as a complete surprise, and Stiva could not stop herself from staring at Chandris in total horror.

He stared back coolly, his eyes, like hers, the dark green color of ghiti flowers.

Eventually Stiva found her voice. "I never wanted Cronn dead. I think you know that, Chandris, even if for no other reason than that his death meant your return, and the end of my freedom. Cronn let me do what I wished. I would have kept him alive forever if I could."

"So I judged," Chandris admitted. "Beyond that, you lack the necessary cruelty, and I highly doubt you could bear to stain your soul with patricide. You've always been so *pure*."

His voice twisted in sarcasm. Stiva clenched her fists.

"I have a good idea," Stiva said, her voice low, "who did kill him."

"So do I." Chandris said flatly. "It was Delora and Orlin, always at our borders. It was Barls, Erad, Ehodris, Chalmers, Fentar, and all the rest of his vassals, who kept him continuously looking over his shoulder. It was Kele and Talia, always fighting so violently. It was Fala, Tyler,

Zerik, and all the others who came to him wanting his help and his alliance against their tyrannical kings, asking men and weapons and giving nothing in return. It was Lara, keeping her distance until the times she chose to be close to him, which were never the times he needed her most. It was Mohr and all the other Reonih constantly telling him to beware this, beware that. The srih, with their intrigues and plots. It was the grief of burying dozens of people he loved. It was us, adding to that stress with our little war. It was a lifetime of eating fried jhar drowned in bluefish oil and five links of chiara sausage every day. His diet would have killed a sea dragon. It was his heart, Stiva," Chandris finished. "It's hardly a surprise that Lara saw it coming. A blind man would have."

But Stiva shook her head, unconvinced. "Two days before he died, he raced Kele and Lyle down the beach and won. Three weeks ago, he wrestled five of the Selin, and beat four of them. He sparred every day, and rode every day. He was tossing Maren around in the sea a few weeks ago as if he weighed no more than a coin. Does that sound like a man with a weak heart?"

"Alright, then." Chandris cocked his head, humoring her. "What do you think happened?"

"I think he was poisoned."

Chandris frowned. "By who?"

"I'm not certain," Stiva told him, reluctant to reveal her suspicions about Cerrow until she could back them up. "But I would advise you to employ a new poison taster."

"I already have," Chandris snapped. She sighed and leaned her head back, suddenly aware of a dryness in her mouth and throat. No sooner had she realized her own thirst than she heard the tinkle of liquid moving as Chandris poured some greenberry wine from an elaborate crystal decanter into a goblet, which he raised to his lips.

They had always shared identical cycles of hunger and thirst, sleep and mood.

"What do you want here, Chandris?" Stiva asked wearily.

He sat down on a cushioned sofa, reclining lazily, and put his feet up on a low table. His tone was thoughtful, even patronizing. "Like any new king, I have to prove myself and establish control over my subjects in the next few seasons. It will be a difficult period. All of our enemies are going to test me at one point or another, more likely sooner than later. Already

I have heard the raids from the other city-states have become bolder and more frequent. Even before Cronn's death, Deloran raiders have grown bold. Itacha is testing us, and will continue pricking us until we bite. There will be war this cycle, lives lost that we cannot afford. You know that as well as I. Aris has not gained land in years. Once we were thriving. Now we barely cling to what we have, at the cost of blood spilt every year. I want more than that. I want more than to hold what was left to me. I want Aris to push forward, to prosper, to conquer."

I want to rule the world.

The child Chandris had been spoke to her across the years, from sunny days lost in time, when they had only played at being king and queen, and spoken those dreams to one another in a flower-filled meadow at the edge of the forest.

Stiva looked at him, a sickening feeling of dread growing in her stomach.

Chandris continued, not seeming to notice the apprehension on her face. "It turned out to be a blessing that I went abroad. I learned much more than I would have here; patterns of thought I had never imagined, tricks Cronn never dreamt of. I learned to question everything, and take nothing for granted. Even you."

"What do you mean?" Stiva heard herself ask.

Chandris put the goblet down and looked her dead in the eye. "I'm giving you a choice, Stiva. As I said, this little war of ours has to stop, one way or another. I have decided that it will end tonight. You will either give me your complete and uncompromised support ... or you will walk out these gates without even a name."

Stiva stared at her twin in complete shock. Then her inner voice reminded her that she would have done the exact same thing, if it was herself being crowned. The ultimatum was blunt, cold, and ruthless ... completely characteristic of Aris. Of him.

"There may come a time," she said acidly, "I find that a preferable choice. I'll keep it in mind."

"No," Chandris said flatly. "You will decide tonight."

Stiva felt the blood drain from her face.

"You want your freedom, Stiva, then go. Now. Tonight. Take what you want and go to the Reonih. Go be a bard, if you want. Live in a wooden cottage, and spend your days and nights drenched in song and

bloody magics. Or take the estate at Starshire; I never much cared for it."
Chandris vaguely motioned to the outside, indicating the world beyond
her window. "I will be crowned tomorrow. The ceremony requires that
you pledge your life, body, and soul to me. I don't want that sort of vow
given callously from anyone, especially you. I know better than to
underestimate your ability to hold a grudge. It matches my own. But
things are different now. There is too much to lose. If you are at the
ceremony, then from this day forward you will look to me as your king
first, and your brother second. You will remain loyal, and you will stand
behind me no matter what. You will consider—as I do—the troubles
between us done and over with, and they will remain in the past. In
return, you will have my protection and my support, your choice of
lands, your choice of husband, so long as you choose from among the
srih. I have no wish to curtail you, Stiva, or to control your every move.
I don't want to have to kill any more of your lovers. But if you cause me
trouble, if you cross me, if you betray me ... I will make an example of
you. And it won't be pretty. I will not tolerate sedition from you any
more than I would from anyone else." He paused. "I cannot change the
past. But the future is yet unwritten, and that, *that*, I can control."

Stiva swallowed. "Chandris, I—"

He cut her off. "You have until dawn to decide."

Stiva searched for words, her thoughts pinwheeling down a jagged,
rocky cliff into a black abyss. She had never, in the thousand days or
thousand nights he had been gone, expected this. He had relished his
control over her too much, that she had never dreamt he would be
willing to give it up forever. To set her free.

He waited a moment, as though debating whether to say more, then
turned abruptly and left, as suddenly as he had come. The door creaked
shut, closing with a final, resolute thud.

Stiva turned her eyes back to the night.

CHAPTER 4

Stiva's mask was an intricate, ethereal creation, delicately constructed of bloodwing feathers, rubies, crimson silk, and rose petals, decorated with glittering jewels, thin gold leaf, crimson kirit scales, and ebony vota claws. Vibrant and brilliant, its colors perfectly matched the blood-and-fire tones of Aris' coat of arms. It was a beautiful piece, though it stood for darker things.

Illusion.

Deception.

Death.

It was tradition in Aris to go masked at formal or festive occasions. The masks were removed during ceremonies; traditionally, this symbolized the shedding of outer facades, the baring of the soul. The underlying meaning was that all formal vows were given in complete honesty, without falseness. But some of the srih never took the masks off at all. Some wore masks of flesh and poise, hiding their souls and purpose behind decorated words and bladed fans.

Several long, straight corridors dissected the castle's vast interior, but the longest twisted, serpentine, upwards and around the outer circumference of the building. This winding corridor was decorated with ceremonial masks worn by countless generations of Arisian royalty and was—quite appropriately—named the Hall of Masks. Hundreds of gilded, eyeless faces stared down on this latest party as they made their way to yet another ceremony.

Chandris' coronation.

Stiva glanced down as she walked, distracted by the shimmer of her crimson gown as the fine satin caught stray bits of light. It reminded her of blood. A vision flashed through her mind, of herself walking at the front of a river of blood, a river that drenched Aris, pulling lives and souls and sorrow into its vicious flow. The metaphor, she realized, was not entirely benign. Behind her walked a long line of srih and Selin, many of whom were clad in red. Between them, they had probably spilled enough blood to fill a sea, never mind a river.

They were masked as she was, silent as she was, and probably as worried as she was. Likely they feared, as she did, the folly of an unproven king, wondered whether he would lead them into madness or glory, death or triumph, decoration or decay. A palpable tension hung in the air. The Reonih diviners had lately been tight-lipped and fretful, and the borders had been uneasily quiet. The Selin had gone about their training and their patrols with a bleak-faced determination, somehow managing to seem even more grim and severe than usual. To judge by what she knew of the mood among the people, Stiva surmised that the rest of Aris was probably not much more optimistic. From farm to castle to the city, within gilded halls and smoky taverns alike, unease hung in the air. One could almost smell the unease. It was as though the people feared they walked and breathed now within the last good times before some black disaster.

At the moment that thought crossed her mind, Stiva moved from the dusky violet shadows of the castle interior into a beam of orange sunlight that fell like a ray of liquid fire from a window. Light bathed her, warming her skin and her soul equally. It gave her a sense of hope, so rare she barely recognized it. It gave her strength, as though dozens of shunar fairies—tiny elemental sun sprites—danced around within that beam of light, transferring the sun's energy to her as she passed.

Revitalized, she lifted her chin higher and moved forward with renewed strength and determination. In later years, the moment returned to her often in dreams. The nightvisions added an aspect her subconscious kept to itself at the time: the touch of solar rays gave her more than a sense of rejuvenation; they provided catharsis and division. Part of her, the child she had once been, remained behind, abandoned forever to the shadows. The rest of her moved forward into a new age, and a passage she walked daily became, this one time, a journey of the soul.

The conical shape of the castle was most evident from the interior at the upper stories. The ceremonial hall occupied the entire top story, which sat like a crown atop the castle. The Hall of Masks was the only way to reach it. Therefore, official processions had to walk the entire circumference of the building several times. The fact that the distance around got smaller with each level ascended was offset by the fact that the slope grew steeper at each turn. It was a long climb, tiring even the physically fit. This was no coincidence. The long-dead architects who had designed the castle knew full well that reaching the hall would take some effort. They wanted it that way. Stiva did not doubt that for a moment. The fatigue that invariably set in by the time one reached the top only intensified the feelings of awe the hall itself inspired. Such was the way of the srih. The warrior aristocracy was expert at manipulating the human mind.

As the procession neared its destination, Stiva glimpsed the elaborate, gilded doors, which were open now. Beyond, the glitter of gold and jewels waited within. The sight rekindled a distant memory, that of her father's coronation, which had taken place when she and Chandris had been very young. Stiva remembered being awestruck and frightened by the discovery of such an amazing room where before there had only been locked doors. The sight of Cronn in full ceremonial dress, with Caro's scepter, crown, and sword, had terrified her. Chandris had comforted her, squeezing her hand. He had watched the ceremony with fascination, holding his chin up proudly, even at such a young age. He had leaned over to whisper to her.

It will be my turn someday, Stiva.

Stiva felt a chill pass over her as she entered the ceremonial hall. The spoils of a hundred wars had made this room. It stood testimony to Aris' power, though it was rarely used. Only the most important ceremonies unfolded within the hall: royal weddings, naming days, and coronations, the occasional military promotion, the granting of an important title. Twice a year, on Lightfest and Darkfest, new dictates were announced. Aside from that, it was left to the ghosts of long-dead kings.

Those ghosts stirred today, hovering in the shadows, watching. They were not alone; the room was filled to capacity. Five hundred or so stood watching. Clothed head to toe in their most glorious outfits, the srih were the halls' final decoration, though theirs was a far more deadly and sinister beauty than that of the hall itself. Top ranking military officials, mostly Selin with a few officers from the general army, srih nobles representing individual Houses, foreign dignitaries, merchant princes, and Reonih officials made up the majority of the audience. The rest consisted of Aris' extended family and a few merchant princes.

Five hundred masked faces … and there was absolutely no way for anyone to know how many or who among them would try to undermine Chandris' rule. Only one thing was certain: somebody would. Aursan thrones did not often change hands without turmoil.

Stiva turned her gaze to the hall itself as the party moved further in. Elaborately carved thi-wood arches, gleaming with lacquer, dissected the room into segments, reaching up to meet in the center of a paneled, painted ceiling. Gold gleamed everywhere: in lamps, on candlesticks, in the veins of the marble tile on the floor. A single ring of skylights, framed in gold set with precious stones, circled above the center of the room, letting in just enough light to give the gilded decor an extra dazzle. Rows of intricately carved benches lined the hall. The carpet alone was worth a fortune: it was of the best Shadrian silk, perfectly dyed to match the blood-red color of Aris' standards. Along the far wall hung a huge tapestry with Aris' coat of arms. There were no other banners. The arms of Aris' srih nobles graced the great hall below and decorated the doors and walls of their reserved living quarters, but they had no place here.

The main focus of the room was a multi-tiered ivory dais. Images of Aris' beasts—both real and mythical—had been carved into the ivory panels. Sriak, raptors, sea serpents, flowers and trees, roses, cats, wolves, gryphons, erlits, and other creatures twisted and turned around intricate patterns and Aorhan runes. The dais itself was breathtaking, its beauty dramatically enhanced by the sunlight that filtered down from the skylight above it, which gave it an ethereal, magical glow. Thus elevated, and highlighted dramatically against the skylights, even a drunkard in muddy, threadbare clothes would have seemed regal atop it. But no citizen with even the remotest interest in survival would ever dare set foot upon it. Only Aris' royalty was allowed onto the lower tiers. The upper tier was reserved for reigning kings and queens. The penalty for breaching the royal dais was automatic and immediate, regardless of age, rank, or reason: death. Even the royal family wasn't exempt, or guaranteed survival, should they breach that protocol. Aris' royalty was subject to the same laws as the rest of its people. This was a matter of honor. This was Aris: harsh, cold, and uncompromising.

Honor. Courage. Serenity.

Chandris graced the upper tier now, and as Stiva raised her eyes to him, the sight of him struck her breathless. Magnificent in red velvet and gold, the colors of their House, Chandris glowed like a flame in the sunlight. He looked like a god. More than that, he projected an aura of power and strength that wove an unseen web through the air, making captives out of his audience. It hurt her to look at him, first emotionally and then physically, as she missed a step and turned her ankle slightly in the effort not to topple.

Moving into place beside her, Shira subtly caught her arm, and Stiva squeezed her hand in unseen gratitude.

"My nose itches," Shira whispered, speaking without moving a muscle on her face. It was a technique they had all perfected long ago, that of speaking without seeming to. One of the hidden traits of royalty, perhaps, or merely the result of long hours spent in ceremony.

"You're making mine itch, too," Stiva whispered back. They fell silent as they came to a weary halt before the dais. Kele alone continued on, climbing the giant, iridescent clamshell steps until he stood on the top tier, a step above Chandris. As acting regent, Kele held a temporary position as king throughout the short period between Cronn's death and Chandris' coronation. Otherwise, the step that took him onto the upper tier would have cost him his life.

Mohr stepped forward to speak. Another ceremony began; an endless stream of elaborate, monotone oaths, followed by puppeted responses, ritualistic gestures, and chanted vows. Normally, Reonih rituals fascinated her, but this one, much stiffer and less mystic than most, seemed to drag on endlessly. An hour grew to adulthood, and birthed another. Even Chandris looked bored. Although those present would tell this story for years to come, embellishing it to make it seem even more dramatic and glamorous, at the moment everyone looked half-asleep. Stiva's back began to hurt, and yet she could not even stretch to ease her discomfort, for honor dictated she remain still as a statue.

At high noon, the sun blazed down, forming a golden circle of light around the dais. Chandris and Kele switched places. Mohr put the crown on Chandris' head. The silence in the room rang out; the moment grew surreal. Stiva watched with unease as the House of Aris changed hands once more, and her twin became king.

It came time for individual vows of loyalty. Aret nudged her, and Stiva shook herself out of her stupor and approached the dais. Once Celor had announced her, she removed her mask and knelt before her brother.

Kele looked at her with bloodshot, bleary eyes in a stony face. He had drunk too much the night before, and would again tonight. His voice was hoarse, gravelly. He had shouted too much the night before, and would again tonight. His face was lined and haggard. He seemed to have aged a decade in the days since Cronn's death. He had buried two brothers now, and a sister, and was now the last of Caro and Zran's children. Stiva met her uncle's eyes, and their gazes locked in a silent exchange.

Then Kele spoke, and his voice boomed out over the hall. "Stiva zri Aris, do you hereby swear loyalty to Chandris zri Aris, and take him as your king? Do you vow to serve him, from now until the day you leave this life? To be loyal, and honest, and true? To protect him with your own life, if necessary? To obey and honor him, before the eyes of both men and gods?"

Stiva swallowed. Despite her nervousness, her voice managed at least some semblance of assurance. "I give oath. I swear by seven moons and seven stars, by the seven rivers of Aris, by forest and sea and sky and flame. Chandris, you are my king."

Stiva's eyes met Chandris', jeweled orbs glittering with vitality. His expression was unreadable. He gave the customary reply, and she curtsied, rose, and climbed the steps to the dais, grateful that she only rarely had to navigate the awkward, inverted shells. Reaching the top without incident, she stopped and straightened, a step below Chandris, opposite Kele.

Chandris turned to her, holding out his hand, inviting her to stand beside him

To rule beside him.

Stiva forgot protocol entirely. Her jaw dropped, and she stared at her twin in shock. Around the room, hundreds of mouths followed suit. A moment later, the srih, who had until then stood quietly, motionless as statues, came to sudden life in one roar, faces breaking into expressions of astonishment and, in some cases, outrage. An excited buzz filled the air. The silence in the room devolved into chaos. Talia hid her reaction behind a ladylike cough, while simultaneous grins split Aret and Maren's faces. Shira only stared, wide-eyed. Cerrow looked utterly shocked.

Of all the possible events that could have marked this coronation as memorable, this was one that no one had considered … including Stiva herself.

"What the hell is this?" Mohr hissed at Chandris under his breath, his voice so low that only they heard him. "You could have warned me. I only brought one crown."

Chandris stood waiting, his eyes fastened onto hers. For a brief, fleeting instant, she saw emotion cross his face, and then it was gone, lost in the cool green depths of his stare. She wondered if his reaction would have been as extreme if she had chosen exile instead of loyalty. *You never would have made it out alive*, a hidden voice whispered, deep in her mind. *Chandris does not know compromise.*

There was movement in the audience. Barls, speaking out of turn. "My lord, this cannot possibly be legal."

Chandris stared coolly at Trin's father. "I have consulted with the keeper of the law on this matter."

Almost as one, everyone turned to look at Huran, the Reonih official law keeper. His reaction would have been almost comical, had the situation been less important. Upon finding himself suddenly the center of attention, he froze, obviously uncomfortable, then regained his composure enough to nod nervously in affirmation. When he realized that five hundred pairs of eyes were now focused on him—and were not going to turn away—Huran cleared his throat loudly and explained. "There is a precedent. A situation that occurred two hundred years ago, most commonly known of through the epic *The Pride of Inake*. A duke had twin sons, and left them to rule jointly. It was made legal at that time."

The only sound in the room was the scratch of Payne's pen as he recorded the turn of events. Stiva would later ponder his words: *Chandris zri Aris began his reign by breaking tradition.*

Thick silence descended over the room like a fog. Everyone in the room was looking at her, waiting. A small dragon screamed in the sky above. Nothing else moved.

Stiva hesitated, a million thoughts rushing through her head. She opened her mouth to refuse, and completely blanked out, unable to find the words. *No,* she kept thinking. *No, I don't want this.*

But then she looked at Maren and Shira, and realized she had a chance to make their world better.

Her heart pounding, Stiva stepped up to stand beside her twin.

In doing so, she became queen of Aris.

"Aris, I give you your queen," Chandris announced loudly.

A clamorous roar of shouts filled the hall. They cheered, whether they meant it or not. Lyle saluted, and the voices of the Selin crashed through the hall like synchronized thunder. Around the outer edges of the hall, the Selin shifted. Stiva saw Vane, the captain of the Black Boot, gesture and murmur something quietly to Dallan, his brother and second. Stiva's guard responded to the change in dynamic both quickly and efficiently, taking a more defensive stance. Stiva nodded at them in recognition of that grim professionalism. Keorl, the youngest of them, shot her a quick thumbs-up. The rest stayed in formation.

Kele sent Rory, the treasurer, to fetch another crown. The room waited. The world waited.

Trin's father looked at her expressionlessly, as though she were a tasteless decoration, a statue.

Stiva was barely aware of the rest of the ceremony. She stood in a daze as the formal procedure ended and the family filed down off the dais. It took her a moment to realize that she was now expected to walk at the head of the procession, beside Chandris.

It took her a moment to realize that she was queen.

The official coronation ceremony was followed by a long parade through the streets of Aris, the second in as many days. The coronation parade differed from Cronn's funeral procession in almost every way possible. Yesterday's solemn convoy had exited the city by the west gate, following a bleak stony trail to the House of the Dead. This one went to the east, towards the sacred King Tree. And, while Aris' people had been reserved and respectful the day before, today, they were celebrating.

The streets were packed. Thousands had come to watch the parade. All of the Selin marched, weapons oiled to a shine, the murdik stones on their uniforms gleaming in the sun. The Reonih too, were part of the procession. Chandris and Stiva sat in a gleaming red wood carriage, which was pulled by six white birds in jeweled tack. The city, so recently subdued by mourning, now came alive with celebration. Dancers and acrobats in brightly colored costumes spun in synchronicity before them, bending and twisting their bodies into seemingly impossible shapes. Fire dancers, mummers, buskers, and mimes took up residence on sidewalks and street corners. A veritable orchestra of Reonih bards beat skin drums in a throbbing rhythm that had even the eldest onlookers tapping their feet, while maidens and children threw flowers and rice. Vendors offered fish pies and pastries to the crowds, and the city fountains flowed with spirits and ale. To mark the occasion, many of Aris' citizens went masked. The citizens took in the sight through the faces of beasts and birds and mythical creatures.

That was Aris, capable of moving rapidly from the depths of sorrow to the extreme of joy, as inclined to song and dance as they were to warfare and violence.

One could see shock passing through the crowd as Aris' citizens realized that they had not only a new king, but also a new queen. The reactions were almost uniform. They blinked, stared, breathed a curse or two of disbelief, spoke excitedly to whoever was standing beside them ... then resumed cheering, some shouting even more loudly. Seeing the twins united once more drove Aris into an uproar. The cheers were deafening. Even the Selin were smiling. As the parade passed, the people of Aris fell in behind it, many of them singing and dancing as they followed the procession to a bright meadow that stood as an informal border between city and wilderness.

The parade ended at a field just outside the city walls, on the east side of the city. A massive rupalier tree stood in the center of that meadow, so tall it seemed to stretch into the very sun, thrusting up from the earth like a giant spear. The meadow grass around it had been flattened into a spiral shape.

The King Tree.

The crowds fell in behind the procession, still dancing and laughing, forming a great circle around the spiral. The Reonih began their part of the ritual. This was the final formality, after which the coronation festivities would truly begin. The rest of the week would be filled with celebration. Bonfires would blaze in fields and along the beaches, and the line of watchtowers that connected Aris from border to border would blaze with colored fire. The faires, feasts, and athletic games would continue for days. In the arena, there would be a week of bloodsport with a truly coveted prize: admission to the Selin. For seven days, there would be hunts and plays and feasts. The harbor and river would host parades of brightly decorated boats. Down on the beaches, drum circles and flame eaters would compete with actors and snake-charmers and bards.

But first, the king must be bound to the land.

The inner circle of this second, shorter ceremony was all Reonih. Chandris was given a second crown, this one woven of shardwood, dyed seaweed, feathers, and bits of thornwall, and adorned with a single, blood-red ruby. He put his hand through a small fire and then vats of water, earth, and herbs. While he did this, Mohr carved the runic version of his name into the tree, and then cut Chandris' arm with the king-sword. Chandris then rubbed some of his blood into the rune Mohr had just inscribed on the tree.

Thus, he bound himself eternally to the land of Aris.

Stiva, as queen, must do these things as well. She felt dazed, even when the kingsword bit her forearm. As much as she respected the ways of the Reonih, she was too overwhelmed to concentrate, and went through the motions numbly, her head still spinning.

Mohr approached as she was binding her wrist to stop the bleeding. Stiva searched the familiar face for a hidden wink, a smile, anything, but his face was unreadable, even harsh.

He cast the runesticks in divination, and Stiva stared at the patterns.

The runecast promised glory and wealth. But they also foretold darker things: blood and betrayal, strife and poverty and trying times. The tense set of Mohr's shoulders belied the concern he felt, though his voice and face remained calm.

Stiva's vision was once more eclipsed by fluttering wings and shadow. She shuddered, ice cold in the daylight.

A shadow crossed the sun.

Omen.

CHAPTER 5

Aris' great hall was alive that night, vibrant and animated, a maelstrom of colors, faces, and sounds. Brightly colored banners bearing the crests of Aris' most powerful srih houses hung on the stone walls. Beneath the twining intricate runes, silk-clad dancers draped in colorful jewels spun like pinwheels as flutes, lyres, pipes and drums filled the air with festive music. The sound of numerous voices competing with the music melted into a senseless din punctuated by bursts of uproarious laughter, disembodied bits of conversation, and the rhythmic thud of pounding feet. A small army of servants maneuvered their way through the crowd of revelers, carefully balancing platters heaped with steaming food or trays of crystal goblets. The coronation banquet had begun in the late afternoon, and would likely continue into the very heart of night.

At the high table, the mood was somewhat darker.

"You could have given us some warning," Kele grumbled sourly through a bite of vru. He dipped a wheth biscuit into a dish of rhinberry sauce as he spoke. "I felt like a fool sending a servant for the second crown. Poor old Rory nearly collapsed from the strain of having to go all the way down to the lower vaults and then rush back up to the ceremonial hall."

"I'm as surprised as you are," Stiva protested. "Chandris said nothing of it to me."

"Or to me," Aret put in. He motioned a serving girl to his side, continuing. "He had his reasons, I'm sure, for keeping silent about it. It certainly saved him the trouble of trying to convince the srih to accept the idea. By the time they found out, it was too late for them to do anything." He pointed his fork at his plate, gesturing to the serving girl. He did not look first to be sure he had her attention. He was srih, a son of the ruling House; he needed no such reassurance. "More roast vhar, steamed kale, and mushroom gravy. And another fried dit."

The servant nervously obliged Aret's request, her brow furrowed slightly in concentration as she carefully measured the correct amount of meat, taking care to hold the knife by the proper joints. Her features showed something close to terror as she approached the small cauldron in the center of the table, which was heated by its own blue fire. Gingerly, the girl took a dit from the nearby platter and dropped the tiny fish into the cauldron, wherein the boiling grease sizzled and spat viciously. Moving slowly, she cautiously extracted the dit with a pair of tongs and put it on Aret's plate, breathing a heavy sigh of relief when it held together. She was new, Stiva realized, and obviously terrified of making some heinous, humiliating mistake. Recalling her own frustration at learning the seemingly endless decorum and protocols of srih dining, Stiva smiled sympathetically at the girl ... and met Talia's look of disapproval with a cool stare.

It was nice to know she could no longer be bullied by her aunt.

To her right, Kele was still muttering. And still dipping the biscuit. "It's lunacy," he grunted. "Always thought you were the mad one, girl, off in your own world with your songs and poems, living a sylvan dream with the Reonih every minute of your life. Turns out *he's* the cracked egg. Seems the years abroad knocked the sense out of his head instead of into it like they were supposed to. Last I knew, you two couldn't even stand to be in the same room. I don't see how you intend to rule together."

Two seats down, Shira winced. Aret looked uncomfortable, keeping his eyes fixed on his plate as the girl meticulously spooned gravy onto the vhar.

"Thrones are not favors, to be tossed around like baubles," Kele went on. "He'll learn that the hard way, I fear." He spared Stiva a sidelong glance, finishing around a mouthful of food. "So will you."

The biscuit fell apart on its next descent into the sauce. Kele looked at the sodden mass in disgust, and then threw it to the floor, where it was immediately snapped up by a dog.

"Almost started a civil war right there," Kele grumbled. He lifted his goblet and drained it in one long gulp, barely waiting for the wine girl to refill it before drinking again. "Madness. Sheer madness. They would have left, I think, walked out, but for the feast."

By "they" he meant the srih; the vassals, princes, aristocrats and warlords that were the fingers of the fist that was the crown, they who held the borders and the choicest lands for the throne, whose men followed Aris' banner to war. Stiva looked around the room, eyeing the tables where the srih were seated. At some of them, drunken laughter and boasts abounded. At others, it was heads close together and lowered voices, eyes moving across the room taking careful stock of the rest as srih judged srih, reckoning enemies and allies, wealth and territory, influence and manpower.

Not a good sign.

A tight lump formed in Stiva's throat. She put her fork down, eyeing the food without appetite.

Stiva had already reckoned that Chandris had acted out of logic and not sentiment. Knowing that rumors of the rift between the twins were widespread and ugly, Chandris had taken the swiftest, surest course to discrediting them, and thus ensured that that feud, at least, could not easily be turned against him. He had also mollified her, taken the edge off whatever anger she still held over Trin's demise. The power she held would be secondary to his, of course. She could never overrule him, or issue major orders without his approval, save perhaps in an emergency. But in the meantime, it was a much higher honor than she had ever expected him to give her.

"Madness," Kele said again. "Best not be planning on having any sons," he said. He was apparently speaking to Stiva, though he didn't look at her.

"Kele," Talia said sharply, "That's enough. You've had enough. Do you purposely intend to make a fool of yourself before the whole kingdom?"

Kele's eyes snapped coldly onto Talia's face. "Shut your mouth, woman. Or I will."

In the midst of the celebration, the high table rang with silence.

Talia went white. "You drunken sod," she hissed. "How dare you speak to me like that in public?"

Kele dropped his fork to level an icy stare at his wife. "I just buried my brother," Kele growled. The growl ended in a roar as Talia opened her mouth to speak: *"Be silent!"*

Even amidst the clamor, Kele's voice carried. The noise level in the hall dropped a notch as srih and servant alike glanced toward the disturbance. Stiva had no doubt that if they had been dining in privacy, the table would have been wiped clear of its contents and possibly even overturned by Kele's notorious fists. Certainly later tonight, the sounds of angry shouting would fill the hall that held their suite.

The room quieted. All eyes turned to the royal family. The music stopped. Servants halted mid-stride. Behind her, Dallan shifted nervously.

Kele stood and loudly toasted Chandris and Stiva, skillfully twisting the attention to his advantage. Roars shook the air. Music and dancing resumed with renewed fervor.

Stiva wanted to crawl under the table.

Below, the dancers spun themselves into a frenzy, drops of vivid color that spun like flowers in a stream. Stiva looked up and caught Lyle watching, his face guarded.

"So do you think me incompetent?" Stiva asked her uncle quietly, when he had regained his seat. "Or merely unacceptable?"

Her question took him off-guard. Kele looked at her slowly, as though realizing for the first time that she was no longer just his niece, but now also his queen, which complicated the family dynamics considerably.

"I didn't mean—"

"I did not ask for this crown," Stiva continued calmly, "but it is mine now, regardless, and I intend to use it wisely. You are right to say I spend my time immersed in songs and poems. I know a hundred kingsongs and a hundred ballads, a hundred histories, a hundred epics, a hundred battle songs. I know every tactic in every war used by every king the Reonih have ever crowned." Without looking, she gestured around the room, indicating the srih. "And I know just as well as you that some of them are likely to protest this with weapons, and some with words, while some will shrug with indifference. Some of them will fight this, and I will have to deal with that; I need your support, Kele, not your temper. Do I have that?"

Kele looked at his plate and sighed, his anger fading. "Of course you do," he said, his tone growing more civil, almost reassuring, "It's not your mind that worries me, Stiva; it's the discord between you and Chandris, which will now pull the throne back and forth with it. He was a fool to crown you, though not because you're incapable. I never thought that. But he's asking for trouble. We've had problems with raiding parties. Then the trouble between you and Chandris …" Kele shook his head. Instead of finishing his sentence, he lifted his goblet and finished that.

The ghost joined them then: Mykhal. Though her cousin had been in his grave nearly four years, Stiva could almost see Mykhal's reflection in his father's eyes.

Talia sniffed. "You're drunk."

"Hold your tongue, woman," Kele growled. "It must be tired by now; let it rest."

Aret shoved his chair back and stood angrily, careless of the servant he nearly tripped.

"Where are you going?" Talia asked him, a puzzled frown pulling her face down.

"To eat with my caste." Aret replied without looking at her. He picked up his plate, took a final sip of wine, and then set the emptied goblet back down on the table. "This is the first decent meal I've had all this cycle, but I can't possibly stomach any of it with you two around."

Talia stared after her son with a shocked expression as he made his way to a table of Selin. Aret did not look back, but the tension on his face eased a bit as his caste-mates loudly greeted his approach with cheers and drunken howls. He was pulled down among them more than he sat, and was quickly immersed in a much more jovial conversation.

Predictably, Talia turned on Kele. "You did this to him. You drove him into the Selin, you pushed him away from us. Did you hear what he said? He despises us."

"Do you blame him?" Kele snapped.

Talia drew back, eyes narrowing.

"Can I go?" Maren piped up. Unanimous denials answered him from all quarters. Pouting, he slouched down into his chair, crossing his arms sullenly.

"You've been asking all week to eat at the high table," Talia snapped. "So eat."

Maren slumped down, kicked the chair leg and popped another fried dit into his mouth.

"Sit up, Maren," Shira murmured, as the music stopped again. "Chandris is coming back."

Chandris made his way across the room towards them, seemingly oblivious to the bows of his subjects, who dipped before them, bending like a wave at his passage. His arm was thrown in camaraderie around the shoulders of the blond man who had been at the funeral. Cerrow followed just behind. Six or seven others stood with them. Some of these were Chandris' old friends, others had apparently returned with him from Vrehn.

Belatedly, Celor, the herald, introduced the blond man as Jahn, a Vrehnian prince whose father's court had been Chandris' home for nearly four cycles. It took only a glance for Stiva to see that the two were close. She frowned, watching the foreign prince more closely. But he too was srih, skilled in the art of deception. Nothing in his face revealed anything of his thoughts.

A million thoughts raced through Stiva's brain. She eyed her twin suspiciously as he settled into the seat that had been Cronn's, wondering at his motives for crowning her. She could by no means dismiss the possibility that he had crowned her only to make her a pawn, a prize to be traded to some distant king to secure a tempting alliance. But the thought slid sideways in her mind, refusing to take hold. Chandris had always hated being separated from her. He could best judge her mood, her intent, her motives by looking into her eyes.

Or from her side, where he now sat frowning at her.

Mohr and Cerrow took their respective places at the table. Kele continued eating, his rage silent now. Talia dabbed at her face with a napkin and pretended to be fascinated by the dancers.

"Mohr," Stiva said quietly. "I'd like a scrying tomorrow. I know Mehran will send me runecasts daily, but if you wouldn't mind, I'd like one from you."

The Reonih High Priest looked at her, his eyes, as always, reminding her of some bird of prey. "Of course, *saya*," he said, giving her the formal title of queen. He turned to Chandris. "I can do another for you as well, if you like."

"No need," he said. He met Mohr's eyes, something of challenge and something of curiosity crossing his face. "There is war in my future, and change. Danger and deception. That is the runecast of any new-crowned king, is it not?"

Mohr raised his eyebrows. "Fair enough," he said, and lifted his goblet. When finished drinking, he cleared his throat and spoke again. "There is an old tradition among the Sijhani, to mark the night of a great change. The ritual begins with a—"

Chandris interrupted him. "Such rituals and symbols have sway because of their effect on the human mind, I suspect. Men find comfort in such things, such traditions. I do not think the fate of the world rests within the shell of an oyster or the fall of bones against stone."

Mohr's brows raised. The high priest spoke carefully. "If there is some advice, some help I can give you—"

"Help *them*," Chandris said quietly, motioning out at those in the hall. "Prophecies never make sense until the events they foretell come to pass. I'd value your opinion on less esoteric matters, but I've learned to put little stock in mysticism."

Clearly somewhat less than thrilled by this answer, Mohr nodded. "My opinion and my wisdom are not always borne of the same source, but both are at your service." He turned to Stiva. "And yours, as well."

Stiva nodded. "Thank you, Mohr," she said sincerely.

"Men create their own destinies." Chandris said. "Your kind open their eyes, that they see things with a wider mind, that they may choose those destinies with thought. But do not mistake your place in this court. Aris rules by the sword, not the staff."

The statement was dressed as a challenge, but Chandris did not seem interested in debate, and Mohr chose not to pursue the topic. Stiva watched her twin looking out over the hall, his gaze taking in the dancers, the detail of the stonework, the bards. Something in his eyes chilled her.

Jahn, the Vhrenian Chandris had brought home with him, seized the moment to raise his glass in a toast. "In my country, we also have traditions for change. Most of them involve alcohol. And so on that note, I would like to bestow the blessings of Vrehn on the New Crown of Aris.

Peace, prosperity, and valor. May the Sun God shine on the lands of Aris."

Chandris lifted his glass. "Thank you, my friend. I hope you will stay on."

Jahn nodded. "Absolutely."

"Jahn, is it?" Kele asked. "You are the crown prince of Vrehn, are you not?"

"Prince, yes, but let's hope the crown never rests on my noggin," Jahn said cheerfully. "I've six brothers, and I prefer the field to the chair."

Kele actually smiled.

Jahn turned to Chandris. "If you will permit, I have a gift that may interest you."

Chandris took a sip from his goblet. "Yes?"

"You were so fascinated by our Relics during your stay," Jahn continued. "I thought you would appreciate this."

Chandris' eyes sharpened with interest as Jahn reached into a pouch and drew out a small object. Everyone at the table craned their necks to see.

Chandris turned it over. "What is it?"

"Here." Jahn reached over and touched it. Suddenly it lit up, emanating a cold, bluish light. Chandris, startled, dropped it onto the table. Jahn retrieved it and fumbled with tiny buttons and switches. "Press this button. You'll see images taken when the Zhur smashed the cities of the Elders. If the device goes dark, put it in the sun for three days, with the screen facing up. Place leaves of rhega and seashells beside it. Watch those images."

Shira gasped. "Is that a Relic? They are forbidden here."

Chandris looked at her, amused. "Are you going to tell the king?"

"Such things should not be toyed with," Cerrow said. "It's dangerous."

"It's quite safe," Jahn said. He turned back to Chandris. "If you'll permit?" Jahn took the device, and showed Chandris a few of the buttons. "This one, and then this one, and see. There."

The device gave off a cold, blue light, almost like starlight. The lights moved, flashing and shifting. Stiva, looking closer, gasped. Images flickered and danced within it. She was able to make out strange, fantastic landscapes, visions of distant, alien lands. The likenesses of people moving and speaking played through the tiny window.

"It's like looking into the past." Chandris was fascinated.

Cerrow's face darkened. "That is a sacred Relic, not a toy. These things are not meant to be handled casually."

"It's from Vrehn," Jahn said. "I've taken none of yours."

Mohr sipped his wine. "Jahn, is it? Cerrow is right in this. The Relics are not toys." He looked Chandris in the eye. "I trust your wisdom and responsibility with regards to this. Such things are dangerous, deceptive. Best left alone."

Stiva shivered, suddenly cold.

"We see things differently, in Vrehn," Jahn said. "In my father's court, such things are openly displayed, so that the people can know they are descended from gods of the sky."

Chandris set the thing down, and stood. The room fell silent. "I wish to welcome you all to my court. Each and every one of you has my sincere vow that I will do everything in my power to not only protect Aris, but to improve it."

A roar of cheers crossed the room, a wave.

Chandris motioned to Cerrow, who was seated at his right hand. "I must recognize the foresight and wisdom of Cerrow, who saw the wisdom in having me fostered abroad, as though he knew exactly what I needed to move forward. Cerrow, you have been the greatest mentor a king could ask for. I wish for you to continue on in the position of Prime Minister."

Cerrow's face was unreadable. He bowed deeply. "I would be honored, *sayo*."

There was a silence over the room, and then applause.

Lyle leaned back against the outer door. He caught Stiva's eyes and nodded, and she knew a brief relief that there was at least one man she had no reason to doubt.

One, among hundreds.

Stiva stood up. The minstrels stopped playing immediately. She blinked, and looked to the door, expecting some newly arrived king, then realized that it was herself they had paused for.

They all looked up at her, curious. Stiva looked at Chandris, who was still seated.

"Dance with me, brother," Stiva told him. "It's tradition."

Shrugging, he rose to oblige, perhaps sensing that it was not truly the dance she sought but brief asylum, a chance to speak privately. Doubtless it would be weeks before things settled enough to give either of them any leisure time.

As they moved into the center of the floor, the other dancers backed away respectfully, giving them room. Stiva looked across the hall to the minstrels' alcove and nodded at Reide. He looked back at her, picking up his lute, but the smile he gave her never reached his eyes.

Song filled the air once more, twining with smoke and the scents of food. Music flowed around them like water. The twins moved in perfect synchronicity, their movements flawlessly matched. The steps were formal, intricate. They handled them alike, with the same fluid grace.

"It's been some time," Chandris said, stating the obvious, "since we've danced together."

"We're much better at it now than we were the last time." Stiva lost herself in the dance as they spun around the room, then looked up at him again. "Why did you do it?"

"Don't you remember?" Chandris tilted his head. "I had planned it since childhood."

Memory stirred; a golden meadow ringed by a rust-shaded wood, a warm day beneath a bright sun. They had chased their cats after shadows and butterflies and played at being king and queen. *I will make Aris a bright shining dream*, he had said to her then. *An empire greater than any other, even the Elders'. And you will help me, Stiva. You will be my queen.*

"That was a long time ago," Stiva mused. "And if I hold you to everything you promised me in childhood, I shall be expecting a purple cat and a vlorship filled with honey pastries to arrive shortly."

Chandris chuckled, but the laughter did not quite reach his eyes.

"You could have warned me, at least."

The dance spun them apart and brought them back together. As had the world.

"No, I couldn't." Chandris caught her hand; she twirled around him. "Not without checking to see if you would stay loyal. I would have been a fool to dangle that sort of power before you and then try to gauge the honesty of your reaction."

"It was honest enough," Stiva muttered. "I nearly fainted."

"I doubt that; you've never been that delicate. I thought Shira was going to, though."

"Chandris," Stiva tried a different approach. "You didn't do this because of anything we said when we were children. You've never been the least bit sentimental. And you didn't do it to make peace. You accomplished that last night. I never asked for this. I don't understand whether you meant it as a gift or punishment."

He shrugged. "Take it as you will," he said. "And make of it what you will."

"I'm not so sure it was a good idea," Stiva said. "I never wanted to rule Aris."

Her twin looked amused by this. "Precisely."

Stiva frowned. "I don't understand."

"You've never shown even the slightest desire for power," Chandris explained. "You have always sought freedom, instead. You've always been much more interested in the Reonih, and in music, than in elevating yourself. I need someone I can trust to stay here when I am away. Someone who cares for Aris, someone the srih and Reonih will respect in my absence. However much you despise me, you love this land. And I imagine you would bare your claws, sister, before you let it be threatened."

"Lyle, Kele, or Aret could have done that."

"If I ride to war, I want them with me." Chandris shook his head. "Or perhaps I should say *when* I ride to war."

Stiva felt her stomach twist. "The crown hasn't even settled onto your head, and already you speak of war."

He regarded her thoughtfully, green eyes unreadable. "Day and night, you and I," Chandris mused quietly. "Yet I always see myself reflected in your eyes."

Something in his tone or his face rang a bell of warning that tolled deep in her soul. "Chandris?"

"I want peace, and unity. I want to bring brightness and knowledge back to this world."

Noble words, and stirring. But in his green eyes, Stiva saw a raging black fire, one that could consume worlds, and kings, and souls. She backed a step, staring at the gilded stranger who shared her soul. For a moment, she forgot the dance, until he casually guided her back into it.

"You've changed," Stiva whispered. "I don't even know you any more, Chandris."

"Of course I've changed," Chandris looked almost amused. "What did you expect, the same boy who went away? I chose that exile. And my eyes were opened for it; I learned a thing or two through its duration. I changed, and I grew, enough to realize that Aris must do the same if we are to survive."

She stared at him, searching for words that eluded her. "You're planning something," Stiva whispered finally. "What?"

"Survival," Chandris whispered, pointedly looking away.

Perplexed, Stiva followed the direction his eyes had taken, and found herself staring at the far side of the room, where three long tables were piled high with gifts. All of the srih, even the border lords who guarded Aris' most distant edges, had come in to pay allegiance to their new king, and, following custom, presented gifts as tokens of their loyalty. Even the poorest families gave something, even if it were only some small token, such as flowers or bread or a piece of scrimshaw. The storage rooms were already overflowing with such things, many of which the commoners had brought to the Zhrue Gate: woven baskets filled with grain or fruits, soft linens, pieces of art. The wealthier houses had brought finer gifts, such as gold, jewelry, weapons, soft furs, reams of choice cloth, incense, exotic oils and spices or painted vases, delicately crafted carvings, fine leather tack, candlesticks, flagons of wine.

In the midst of all that bounty lay a plain, burlap sack, not only used, but dirty and soiled and stuffed with straw. Stiva gasped aloud. No less than a blatant insult, that; it was a slap in Chandris' face, a brazen, shameless defiance of not only tradition and goodwill, but also the honor of the crown. The gift tables were not about wealth. They stood for respect, love, and loyalty. Theoretically, at least. Looking more closely, she spotted not one, not two, but three other sacks. A fourth joined them as she watched, falling from the outstretched hand of the lord of Barls.

Trin's father turned to look at them, a cold contemplative stare fixed on Chandris. His gaze moved to the high table, eventually fixing on Cerrow. A look passed between them. It was just a glimpse, a fleeting moment, but Stiva felt chills run down her spine. Then he turned and marched out, without even bothering to pay his respects.

Cerrow stood to the side of the room, watching the twins. His face was hard to read, a mask of age and twisted thoughts. Something cold twined through Stiva's guts, ringing like the chime of a bleak funeral bell.

Barls' hatred for Chandris had never been clear to her until that moment. She had always thought that he blamed her for Trin's death. Now she knew it was Chandris. And that was trouble, breeding and festering, deception brewing against a new king, even as they drank the first of his wine, the old king not yet settled into his tomb. Barls was a powerful house, capable of insurrection that would not be easily quelled.

Aris had been breeding such enemies for centuries.

War danced already on the smoky strands of incense trailing through the air. War laughed in the fires of the torches in sconces on the walls. War sang in the minstrels' voices.

Stiva felt the eyes of her twin boring into her.

"Did you see that?" Chandris asked her quietly. "Do you see, Stiva?"

She nodded, staring after Barls' retreating back.

"It begins," Chandris whispered.

"Chandris—" She choked on his name and could say no more.

"I need your help, Stiva." Chandris gave her a frank look. "If you do not care enough about Aris to help me fight for it, then abdicate now. There'll be little resistance, if any."

It was a chaotic world they had been born to, one slashed by politics and fear and eternal war. A chaotic world they now ruled, and had to, somehow, protect and keep whole. Stiva stared around the room and realized that the lives of those who filled if were now her responsibility. Panic coursed through her as she realized the sheer scope of her new title, the power and responsibility it entailed. It was not the first time that day she had regretted her decision, for she knew that she had just bound herself to everything she despised about the srih; their serpentine politics, their bloody greed, their cruel casualty about human lives.

But something in her soul stopped her from walking away.

Taking a deep breath, she looked up at her twin, meeting eyes that were mirrors to her own. "No," she said. "I stand with you, Chandris. For Aris."

The music stopped. The dance ended. Polite clapping filled the room. It had nothing to do with their skill. They would have clapped even if the twins had missed every possible step. Chandris bowed; Stiva curtsied. They left the floor together. Almost immediately, the displaced dancers returned, and song once more filled the air.

The high table waited. Stiva could see Kele and Talia still arguing, while poor Maren squirmed in his seat and Shira stared miserably at her food. Cerrow drew Chandris into conversation as soon as he sat down.

Stiva grimaced. At the moment, the dungeon seemed more welcoming. Looking around the crowded hall, she spotted Reide, Twyla, and Marcelle in the same small minstrels' alcove that they almost always passed these nights in.

A path automatically cleared for her as she made her way towards them. They rose as she approached, which they had never done before. She froze, unaccustomed to the deference, just barely stopping herself from looking over her shoulder for her parents as they greeted her with the proper terms.

"Relax." Stiva motioned to their seats with her hand as some of the Black Boot positioned themselves at the entrance to the alcove.

"You had quite a day. No, sit here." Reide offered her his seat, the best in the alcove. "How are you holding up?"

"I feel like I'm dreaming." Stiva said, accepting the seat. She lowered her voice. "Did you see Barls?"

Reide nodded. "Best watch that one."

Stiva held out her hand, and a servant immediately put a goblet into it.

Aret approached, accompanied by his friend and caste-mate, Khren.

"I can't believe Barls did that," Aret said, sitting down. Firelight gleamed against the murdik stones on both his uniform and Khren's. The gems were engraved with the glyphs that named his rank, caste, and house. The last two were nearly identical in Aret's case, as Kele's arms differed only slightly from Cronn's.

"Should we ride after him?" Khren asked Stiva. There was an eager note to his voice. He was Selin to the bone, that one, always spoiling for a fight.

Stiva shook her head. "Not tonight."

"Chandris will not let such an insult pass."

Stiva looked across the room at her brother, and the darkness on his face. "This is no night for bloodshed."

"Idiot." Aret reached for the flagon. "He's only set himself up to be made an example of ... and saved Chandris the trouble of finding one."

Stiva bit her lip, recalling nights when Trin had sat with them all.

Khren reached over the low table in the center of the alcove and helped himself to some cheese. "Chandris' first challenge will be bringing the vassals to heel. He's got his work cut out for him."

"War, this cycle," Reide commented.

That was nothing new, but the thought, regardless, sobered them. All of them, that is, save Aret and Khren, who, being Selin, clinked glasses and looked cheered by the prospect of battle.

"Are you coming to the arena tomorrow, Stiva?" Marcelle asked.

Stiva looked at her blankly. "What?"

"The gladiator fights? The winners will be allowed to join the Selin."

Stiva had forgotten. It was a tradition that after the death of a king, bloodsport provided an open door to the elite guard. She shook her head. "I don't think so. I am not really in a mood for more death."

"Your mother doesn't look very happy," Khren said to Aret.

"Is she ever?" Aret snorted. He glanced at the high table, where Kele and Talia were clearly beginning to argue. The music drowned out their words, fortunately. "She doesn't know what happiness is."

Stiva jabbed her cousin lightly with her elbow. "Look: Ghodrik's dancing."

They both chuckled at the sight of their old tutor, a grim, ancient Reonih, merrily kicking up his heels with Adele, one of Stiva's maids. Twyla giggled, and then hiccupped loudly, which set the rest of them to good-natured teasing.

"Where is your wife?" Marcelle asked Khren.

"Sleeping. She's due soon. She waddled along to her brother's house after the ceremony." Khren chuckled. "She scared me earlier. Got so pale, I thought she was going to drop the child in the middle of the ceremony."

Marcelle turned to Reide. "Is there a precedent for that?"

The bard frowned, thinking. "No, but one of Trian's kings sneezed through his coronation. And one of Delora's had gas."

"All Delorans have gas," Aret said. "It's their food."

They all laughed.

"Who is that?" Marcelle craned her neck to get a better look at some young srih.

Stiva followed Marcelle's gaze. "Ceth," she said. "They're a smaller house, outside of Horenfort. That's one of the younger sons."

"Oh." Marcelle sounded disappointed. "And that one, in the red?"

It was an old game between them, which had kept them amused through countless formal occasions. Guess who this one was, guess who that one was, guess who had more land, more livestock, more gold. Marcelle and Stiva had become close in the time Chandris had been gone. Marcelle was technically a hostage, a lower princess of Jara's court, sent to Aris as a token of an uneasy peace. It was tradition in Aursa for kings and srih to send such hostages to foster at one another's courts. This was done in the name of alliance, though it did not always end as such. Aris had cousins in numerous courts, though it went unspoken that these hostages did not necessarily ensure peace. Nothing did.

They passed a flagon of spirits around, as they always did. The room sped up, or seemed to. Conversation danced among them, but it was less familiar, less relaxed, than it had been. Stiva had been at court her entire life, but in the space of a day, of a breath, the dynamics of her world and her inner circle had changed. Her oldest, dearest friends were now slightly nervous around her. It wasn't just the group dynamic that seemed different. The entire court had changed. Cronn's voice was missing from the noise, and Lara's silent grace seemed to haunt the room. Despite the festive atmosphere, grief came over Stiva like a cloud. Lara's absence seemed to burn a hole in the room. A lump rose in her throat, and she bit her lip, holding back a sudden flood of tears.

Reide, somehow sensing her sorrow, laid a hand on her shoulder, careless of protocol. "Are you alright, Stiva?"

"Just sad, and still in shock." She smiled up at him gratefully. "I want you with me, Reide," she said. "Do you understand? There are few I trust, and none so much as you."

"I am a bard," Reide said, "Not srih. I belong in the bard's alcove, not at the high table."

"You belong," Marcelle cut in, "in a theorica with the rest of the madmen."

Reide ignored the joke. "Anything you ask, Stiva," he said. "Only promise me we'll still sing together."

"I promise," Stiva said. "Then you'll stay on at the castle?"

Reide nodded. "Of course," he said. But his eyes were uneasy.

A sudden crash from the high table made them all turn and look. Chandris was standing up, half-turned around, his arm falling in a manner which suggested he had just struck someone. And he had, though it was a moment before Stiva found his victim.

The serving girl, the new one, lay crumpled into a heap at Chandris' feet, writhing in pain and wailing. It at first seemed a bit of an extreme reaction, even to a solid blow, and Stiva frowned, puzzled. Then she saw the overturned cauldron of hot grease, its contents sizzling and steaming on the floor, saw the steam and smoke coming from the girl, saw her clothing wet and stained, saw the way her hands clutched at her face. The horrible stench of burning flesh reached Stiva's nostrils, and she gagged. Realization struck her like a physical blow.

Chandris had burned her with the oil. Deliberately.

Silence was instant and complete, even at the heart of the disturbance. Everyone froze. Even the bards stopped playing. Of the hundreds in the hall, not one spoke. Only the girl's screams broke the quiet.

Chandris sat down again and calmly resumed eating, as though nothing had happened. Two other servants, pale-faced and stricken, carried the poor girl away. Her screams echoed eerily through the halls before fading.

Shock chased horror through Stiva's soul. Chandris had always been arrogant, cunning, even cold, but he had never been purposely cruel. And then she realized, in that way that she sensed his thoughts, knew his thoughts as though they were her own, that he had done it to make a statement, a demand for respect. Glancing around at the expressions on the faces of the srih, which ranged from shock to deep thought, she knew he had won it. They were reconsidering him now, quite seriously.

And that poor wretched girl had paid the price, likely with something as trivial as a dropped crumb or a splash of gravy.

"My gods," Marcelle breathed.

Aret looked sick. Stiva felt sick. Shira *was* sick, judging by the way she fled the high table.

Hesitantly, the minstrels resumed playing. Conversation picked up again, though it was more subdued. Some of the srih, Stiva noted, seemed to have lost their appetites, while others did not seem the least bit bothered by the incident. There were srih, she knew, that treated their own servants with a brutality she found sickening. Some refused to release serfs from their lands. Others demanded more work from them than they should, or took a greater portion of their serfs' produce than they should. But Aris had never been such a house. They had always treated their castle staff extremely well, and expected their own subjects to do the same. The serfs who rented properties on Aris' country manors were required to work only one day a week for Aris to pay their share, and were given larger shares of land than most srih offered. This was, to be fair, not just for benevolence: it also helped keep the serfs loyal. Here, in the castle, even the lowest scullery maid or stableboy was well-fed and healthy, decently clothed, not overworked or beaten, sheltered safe and warm in winter, allowed to marry freely, given medicine and access to healers when they were sick, and set to light duties when they were pregnant, nursing, or old.

But they were, on occasion, made examples of.

The room seemed to fold in upon itself, choking her. Stiva felt the blood drain from her face. Her stomach twisted into a knot, and she felt overwhelmed with both fear and nausea. She dealt with it the only way she could.

She fled.

The music paused as she exited, then resumed, fading away behind her as she left the great hall behind, trading its poisoned brightness for Aris' cool shadowed halls. Once past the rotunda, and thus freed of prying eyes, she ran, careless of her dress, careless of the whispers that rose up behind her, careless of the Black Boot jogging along behind her, careless of everything but the sudden need to put as much distance between herself and her twin as possible.

As large as the castle was, she ran out of breath before she ran out of room. She found herself looking down into the smallest of the three main courtyards in the castle complex, the one commonly known as the Third.

An ugly sibling to the other two main courtyards, the Third paled next to the statue-and-mosaic embellished First. It owned none of the Second's imposing military starkness. Strangely, however, neither the First or Second was the most interesting place to watch. That distinctive honor went to the Third, the plainest courtyard, often a muddy mess that occupied the space between the stable complexes that held horses, birds, and cats; mews and kennels; and Aris' crafters' hall. The Third, traversed by a continuous stream of servants, clerks, couriers, and animals, was constantly busy. Stiva had witnessed everything from lovers' trysts to ridiculous drunken challenges to all-out brawls between the servants while watching the Third. Now, however, it was silent and abandoned, and there was nothing to watch but moonlight reflecting on puddles, and she paused there, allowing herself to catch her breath and ponder the day's events.

A few moments later, she found herself contemplating the look that had crossed between Cerrow and Barls. She could not put a finger on exactly what it was about Cerrow she disliked. The twins had been eight or nine cycles old when he had succeeded old Granion as prime minister, and he had been like an uncle to them, buying them gifts from the great traders' market in the city, telling them stories, taking them to the beach. He had served Cronn loyally enough, only butting heads with him occasionally, yet a few years ago a single instant had cost him Stiva's trust, a look she had found unexpectedly on his face when he thought she wasn't looking, a look of hatred, aimed not at Cronn, but at Chandris and herself. Chills had come over her in that moment.

Came a step behind her, a soft rustle in the night. She heard armor as her guards moved, and turned to see Mohr approaching. She nodded; they let him through, and he went to stand beside her.

"You have journeyed far, these past days," Mohr said quietly.

Swallowing a lump in her throat, Stiva looked up at the sky. "Not as far as some."

She thought she saw something moving in the clouds, and froze. But nothing further revealed itself, and she turned her gaze earthward again. The memory of the nightwing flashed through her mind. "I saw a nightwing the day of the funeral."

Mohr's brow creased. "Are you certain?"

Stiva nodded. "Absolutely. It broke my window."

She was about to ask him about the dreams, the painting, but something in Mohr's gaze froze the words in her throat. Instead she drew a deep breath. "You saw what happened back there," she said quietly. "What he did."

Mohr offered nothing beyond a nod as confirmation. "You have been given a great thing. Power. Use it wisely, Stiva, else it will use you."

They were quiet a moment. The sounds of revelry still filled the city, the night. "Did you see this coming?" Stiva asked, after a moment. "My coronation?"

He was quiet for a moment. "Everything has its counter, its balance," he said. "Every word, every action, every age."

Stiva pondered that. That was the way of the Reonih. They rarely gave straight answers, but made one decipher things for themselves.

"I hope you don't mind me asking for scrying," Stiva told him. "I know Mehran will send me runecasts, and I know you are busy, but … I do not ask lightly, Mohr. I know you advised my mother. I … I would …" She trailed off, fighting back a rush of tears. "I will need your support."

"And I yours." Mohr studied her, his face unreadable. "You would like to continue the ways of your mother."

"Yes." Her voice was small.

"Very well," Mohr bowed his head. "I—we—are at your disposal. As to the scrying, I think you already know what I'm going to tell you."

She looked at him askance, a lump tightening in her throat. "War," she whispered. "You don't need a runecast to see that."

Mohr paused, choosing his words carefully, "Your reign is going to be crucial. That we have seen, and that I suspect you yourself have already sensed."

Stiva looked out at the night, at sky and sea and city. "I've dreams," she said. "Visions."

"Change comes," he said quietly. "Like the tides that twist and turn in the oceans, like a fire raging in a forest, change washes over the world, bringing in wreckage from past ages, leveling cities, Houses, entire cultures. This age will end, and another will rise. It does not require a seer to know this. That is the way of the universe. Do not fight it, for that will be your demise, as well as ours." Then he rubbed his eyes, and in the next moment, he seemed less mystic, more human. "Now, by your leave, my queen, these old bones are begging for some rest."

"Of course." Stiva looked at him inquisitively. "You'll stay the night?"

He nodded. "Reide's given me his bed. I expect he'll find a more inviting one." Mohr bowed. "Goodnight, St—" He stopped himself from addressing her by name. "Goodnight, *saya*."

Trailed by two Selin, Stiva walked back to her rooms slowly, wandering the maze of Aris' stone halls until she found herself at last outside the door to her own suite. Twyla was waiting outside with Vane, the captain of the Black Boot, and Keorl, another of her guards. Stiva started walking past them, then paused and turned to face them.

"Is something wrong, Stiva?" Twyla suddenly blanched. "I mean, *saya*."

"Don't, Twyla," Stiva said quietly. "I am Stiva to you, as I always have been. At least here, at this door and beyond it." She hesitated, thinking, then looked Twyla in the eye. "I suppose I will need more maids now, but you will always be first and foremost among them. In fact, one of the first things I will do is title you. You have always been my sister, Twyla, even if our father never acknowledged it."

Stiva waited, anticipating a look of joy crossing Twyla's face, but instead Twyla bit her lip and shook her head. "No," she said, "I'm a bastard, and to title me would open a can of worms. I'm not the only Lightfest child Cronn sired. Besides, Chandris would have me married off to some fat old march lord and sent to some distant castle on the borders in a heartbeat. I'd rather stay here, with you."

"Are you sure?"

Twyla nodded. "I am your eyes, Stiva. I've no desire to get further involved in court."

Stiva nodded and held out her hand. Twyla squeezed it. "Go on to bed, Twyla, or go back out, if you wish. I'm alright here."

Stiva moved to step inside, then stopped again. "That girl," Stiva said softly, "the one Chandris burned. See to it that she is paid full blood-debt for her injury. I want Galen to treat her himself. Have him summoned to the sick room immediately. She will not work until she is healed, and then she can choose if she wants to stay with us. If not, I will give her a house. If she wishes to stay, she can have light duties, pleasant ones."

Twyla nodded. "As you wish."

Having matched Chandris' cruelty with kindness, Stiva retreated.

It wasn't until later that she realized she had power to help more than one burned servant.

So began a long cycle.

CHAPTER 6

"You're going to get yourself killed," Cassandra said.

She was naked, sprawled nonchalantly across the soft down quilt that covered the massive bed, in a manner very unlike that of the genteel world she was supposed to belong to. From her vantage, she could not directly see the man she spoke to, for his back was to her. Though she much admired that view, she focused instead on the reflection of his face in the mirror he stood before.

The face in the mirror gave no reaction, but to tilt slightly so that the hand shaving it could reach beneath the chin. "Perhaps," the image said, unconcerned.

Cassandra rolled onto her back, putting a pillow on her stomach.

Khirin surveyed himself in the mirror, scowling. The grim expression was not a reaction to his appearance. He kept himself in good shape physically. His body was fit and hard-muscled, his skin clear and smooth, the planes of his face clean and well-angled, pleasing to look at. Straight dark hair hung loose and long past his shoulders, shining richly, a dark veil that shaded dark eyes. The seriousness in his eyes matched the small arsenal of weapons laid out on the floor around him.

Cassandra watched him dress, scrunching her face into a pout that had melted the hearts of more srih than she could count, most of whom had since gone to early graves. "I won't watch," she said. "I'm not going to go see you off to die, even if every noble in the land is there."

"You've enjoyed it well enough the last three years," Khirin told her calmly.

"That was fun. This is stupid. I thought you would have come to your senses by now." Cassandra twined herself into a more enticing position, arranging herself so that the curve of her leg fell right over his face in the mirror.

Khirin dipped the straight razor into the basin one last time before aiming it at the curve of his chin, scraping away the last of the stubble. "I told you I have chosen this."

"Chosen what? The life of a Selin? Serfs live more comfortably."

Silence hung in the air for a moment, during which the sounds of the inn infiltrated the room: the now-familiar screech of the owner's wife berating a scullery girl, the squawk of the poultry in the courtyard, the never-ending rumble of voices in the tavern below.

A nudge at the thick velvet drapes revealed the sun sinking rapidly beneath the waves of the amethyst Oburion ocean. From below, the sounds of the first patrons entering the tavern made a distant murmur. The room he had taken was the best the Inn of the Speckled Jhar had to offer, but it was still indicative of the inn's true atmosphere: dark, smoky, and rather shabby. It was a tarnished wealth, the inn owned. The once-elegant thi-wood furnishings were scarred and stained, the thick Shadrian carpets were nearly threadbare, and the heavy velvet drapes were run-down and faded with age. Rats, mice, and erlits shared the rooms with guests, and the food was mediocre at best.

For Khirin, it was perfect.

The staff was extremely discreet, though he wasn't certain if this was a cause or effect of the volume of shady business that went on within its walls. The crowded, dim-lit tavern appealed to outlaws and srih alike. It was a rough place, by any account, but the prices were cheap, the drink palpable, and, most importantly, the tavern was large enough and dark enough for any manner of dealing. The tavern's usual clientele consisted of prostitutes, smugglers, outlaws, the occasional gladiator, the occasional ex-Selin, mercenaries, and, of course, run-of-the-mill neighborhood drunkards. Khirin went unnoticed among such company.

As he preferred.

Seeing that he would not be seduced (at least not for the moment), Cassandra rolled into a sitting position, hugging her knees. "You're walking into a trap. Do you think it will be so easy to get out? You can't walk away from the Selin. You'll have every bounty hunter, Selin, and citizen looking for you."

"Not necessarily." Khirin checked the razor blade, scowling at the nick he found there.

She glared at him.

Their eyes met and locked. Memories and unspoken words flowed between them, forming a silent chain.

"I'm not going," Cassandra said. "I don't want to watch you die. And I don't want to watch you win. I've had enough bloodsport."

"That's fine," he said.

Cassandra looked away first, drawing a deep, shaky breath. "What if you lose?"

"If I lose," Khirin said quietly, "I will be dead by nightfall."

"If you win, you put on those colors. And they will never let you go." Cassandra whispered.

Silence.

"Stay if you like," he said.

"And do what? Run the potato patch they give you? Bear sons to carry Selin shields after you?" Cassandra's pretty face twisted into a scowl. "Do you expect me to spend my days peeling vegetables and spinning wool, tending roses and midwifing cattle? Spitting out sons that would run off to die as soon as they turn six?"

"Seven. They go to the institutions when they are seven." He had started his own training even before that, but it was useless to point that out.

"I'd die of boredom within a year. Besides, I hate Aris." She stretched out her arm, absently admiring the gold bracelet on her wrist. "It's cold and dreary, and my work here will be done when the coronation ceremonies end. I'm going back to Vrehn. Or Turrel. Or Jara, perhaps. Somewhere warm." Her blue eyes met his dark ones in the mirror. "Come with me."

"I'm not asking your approval," Khirin said. "I've chosen this."

He put the razor down and opened the single chest he had brought with him, and pulled out a boiled leather greave, and rummaged around for the other one. She had been through his things again. The greaves had been on top of the silver dagger, rather than below it. It did not infuriate him that she had gone through his things, but he found himself annoyed that she was goading him.

Cassandra only left trails when she wished.

Her blue eyes fixed on his. "I won't ask you again," she said, "because I know what you'll say. Don't do this, Khirin."

He didn't answer.

"What of your contract?"

"Settled," Khirin said. "Our benevolent leader has given me his blessing."

"And how many will die for this foolishness?"

He knew better than to answer that. He knew, also, exactly what she meant.

The Dralek rarely pulled the invisible reins.

Cassandra launched herself from the bed in one graceful leap, and picked up her clothes from where they lay in a tangled heap on the floor. She was dressed within a moment, without a word.

She turned to leave, then, pausing, turned back. "Khirin," she said quietly. "Don't do this. This is not your game."

"The game," he said, "is always the same. The courts you play it in are not so different that the ring. It only pretends to be more civil. The sword is kinder than the poison, in the end. More honest."

"Steel doesn't lie," she said, "but one day you will find yourself on the wrong end of it." Her voice dropped. "You cannot hide what you are. They will kill you."

He pointed out the window. "The coronation games happen once in a lifetime. They're asking no questions. And if they did, so what? I've killed no one they care about." Khirin adjusted his bracer.

The reverse, of course, was not true. But he would not speak of that.

"You will go to war with them," she said. "And die for a king you owe no allegiance to."

"Perhaps."

"There will be war," Cassandra sniffed. "Soon. This season, perhaps. Delora is sniffing around, smelling blood. There are rumors that Trian is finally cracking under siege from Orlin. If that war ends soon, Aris will have to watch that border as well."

He kept packing. "Stay," he said, "Or be silent. You won't change my mind. Delora and Aris have been battling since long before we were born, and they'll keep fighting after we're dead."

Cassandra looked at him, her blue eyes filled with sorrow. She hesitated, but her indecision—if that was truly what she felt—was short-lived. She smoothed her hair, picked up her cloak, and opened the door. She did not wish him luck or give him some token to hold for luck. That was the type of person she pretended to be, but with him, she never pretended anything.

She glanced back once. "Take care, Khirin. Try not to get yourself killed."

"You too," he said.

There was no point in saying anything more.

Cassandra never begged.

A moment later, she was gone, slipping into the crowds that were already spilling into the streets.

Extinguishing the lanterns, Khirin left the rooms in darkness. He paid his tab and left his few belongings in the innkeeper's care, with instruction that if he did not return within a week, they were to be sold. If he were to meet his death in the arena, he wanted nothing unsettled to tie him to this earth.

The arena was packed, as it had been for the last several days. Aris was notorious for its taste for blood sport. Most of the men who set foot in the arena did so seeking fame and fortune. A good gladiator often enjoyed both fortune and celebrity status. With luck and skill, a single game could net a good fighter enough for early retirement and an easier life. Death was a risk they took, but the arena was, in a way, not much riskier than a career fishing Aris' rough seas. In any case, there were enough men willing to risk life and limb for a chance at a better life to keep the arena busy.

But the coronation games were different.

These games would last for days, but the sand in the ring would be red long before that. Each day a hundred men went in, to stand in the dust among the bones and souls of those who had gone before. Those who did so faced a variety of challenges and a variety of opponents. Thirty matches per day. Five men per match.

One winner of each, who would then gain the prize.

Admission to the ranks of Selin.

It said something for the status held by the elite army of Aris, that men would die for entrance. It said something for the exclusivity of the Selin, that only upon the death of a king could an ordinary man even hope to gain admission. Normally, the only way to get into the Selin was either to be born Selin, or get promoted from the general army.

The arena was ancient, and was both the oldest and largest building in Aris. Originally built by the Elders, it had somehow managed to remain standing through the centuries. Shellscale glittered on the walls, and thick canvas tapestries had been unfurled to form a sort of ceiling, offering shade to the masses within. The bleachers were packed. Thousands of bystanders filled the stands, their voices melding into a dull roar. Girls with baskets of flowers, food, and drink made their way through the crowd, offering refreshments and souvenir trinkets, along with favors to throw at the day's winners.

Once inside the main door, Khirin was directed to a large hall with a split stair. Most of the people entering went up, to join the crowd, but his path took him down, into the shadows beneath the bleachers. The corridor led him past a series of gyms and offices, to a large chamber where the competitors were gathering. Sunlight poured in through a grated window. He glanced outside, and found his nose was roughly ground level with the arena floor.

Red; that was the world one saw from the arena. The sand was stained with it. The crimson and gold banners of Aris' royal house decorated the stadium. And the crowd itself, filled with Selin, was red as well.

Khirin had spent the last few days on the other side of this room's ceiling, among the crowd, a spectator. Though it was only a short distance away, he knew that world was lost to him forever.

The day was unusually warm for that time of the cycle. Khirin waited beneath a burning sun, ignoring the growing discomfort as his armor grew hot. He paid no attention to the chatter of the men around him, though he watched them closely. At the head of the arena, a ring of Selin stood before the royal box. Khirin squinted, but could not identify the occupants.

Eventually, one of the Reonih came around with a large urn filled with colored stones. He paused before each man, allowing each to reach in and pull out a stone. This was the lottery that decided the order in which they were to fight. Some whispered prayers, drew runes on themselves, or rubbed amulets for luck. Khirin had no such compulsions. When the time came for him to draw, he simply reached in and plucked the first stone he felt.

Luck seemed to favor him anyway. He drew for the second match, which was the one he would have chosen. The sand would not yet be too wet, and the men would not have the crazed adrenaline madness that seemed to always mark the first match. Seeing the bodies of those who were wounded or killed in the first would temper them somewhat, but they would not quite be so grimly determined as those who fought last.

They were organized into groups then, according to the lots they had drawn. Like everyone else, Khirin studied those who had drawn his match. They varied widely in size, shape and coloring. A scrawny looking Sijhani stood next to the door, stretching. Beside him, a wiry, bearded redhead wearing the bone necklace that marked him as Subian exchanged insults with a massive, bald, tattooed man. A dark-skinned man sat quietly on a bench, watching everything, but saying nothing.

He had learned long ago not to judge skill by appearance. Heavily muscled men were not always slow and stupid, and lithe ones weren't necessarily quick and clever. It was not their physique he studied, but the looks in their eyes, the manner in which they stood, their choice of weapons, the condition of their gear. He noted the placement and number of scars on their bodies. He watched to see who stretched and how they stretched, judging flexibility and training. He saw who shifted nervously, who waited quietly, who focused on the other combatants, and who watched the arena.

They were led into the bowels of the arena, to wait beneath the crowds. In the staging area, the sun fell only in a few thin lines that passed through the iron grate of the massive gate that opened into the ring. Stale odors hung thick in the shadowy, humid air. The sharp tangs of sweat, urine, vomit, feces, and blood seemed to belong more to a battlefield than an athlete's arena.

A Reonih scribe appeared with a scroll. He approached each of them in turn, taking down names and lands of origin, and noting brief descriptions of each contestant.

A hundred and fifty men waited in a strange, surreal silence. Though they bore one another no hostility, there was little point in forming friendships: they were about to try to kill each other. They did not speak. There was nothing to say.

The roar of the crowd, and the blood on the sand, said it all.

The arena master appeared out of the shadows at the far side of the room. He was dressed like a gladiator himself, in a large red cloak, a mask, and a leather tunic. Only the gold mask on his face, and the quality of the torc around his neck, distinguished him from the other fighters. His physique provided an odd contrast to his uniform. He was massive, but his muscle had begun to run to fat, though Khirin noted by his reflexes and the way he held himself that he had not gone entirely soft. Two other masked men flanked him, heavily muscled and stone faced. Gladiators, Khirin figured, who had no interest in joining the Selin.

His voice, in odd contrast to his appearance, was thin and nasal, almost feminine. Still, his voice filled the room perfectly, almost as though he knew exactly how to project the precise amount of volume needed to carry into its nooks and crevasses. "If any of you are branded as thieves or murderers," he said, "you may withdraw now without penalty. You should be branded a fool if you do not, for the Selin will not have you, even if you win. There are over a hundred of you in here. Many of you will die, or suffer severe injury. If you die, the Reonih will perform the death rites for you tonight. If any of you hold to a different religion, let the scribes know now. Otherwise you will be going to our gods tonight, and not your own." He looked around at them all. "You've all given your information to the scribes?"

Affirmations filled the room, a low roll of distant thunder.

The arena master looked around at each of them. "Understand one thing: once you walk through that gate, the only choice you will have is between survival and death. If you hope to escape with a wound, you're even less suited to the Selin than you are to the ring. There is no way out of the arena. There is only one rule on the sand, and it is a simple one: there are no rules." He paused a moment to let them absorb that, and then bowed. "Die well," he said, and spoke no more.

He looked back into the shadows of the hall beyond, and nodded.

Another man stepped forward, this one wearing the red that marked him as Selin. Hawk-nosed and sharp-eyed, he seemed to be leaning toward the far end of middle age. There was no welcome in the man's face or eyes, both of which trapped the icy callousness of an experienced warrior. His chest glittered with murdik stones; his eyes glittered with the lessons of more battles that he could probably count. A scar crossed the left side of his face, bisecting it.

So this was Lyle, the famous general, commander of the Selin.

He looked around the room, surveying them all before speaking.

"The Selin are more than a military unit. We are our own society. These men have a bond tighter than blood. Many of the castes have been together since they entered the institutions at the age of seven. They have grown together, bled together, and sweated together. They have trained together, each and every day, and pushed themselves past their limits, each and every day. They eat, sleep, fight, drink, and die with their caste-mates. They may see their own families once or twice a season. Less, in times of war. My men have been handed nothing. Not even their meals. They provide for themselves, as will you. We have no use for a boy—or man—unresourceful enough to let himself starve. We have no use for those who cannot tolerate pain. Compared to the institutions, battle is easy."

The roar of the crowd faded to a distant din.

"There are benefits to being Selin. Those of you who make it will be granted a plot of land, grain, seed, and cattle, as well as the funds to contract serfs to work it. Your sons will join the Selin institutions. Your daughters will have the opportunity to marry from among the Selin or srih, and you'll have access to the Reonih for your needs. The term of service is twenty-five years. If you survive that long, you can retire to a life of leisure. *If* you survive that long."

Lyle glared at them. He stepped into shadow, and the scar on his face became a dark line. "Normally, the only way for an outsider to be admitted into the ranks of the Selin is through the general army, as a reward for acts of extreme courage or valor on the battlefield. The right to wear the uniform, to be Selin, is won through sweat, pain, and hardship, and through a decade at the institutions. The right to enter our institutions is passed down from father to son. It is not a prize handed down to scum who slink about in alleys knifing civilians for mere coppers. This sort of enrollment happens only at coronations and royal births, and, once in a while, if a war depletes our numbers too badly. We only want the best of you. And even then, scum still manage to slip in."

Khirin's lips tightened, yet he held himself quiet.

Lyle's eyes raked over him. "The same rules will apply to you as do any other Selin. Fear or failure in battle, insubordination, hesitation, failure to provide for your caste, failure to follow orders … those are all breaches of conduct we will not tolerate. If anything like that happens, you will be stripped of all rank, caste, property, and quite possibly, life or limb. If you're lucky, you'll be beaten to within an inch of death, branded, pissed on, and left naked in an alley. Is that clear?"

A chorus of "Yes" and "Aye" answers filled the room.

"You are here by choice. You are here of your own free will. The fact that you are willing to die to join our ranks speaks volumes. Each man who dies wins a place in the Selin for one son. Make sure the scribes have the names of your boys. If you are severely wounded, the Reonih will care for you until you either recover or die. Those of you who survive are to report to me. You'll go through an intensive training course at the institute near Starshire. If you make it through that, you'll be assigned to an existing caste. The last day of the games will be among the champions of the previous days. Winners of those matches will be admitted with higher rank, and will also get better lands."

Lyle opened his mouth to speak again, but was cut off by a thunderous roar. The ceiling above them shook as the crowd shifted. Though he could not see from his vantage, Khirin knew that the new king had just stood up in his box, signaling a start to the games. The sound of music filled the air as Reonih bards opened the day's events.

The roar of the crowd receded into the distance, like the waves of an ocean.

The gate opened, and the first group of men went through.

Khirin watched the first match closely, noticing the details he had not seen so clearly from his rented box: the slight bump in the wall, the half-buried chain in the sand, the pattern of sun and shade. There was always some added challenge to the arena. One day the men had fought blindfolded. The second day, the game masters had put vipers in the sand for them to dodge. On the third, they had fought without weapons.

Today's bonus revealed itself fairly quickly, when a combatant rolled to escape a blow, only to rise up bleeding from several shallow wounds. The sand was mixed with shards of glass, thornwall splinters, sharp shells, and bits of steel, making the ground itself a deadly foe.

Five men went in. Khirin watched them fall one by one. A scrawny man with a thick beard won the first match, disemboweling one opponent, hamstringing another, and breaking another's arm. His final opponent opened a gash in his back, but he bounced back from that, sinking a shard of glass into the man's eye. The crowd did not seem to care for him overmuch. Though there were literally hundreds of girls selling flower petals by the handful, the day's first champion only scored a few buckets' worth.

Once the first match was over, the Reonih entered the arena to collect the bodies of the fallen. The dead would be taken to the arena's shrine, and given the death rites of a fallen warrior. The wounded would go to a Reonih theorica to recuperate.

Khirin looked up at the royal box, but could not see his target.

Silence fell.

The gate opened again.

Khirin walked out into the sunlight and began to kill.

CHAPTER 7

Stiva swept through the halls of Aris with a quick, purposeful stride. Marcelle and Twyla walked at her side. A step behind them, Vane and Jarvor trailed the trio through long cold halls hung with glittering arms, through galleries that smelled eternally of dust and paint and damp sea air.

The faces she saw along the way were familiar. The reactions were not. The initial instinct among Aris' staff was still to do what they had always done at her approach, which was to take silent note of her presence, nod briefly in acknowledgment, and then go about their business. Now they froze when they saw her, sliding out of her way as though moved by an unseen hand, nervously pausing to bow or curtsy as she passed. They waited until she had gone before resuming their work.

Once they had seen Lara when they looked at her, the living shadow of a pale, wistful queen.

Now they saw Chandris.

A single bird sang in a golden cage as she passed it. Other voices fell silent, as though hushed by her approaching step.

There were so many things she had never taken note of. So many names and faces she had taken for granted, so many she had always thought of as loyal that she could no longer be entirely sure of. But for all the clouds and shadows, for the trouble in the air and the silent, ravenous fear that had been gnawing at her soul since her father's death, at the moment Aris glowed with firelight on a rain-chilled day, and the scents of cinnamon and yrehn mingled pleasantly with fragrant woodsmoke on air that rang with children's laughter.

It was a world worth saving. A world worth fighting for.

"Are you certain you want to do this?" Twyla asked for the tenth or eleventh time as they crossed over the mosaic of Aris' crest that embellished the quarkstone floor in the main rotunda.

Stiva did not look at her as she answered. "Quite. I am not going to be some mindless empty figurehead at Chandris' side, a crowned doll with no idea what is going on in the land."

Marcelle tilted her head. "You might stir up something."

"I might," Stiva acknowledged darkly. "I might even start a war or two."

She was only half joking.

Marcelle frowned, not amused. She measured her steps carefully, the epitome of grace and ladylike poise. "No queen has sat on Aris' council since …"

She trailed off, uncertain, and then flushed with embarrassment. A princess, foreign or not, was expected to be educated in such matters. Marcelle, though keen and quite intelligent, and endowed with a generous streak of cunning, had neither the patience nor the inclination for formal education. Stiva had always liked her impudence. Now, it seemed slightly insulting.

"Migatha." Stiva supplied the name Marcelle had forgotten with a faint smile. "Caro's grandmother. She ruled as Royce's regent until he came of age. That was over a century ago. And my mother … well, she was quite well informed. She advised my father privately." Stiva's voice trembled slightly. Lara's death was still too fresh, too painful, for her to be able to speak of her mother without tears.

But she was queen now, and she must keep such things hidden.

Marcelle glanced at her. "What advice did Mehran send you this morning?"

Stiva lowered her voice as they passed a small crowd of srih. "He told me to beware serpents."

"Do you think he meant Cerrow?" Marcelle questioned.

Stiva paused as an erlit dove in front of her. "He may have meant you."

Marcelle feigned shock, but giggled before a retort left her mouth. Stiva said nothing, though her eyes belied mirth. Marcelle's laughter had a way of being contagious, of drawing others into it, and she found herself smiling too. But the smiles fell from their faces as they ascended the stairs to the second story, at the top of which were clustered a group of srih and dignitaries.

The crowd parted soundlessly to let them through, bowing down before them like a row of silk-clad trees bending in a breeze. Stiva felt her heart pounding as they approached the great, gleaming doors of the Council chamber.

The Selin posted outside the Council Chamber stepped aside to let her pass, moving quickly and efficiently despite the puzzlement on their faces.

"Good luck," Twyla whispered.

The doors swung silently open before her. Despite the chill of the day, the room within was hot: a vast fireplace in the center of the room was going full blast, giving off enough heat to warm the chamber on a frozen day.

Cerrow's voice echoed across the council chamber as Stiva entered. "Garrison the outlands, my lord; that is my counsel. I tell you, the Delorans have grown too bold. Itacha's men have crossed the border a dozen times this cycle, and whether by incompetence, treachery, or laziness, the northern lords let them through. This latest raid struck Horenfort, a full thirty mils inland. If this continues, they'll burn a path to your doorstep before the cycle is out."

Around the room, srih shifted uneasily in their seats, cooling themselves with bladed fans. Almost as one, they turned towards the door as Stiva entered. Noticing the disturbance, Cerrow also looked. He fell silent, seeing her.

Slowly Stiva's eyes grew accustomed to the darkness within, which was in truth dark only in relation to the hall just outside. First shadows and then polished, carved thi-wood slid away from the edges of her vision, to be replaced by a much more imposing sight.

About three dozen greybeards waited inside. These were the srih, Selin officers, and Reonih that made up Aris' council. Colors and sigils and houses flashed through her memory as she surveyed them, taking stock of who was present and who was not. Huran, the Reonih official law keeper, sat beside Mohr and Cerrow. She scanned the faces in the audience. Lavos, Chorin, Barls, Adan, Rithab, Ceth: all of them had pledged fealty. But their faces were drawn and hard.

Chandris sat at their head, a glittering, golden icon. His only visible reaction to her appearance was to frown slightly, as perplexed by her sudden arrival as the rest of them. That was only to be expected, perhaps, for she had given him no word of her intentions.

Belatedly, the audience rose in obeisance as she passed. Stiva lifted her chin, though her palms were clammy with sweat, and took her place beside her brother. "Good afternoon, my lords."

"Stiva." Chandris greeted her coolly as though they were alone, casually ignorant of both the generally formal tone of council meetings and of the council itself. "What are you doing here?"

"What does it look like?" Stiva asked airily, crossing the room. "I've come to sit in Council."

It sounded thin and weak, childish even, but, seeing as she was their queen, there was not one of them who would dare say so. At least, not to her face. No, they would save that for later, in darkened rooms. Her name would grace the air over their cups tonight. Of that much, Stiva was certain.

She was not quite so sure what it was they would say.

Chandris looked amused. Cerrow did not. The prime minister turned and gave her a stiff, formal bow. "My queen," he said cautiously, keeping his tone carefully neutral, "We are highly honored by your grace and your beauty. We were just discussing a matter of grave importance, the—"

"Then by all means," Stiva said coldly, "continue."

Her twin looked at her curiously as she sat down beside him, but he said nothing, instead turning his attention back to Cerrow, at whom he directed an ambiguous wave.

Cerrow cleared his throat. "As I was saying, my lord, I strongly advise you to send more of your force to the borders."

"Lyle." Chandris turned to the Selin commander. "What say you?"

Rubbing his mustache, Lyle answered slowly, choosing his words carefully. "An increase in defense along the borders is certainly not a bad idea, sire. It is true that the Delorans been bold with their raids lately. Though I do not think they are a severe threat, if we don't deal with them soon, they may become one. I would increase patrols, for a time, and perhaps move some of the greener troops to the border."

"I agree," Kele said. "If we cannot police our borders well enough to keep them free of brigands, then eyebrows will begin to raise in the other city-states, and kings bent to war may be tempted. Orlin has parleyed terms with Trian. They might decide to try us, hard, if we do not run them away like the curs they are."

"Right." Lyle nodded. "But to be honest, we haven't the men to spare. The force would have to come from the city. The men patrolling the east have their hands full watching Orlin, and the highways are too infested with bandits to leave the midlands unguarded."

"Let the merchants hire their own swords," Ehodris suggested. The lord of Fahrin—Talia's father—had a bad cold; his words were clipped and awkward. "They can afford it."

"The last thing we need," Kele said gruffly, "is to make Aris a promising place for mercenaries out of work."

Lyle gave Kele a brief but respectful nod of acknowledgment. He toyed absently with the golden goblet before him as he continued. "Cerrow is right about one thing. They must be dealt with." He paused, absently tracing his scar.

Kele snorted. "We have dealt with the mountain kings several times already. They refuse to let a lesson stay learned."

"There have been rumors that they are building warships," Lyle said. "While I doubt they have many sailors in their ranks, they do have enough harbors to keep a fleet."

"I don't like leaving the city open," Chandris mused. "Nor do I relish the vulnerability of an unguarded harbor. That would be too tempting a prize for the Jaran fleet, I think, not to mention pirates."

"What of the temptation of undefended fields, villages, and manors?" Kele snapped. "Are they of less concern?"

Cerrow turned to face Kele. "No one's attacked the city in—"

"Twelve years." Stiva spoke crisply, cutting him off mid-sentence. "I remember it well, my lord Cerrow, if you do not. And that assault was indeed launched from the waves of the Oburion. We barely stood. That attack convinced my father to pull men in from the borders."

"We weren't being raided then," Cerrow said, rebutting her argument as though he were dismissing the silly notions of a precocious child. "Besides, the harbor practically defends itself. The reefs break apart even our own vessels sometimes."

"As do many harbors. Ships manage it daily, however. As to the harbor defending itself, I could refer you to a dozen tales that say otherwise."

Cerrow spoke into the silence that followed, obliterating it; he looked directly at Chandris as he spoke. "The march lords are asking for help. You can either oblige or refuse, and there are consequences to each. You have had little contact with them so far. If they think you are careless as to their plight, they will begin to grumble, and that you most certainly do not want. The men of the north, particularly, are known for shifting alliances. Huntik, for one. Delora may tempt him too easily, and I wouldn't put it above Itacha to bribe or blackmail him. A choice between gold or burnt crops is exactly that to him, and he is ruefully slow to call out his men."

The srih watched this coldly, bladed fans slicing the air.

Chandris frowned. "He was loyal to my father."

"Aye," Cerrow agreed, "but you are not your father, for one thing, and for another, Cronn spent a good amount of time keeping him in line."

Chandris' frown deepened into a scowl. "Then I am of half a mind to take an army into the north and teach him some manners myself. If the march lords cannot hold the territory entrusted to them, what use are they at all? Perhaps they should be replaced."

"You could end with a full-scale war on your hands if you do that," Lyle warned, speaking even as Cerrow opened his mouth to reply. "The northern Houses have held their lands for centuries. If you depose them, you will have the south on edge as well, and the men who replace them will have resentful strangers in their ranks."

Mohr spoke then for the first time since Stiva had entered. "I, for one, would not trust Orlin not to strike from the northeast, if you call the southern vassals to war deposing the men who hold the north. Redistribute, but do not leave the city open. That is my counsel."

Chandris paused, considering. Then he cast a sharp, emerald gaze around the room, inviting debate. "Has anyone else an opinion on this matter?"

"I agree with Cerrow," Barls said. He scanned the room with a sharp stare before continuing. "Increase the garrisons along the border. Double patrols if you must. It's only a matter of time before we catch some barbarian dogs sniffing around."

Cerrow looked at Chandris. "Send the Selin."

"Folly!" Kele shook his head vehemently. "We cannot leave the city open."

"He's right," Lyle said. "It's too much of a risk."

"We cannot leave the north unguarded." Cerrow countered Kele's heat with coolness, speaking calmly. "It must be one or the other. If you intend to keep the march lords loyal, you must pay these mountain goats back in blood for what they have taken and destroyed. To do that, you must send more men to the outlands. And if you send more men to the outlands, you must take them from here." He looked back at Chandris. "See to the borders, my lord, else they will find their way inland."

"Perhaps you are right." Chandris frowned thoughtfully. He turned again to Lyle. "How many men can you spare?"

Lyle's voice and face were grim. "Twenty castes, now. Ten more when this year's batch comes out of training."

"That's it?" Chandris asked sharply. "Six hundred, and a third of them green as old bread?" He grimaced. "I may as well send the general army."

"They're needed for the harvest," Cerrow said.

Chandris fixed Cerrow with a cold stare. "What would you?"

"You haven't a choice," Cerrow said flatly. "Garrison the outlands."

Argument broke out then, loud and tempered. Stiva settled back, reckoning motives and connections, and liked nothing of what she saw. Her mind spun from the weight of problems descending upon it.

She found one waiting, in the layout of the room.

Stiva spoke into the melee of clashing voices. Her voice cut through the air like a knife.

"It isn't force we lack," she said crisply. "It's mobility."

The room descended into thick, tense quiet.

Chandris' head snapped around to face her. "What?"

She turned and faced him. The bard's blood in her tended to manifest at odd times. Her words slid crisp and sharp into the air. Almost unconsciously, she drew into her Reonih training, putting an energy into her voice that drew the attention of everyone in the room as she spoke. "What use are roads that trap our wheels in mud, so that it is often better to travel alongside the road that on it? What use are garrisons that take days to travel from one keep to the next? Even when the towers are lit before the raiders arrive, the reinforcements get there too late to do anything. Itacha is not interested in battle: he strikes and retreats, cutting a thousand shallow wounds through our borders. We are not fools, that do not understand the benefits of paving. And yet we labor down these muddy sodden tracks without a second thought, season after season. How many times have messages been delayed for bad roads, messages that could have saved lives?"

The room had gone deathly still.

"My lady," Cerrow spoke carefully. "Perhaps you should like us to check and see if the crops run in straight lines. The roads are not the issue here."

Stiva went white. Chandris looked at her evenly, watching to see what she would do.

To her surprise, it was Lyle who came to her defense.

"She's right." Lyle gave Cerrow a cool look. Stiva realized with some relief that she was not the only one who distrusted him. "And she is your queen, and you'll face a straight line of steel the next time you forget that."

"My apologies," Cerrow said tightly. "I meant no disrespect."

Chandris rubbed the stubble on his chin thoughtfully. He reminded Stiva in that moment so much of Cronn that she looked away, feeling a sudden lump rise in her throat.

For the next four hours, Stiva sat silently and listened to the voices going back and forth over a great many issues, a delicate game of point and counterpoint. It was rather like a sparring match, only here, every motive was cloaked in formal dialogue and courtesy, examples dredged up from history. They spoke of the issue of dishonest millers, who tipped the scale on measured grain, mixed poor grades in with the finer ones, and therefore stole shamelessly from both commoners and lords. They debated the long, bitter friction between the Selin and the lesser armies; the trouble of exchanging currency among the other city-states, each of which followed independent systems; and of the less than bountiful harvest that Aris had yielded this year.

She should not have been surprised at the weight of the problems facing Aris. She had known about the issues long before her parents had died, though she had honestly found many of them boring. Now, as each new subject was brought up, Stiva felt the burden of the crown weigh more and more heavily on her. Simply keeping the city-state from collapse began to seem impossible.

As the Council adjourned, grim-faced and somber, Stiva looked at her brother and found his face lined with worry.

The ghosts of a hundred bloodthirsty kings watched from the shadows.

CHAPTER 8

"No, no, no. Wait. Stop." Kira shook her head in frustration, holding up a hand. Music unraveled into fragments, then fell into sunlit silence. "The fourth chorus has the high soprano harmony. The first three are descending triads. Think of the lyrics. The first verses tell of how the Elders journeyed for centuries across the sky until at last they found this place. It describes how they descended to earth from the stars, and found the land we now call home. *Descent.* The entire melody *descends.* It's only the fourth that tells of their great shining cities, of the golden society they created, that the melody begins to ascend. The next three descend again, along with their tale. But you know the parts about the Skyborne well enough, do you not?"

Kira's gaze was suddenly intense.

Stiva stiffened. "What do you mean?"

Kira shook her head; she would go no further with that particular subject. "The last verses ascend again as the lyrics again tell of success, redemption, of how last of the Elders formed the first Reonih tribe, and took charge of the Relics. Think of hope, glory, triumph. An end to darkness and chaos. That was when the shadow of the Zhur was finally lifted. The song crescendos and changes octave. *Triumph* lifts the melody up. And you have to be more precise in your enunciation. You're distorting some of the words again. Don't give me that look, Stiva. You know every performance of a historical ballad has to be perfect, down to the last detail. It's the only way to be certain our history is preserved correctly. Now try it again."

Kira counted out the time, then cocked her head to listen as sound filled the air once more.

This time even the Reonih master bard could find no fault. When the song ended, she broke into a huge smile. "Stiva, you have the voice of a bird. I think you have that talent to thank for the fact that the gods put you in the womb of a queen, so that you would be heard by kings and queens. Of course, even if you'd been born in a hovel, I think your voice would have found your way into royal ears anyway."

"I wish I had more time for it." Stiva sighed, waving away a servant who approached with a tray of trutes' brains, sugared rose petals, and chilled arithyn eyeballs.

"You could always present your speeches musically." Reide took a sip of greenberry wine, then launched into a musical caricature. "I'd like to o-o-pen today's se-ssion with a—"

Stiva raised an eyebrow. "And you can always practice from the dungeon."

They all laughed, a bit too brightly. That, she had learned, was part of wearing the crown. When she laughed, the court laughed. When she danced, they danced. Whatever she did, or Chandris, the srih around them reflected it, mirroring even the palest emotion.

Chandris loved it. Stiva found it revolting.

"I'd be careful, Reide," Marcelle spoke up. "She's picturing you in chains and manacles. You should be honored, for now you can rank yourself up there with Chandris, Talia, and a host of foreign diplomats."

Reide coughed, suddenly deeply interested in adjusting his tuning. Carin and Fiurn, the two Reonih bards who were providing accompaniment, stared uncomfortably around the garden. Shira, who sat beside Marcelle on a nearby bench, shifted uneasily, and popped a candied flower into her mouth. Twyla pretended to be absorbed in watching the Selin, who were training in the Second, below them. And Kira looked at Stiva with enough reproach to fill a lecture.

Once, not so long ago, Reide would have laughed heartily at the same comment. Once, Carin and Fiurn would have come brimming with cheerful sarcasm and risqué jokes instead of sitting quietly in composed serenity. Kira would have complimented her not with words of praise, but with a curt nod.

Once they had seen her as a person, and not a symbol.

Despite the sunlight, the world darkened a shade around her.

Somewhere in the pale sky, a black bird screamed at the sun. Visions struck her thoughts. She saw the courtyard stained with blood, lifeless bodies strewn across the stones and benches. The premonition left her pale and shaking.

Like Lara before her, Stiva had the Sight. She had seen omens before Cronn's death, before Caro's, before Trin's and Mykhal's. She had even seen one of the Earthborne once, in childhood when, against the strictest orders, she had first ventured past the thornwall and wandered into the deep forest. She had found it enchanted, a dreaming place wrapped in a shadowy, haunting beauty. And the Zhurlord? A pale, dream-wrapped thing, slender and ethereal, it had seemed almost human, but for its eyes, which burned with cold fire, and the aura it gave off. The creature had not harmed her. It had not touched her, or spoken to her; it only stood there and watched her for a time, mystical, beautiful, deadly. Time had stopped, or seemed to. Then it had faded, the being, stepped into the forest and vanished, as though it had been absorbed into brambles and mist and fallen leaves. One minute, it was there. In the next, it was gone. Only once its presence dissipated had the moments resumed breathing again.

Stiva had ceased to fear the woods at that moment.

When she'd returned, she'd found the castle in an uproar. When Chandris told her she'd been missing for a week, she hadn't believed him, until Lara confirmed it.

Instead of frightening her, the incident had the opposite effect. Since that day, she had tread the forbidden ground beyond the thornwall time and again. In time, Mohr had given her leave to walk the forest. Lara had pulled strings for that, Stiva knew. But in the end, it was neither Lara's influence nor the fact that Reonih blood ran through her veins that had won her that right to learn the bard's way. It had been Stiva herself, who had unknowingly chanced to raise her voice to the sky one day within Kira's earshot. Stiva had returned home to find Kira already waiting for an audience with Cronn. A voice like that was a boon from the gods, Kira had said, and should not be wasted.

Stiva had been trained informally, for her father refused to release her from court for the years of study it took to become a true robed bard. She was royalty, and her life must belong to Aris. Stiva had accepted that years ago. To defy it would be dishonorable, and neither defiance nor dishonor was her way. She knew full well that she would never wear the blue robes, though she wanted nothing more. Nor would she ever have a true Reonih instrument, though she owned several fine lyres and a dulcimer. The Reonih acknowledged music as a magical force. Thus, the creation of a musical instrument required the sacrifice of a living creature and the cutting of a sacred tree. The soul of that being was then bound to the instrument, and that soul sang in the tones that it produced.

The Reonih held that music, dance, poetry, and painting were sacred, a gift from the universe. The arts, as such, were divine, and should be treated as such.

They would never offer her the robes. But the bard lore, they had given her.

A gift indeed, that voice, and one she had no right to. One that had no right to her. Knowing her dream for the illusion it was took away none of its appeal.

A bronze kirit lizard crawled along the face of a statue and settled onto the nose, near some pink lichens, baking its jewel scales in the sun. The stone warrior, weapons raised against some ancient enemy, wore the tiny dragon like a badge. A piece of the lichen moved, lightning fast, and wrapped itself around the lizard, crushing it in a camouflaged tendril. In a moment, the snake pulled the captive lizard under the lichens to die.

That was Aris: death, waiting beneath beauty.

Stiva looked around, the vision fading from her thoughts. The light season was waxing, and the land was alive, vibrant, buzzing with life, not yet wilted by the heat of high season. The Overlook, as this particular garden was called, was an enclosed but breathtaking arrangement of potted trees, ivy-draped trellises, fountains, fishponds, and manicured raised flowerbeds, situated on the roof of the storage building that divided two of the three main courtyards. The southern wall looked down onto the gigantic Zhrue Gate and the main courtyard, which was known as the First. The Zhrue Gate was the main entrance to the castle complex, and the only public access. Since pretty much everyone and anyone with right and reason to visit the castle came in through the Zhrue, the First was a constant bustle of activity, hosting a ceaseless stream of traffic.

On the other side of the Overlook, the northern wall provided a view of the Crimson Gate, which led, via a series of passages, from the Zhrue Gate into the Second courtyard and the military barracks. Surrounded by barracks, gyms, and armories, the Second was usually filled with Selin, who used it as a training ground. The nature of the Second was the nature of the Selin: militaristic, severe, proud, and brutal. When the Selin moved or spoke in synchronicity, the air in the Second resonated like thunder. Over the centuries, the tread of thousands of feet had worn the paving smooth. The walls were speckled with drops of blood, a testament to the brutality of the Selin lifestyle. Despite this, the sound of laughter was not uncommon. It also wasn't unusual to witness practical jokes—or the aftermath of them—ranging from the mundane to the absurd. The Selin worked hard and played hard.

Kira stretched, raising her face to the sun, and then called out for their attention again. "Enough of that one for today. Run through 'The Vengeance of the Zhur.'"

A darker song, this one, and much more poignant. It was shadow slithering through the sunshine. It was the scent of death floating along the perfume of open-faced flowers, a cold current twisting in a warm bright spring.

A childish brightness rang out at its end, as Maren piped up from his seat at the edge of an elaborately constructed fishpond. "Did it really happen that way?" he asked. "The Skyborne coming out of the skies to kill people, the Seaborne pulling down ships, guarding every stream, every pond? Did the Fireborne really burn all those people and their land? Did the Earthborne split the mountains, and put magic spells on worked metal, stealing bodies to make their own?"

Kira turned to answer, and then froze, her shoulders shaking slightly as she stifled a giggle. The little boy was soaked to the bone from an earlier adventure involving that same fishpond. Beside him, the puppy Kele had given him for his birthday was licking the crumbs from a plate. It was rare that Maren sat still long enough to hear an entire song, but tales of the Zhur fascinated him, as they did Stiva.

Lara's heritage, that.

Kira answered the young prince gravely. "Our ballads are always truthful, however ugly that truth may be. There really was a brutal, bloody war between humanity and the Zhur. There aren't many songs left from that age, but the ones that we do have are all grim. Were it not for the songs, Maren, we would know little about it. The true purpose of Reonih bards is to preserve history, not merely to entertain. That's why formal training takes so long. All those songs must be pounded into memory so deeply and perfectly that no song, however obscure, is learned incorrectly. If not for the bard lore, our whole history would be forgotten. We keep the past alive, as best we can, for the spirits of those who lived it walk this earth still, and need to be reminded. For some cultures, words carved in stone or wood, or drawn on paper is enough … but look at what happens. Can we read their glyphs? And the ruins of the Elders' cities are even more incomprehensible. They saved their knowledge in machines, and the machines rusted away. Most of their wisdom was lost. Their culture did not survive the journey from Denebola. We have little history of that time, and less of the ages before it." Kira's face grew somber, pensive. "Perhaps it is as well."

Maren blinked, having anticipated a much shorter answer. "But where are the Zhur now?"

Kira's answer was a whisper borne on a sudden breeze. "They walk the world still, child. The treaty the first Reonih made with them holds them at bay. Somewhat."

"And they will come after you, if you don't behave," Reide growled, pretending a threatening face. The little boy shrieked in mock terror, giggling. The puppy, alarmed by the noise, started and took cover behind a huge vase, peeking out cautiously before hesitantly edging back to Maren's side.

Kira changed the subject—and her tone—to something brighter, turning to Reide. "Is there anything else you need to work on before the kingsong? I'd like to be home before dark."

Reide looked at Stiva, who glanced away guiltily. In the season that had passed since she had become queen, her free time had diminished to almost nothing, and the time she had left over to work with Reide and Kira was even more sparse. Stiva had begun to look at that loss as yet another sacrifice Aris had demanded of her. For years, she had given every free moment she had to music. Now it was hard even to look at Reide, knowing she had robbed them both of something special. Reide had always insisted that the songs they created together were far better than anything either could accomplish alone.

Talia made her way towards them, followed by a cluster of maids.

"I'd like to do that saltarello Lara used to sing," Stiva said, swallowing.

"I never heard Lara sing," Maren piped up.

"That's because by the time you were old enough to listen, Stiva had found her voice, and Lara was overshadowed." Kira told him. "She often accompanied Pahnryn to court as a bard, and was renowned in her youth. She lost some of her song here, and would rather hear Stiva's voice than sing herself. In her day, though, few bards were more renowned than your mother. Not just in Aris, either."

"Lara was a bard?" Maren asked, surprised. "I thought she came from Shadri. From the mushroom forests."

"She did," Shira said softly, in that gentle, musical tone of hers. "She wore the blue robes for years, and was very much in demand. When her voice found Cronn's ears, he was so taken that he married her. So she gave up her robes and came here."

"Are you sure?" Maren said disdainfully. "I didn't know Shadri had any bards. I thought there were only mushrooms and big mountains there."

"There are bards everywhere in Aursa, Maren," Stiva told him. "Even in Kralin and Orlin, there are Reonih. And while Shadri does have mushroom forests and big mountains. The mountains of Shadri are called the Arriks. You'd know all sorts of interesting things about Shadri and the other city states if you actually listened to your tutors instead of just pretending to."

Maren made a face. "I don't like Ghodrik. He makes me do boring things like counting. I like the songs better. They talk about the Zhur and kings and wars instead of boring things like laws." He stomped his foot. "I don't need any of that. I'm to be Selin one …. What is that?"

Maren cut himself, twisting around to stare intently at a moving squiggle on the ground. The puppy wiggled frantically in his arms, its banded tail lashing.

"Looks like a ruby snake," Stiva told him. "Put him down before he bites you, Maren."

"I want to hear the kingsong." Maren put the puppy down. The dog, apparently of the same mind as Maren, immediately went after the ruby snake, which slithered down a drain grate, its jewel-colored scales flashing in the sun before it slipped into the darkness below.

"Then be quiet and behave, or we won't let you listen," Shira said coolly.

Maren stood straighter, a perfect picture of innocence.

"Is Cronn's song nearly finished?" Marcelle asked Reide.

Reide nodded, running a hand through his light brown hair. "That's why Kira's here today, to approve it."

"Why?" Maren asked. "Can't you tell if it's any good?"

"A kingsong has to be approved by a Master bard. And it's judgment day." Reide struck a gloomy, ominous note on his lyre, his brown eyes gleaming mischievously. But still, he glanced at the sun with a deliberate frown.

"I know, it's getting late." Kira picked up his line of thought immediately. "But first … Stiva, if I might have a moment of your time?"

"Of course," Stiva said immediately. They walked to the center of the garden, among the potted trees and statues, where no one could overhear them.

"Stiva." Kira spoke quietly, in a serious tone. "I think you understand our ways fairly well. We do not take half-wits as apprentices. We are an order of knowledge; nothing more, nothing less, though that knowledge is multi-faceted. We are healers, arbitrators—"

"I understand what the Reonih do, Kira. I've known that since childhood." Stiva cut her off, frowning slightly. "What is this about?"

Kira took a deep breath, suddenly nervous. "You know there are things which are kept to the separate sects. The sages hold the secrets of the stars' dance, the laws, all of the higher magics, the writing and reading of the Aorhan runes—"

Stiva waved impatiently. "I've known that since I was Maren's age. Get to the point."

Kira drew and released a deep breath. "Most of the things I just mentioned are the areas of the other sects, the healers and the sages. It's the bard's way I want to speak of."

Stiva waited impatiently.

"You have immense talent, Stiva; if you were not of royal blood, I would love to complete your training and give you the robes."

But we both know Aris will not let you go. He will not let you go.

Echoes of an earlier conversation, one that had taken place years ago.

A bitter pang of regret soured in Stiva's throat. Her annoyance fell away, falling into sun-drenched air. She spoke quietly. "To be honest, Kira, I would have preferred that way. But though you know how much I want to wear the robes, you don't have to apologize for the fact that I never will. I knew it years ago."

"So did I." Kira sighed. "I think you may have gone that route already in a former life, though you would not remember it. But that's not the point I'm trying to make."

Stiva frowned, puzzled. "What, then?"

Kira looked Stiva square in the eye. "You are of Aris. You live within the walls, in the court. And yet I see the Reonih in you. That is the difference between you and your siblings. Chandris and Shira show little of that blood, and Maren already fancies himself a warrior. But you will all walk the path fate has set for you, and it is not mine to say where and if you should venture from it."

Stiva stiffened. "What are you getting at, Kira?"

Showing an uncertainty, a nervousness that was entirely unlike her, Kira looked at her feet, wrung her hands, and then took another deep breath before continuing. "Our seers have cast many readings into the future of Aris as of late. We have foreseen some drastic changes. Both prosperity and severe hardship wait in your future, and in Chandris'."

"Since when has divination become a concern of the bards?" Stiva asked sharply, growing uneasy.

"The future concerns us all." Kira hesitated. "One thing we saw years ago was that song will continue to have an influence in your life. At some point, it will become crucial. This came up in scrying after scrying. That is why Lara begged Cronn to let you study, and why he allowed us to teach you the bard lore, even knowing you would never wear the robes. We have also seen danger ahead of you, Stiva. The Otherworld has some stake in you, though I have no idea what it is."

Stiva was spellbound now, hanging on Kira's every word.

"Stiva," Kira said quietly, "what I am about to tell you is extremely confidential. I beg you, keep it to yourself. Tell no one, not even Chandris. It is not usually—in fact, *ever*—something we reveal to any who aren't fully robed. But Mohr and I both feel that, in your case, the benefits outweigh the risks."

"You know I can't promise that, Kira." Stiva sighed. "Chandris has this way of reading my mind."

Kira studied her carefully. Her face, when she finally nodded, was untouched by anger. "Then promise me you won't unless you absolutely must," Kira said. "That you will prevent his knowledge so long as you may, without endangering him."

After a moment, Stiva nodded. "Of course."

Kira checked the progress of the sun in the sky, squinting. "Did you ever wonder how Lara kept Cronn informed, when the messengers and spies reported to him?"

"I hadn't really thought about it," Stiva admitted.

"Some of it was her Sight. Lara had a strong talent. She could have been a seeress as easily as a bard. But the constant stream of traveling bards that came in and out the Zhrue Gate … they had their role in it too. Reide knows the language. It was one reason she urged Cronn to become his patron." Kira's eyes met hers, steely with resolve. "There is another meaning to the songs. Another layer of meaning. The ballads are more than history, Stiva. They are a language of their own."

Stiva shook her head. "I don't understand."

Kira explained quietly. "As you know, the songs are ingrained into memory, word for word, note for note, over and over, through decades of training, until they are as deeply embedded into a bard's mind as their very names. No robed bard will err much, if at all. This is done to ensure that history, the songs, are preserved correctly, and not altered over generations. Therefore, the slightest deviation—a single note or chord changed, a phrase adjusted, a tempo altered—would be instantly noticeable to another Reonih. But not so noticeable to anyone else."

Stiva stared at her mentor.

"I see that you begin to understand," Kira said. "There is a rather simple but very clever system by which one can give and receive coded messages. Only a few dozen songs are code songs. They're all popular songs, though they aren't played that often. Minor variations in these songs, as well as certain gestures and embellishments, give them shades of meaning that, while subtle, can be very revealing. To the untrained ear, these changes are either unnoticeable, or dismissed as a bard putting a slightly different twist on a song. That isn't done, of course, but only the bards themselves know the rules of our ways. You know the songs already. 'The Carrion Queen' is one. 'The Ballad of Arctina.' 'The Song of Solara.' There are others.

"I can teach you the codes in the space of a few days. I don't dare do it here, though. If you can come to the forest, it would be better."

Stiva nodded, finding her voice. "Absolutely."

"This has, in the past," Kira continued, "served us well in times of need, as a swift, secret means of communication. We send and receive word through the land, without fear of spies."

"The traveling bards." Stiva spoke quietly.

"Aye," Kira nodded. "Lara was in communication with Shadri the entire time she was here. With Pahnryn, and the Reonih elsewhere. You are queen now, Stiva. You cannot afford to be naïve any longer, or to be uninformed. You aren't only responsible for your own life, but the lives and welfare of all Aris' people."

Stiva took a moment to absorb what Kira had told her, her mind spinning in several directions at once, and then looked Kira straight in the eye. "You fear," she said flatly. "You didn't give me knowledge of this out of generosity. And I don't think you would have told me this at all, had Chandris not crowned me."

Kira looked back at her calmly, her gaze reminding Stiva of the sea. "Question everything, Stiva," she said. "Even your own heart. You can't afford not to."

A high-pitched squeal echoed through the garden, followed by the crash of pottery breaking. All heads turned as one, to find Maren frozen in place beside the remains of what had been an exquisite vase, his face caught between guilt and fear. Tears welled in his eyes, but he fought them back, instead stepping back so the servants could clean up the mess.

Stiva dreamt of blood that night, a banquet, at the hall of some fallen king, where the guests at a great feast slumped over their dishes, bloody and unmoving, staring at her through glassy eyes. She dreamt of screams and flames and dark things that crawled the night. She saw herself singing lullabies to the dead, while corpses and shadows and ghosts crept like mist through dark forests. Wings came down from the night sky, fluttering beneath pale, dim moons that were draped in thin clouds. Trees reached bony fingers out for a red swollen moon, as though wanting touch the gods that danced in the air.

In the last vision, she found herself in a stone circle. There was blood on the ground before her, and the strange, disembodied sound of a flute filled the air.

The winged god landed gracefully and looked her in the eye.

You are not long for this world, came the voice in her mind. *You will be ours one day. This is your dream of glory.*

And the world turned to blood around her.

CHAPTER 9

A sunlit day, early in the dark season.

The first chills of frost had touched the land, but the sun shone brightly in a pale gold sky. Aris' people went about red-nosed, their breath forming clouds of mist on crisp air laced with the scents of apple and cinnamon, and gerfruit pies.

But summer—the season of earth—did not fade quietly. After a few weeks of cold, the days grew warmer again, and the sun shone down on forests that blazed even brighter red as the cold season approached. The land had warmed again briefly, after the initial icy touch of winter. It was only a brief respite from the biting cold, but Aris welcomed it as heartily as the first greening of the light season. *Second fire*, these warm stretches were called. In the fields outside the city walls, the commoners loaded the last harvest of the season onto carts and wagons. Shepherds and wranglers drove the cattle herds in from summer pastures, moving them to their winter grounds. A steady line of traffic flowed through the millers' halls and granaries, and Aris' stewards bustled back and forth between them and the castles and manors, carefully measuring the year's take and calculating tribute and taxes. The inns were packed with bards, merchants, actors' troupes, and hunters making final treks before the dark season brought sleet and icy winds and the cold dark nights. It was not uncommon to see the banners of four, five, or even six srih lords hanging outside a single inn; within, it was often an uneasy peace, kept or broken by mead and spirits, as men drank hot spiced wine and told war stories, or accused each other of thievery and drew steel upon those words.

On one such day, Aret sought Stiva out in one of the libraries on the second floor, where she was reading. Marcelle and Twyla were sitting nearby, writing letters and sewing, respectively. Reide had set up on a sofa near the fire, working on a new song.

"Aret!" Stiva greeted her cousin with a delighted smile. "I thought you were leaving for border patrol!"

"I am." He descended to one knee, showing her a more formal greeting than her own. "We've been assigned to the eastern border, at Thricer's Crossing. But we had to come through the area anyway."

Stiva caught the twinkle in Aret's eye and laughed. "And so close to Darkfest, you had to stop in for some vodrik and mushroom sauce. You'll join us for the feast, of course?"

Aret bowed deeply. "As you wish, my queen."

"Stop with the formality." Stiva rolled her eyes. "I finally get to speak with someone who has never balked at yanking my hair or hiding frogs in my bed, and what do you do? You begin to act like everyone else? No! I forbid it. And if you agree with every word I say, I'll have you whipped."

Aret's severe expression did not change, though his eyes twinkled with mirth. "As you wish, my queen."

"It's been too long," Stiva said.

"It has," Aret agreed. "How are you holding up?"

"Well enough." Stiva sighed. "I know it's selfish to complain, but sometimes I think Chandris crowned me just torment me. I cannot do anything I used to enjoy. Especially the things I wasn't supposed to do in the first place, like listen to Eldon telling dirty jokes while he worked the forge. Now it's 'Your Grace' this, and 'Your Excellence' that, and I have to order a joke. And then when he tells one, they're all strictly proper. I can't visit the mews anymore. Instead of letting me help him, Graig fusses over me or worries that I might get straw in my hair or dust on my dress. Even when I visit the nursery, Zinnia immediately hushes up the children so they'll be on their best behavior. That's no fun at all."

Aret gave a slight frown. "Stiva—forgive me if I sound like my mother—it is somewhat beneath you to spend your morning listening to child's tales."

"Shard-worms." Stiva waved disdainfully. "You're never too old to hear the tale of Tikina and the falling apple. Besides, I like children." Her voice darkened, slipped from sunlight to shadow. "They're honest."

The last of the laughter fell from his eyes. "Ah," Aret said, "I see. The poisonous tongues of the srih have you on edge."

Stiva's brow furrowed. "They trip over themselves trying to win a smile or a compliment, and they copy everything I do. They all bow and smile, but there are razors in their eyes, and their petty intrigues bleed into everything. The simplest conversation is marinated in politics. If I say something that doesn't precisely match Chandris' opinions, the gossip begins immediately. There are enough people waiting to drive a wedge between us to populate a small kingdom."

Aret frowned. "I heard something about a duel. What happened?"

"It was stupid." Stiva sighed. "I was in a bad mood, just so irritated with people being fake, that I started trying to goad people into arguing with me. Do you remember that horrid performance of *A Cause for Surrender* that Trianic acting troupe did a few years ago? The one about pirates on the Yeverad Sea?"

Aret grimaced. "Unfortunately, I do. I've been trying to forget it for years."

"Well, the subject came up, and I said it was the best play I had ever seen. I just wanted to see if there was even one person honest enough to dispute me. Well, someone did: the Viore of Erad's eldest son. As soon as he said something, one of the Rithans accused him of treachery and challenged him on the spot. And drove his sword through him. It wasn't a death challenge. But it caused problems between the Houses of Rithan and Erad. Then Fentar got involved. It's been a mess."

Stiva realized too late that her words recalled another ill-fated duel. She bit her lip. "Aret, I'm sorry, I didn't mean to—"

"It's alright," Aret said quietly. "Erad has never been easily subdued," he said, steering the conversation to a safer topic. "That is a clan to watch."

"They all are," Stiva said bitterly.

"Stiva." Twyla stood up, and moved to the window. "There's something happening in the Second."

Stiva, Marcelle, and Aret got up and went to join Twyla at the window.

"Can you see what it is?" Marcelle asked.

The dusty courtyard was filled with Selin, and more were arriving by the moment. All of them seemed to be straining for a view of the center of the courtyard, where a large circular area was the only place not packed with bodies. As they watched, an officer used his scabbard to describe a large circle in the dust. The crowd shifted back a little, away from the circle.

"Probably two of the officers," Reide commented. "There's a lot of gemstones in that crowd."

His observation was correct. The flash of sunlight reflecting off the Murdik stones emblazoned onto red Selin uniforms belied the presence of several ranking officers in the throng of onlookers. As Stiva searched the crowd, it parted to let two men enter from separate directions.

"Is that Lyle?" Marcelle asked. Her question was not directed at anyone in particular, nor did it require an answer; the commander of the Selin was impossible to mistake. Lyle's dark hair was pulled back into a tight tail, revealing the familiar sharp, hawk-nosed profile.

"No wonder there's such a crowd," Reide said. "Only an idiot would take him on. Ah, here comes his opponent."

As Lyle's opponent stepped into the circle, Stiva gasped.

It was Chandris.

This was not the boy had last seen stripped to the waist, at the beach, years ago, just before the trouble had started. This was a full-grown man. He was, for one, much more fit now than he had been then. Not an ounce of fat could be seen on him, and his muscles moved visibly under his skin. He had scars she had never seen. This both startled and upset her, though it did explain why she had sometimes felt unaccountable pains and aches during their separation. Though it was only reasonable to assume that his training or his life had, at some point, dealt him injuries, that he might have found some reason to duel in Jara, Turrel, or Vrehn or any of the other places he had been, she had never truly considered that he might actually be wounded seriously. She'd had no word of such incidents, neither before nor after his return … yet here was the proof before her eyes.

Proof of the distance grown between them.

Every eye in the place was on Chandris, yet he did not appear to be the slightest bit uncomfortable. He bore himself now with a steely grace he had not owned in childhood, a bearing that set him apart even from the Selin. His face and eyes were hard, cold and confidant. He gave off an aura of power that was almost visible. Like Mohr, he inspired awe, rather than commanding it.

Stiva turned and left the library, headed straight for the Overlook, where she could get a better view. The others followed behind her. Vane and Keorl fell into step behind them.

There were already several people at the half wall where the Overlook—holding up to its name—looked over the Second. They moved aside as Stiva's party arrived, giving her the best view. Shira joined them at the last minute.

Chandris saw her then. His eyes met hers, gazes locked in wordless communication.

Then he nodded turned to face his opponent.

His teacher.

His general.

Silence fell over the crowd.

"They're baring steel," Shira whispered to Stiva, horrified. "What is he doing?"

It was hard to say who made the first move. One moment Chandris and Lyle were circling each other, and the next they were dodging steel. Lyle's movements were expert, precise and fast, executed so smoothly that even the most complex patterns looked easy. Decades of experience had honed the Selin commander into a walking weapon. He had seen Cronn through decades of warfare, and had no qualms about making occasional examples out of his men.

Stiva watched with baited breath, expecting Chandris to lose quickly: not because he was unskilled, but because Lyle was so formidable. However, her twin was holding his own against his former teacher. Chandris' martial training in Aris had brought him to considerable skill even before he had gone overseas. Now, the additional training he had received in Jara showed itself. Apparently, he had studied Oho-Maka and another, less familiar martial art. Stiva recognized some of the styles, having sat through numerous duels, training sessions, and gladiator fights. Chandris moved with a subtle, fluid grace, his muscles rippling smoothly under his skin.

The sound of running footsteps preceded the arrival of another group of onlookers, these from inside the castle. Stiva's party was suddenly engulfed by a large group of srih and staff members, all rushing towards the tiniest spark of excitement on a slightly dull day. It was rare, though not unheard of, for a king to spar with his captain. Cronn had often fenced with Lyle. In fact, the two had been notorious for wrestling and even exchanging blows. But he had never faced his general with bared steel.

Talia was among the newcomers, and she spoke up immediately, commenting loudly. "Ah, so Chandris has decided to prove himself worthy before the Selin. He should save his skill for battle, not demonstrations."

"Chandris has nothing to prove to them," Stiva said quietly. "This isn't about that."

"What, then?"

"A wager," Stiva said thoughtfully.

It was one of those things she sensed about her twin without being told. His mood fell over her own emotions like a veil, and she could not help but absorb it. Another might never see it, but Stiva could decipher the intent hidden in the set of his jaw, the determination in his eyes. Chandris wasn't interested in testing Lyle's limits. He wasn't trying to see how Lyle had stood the test of time. For though Lyle had aged—there was silver in his hair now, and his skin was loosening, especially on his face—he was clearly still in top form. There was more to it than that. Looking at the way the two looked at each other, Stiva realized that they both had the look of gamblers.

Chandris moved quickly, liquid silver speed, neither attack nor defense, but merely a repositioning. He moved himself so that Lyle was facing the sun, and then waited for his commander to make the next move. Lyle himself had taught him many of the tricks he was using: to judge an opponent by forcing them to attack, letting them tire themselves as though they were attacking a wall. As fatigue set in, the weakness became obvious. Chandris was using Lyle's own tricks against him.

Lyle had made him into a warrior, over the course of countless long dusty afternoons they had spent in that very same courtyard, under the same blazing sun, man and boy, teacher and student, general and prince. Chandris had been forged, reshaped, by endless hot days when Lyle—

demanding, unrelenting, Selin—had pushed a young boy to the limits of his endurance and beyond, and, in doing so, made him a warrior.

Something in Chandris' face changed. Stiva saw a new Chandris, one who didn't want to merely survive his reign, or to hold the lands he'd inherited, but to conquer. A hunger grew in his eyes. It was the same battle lust their ancestors had always been known for. A cold chill danced down her back as she watched her brother set himself against his former idol with such cold determination.

It soon became obvious that neither king nor general was holding back. More and more, Lyle found himself hard pressed to defend himself against the very man whose life he was sworn to protect. The two men in the circle held their audience rapt, steel kissing steel, their swords' clashing discord ringing like a bell through the warm air, meeting, turning, dancing, each deflecting what could have been deadly blows. Lyle did not look happy, but he was too smart to let emotion interfere with his instincts, lest it take over. His face was calm, as though set in stone.

A gasp escaped dozens of throats at once, followed by a communal murmur, as Lyle's blade swept close and a thin line of blood appeared on Chandris' chest. Chandris twisted, catching Lyle with a sudden kick to the ribs. Lyle moved, readjusting his balance, spinning low and then slashing upward to try and cut up under Chandris' defense. Chandris saw it and adjusted his guard, neatly deflecting Lyle's blade. Lyle retreated, not in defeat but in feint; halfway into the retreat he attacked again, coming at Chandris hard and fast, forcing him to defend, to retreat.

Chandris did not give so easily. A sheen of sweat glistened on his skin. Lyle was sweating as well. The crowd watched in utter silence. The only sound in the vicinity was the clash of weapons repelling each other.

Chandris turned, ducked low, brought the sword up and across. Lyle barely evaded the blade, and Chandris pressed forward with a series of thrusts, forcing him to the right, forcing him to use his bad left knee, which had been broken badly in some long-ago battle he had fought at Cronn's side.

Lyle advanced again. He was quick, but not quite quick enough.

Chandris kicked hard and Lyle went down, his sword missing Chandris' throat by a hair. Chandris spun, dropped and rolled, rose again up at Lyle other side. Lyle twisted, paling slightly as the knee protested, turned the next blow. Chandris feinted, parried, thrust, and lunged, every muscle in his body under precise control. Lyle dodged, red-faced now with exertion. But he refused to give in. He pressed forward, his own defense impenetrable.

Almost.

Chandris thrust. Lyle stepped back, evading the blade. The years had taken their toll. Lyle fell.

The crowd drew breath, almost as one. A great, collective gasp rose through the air. A moment later, Chandris' blade was against Lyle's throat. Utter stillness descended upon the yard, as the crowd waited with baited breath to see what Chandris would do.

Chandris had always hated being handed an easy win, whether it was at a race or a game or in battle. Nor did he enjoy losing. But now, something new had joined these other traits, a by-product, perhaps, of royal blood. He did not defeat, he did not defend, he *conquered*. And something left Lyle's face that day, that moment, which never returned, a part of his confidence, of his self-esteem, of the pride he held in himself. Student had defeated master; such was the desired eventual outcome of any tutelage worth its while. Lyle, who had been general of the Selin for longer than Stiva and Chandris had been alive, had been defeated not by his student, but by some other teacher, it seemed.

From the fishpond, there came a sudden splash, as a serpent killed one of the fish.

Chandris lowered the blade slowly and offered his hand instead. Deafening shouts thundered into the air as Chandris and Lyle met once more, this time in a boyish bear hug. And the Selin commander forgot protocol long enough to muss Chandris' hair.

The crowd dispersed slowly, trailing a buzz of excited voices in their wake. The group in the garden stirred, as though released from a spell.

It did not take long for it to become clear just what it was Chandris and Lyle had decided to settle with steel.

The next day, Chandris sent the bulk of their forces to the border.

CHAPTER 10

Khirin moved like a ghost through the city, wandering the twists and turns of Aris' maze of cobbled streets. He had walked these streets before, but his scouting then had been purely militaristic. This time, he took note of more than guard posts and hiding places. It was the soul of the city he was after, the silent unseen heart that beat within the city.

Gradually, layer by layer, he found it. In the cafes and shops that lined the market square, it was bohemian, artistic, and vivacious. Near the arena, where the gladiators trained, the city took on a more brutal image; Aris ranked the arts of war as equally fascinating as the arts of song and dance, and found a gruesome death every bit as entertaining as a good play. In the wharf-side taverns and inns, it had a darker nature, thriving on seedier pastimes. Equipped with both sea and river ports, Aris had developed a formidable underworld. The foundations of it were based on illegal trade, most of which took place both behind and beneath the constant bustle of the usual harbor traffic. Aris' city guard had been playing cat-and-mouse with thieves, slavers, and smugglers for centuries. Every time one crimelord was caught, three more replaced him.

The wind grew angrier. The skies wept. The sea lashed the docks with the promise of a coming storm. Still Khirin wandered, slipping silently through the run-down areas of the lower city, where hunger and poverty dwelt among squat crumbling buildings, and disease romped and played in the streets with thin, dirty children. Turning, he wove back through the garden quarter, where small elegant castles sat behind high walls, surrounded by fragrant orchards and lush gardens. In the summer, vividly colored flowers bloomed, giving off clouds of sweet, musky perfume. These were the houses of the srih and the merchant princes. Through it all, he noted an odd overlap of culture. Aris' seedier neighborhoods were, in some cases, just a block away from the manors of the wealthy. He began to realize that the heart of Aris beat not in the serpentine castle that squatted on the hills above the city, draconian and blood-colored: it was in Aris' great market, the soukh, and in the taverns, shops, and gambling hells around it. He browsed around in a Sijhani-owned hunting shop, where one might buy sinew thread and polished stone spearheads, intricately woven blankets, soft leather and suede clothing, bone needles, or the furs or tanned skins of the great vaianths, the furred elephants of the eastern plains. These things were but one step removed from nature, work traded from the tribes in the north. And right next door to this shop was a store that dealt in antiquities, the lesser relics that were the icons of the fallen age of the Elders. They were sold as baubles, these artifacts, things not deemed important enough to be held in the care of the Reonih. Yet one wondered, one marveled, to hold in one's hand a thing made by a long-dead craftsman from across the stars. One could not help but speculate as to whether or not humanity would ever again reach such heights.

Rumor had it that Chandris held such things in a fascination that bordered on obsession. The city of Aris spoke of ancient mysteries and dreamt the wonders of a fallen age. Here and there, one could see it, in the alien curve of a bridge, in the icons frozen in bas-relief, in the mosaic paths that wove through the parks. The city was beautiful and ugly, graceful and hideous, placid and warlike.

So that was Aris, a place where death and blood walked hand in hand with beauty and elegance, a place where dream and nightmare slept together, where past and future collided.

There was another layer yet.

The forest itself cast its own spell over the city. Here and there, from higher vantage points, one could see past the city walls and the outlying fields, to the woods, that mystic, ancient world, threaded with the magic of the Reonih and the gods they served. That influence too was draped over the city, in the parks and groves which popped up here and there, where not so much as a single stone had been turned by man, and on the wells, where skulls of the dead guarded entrances to the Otherworld.

As for the castle that sat above the city, Khirin had not yet discerned its nature, but that place cast a deep shadow. In this weather, the shellscale coating did not blaze with the glorious, rainbow-tinted gold it owned beneath the light season sun. Instead, it was a ruddy reddish color that reminded him of blood.

Blood, and the crimson of the Selin colors.

The day wore on, the clouds drew in ever thicker, and eventually Khirin made his way to the Three Cups Cafe. He was a bit earlier than the appointed time, but that was easily remedied with a cup of fish stew.

Khirin lingered in the cafe a time, watching the citizens go by. Days before, he had secured passage on a ship leaving port later that afternoon. He had known, even as he was forking over his coin, that he would not use the place he had bought. That would have been cowardice, something he had never been able to live with. Money wasted … he had no care of that. Still, it had made him feel better, knowing that he had a way out, if he was desperate or foolish enough to try it. In truth, he was neither. He was strangely calm, almost ambivalent, but for one image that nagged at his thoughts, a laugh that haunted his dreams like a ghost.

Cassandra was gone. He did not know where. Perhaps she had been called back to Zors, to the great desert wasteland that began south of Vrehn's bottom reaches. Or maybe the Dralek had sent her to spin her web upon some other Aursan warlord or king. It mattered not. They would not let her go, not that he was at all certain she *wanted* to go. She enjoyed the life she led. At times, anyway. Still, in the years he had known her, he had lost count of the number of times she had slipped off unannounced, only to reappear almost at random, weeks or even seasons later.

He knew better than to question it. She knew better than to offer information.

Her last message had been clear. The seal that bore her insignia was, in itself, a missive.

Three Cups Cafe. Octavian Solstice, thirteenth hour.

Words from the past filtered into his mind like smoke. He thought again about the message he had received only the night before.

You remain bound to us, until I determine that it is time to release you. Yet it is my hope to see you through this, to all of our benefit. A rare chance sits before you. Take it, Khirin. You have served me well. It seems only right that you should be given this chance. Go, with my blessing. But know this: honor is a heavy burden to bear. As heavy as shame, in its own way.

"Lord?"

Khirin blinked. A dirty face was peering at him. "Nice day, is it? Have you tried the snapfish?"

The messenger was more or less what Khirin had expected, an unremarkable, rather plain-looking man of middle years.

"Excellent," Khirin said, "But a bit bland. Needs pepper. And a bit of citrus, I think."

The man nodded and tilted his hat. A nut dropped onto the floor as he did.

Khirin retrieved the nut with his shoe, and then leaned down to grab it. Once it was in his sleeve, he stood.

He left the last of his Vrehnian coins on the scarred wooden table, which it had not even settled upon before being snatched up by a grimy hand. The face peered down at the coin, scrutinizing it carefully for a moment before looking back at Khirin with a strange, bewildered expression. But Khirin was gone, his black cloak billowing as a harsh burst of wind gusted through the shadows of the alley that twisted away behind the cafe.

He opened the nut in the alley, carefully extracting two intricately folded pieces of paper. One was a cipher, which he would use to decode further instructions.

The second message was simple enough, blunt and to the point.

You'll be in the ground before Darkfest. He knows.

Cassandra never had been one for emotional farewells.

Eventually the time passed when the ship would have left the harbor, and with a single glance at the moons, Khirin knew that by not choosing to leave, he had chosen to stay. Only then did he return to the Inn of the Speckled Jhar to pick up the single satchel that held his personal possessions, before finally beginning the long walk up the hill.

The castle swallowed him without a stir.

The arena master had given him confirmation; a stamped letter, a password for the Crimson Gate and the name of the man he was to report to. With this, entry through the Crimson Gate proved simple. Finding his way to his check-in point was somewhat more taxing. Navigating the castle's interior was not nearly as easy as he had thought. The construction of numerous additions to the original structure had made the castle into something of a labyrinth. This had been done deliberately: the additions' confusing schematics were intentionally maze-like, designed to confuse invaders. As if that weren't enough, many areas had more than one nickname. Wandering at whim, he discovered for himself the layout of the castle, which was one of the first things he had intended to do anyway.

As he walked, he memorized the paths he took. Despite all the tricks and techniques he had been taught, it was impossible to capture the castle's schematics in one outing. Aris was nothing if not confusing. He suspected he would find himself frequently lost at first, regardless of how many tricks he employed.

But, over the course of a few hours, he began to get a feel for the place.

The ground floor contained the great hall, surrounded by its honeycomb of alcoves, many of which branched off into other rooms and hallways. On the first floor were also ballrooms, sitting rooms, and galleries, in addition to the kitchen and pantry complex and several outbuildings. The second floor held offices for Reonih clerks, stewards, and bailiffs, as well as other officials, a map room, libraries, meeting halls, and dining rooms. The third level consisted only of living quarters for both the royal family and visiting dignitaries, while the fourth story contained accommodations for noble guests, ranking staff, and resident srih. The fifth floor was utilized mostly by nurseries, sewing rooms, and children's quarters, while the sixth contained a series of guest rooms, music rooms, a theater, and several studies. The seventh floor was almost entirely used for storage and servants' quarters, and the eighth held only the grand hall. There were three sub-levels, containing wine cellars, pantries, dungeons, more storage, and a cistern.

Four separate major additions surrounded the main castle. Of the four, all of which were castles in their own rights, each had their own, smaller additions. One was a stable and granary complex, and one a craft hall, where the smithy, carpenters' hall, tannery, butchery, weavers, apothecary, and smokehouse took up residence. A third served as an armory.

The fourth, and largest, was occupied solely by the Selin.

One of the Selin provided directions to Lyle's office by way of a curt pointing gesture. The difference between the extravagant decor of the main castle and that of the Selin compound was startling. In contrast to the caste's grandeur, the military station was stark, even severe, in aspect. The whitewashed walls were bare of all but the simplest adornments, the doorways and torch fixtures without ornamentation. Khirin had expected as much. Everyone knew of the bleak, austere conditions in the training camps, where Selin initiates were forged into warriors. Though the training at times, it was said, bordered on torture, the brutal catechisms inflicted there were not done for negligence or maliciousness, but rather the opposite. The Selin deliberately chose harsh, sometimes deadly methods to harden their apprentices and weed out any weaklings. This was a matter of pride among the Selin, rather than one of shame. They had paid a price to wear that red, each and every one of them, a blood price.

And one felt it, in these barren halls. The stark corridors rang with the footsteps of a hundred generations of warriors, the proud, deadly ghosts of Aris' past. The truth in those bloodstained stories reached out, wrapping itself around him, trailing its essence everywhere through these stark, unwelcoming corridors. It was not surprising, therefore, to find that the figures that traversed these bleak, plain passages were also severe. They carried themselves with strength and pride, did the Selin. Blades waited at hips and in eyes. Not one smile greeted him; not a trace of sluggishness or idleness hovered about these warriors. The Selin were more than a private guard. They were an elite, deadly force, born, bred, and raised to war. They were also notoriously brutal in their rejection of those they considered inferior, which was more or less everyone. He knew more than one ex-Selin gone outlaw, gone mercenary, men who had been banished for some act of betrayal or weakness. He wished belatedly he had been interested in learning more of them than martial tactics.

He reached a rotunda that was slightly more garnished than the rest of the place. Khirin realized, judging by the increased number of murdik stones on the chests of the Selin in this area, that he had neared the office of the Selin commander. He rubbed his eyes, feeling a sting there from lack of sleep. Shaking it off, he asked a page for directions, and then approached the elaborately carved double doors on the far end of the rotunda.

The guards on duty tried to bar Khirin from entering Lyle's office. He had expected this. He would have been alarmed if they had not halted him. He had no wish to join the ranks of an incompetent army. Not that he had any fear of that being the case.

They sent one of the younger boys for confirmation from Lyle before allowing him entry. Cold gazes raked over him as they waited in silence for the page's return.

The reply came as expected. The door opened, and one of the guards roughly shoved him inside. Khirin turned angrily, ready to retaliate, but the door was already swinging shut. He turned to the man before him, and then straightened, his face and voice expressionless. "I was told to report here. I am—"

Lyle surveyed Khirin with an icy stare. "I know who you are."

Khirin met that iciness with a raised eyebrow. "It was my understanding that—"

Khirin's words were effectively cut short by a dagger—Lyle's—which he found suddenly hurtling towards him. He dodged the blade easily, by simply leaning away from it. The knife buried itself in the thick wood of the door.

"You will have to unlearn that reflex," Lyle observed, leaning back slightly in his chair. The movement gave the illusion of relaxation, but Khirin was not fooled. "Your job here is to intercept blades, not dodge them."

Khirin tilted his head slightly. "Somehow that lacks the warm, comforting tone of welcome I had expected."

"You'll get that later," Lyle retorted.

"Will I?"

"Sit down," Lyle growled. "*Captain.*"

Khirin waited, deliberately measuring the amount of time it took for Lyle's icy disdain to melt into silent rage. He saw the moment pass, and waited a moment longer before plopping himself down into one of the wooden chairs before Lyle's desk. "Shall I return the blade?"

"Sir!" Lyle barked. "This is the headquarters of the Selin, not the camp of some hedge-lord. You will use the proper honorific at all times when speaking to your superiors, or you will be punished the way these men were punished when they stepped out of line as children."

"Shall I return the blade, *sir*?"

Lyle ignored the question. Somewhere across the city, a bell tolled, marking the turn of the hour. Khirin casually tossed the knife, hardly looking. It stuck into a wooden beam.

Lyle observed this, his face expressionless. When he spoke, his tone was flat. "I protested your new position, if that's what you're wondering. It wasn't my idea. And, just to avoid any confusion on the matter, I'll be frank. I don't want you here. Regardless of how many men you managed to kill in the southern lands, in the arena, in the world outside Aris, I still think that your presence here is a disgrace to the Selin, and everything we stand for. If it were my choice, you'd never gotten within a mil of this castle. None of you would. We don't kill for sport, or for fun. We defend our lands, our families, and our king. But you impressed Chandris in the arena. He wanted you brought into this position, and I do what my king tells me. As will you."

"I do what I get paid to do." Khirin snapped, losing patience.

"Oh, you'll be paid." Lyle's eyes glittered. "In cold steel, or in gold. You decide. If you can't keep up with your caste, they'll slit your throat themselves."

Khirin said nothing.

Lyle turned a sharp, calculating gaze on him, estimating him as one would judge or a horse or a cat at an auction. The scar on his cheek was paler than the rest of his face. It slid down his cheek, almost snake like in appearance. He rose, and walked a slow circle around Khirin. "You are srih, or you pretend to be," he said. "You have the accent of nobility. Your nails are neatly manicured, but your hands are callused. You've a taste for finery, no doubt." He paused, eyes narrowing. "That appetite will be neglected here. You will eat what your castemates provide, be it soup, stolen food, or gruel. You will sleep on a board, when you have time to sleep. You will own nothing here that you cannot carry. You seem to be in excellent physical shape. The Starshire institute said you excelled throughout your training there."

Khirin said nothing.

Lyle's brow pursed thoughtfully. When he continued, his tone was slightly less hostile. "I don't think you have the slightest idea what we are. I don't think you understand what it means to be a soldier, never mind Selin. Entire armies have turned and run just at the sight of us."

"So I've heard," Khirin said, "though not recently, I think."

Lyle fixed Khirin with an eagle stare. "One step out of line," he said, "and I will kill you myself. Is that clear?"

"Crystal," Khirin snapped. "I'm not here because I make mistakes."

"Sir!" Lyle barked. "Chandris chose to promote you to a position of high rank, due to your skills and your prowess at killing. You are now part of the Grey Bull, which is auxiliary to the Black Boot, part of the royal guard. The position does not come freely. There are obligations you must fulfill. Failure to do so is as much a disgrace as failure in battle. You will be held to high standards regarding physical and martial fitness, behavior, tidiness, and supply coordination. I'll provide you with a scribe to read the code requirements."

"No need," Khirin told him. "I can read."

"Really?" Lyle asked, a tone of cunning coloring his voice. Khirin saw a thick scroll coming at him. He reached out and caught it reflexively, his hand moving almost of its own accord.

"These are the regulations," Lyle told him brusquely. "Memorize them. As with any other Selin, you will be provided with a small holding of lands, including housing for tenants that work the land. The harvests reaped from your lands will be used to supply your unit. This is a duty that rotates among every Selin by turn, without exception. If the crops fail when it is your turn, if your tenants steal your food and run, if your property is damaged by flood or fire, if *anything* happens, you will find some other way to feed them. Failure to provide for your caste is grounds for discipline up to demotion and dismissal."

"Anything else?" Khirin asked calmly.

Lyle's eyes narrowed slightly, into a look Khirin knew well. It was the look of a killer homing in on his prey. "I'm warning you once. Cross me, and you will die. Unpleasantly. And don't expect Chandris to save you. He won't. If you look at either of the twins, the Selin will slice you open and give Chandris your balls."

"Understood," Khirin said. "I knew exactly what I was signing on for."

"I was Cronn's general for decades. I was commanding the Selin before the twins were even born. And I will die in command."

Khirin waited.

Lyle's voice took on a more civil tone. "I will be honest with you, to this extent. Aris is not in good shape. We are surrounded by enemies. Itacha has been trying Aris' borders, and just last week a raiding party got as far inland as Leth. The srih are roused, already testing Chandris and Stiva. We're moving more forces to the borders, so those left guarding the castle will be pulling a lot of long shifts. I haven't the time to babysit your ass. Maybe you'll survive the year. I doubt it."

Khirin considered that. Lyle had just told him more than his words alone could account for. That the srih were dissatisfied brought a variety of possible situations into the light.

Lyle stamped something on a piece of parchment and handed it to Khirin. "Take this to the sewing rooms. You'll be fitted with a uniform. Then you may report to the armory and select standard weapons. We use short swords in battle, but you can supplement that with other weapons."

Khirin had no intention of giving up his own sword, but he merely shrugged. "Is that it?"

"That's all," Lyle said. "You will report directly to Baros, the captain of the Grey Bull. Chandris himself will formally swear you in later tonight. Your ties to the outside world have been severed. You belong to me now."

Khirin nodded. "Understood."

"Questions?"

Khirin shook his head. "I'm ready," he said calmly, "to meet my caste."

"Then do so," Lyle said. "You'll find them in the barracks, or the Second. But don't expect a warm welcome."

Khirin got to his feet, shouldered his bag, and walked out. The two guards at the door said nothing to him, but a thin ghost of a snicker escaped the first.

Neither of them were expecting what happened next. Khirin lashed out, effectively kicking one's legs out from under him, while almost simultaneously turning to deal with the second. His attack was quick, brutal, and effective.

Both guards were sprawled on the floor when Lyle opened the door a moment later to see what had caused the commotion.

Khirin returned to the barracks, and eventually found the door scripted with the symbol matching the one on his papers, and paused outside.

There were voices within.

Khirin pushed the door open and walked in, glancing around at his new surroundings. Three-tiered bunks lined a barren, whitewashed room … if a few planks of wood with a thin folded blanket atop them could be called bunks. Small cupboards and cubbyholes lined the walls between each set of bunks. A long table and wooden benches filled the center of the room. Several men sat there, eating soup. The far end contained a small kitchen, pantry, and two water closets.

He had seen dungeon cells that were more comfortable.

Something like a dozen men fell silent as he entered. From various positions on bunks, at the table, on the floor, they stared at him, at each other, and then back at him.

"I was told to report to Baros," Khirin told them.

"Who in hell are you?" One asked, finally, a red-headed man with a scar on his cheek.

"My name is Khirin. I'm your new castemate."

Silence.

A dark-skinned man looked at him coldly, his tone no more welcoming than Lyle's had been. "What caste are you from?"

"None," Khirin said simply. "I won entrance in the arena."

That was all it took. The room exploded into a chorus of curses and protests. Several of them stormed out. As for the rest, they cursed more quietly or grumbled, or said nothing at all. But they all looked at him with varying degrees of the same expression. Hatred.

"You aren't just handed the red," one of them said. "You have to earn it."

A pale, blond man appeared at the door. "What the vulk is going on in here?"

"Dallan. Just in time." The dark-skinned man jerked his thumb at Khirin. "We got ourselves a pet gladiator."

Dallan shook his head. "That's got to be a mistake. The arena intakes are supposed to be integrating with the castes that are graduating."

"There's no mistake," Khirin said coldly. "Lyle sent me himself."

"I saw you fight," one of them said. "He's good."

Dallan cursed loudly, and started towards Khirin. "Let's find out."

In a moment, Dallan was lying on the floor, barely conscious, touching a finger to the thin stream of blood running from his nose.

The dark-haired man shrugged and went back to his soup. "Least he can fight."

It would take more than that for them to accept him. This first incident was a given. He had expected something of the sort, even before Lyle's warning. But as he surveyed the hardened faces around him, a twinge of jealousy swept through him. These men had something he would never have; a sense of brotherhood.

And yet he was bound to them now.

Not for the first time, he wondered what he was doing. He dabbed a finger at a tingling spot on his mouth, his finger came back bloody. Dallan had gotten a few solid blows in.

So he bled. Crimson drops fell to the floor.

Selin blood, now.

CHAPTER 11

The dark season brought a cluster of bleak, grey-brown days in its beginnings, throughout which raged a cold wind laced with drizzles of rain. It was the sort of weather that enticed people to stay indoors if possible, or to pull their cloaks tight and hurry, if they must venture out. Aris' streets were somewhat emptier than usual, for no one was particularly inclined to linger outside in the frigid cold simply to chat. Frost-laced windows glowed with a warm golden light, promising the comfort of a cozy fire and perhaps a steaming mug of yrehn. The fortunate ones would find respite from the wind behind such windows. The unlucky huddled miserably in whatever shelter they could find, their eyes filled with the broken dreams of warmer lands.

Outside the thick walls, the winds screamed and set banners to dancing and whipping furiously. They were mischievous winds, which reached into every nook and cranny, as though they were ravenous and determined to feed on even the slightest pocket of warmth. The winds of death, the commoners called them, for every year the corpses of unlucky transients invariably turned up in the streets and alleys throughout the dark season, frozen solid in their sleep. Pneumonia and influenza took their share of the weak and the elderly. The Reonih offered shelter to the destitute and the mad in their theoricas, and the srih gave food to the poor, but it was never enough.

The Reonih predicted a harsh winter.

It was never a good sign when the land welcomed a new king with particularly harsh weather, and the coming winter—the season of air—promised to be brutal indeed. Aris' women kept worried eyes on the meager stores they had in their cellars, while their menfolk went around with furrowed brows. Hunting parties set out, grimly determined, seeking the great fish that braved the purple and black depths of the Oburion, and the massive shaggy vaianth herds that fed upon the grassy plains and tundras to the north.

Behind closed doors, in drafty, fire-warmed halls, the cycle of life continued. The women of Aris spent much of the winter gathered in the craft halls, sewing and weaving. Some created intricate tapestries, while others worked on clothing, bedding, or carpets. Reonih bards set up in corners, playing music to make the time go more pleasantly. In the streets, children ran, shouted, and threw snowballs at one another. In the city, crafters and artisans focused on the goods they would sell in the spring.

Reonih sang for a frozen world. The skies bled ice.

In the castle, in the tower, words and gazes were as chilled as the air.

The Selin posted outside the tower suite were of the Gold Braid caste, and thus were entirely and exclusively concerned with Chandris' safety. Stiva knew them both, though Delis and Vane, who were one step behind her, were probably much better acquainted. Yet for all the camaraderie the Gold Braid generally showed the Black Boot, at this moment, they could have been strangers.

They did not move as Stiva approached.

Stiva drew to a halt. Keorl and Dallan, two steps behind her, did the same. Brow furrowing, she looked at the one nearest the door handle. Memory found a name for him, the taller of the two: Terne. "Open the door, Terne."

The Selin shook his head slightly. Something rattled on his helmet. "I'm sorry, *saya*. He said no disturbances."

"Open the door."

Terne shook his head again, apologetic, but firm. "He did not state exception."

An erlit swooped down behind her. Stiva flinched, but otherwise did not react. She gave her brother's bodyguard an icy stare. "Stand aside. You know better than to deny me."

But the guard only shook his head again. "When he emerges, *saya*, I will immediately tell him that you have come, seeking audience. But that is all I can do. He was quite clear in his orders. Had he not been so specific. I would of course admit you at once."

"You realize I can just go around." Stiva said flatly.

Terne's face remained impassive.

Stiva cursed and went back the way she had come. A few doors down, she stepped past two more Gold Braid soldiers, who were guarding the second entrance to the suite that had once been Lara's. After the coronation, Chandris had taken over the patriarch's suite, and Stiva had gained possession of the matriarch's suite, which adjoined them via a series of shared parlors. Though the matriarch's suite was hers, officially, Stiva had opted to stay in her own apartments. Besides, she would have eventually had to move back anyway, when Chandris took a bride.

The Gold Braid could hardly forbid her from entering her own rooms.

She left Keorl and Dallan outside with the Gold Braid, and stepped in.

Lara's apartments remained mostly unchanged. Sheets covered the intricately carved thi-wood furniture. The fur throws and pillows had been stored away, and the Shadrian silk rugs had been rolled up and put into storage. Lara's things still hung on the walls: elegant sconces, wood carvings, and paintings and tapestries, most of which depicted Shadri's stunning mushroom forests or rocky coasts, or the Arriks. Stiva passed through her mother's rooms quickly, fighting to suppress the rising tide of memories that swelled through her thoughts.

The suite of parlors and libraries that connected Lara's chambers to the patriarch suite were also unchanged. Stiva reached the inner door, which led to the rooms her brother had claimed, and lifted her hand to knock. She struck the wood twice before remembering the secret knock she and Chandris had used as children.

Rap! Rap rap rap. Rap! Rap rap.

The reply—an echo of the first pattern—was only seconds in coming.

Stiva opened the door that led to her brother's rooms, stepped inside, and then stopped short, staring around.

The rooms within were nearly unrecognizable. When their parents had lived here, Lara had decorated both apartments, and in the same fashion. The apartments had had a natural feel, with potted cyris trees and vases of fragrant ghiti flowers, delicate seashells, candles, woodworking, and pottery. Thick fur blankets and Shadrian silk carpets had given the rooms a cozy, yet elegant air. The suite had felt both peaceful and powerful then, and in harmony with the earth and land around them, an air that owed more to Reonih dwellings than the mansions of Arisian royalty.

Chandris had dismantled that peace and built something else entirely.

Everything Stiva remembered was gone, save only the finest pieces of furniture. Sofas that had been piled with soft furs now held brightly colored silk pillows. The carpets on the floor bore strange, intricate patterns that looked nothing like the work Aursan weavers produced. Even the elegant Shadrian tapestries were gone, save for one: a scene of a silver ship descending from a starry night sky. Huge paintings, mostly depicting the Elders, hung in their places. Jaran vases had replaced the potted trees, and the thick candles had been switched out for gleaming Zorish oil lamps.

The new decor was only the tip of the iceberg. Foreign items occupied the spaces previously filled with statues and woodwork. Here and there, Stiva recognized the intricate style of Turrel metalwork. While some of the boxes and items were obviously from Jara, Vrehn, or Turrel, the majority of the new things had a different feel altogether, a sleek, alien look that could not be mistaken.

Elders' craft.

They were not precisely Relics, from what she could see. These were the sort of things men salvaged from the ruined cities, or—some said— scavenged from the ruins of actual ships. They did not seem to be weapons or devices of great significance, though with Elders' artifacts it was often hard to tell. Stiva was stunned at the amount of goods Chandris had acquired. Then again, what was available in Aris was mostly useless debris. According to long-standing laws, the Reonih controlled the Relics. At the end of the war with the Zhur, they had confiscated all but the most trivial baubles. The lands overseas had no qualms about keeping such things. Their scavengers reaped the benefits of a dead age. Relic hunters and grave robbers of Jara and Vrehn held no compunctions about venturing into the bones of a fallen society and bringing out a plethora of goods to sell.

Some of the articles had survived millennia easily. Other things were rusted or broken. Apparently, Chandris had little care for their condition. He cared only about the objects' origin. Several items lay about dismantled, their components and tiny inner parts carefully set out around them, as though they had been dissected, further proof of his infatuation with the lost technology. Some of the objects were so complex and wondrous that in most cases one could only guess at their use. Others clearly stated their purpose. A pipe, a flask, a comb. The room had an alien feel, as though it were not even in Aris, but deep within one of the ancient ships.

An inexplicable feeling of dread twisted up in Stiva's stomach.

Chandris sat in a plush leather chair, reading a scroll which bore, Stiva noted, the red and gold braid that marked it as one of Rory's. She regretted disturbing him when he was involved in something so crucial as the state of the treasury, but she rarely had the chance to talk to him alone, and she was not about to let the opportunity pass her by.

Chandris, glancing up, seemed, if anything, relieved by her interruption. He even did her the honor of standing. "Stiva." He welcomed her with a strained, troubled cheer. "An unexpected guest."

Automatically, she went to him and kissed his cheeks in semi-formal greeting. He smelled of dust and wood smoke, as though he had not ventured into the sun in days.

Stiva stood there, silently surveying the golden stranger who was her twin, and reconsidering the grim implications of the message Mohr had sent her that morning.

Listen to the whisper, not the roar.

Chandris motioned her to a chair, settling down again into his own.

"What are you doing?" Stiva asked curiously.

His answer was short, sour. "Trying to find some more money."

She frowned. "We have clerks and stewards for that."

"I know." Chandris sounded annoyed. "I was hoping at least one of them was incompetent, or a thief. Unfortunately, it seems they're all quite efficient." He rubbed his eyes and looked at her. "It's bad, Stiva."

He coughed. There was an alarming rattle to the sound. She noticed, not for the first time, how weary he looked. The golden color had drained from his skin, replaced by pallor. The laughter that had once resided in his eyes was gone. He had lost weight; his clothes hung loosely on his frame. His eyes were bloodshot.

"Chandris, you look exhausted." Stiva spoke quietly. "You have too much on your shoulders right now. You'll make yourself sick if you keep pushing this hard. You should just relax for a few days, get some rest. The castle won't crumble in the time it takes for you to get a decent amount of sleep."

He looked at her, a steely determination in his voice and eyes. "I'll rest when I'm in my tomb. I haven't time now."

"You'll be in your tomb sooner rather than later if you don't take better care of yourself."

This was, she knew, the pot calling the kettle black. Her own initial determination to reserve afternoons for reading and music had eroded. Every morning was a seemingly endless pile of decisions: people seeking favor, asking debt forgiveness or wanting old titles restored. It never ended. She was lucky if she had a few hours to relax after dinner.

Chandris rolled his eyes in annoyance, then stood and stretched. He made a halfhearted attempt to straighten out his mussed hair, then gave it up and went instead to the bowl of rolaris leaves that lay on a nearby table. Stiva watched with a creasing brow as he carefully peeled the outer layer back from one and pressed the moist interior of the leaf against his wrist. Almost immediately, his appearance changed. He looked a bit more alive, but it was a false vitality, one that was in the end more draining than it was rejuvenating. "Is there some reason you dragged yourself into my presence," he asked her, "Or did you merely come to see if I were still breathing?"

"A bit of both, truth be told," Stiva said. "I've hardly seen you this last season."

"You saw me at supper last night."

"I saw a king, draped in jewels and serpents."

Her laconic description of the srih drew a burst of laughter from him, rare these days. But the laughter never reached his eyes. "That you did," he sighed. "Which of them sent you here?"

"The jewels."

He frowned.

"I had a message from Mohr today," Stiva made her tone deliberately casual. "It seems the Reonih have not yet received their full tithes."

Chandris did not answer her. Instead, he went to the window and stood looking out at the dusk. The lights of Aris spread out below him, a blanket of golden stars against a sky fiery with sunset's fury.

Stiva continued. "He wasn't angry. He said he was certain it was an oversight, with this still being somewhat new to us, and—"

He looked at her then, with a gaze that spoke volumes.

She trailed off, uncertain.

"It was no oversight," Chandris said quietly.

Stiva blinked. "What?"

"It wasn't an oversight." He turned back to the window, avoiding her eyes, instead staring down at the city as he spoke. "I know they haven't been fully paid yet. Nor will they be."

Stiva frowned. "I don't understand. Why wouldn't you pay them?"

"I'm revisiting our finances: our taxes, our tithes, everything. I'm making changes that I think will benefit us and our people. I saw the world." His voice dropped. "I saw the ruins of a greater age, and saw what we have sunk to."

"We would have sunk further," Stiva said, "if not for the Reonih."

"I knew you would fight for them," Chandris said, his tone quiet now, the fury ebbing from his eyes. "Let me ask you something: why?"

Stiva blinked. "Why? *Why?* Because they are the only thing keeping Aursa from sinking into complete barbarity! The Reonih are our guidance, and the guardians of our heritage, the last links with our ancestors. They are our blood. Or have you forgotten where our mother came from?"

"They more or less disowned her when she married Cronn," Chandris retorted. "I haven't forgotten *that*. Nor have I forgotten that we have yet to receive a single communication from Lara's tribe, but for one formal letter. Our beloved grandfather Pahnryn has not even bothered to personally acknowledge her death or our coronation. We have never met our Reonih kin, and probably never will. That is our blood, Stiva; faceless, voiceless relatives deep in the mushroom forests of Shadri." His voice twisted with sarcasm. "Shadri, Shadri, the old country, the land of violent storms and ancient forests, the place where the Elders planted their brave new world in the shadow of the Arriks. If the old tribes are keeping the wisdom of the ancients alive in the mushroom forests, it's hardly doing us any good, is it? Whatever silent traces of knowledge they retain, they keep entirely to themselves. They refuse to use it, they refuse to share it, they refuse to rebuild it, and their laws make it blasphemy for anyone else to even study it. How does that benefit anyone?"

Stiva stared at her twin, a bleak dawning in her thoughts. Her voice dropped to a whisper. "Gods," she breathed. "That's what this is really about, isn't it? You want the Relics. You want to study the Elders' sciences, to reawaken their power."

Chandris spoke calmly, but his green eyes flashed with an intensity that caused her to shrink away from him a bit. "Stiva, there are things in this room, in our attics, that we cannot even identify. Mankind has fallen. We have literally fallen from the stars and sunk into the mud. We came from a civilization that crossed the stars. And here we are, hacking each other up, turning this land into a bloody chaos of warfare and hatred." He picked up one of his baubles at random and held it up, brandishing it like a weapon. "Do you know what this does? Or how it works? No, of course not. But they do. *They do.* This is our heritage, and they have no right to keep it from us."

Chandris tossed the artifact into the fire. It exploded in a little burst; Stiva jumped, despite herself, and loosed a little yelp of surprise.

But her brother was not finished.

"Terror, *terror.*" Chandris raised his arms in aggravated flourish, mimicking the exaggerated tone of an actor performing a part. "Any who venture into the ruined cities will be struck down by angry gods. Any who attempt to use the Elder's weapons shall be taken by the Zhur and torn into little bloody pieces. Any who try to reconstruct their science shall be damned. Do you really believe that? *Really?*"

Stiva could only stare at him, speechless. "I believe in the Reonih," she said. "And I believe in the Zhur. I've seen them."

Chandris gave a little sigh, as though humoring her. "I'm sure you have." He held up another Relic. "These are power, Stiva. They aren't just weapons. They're tools." He looked at her. "Tools to help us build a better world."

Stiva surveyed her brother warily, well able to interpret the sudden fire in his eyes. A sinking feeling clawed its way to the depths of her stomach.

"Come," he said. He turned on his heels and led her to a bookshelf, which, at the touch of a lever, moved aside to reveal a room Stiva had never known of. Chandris grabbed a torch from the wall. Stiva followed him inside.

The room was used for storage, it seemed, though likely in the past it had been a convenient place to hide a mistress from unexpected guests. The furniture was covered with sheets. Piles of chests were stacked up in the corners. A thick layer of dust covered everything in a grey-brown coating.

Stiva's eyes immediately watered. Her twin's did as well.

They sneezed in perfect synchronicity.

He pointed to a collection of paintings leaning against a wall. Positioning himself so that the light fell on them, he gestured towards the stack. "Go on, look. They're amazing."

Stiva flipped through them, taking in scene after scene of the Elders cities and their wonders, and of the Zhur, who had risen to destroy the Elders. Some depicted the shadow age, the dark time after the Zhur had destroyed the Elders. The Sijhani and Reonih meeting at the first council, securing peace. In one, a fiery cloud rose over an alien land. In another, a huge wave of earth crashed over the Elders' city.

Some, Stiva realized, were not paintings, or if they were, they were so well done as to appear real.

Chandris continued in a calmer tone. "We have a legacy that is wasting away, Stiva, a legacy of wisdom we can no longer even begin to comprehend. Don't you think it's time this adopted world of ours came into its own? It has been a thousand years since the Elders brought us here, and still we huddle in the shadows of their ruins and tremble before the ghosts of their gods. They were fools, if you ask me. An entire new planet, and they fought so bitterly for control of it that they made Aursa a battlefield. And what have we kept? What knowledge? What truth? The ability to mine, to raise crops, to make war and wine. To fuck. Do you know how to fly? How to harness the fire in the sky? Do you know what planet we came from, or why or how? We can point to Denebola on Lightfest Eve, but what else do we know of it? What world had Denebola as a sun?"

"Xeros," Stiva said softly.

Chandris stared at her. Their gazes locked, identical green, a silent battle playing out within that stare.

The last painting was of a nightwing. The beast, a thing of smoky feathers, ebony claws, ink-black eyes, and silken wings, looked nearly identical to the one she had seen outside her window. Stiva pushed the stack back in place and stood.

"They remember," Stiva said quietly. "The bards know that, and more. You forget I was an initiate before you made me a queen. There are songs that are not sung, Chandris. Even the oldest. *Especially* the oldest. We—they—do not sing those ballads at court. But do not assume those songs are lost."

Stiva watched her words sink into his mind, and realized with a sickening feeling that she had, in effect, just betrayed the Reonih. If there was one thing they held sacred above all else, it was secrecy. She had no right to tell him that.

And Chandris seemed to know this too, for he studied her acutely, his brow creased by a faint line. "You plead their cause and then betray their secrets so easily. Would they forgive that, if they knew?"

Stiva had known for years that Chandris' reverence for the Reonih was nowhere near as strong as her own, but to hear him speak so vehemently against them came as a complete shock. She took a deep breath, then exhaled slowly, choosing her words carefully. "I do not deny that it is brave of you to seek the wisdom of the past. But those powers, the knowledge that you crave, they do not come without cost. The Reonih know the dangers that lie down that path. That is why they guard the Relics so carefully. We are safer without it."

"I'm not so sure of that." Chandris went to an elaborately carved thi-wood dresser. Taking a key from a chain on his neck, he unlocked it, and then withdrew a small object.

She recognized it as the item Jahn had given him at their coronation.

"Come here," Chandris said.

She went to stand beside him. Chandris pressed a button, and suddenly they were looking at a window into the Otherworld. A world at war, it seemed. And as Stiva stared in disbelief, she saw images of men ripped apart by bolts of power. Huge buildings crumbled into dust before their eyes. A vast wave crossed a strange land, a wave not of water, but of earth. It flattened everything in its path, leaving only devastation behind. A mushroom-shaped cloud of fire obliterated a blue sky.

Words flickered onto the screen: *I am as death, the destroyer of worlds.*

Stiva looked away, sickened. But Chandris stared at the images with a keen fascination.

A chill shivered across her skin at that look. A new hunger had risen in him, and she felt it gnawing at him as the newly-awakened beast within him chewed at his emotions, ravenous and enraged.

Power hungry, Stiva thought. *A craving that may kill us all.*

"This thing takes its power from the sun," he said. "Those weapons do the same. The Reonih must have them. I have found them in old paintings. What army could stand against that?" He looked at her, facing her with eyes that were identical to hers, but filled with darker dreams. "Who would raid us? Who would send an army against us? We would be strong, Stiva. And we would have peace. Isn't that what you want? Or do you think we can stand through another five hundred years of war?"

"Of course I want that," Stiva said. "But—"

He cut her off. "Everything I do, from this moment on, is for the benefit of Aris. *All* of Aris, including the Reonih. I expect you to do the same."

She nodded. Her head was spinning, and she felt suddenly dizzy. "I'll leave you to it," she said. "But please, send funds for the theoricas and the healers. They care for the weak and the sick. They have nothing to do with any of this."

"Of course." Chandris nodded. "I agree, that they are beneficial, even crucial."

She turned to leave.

He called after her. "Stiva!"

She stopped and turned.

"I would have told you in the morning, but you may as well know now. There was another raid today. I'm riding to the borders with the Selin tomorrow. The Delorans have grown bolder quickly. Cerrow was right about garrisoning the outlands. I'm seeing to it myself. You'll be in charge here."

"Be safe," she told him.

He nodded. "Be on your guard," he said. "There are changes coming."

With that, he went back to his scroll, dismissing her.

She left quietly, her thoughts spinning troubled through her mind.

CHAPTER 12

All seven moons hung full in the sky, tinting the darkness with deep, rich hues of color. The Elders had believed the colors were natural, born of chemical reactions. They had seen only blackness when they stared into the night sky, when they conquered the abyss between stars. Mohr had never entirely understood this. The only answer he had for the children who, invariably, unfailingly, asked him *why* was that they had made themselves into gods, and therefore cared nothing for true deities.

Each moon had its own story and song. The two large moons, Octavian and Calista, ruled war and love, respectively. The myths and legends woven around them had begun, long ago, as Sijhani stories. They had changed, somewhat, over the years and generations. Become colder, harder, perhaps, as well as more ethereal.

Aris was, as its moons, a child of two parent societies: the Sijhani and the Elders.

Both had abandoned it.

The Reonih, having once found themselves at a crossroads between the two paths of thought, had, when possible, straddled the line between them. When not, they chose the Sijhani ways, thus binding themselves to their adopted world. The tribes had taught them herblore and planting methods. They had taught them about beasts and seasonal changes of this strange new land. The Reonih, in turn, had shared what knowledge the Sijhani would accept: smithing, some medicine, the making of paper. The sages who ruled the Sijhani knew better than to tamper with the balance nature provided.

The Elders had known no such restraint.

Wings crossed the moons. The nocturnal creatures, the birds and dragons and bats, danced before them in silent celebration. The forest filled with the howls and screeches of the wild hunters. Tomorrow, the scavengers would feast on bones, and the soil would be rich with blood.

From the village nearby, he heard the faint strains of music and laughter, and as the grove welcomed him in silence, he allowed himself a moment of regret, that he would miss the celebration.

The godtree waited.

Mohr walked into the shadows.

At first, he could see nothing. Neither the passing years nor the numerous prior visits had done much to diminish the fear he always felt at those few first steps. Within, the atmosphere was thick and tense, raising goosebumps on his thin, withering skin. Despite his years, an old, irrational fear rose up through his thoughts to haunt him; that of monsters in the dark. Unseen eyes watched him from the gloom. His tongue grew thick in his mouth. The base of his spine tickled. His heart pounded faster. Beads of sweat broke out on his forehead, despite the chill.

The presence of the dead and the unborn, whose souls in turn strengthened the gate, hung thick in the air. The Otherworld was close, here, the veil between dimensions worn thin. The Zhur waited within, in darkness never broken by the light of the sun, with primordial gods and beings he could neither name nor truly comprehend. Terror slowed his step. He shut his eyes, started a breathing pattern, and brought his pounding pulse under control.

The little red dog beside him sniffed the shadows warily, and then looked up at him, as though asking why they were there.

"You could have stayed in your bed," Mohr told it. "You chose to come. Now wait. This place is not for you."

The little dog cocked its head and settled down with a sigh.

The interior chamber was not very large at all, perhaps a half-dozen steps across. A small well, edged by stone walls carved with Aorhan runes, occupied its center. There was never a current in the waters, yet they remained clear. A small platform—more of a shelf, really—had been cleverly constructed above the well, its wrought iron legs curving above the waters, making a simple altar. The chamber was empty, otherwise.

Mohr made his way carefully across the small chamber, lantern in hand, feeling his way over the uneven dirt floor. He could hear the winds now, dancing across the outside of the tree. His bones creaked and popped as he knelt before the pool and altar. Some tiny voice inside him cussed, belligerent at the pain such a simple thing as kneeling now caused him. The dampness that hung in the air was hardly a warm welcome to an aging Reonih High Priest whose bones ached throughout the season of wind. But the fire must always be started anew, from sacred wood. He took out the kindling he had brought, and set to it.

Mohr shivered, a shudder not entirely born of the chill. The air felt abnormally thick around him, livid. The sense of being watched was distinctly palpable. The scream of the wind rose sharply into a cacophony of screeches and howls, faded away to a whisper, and then fell into silence, leaving him in a stillness so thick it seemed the entire world had ceased to exist. Suddenly, the sound of the sticks rubbing together seemed deafening.

He wondered—not for the first time—if it soon might.

A thin curl of smoke drifted up from the tinder. He blew on it carefully, and then fought a wave of dizziness: his lungs weren't as strong as they had once been. The spark grew, and he put the tinder into the firepot on the small altar. As the flames crackled into life, a ruddy, bloody light filled the chamber. Mohr raised his eyes from the altar slowly, his heart beating quickly with anticipation.

Though he knew what he would see, the sight always took his breath away.

The godtree was massive. In truth, it was not one tree, but several, which had grown, entangled together, over the pool, forming a sort of conical tent out of living wood. The sacred space within was made of both trunk and root, but was, in effect, more of a temple than a hollow.

The tree, from the outside, was formidable, but not entirely uncommon. The sacred rogan trees often grew together. What was remarkable about the godtree was what lay within. Carved faces covered nearly every visible inch of the tree. There were angry faces and gentle ones, beautiful maidens and withered crones, fierce-eyed warriors and benevolent sages, children and elders, srih and commoners, kings and queens and infants. Some of them had jewels for eyes. Rubies and amethyst and emeralds gleamed in the flickering light. The wooden faces staring at him were incredibly lifelike. Even the tiniest detail had been created with astounding precision, from hair to jewelry to facial features, right down to eyelashes and even, in the case of one unfortunate youth, acne.

The faces looked a little different each time. Mohr would have sworn that they moved around, switching places, moving closer to or away from one another. Some also seemed to change expression. One that he recalled as weeping previously now smiled down at him. Another was yawning. Mohr marveled anew at the detail with which the teeth were depicted. Memory nudged him, insisting that this face had seemed only bored before.

Such were the places the Zhur walked.

It was time for the ceremony. He lit the incense, threw the herbs onto the fire, and drank the potion in his drinking horn. When he felt the world begin to lose its hold on him, he drew the runesticks and cast them, studying the patterns intently. The feather-like etchings on the polished bones spoke volumes, to one such as he. The runecast revealed more than shapes. Sounds, symbols, and even names disclosed themselves in the tangle of bones.

One never knew what the godtree would offer. Sometimes it was the Seaborne, spoke to him, giving him visions in the water. Sometimes the Fireborne cast images into flame. Sometimes it was the Earthborne, whose messages played out in wood and dirt. Sometimes it was the Skyborne, hovering in the smoke above the fire.

He stared at the flames until a face appeared, and began to whisper dreams of fire and shadow to him. The Zhur in the inferno changed, constantly, her face morphing from one to another.

Time shifted. His mind expanded, a drop of water melting into the ocean of universe. He saw the other realms, as he had before. Strange and beautiful beings twisted around him as he journeyed to a dark star the Elders had long since forgotten. He saw four white horses, three red cats, and six black albatross, all crossing a golden field. The field cracked and turned to dust beneath them, and snakes slithered out of the cracks. The snakes wrapped themselves around him, hissing secrets from obliteration.

Voices from the void tore his thoughts open, sent them into the abyss, to slip through dying starlight, to float through clouds of poison gas.

He found himself in a smooth, metal chamber, in the center of which was a podium. A book lay upon it, shielded by a glass dome. He approached cautiously, but could not open the dome. The words on the pages danced and changed before his eyes, filling his brain, his thoughts, and—later—his dreams, with apocalypse.

The meditation lasted several hours. It was not his first journey into the Otherworld. Nor did he expect it to be his last.

But it was, without a doubt, the most disturbing.

The things revealed to him were neither comforting nor surprising. When the Otherworld released him, he felt sickened and uneasy, and he felt the weight of dread draped around his shoulders like a lead cloak.

The air grew cold, of a sudden. A bone-chilling wind gusted in through some unseen crack or crevasse. The fire gusted, and then nearly went out.

Mohr stood wearily, gritting his teeth as pain laced through his joints. As he turned to leave, something on the tree caught his eye. He turned and stepped closer to study it, his eyes widening as he noticed two new faces, their familiar features done in such perfect detail that he could have no doubt as to their identity.

Chandris and Stiva.

He stepped out of the sacred space, feeling the ground again beneath his feet. The Otherworld released him, and the forest took him back into its cool, musky depths. The little red dog lifted its head and jumped up to greet him, bounding in happy circles around his feet.

A figure in white robes waited at the edge of the grove.

"Hailte," Mohr said, trying to hide his irritation. He wanted to go home, to his cozy fire and his favorite chair, which was piled high with thick valianth fur. He wanted yrehn, cinnamon bread, and bed, in that order. He wanted sleep, and his bear fur slippers.

But he never shirked his duties.

Cerrow bowed his head. "I hope you don't object to me having my own time in the godtree."

Mohr frowned. "It is yours to use," he said, "as much as mine."

"And what did you see?"

"The same thing you will, I suspect," Mohr said. "Death. Madness. Lust for gold and blood and flesh. The wheel of time is turning. Our age is moving into another era. In the sky, the lion is swallowing the hawk."

He looked down at his feet, where the little dog sat patiently waiting. "The wheel turns."

"That it does," Cerrow said. "You've heard of Chandris' latest decree?"

"Regarding the Relics? Yes. He wants a full accounting of what we have."

"He refused to back down from it," Cerrow said. "I tried to dissuade him. He's as bullheaded as Cronn, if not worse."

Mohr studied Cerrow. They did not entirely trust each other. They had, at various times over the decades, found themselves both ally and antagonist, sometimes on opposite sides of Aris' issues, sometimes on the same side. Yet they had a mutual respect, that the years had forged into something more akin to a relationship amidst siblings or kin.

"And what will you do?" Cerrow demanded.

Mohr didn't answer for a long time. "Grow," he said finally.

"Is that your path? Acceptance?"

"It's useless to fight change. You can't stop the seasons, or keep a child from growing. Change has followed us to the stars, and beyond them. Fighting it is like stabbing waves with a sword."

"Change is one thing. This king will drown the land in blood." Cerrow rubbed his forehead.

"Aris' destiny was never ours to control," Mohr said. "We can only do what we can to guide the twins. Keep their heads on straight, if we can."

"And if he demands the Relics?"

"I won't raise a hand to them," Mohr said. "The moment there is bloodshed between forest and crown, war will engulf Aris. Do you think we can stand against the Selin? We cannot win that way, Cerrow."

"You're getting soft, old man," Cerrow said quietly. "You don't have the stones you once did. You won't stand up to Chandris, any more than you did Cronn."

"I am not one for stabbing rivers," Mohr said. "Every scrying I have done shows the same. Mehran's, too. The future is the way of the past. The science of the Elders is writ in the fabric of the universe. The Elders did not create it. They *discovered* it. Their children will discover it again. There is nothing we can do to stop that. Relics or no Relics, Aursa's future belongs to engines and machines. Aris will learn again to harness lightning and bend fire to its will to make things with no soul, things with the most trivial purposes. The alchemists are already discovering things in the towers of Jara that will change the world. We cannot stop it, Cerrow. Our age is ending."

Once, he would have raged at such a thought. Once he—like Cerrow—would have sought to stop the tides of change. But now he only felt sorrow, and a deep, pure love for his people.

Cerrow wasn't done yet. "You know what that alchemy did to Denebola. You've seen the pictures, read the accounts. Are you just going to let us go that way? Towards a future in which millions starve while a few srih control the majority of the wealth? You've seen it, Mohr. *I've* seen it. Don't tell me that—"

"Change happens," Mohr said sharply. "Mankind is curious and intelligent. We cracked the code of spaceflight once. Do you not think it will happen again?"

Cerrow lifted an arm, gesturing around him. "If we go that route, in three hundred years, these forests will be razed. In four hundred, there will be nothing left. That is the future. Every vision brings me to the same end. There will be an age of prosperity, but, like the rush of good wine, the glamour will fade, the lights will dim. And in the end, there will be nothing but bones and dust."

"Everything ends, Cerrow." Mohr said. "Things are changing. The world spins faster and faster through the abyss. Chandris' obsession with the Relics has spread to the srih."

"And what will you do to stop it?"

"We cannot stop it, Cerrow. Our fight is to stop the land from falling into another shadow age."

"And how do you propose to do that? From the interior of the godtree? You sit in comfort in your forest, with your dog and your pipe, and you write pretty speeches about what Aris needs, but at the end of the day, you're weak. You're just another cog in the wheel. You fear the Selin, when a fraction of those weapons would destroy them entirely."

"And then what? We are back to fighting the Zhur, back to the madness we were in before the treaty." Mohr's voice was thin and weak: it curled around Cerrow like the smoke from a fire. "Your way will make the king an enemy. We need him to be an ally, Cerrow. Do you not see that?"

"We tried your way," Cerrow's eyes glittered. "We followed your urging. *Send the boy away. Broaden his mind.* Instead he returned with a desire for the Relics."

"You cannot change fate," Mohr said.

Cerrow smiled. "I only need to change a man's mind," he said.

"You hold influence over him," Mohr said. "You swore to me that he would bend to your will like a piece of leather. Instead, he hardens against us by the day. Do you not understand what we are looking at, Cerrow? Obliteration. If he takes that path, we will not survive. That is death. Ours, and all of Aris'."

"Keep birds ready," Cerrow looked at Mohr. "I'll take care of it."

"What is that supposed to mean?"

"You take your road," Cerrow said, "I'll take mine."

With that, Cerrow turned and walked into the godtree. The shadows within swallowed his form silently. The dog at Mohr's feet whimpered, wanting supper, a soft bed, and belly rubs, in that order.

See what the gods tell you, Mohr thought. *If you see anything but death ahead of us, I'll be shocked.*

He turned and walked away, the red dog trotting along at his feet.

CHAPTER 13

Starshire, the summer estate: a sunny, flower-laden hillside, golden with the summer's last warmth. A jewel in the midst of the forest, a place for song and laughter, Starshire stretched out over mils of forest and countryside to the north and east of the city. Stiva had always loved it there. Like Lara, she felt more peace in a minute outside the city walls than in an entire cycle within them. Starshire was a place where even queens might bask in the sunlight. From her vantage on a flower-dotted hillside, every direction Stiva looked in offered a breathtaking view of the forest and hillsides. To the north, forest and mountains rolled away into the wild, to lands held by the Reonih and, further on, the Sijhani. To the south, Stiva could just make out the spires of the ancient, weatherworn stone castle. The lake beside it reflected the sunlight and landscape perfectly. East and west offered similar views, of valleys and fields falling gently away to the distance.

This was the Aris Stiva loved most, the gorgeous, rolling golden hills, the gardens, the crystal-clear waters of the lake tucked in behind the orchards. The sprawling villa below held nothing of the castle's severity. Spinflowers were in season, and tiny dots of color tumbled down the steeper hills. On days like this, Starshire was paradise.

A short distance away from where she, Shira, Twyla, and Mina were picking flowers, Reide, Carin, Fiurn, and Kira sat beneath a large shade tree, playing songs to a group of young adults. Marcelle and Aret sat together, passing a flask between them. A small horde of boys from the nearby Selin institution moved back and forth across the meadow below, tossing a pigskin around. Two Reonih walked alongside a thin silver stream, graceful in their robes. They seemed a part of the landscape, completely at ease with the natural world. Even the Black Boot and the Grey Bull, who were spread out almost randomly over the hillside, looked relaxed. Vane and Dallan were playing dice, their pale hair shining like silver in the sun. Others were wrestling, sparring, or sharpening weapons. In the fields and meadows beyond them, birds, cats, and horses soaked up the sun in various paddocks and cages. Beyond these, herds of horses and cattle moved around on the green-gold fields.

Stiva got goosebumps, looking at them all. A lump rose in her throat. This was her land. The land she had sworn to die to protect.

In her mind's eye, the bucolic scene around her was replaced by a darker one. Visions rose through her thoughts: greasy black smoke rising into the air, the cruel hiss of flames, blood on the ground.

This time, she did not have to wonder what the visions meant.

As soon as the winter snows had melted, the Delorans had started raiding again from the north. Cronn had barely held them in line through his reign, so it was no surprise to anyone when Itacha, the Deloran king, moved more of his forces to the border. His bands of raiders, knowing that the Selin would arrive too late, had grown more and more bold. And inside Aris' borders, the thieves were growing ever more bold. Highway robbery, always a problem, had reached crisis proportions. The robbers and raiders, unchecked, grew bolder and more and more violent almost by the day. Chandris had ridden out weeks ago to appraise things.

Stiva had been anticipating the Lightfest retreat for weeks. She had hoped to be able to spend at least a few days relaxing and enjoying herself without a flock of srih jabbering for her attention. After the turbulence and trauma of the last season, the annual Lightfest trip to Starshire promised a much-welcomed respite from the pressures of ruling.

Or so she had thought.

They had ridden two days, arriving to find a veritable flock of messenger birds already waiting for them. In that time, that short time, a whole crop of new issues had sprouted up.

It seemed that it would always be that way, problem after problem and never-ending lists of decisions to make.

The crown, Stiva realized, could not be left behind. It gave her no peace, no respite, but weighted on her every waking thought, intruding even into the brightest, most relaxed hours, like a snake in the sunshine. She had, upon first being crowned, tried to keep her afternoons and evenings clear. More and more, she found herself kept busy until supper. That crown dragged the problems of an entire city-state behind it, whispering worry into each thought, each dream that crossed her mind. The pressure of responsibility regularly left her cold and shaking in her bed.

More and more, she heard her father's voice trailing into her thoughts … not the father she had buried, but the one she had known as a child, stern and strong and invincible Cronn, who had solemnly repeated Aris' creed before a pair of bright-eyed twins.

Honor. Courage. Serenity.

It should have been altered, Stiva thought, *to unending patience, blind luck, and bluffing.*

The hillside was bright and peaceful, but the world around it whispered blood and war.

A voice interrupted her thoughts. "Stiva?"

Stiva turned. It was Twyla, holding out a basket of flowers for Stiva to inspect. "How many do we need?"

Stiva glanced down at the basket at her feet, which was filled with fragrant flowers. A second basket sat nearby, attracting bees. Two more rested near Shira, who was working on her third, as were Adele and Mina. "I don't think we have enough for the garlands quite yet," Twyla continued, "But we need to be back in time to change for supper."

Stiva glanced at the baskets again, then looked up at the sky, mentally calculating the time. "Another hour."

Shira walked up to them from her former spot a bit further down the hill. "Honestly," she said, wiping a sheen of sweat from her brow. "I don't know why you insist on doing this yourself. It's not like we don't have servants for this kind of thing."

Stiva waited patiently for a bee to finish copulating with the flower she wished to pick. "Because for one, I have been dying for fresh air and warm sunshine and some form of movement. And secondly, the servants are busy preparing for the feast."

"Chandris is coming today, isn't he?" Twyla asked.

"He's on his way, I think."

"Have you had word from him?" Shira asked.

I've dreamt his dreams, the visions he sees. The burning lands, the corpses, the crying, dirty orphans sleeping in pig hovels. Stiva wanted to say these things, but she did not. "He sends me letters regularly," she said. "One of his birds arrived earlier this morning. He should be here before nightfall."

The Selin children spotted Ghodrik, the head Reonih tutor, by the stream and ran at him, squealing and laughing. A moment later, Ghodrik was rolling around in the grass, a gaggle of children gleefully tackling him. Kira and Lorin, nearby, nearly bent over with laughter. Stiva loved seeing the children playing in the sun. Life in the Selin institutions was hard on the boys. It was meant to be. But even the Selin were allowed to relax around the holidays.

Her distraction gained her a sharp bite of pain on her thumb, and Stiva looked down to see blood on her hand. She had absently grasped a heather rose by its thorny stem. Frowning, she inspected her thumb and found it already swelling from the flower's venom. Sighing, she drew it to her mouth and sucked it, her thoughts like ice in the warmth of the rising sun. Blood welled up, and a few drops fell from her hand, mingling in the soil. The dirt seemed to suck up the crimson liquid, drinking it. She touched the soil, finding herself slightly dizzy and suddenly completely in tune with the land beneath her.

Stiva shut her eyes, clenching her fist as her blood fell onto the earth. *Fool*, she told herself angrily. *How am I to rule this land, when I cannot even pick its flowers?*

"Stiva? Did you hurt yourself?"

She turned, and found Shira beside her, a slight crease marring her pale brow. That was Shira, always full of concern for everyone else. "I tried to pick a heather rose that would have preferred to stay in the ground." Stiva glanced at her hand, which was turning slightly blue. "I'll have one of the Reonih make a nettle poultice for it later."

Shira looked at the sting and winced. "You should," she said.

Stiva looked at her sister more closely. A faint sheen of sweat glistened on her face, and she looked pale and stricken. Neither the temperature nor the mild exercise of picking flowers could account for that perspiration, or for the flushed look Shira's skin. Shira had always been fragile, but she never complained. To the contrary, Shira would likely drop dead of an illness before breathing a word of it to anyone.

Stiva frowned. "Are you ill?"

"Just nausea. Breakfast didn't agree with me." Shira looked at the swelling, and seemed to decide that her sister's life was not in immediate jeopardy. She untied her apron and carefully spread it on the ground before sitting down on it, setting her overflowing baskets beside her. "Mother tried to teach me about plants and herbs so many times ..." She trailed off, and was silent for a moment before finishing in a whisper. "I just never remembered what she told me."

Sorrow, Stiva decided. That was what she saw in her sister. A gentle, unending sorrow. Not that her own grief had lessened much. Lara's death still felt like a dagger in her heart, but the pain was beginning to fade with time. Shira, on the other hand, seemed to be merging with hers, as though the sadness was becoming a part of her.

Stiva smiled gently. "You'll never need to, Shira. The Reonih know it for you. And you know how to make a perfect stitch, whereas mine look more like puzzles or runes."

Maren, too young to join the game taking place further down in the meadow, was rolling about with his puppy, surrounded by a group of his friends. Every now and then, he shrieked playfully, and the little bright notes of his glee rang through the sunny meadow like golden bells. Now he stood up, raced towards them, and stood there, panting. "When do we eat?"

"Maren, all you've done is eat since we arrived." Stiva couldn't help smiling at her brother's rumpled hair. He looked, in that moment, just like a younger Chandris.

"Here," Shira reached into her pocket, and then held out a small red object. "I brought a gerfruit. You can have it."

Maren raced to take the fruit. She hid it playfully as he approached. "I want a kiss."

Maren made a disgusted face. "Can't you kiss the puppy?"

Shira tapped her cheek. Maren approached reluctantly, only to be grabbed and tickled. Shira released him, and he ran off again, grinning.

Stiva sat down beside her sister, not caring, at that moment, that it was completely improper for a queen to sit on the ground. They sat quietly for a few minutes, basking in the sun.

"Are you and Chandris getting along?" Shira asked her, changing the subject.

"We must be," Stiva said darkly. "Neither of us is dead yet."

"What's going on, Stiva?" Shira asked quietly. "Chandris is concentrating nearly all his forces around the northern border."

"Cerrow's doing, that." Stiva nodded. "Half the barracks are empty. The border raids have been growing worse. We stand to lose control of the western border to Delora."

"I heard as much; to be honest, I had expected it. But does that warrant such huge garrisons and patrols?"

"Cerrow thinks so, and Chandris listens to every word from his mouth, as though he were a god." Stiva shrugged. "I don't know, Shira. We have lost crops and lives, and Chandris will not sit back and do nothing. Some fear the border lords are dealing with Itacha, and allowing the Delorans passage through their lands. Huntik is under arrest, in fact. Chandris suspects that may also be treachery among the vassals in the east, on the border of Orlin. He thinks the march lords—or their men—are taking payment and letting the raiders through."

"That's a sticky floor to cross." Shira tried to reassure her. "But Aris has never been taken."

"Aris has never been so poorly garrisoned." Stiva bit her lip, looking at him with a pensive frown. "And the last time Trian struck, when they came in from the sea … you were very young, Shira, but I remember it. We barely held. I'm worried, Shira."

"Chandris knew he would be tested." Shira told her. "He knew that our enemies—both inside Aris and out—would see him as fresh meat. He must prove himself. If the border lords want more protection, he is wise to give it to them, rather than risk their betrayal. If they turn against us, more than Deloran raiding parties will be coming into our lands."

"I know," Stiva said. "It was bad, what he found up there. He's sent letters."

She did not go into detail. She did not have to. Word of the raids had spread through Aris like wildfire. The contents of Chandris' messages had given her nightmares. Every morning, a black bird flew to Stiva's window, bearing messages of death. *Burned out fields, blackened and shriveled, covering the land from horizon to horizon. The stench of death hanging thick in the air. Here and there, pockets of earth still smolder, and towers of smoke rise to the sky. Our lands should be prosperous, gold with wheat and green with produce, but they are grey and black and lifeless now, crops wasted. The piles of bodies were stacked higher that what remained of the walls, men women and children alike, tossed carelessly atop cattle. They had killed the herds too. They took the best for breeding stock, and slaughtered the rest. Even young calves and foals.*

Sorrow and shock had tempered the early messages. The more recent ones bore a colder outlook.

Her twin's rage reached red tendrils into her paler hours, darkening even moments like this.

"I'm sure he'll tell us more when he arrives," Stiva said. "But it isn't pretty."

They sat quietly a moment, enjoying the sun.

"Do you know what I just realized?" Shira asked suddenly. "I haven't been here in two years. I was sick last year, and the Lightfest before that, we were at Kele and Talia's estate. It seems so much longer than that, though. You know, the last time we were all here was the Lightfest before …"

Shira trailed off again, realizing that she had wandered onto delicate ground. She finished quietly. "Before Chandris left."

Before the trouble started. Before Mykhal died.

It went unspoken.

Stiva looked away, biting her lip. A tree frog somewhere buzzed, and the world seemed to pause in that moment, to pulse.

"Chandris wants me married soon," Shira said. She looked into the sun, squinting. "Next Lightfest. He sent me a list of possibilities to choose from. I am to narrow it down to four, and those four shall present themselves at court." Shira looked at her elder sister. "Did he tell you?"

"I know it was on his mind." Stiva picked a bit of grass off his sleeve. "I didn't know he had narrowed down your options. I haven't seen him much."

Chandris himself had generated a good amount of friction among his advisors by flatly declaring that he would not marry until his hold on the throne was secured by more than the blood in his veins.

"And you?"

"I don't want to marry," Stiva said shortly.

Chandris would never allow her to marry before he had sired at least one heir, probably more. To do that would be to risk her having sons that could threaten his own heirs in the line of succession. He would not risk that, regardless of how well things went between them. It went unsaid, unspoken, but they all knew it. Stiva, for her part, did not mind in the least. She had no desire to marry, to leave Aris. Not yet, anyway. But she wasn't happy to realize that Shira was a bargaining chip. Her marriage would have one purpose only: to secure some alliance or another. That was marriage among the srih. A power play, a political thing. Rarely was a match among nobility made in love.

"Who is on the list?" Stiva asked, changing the topic. "I know he mentioned Taibon, of Shadri."

Shira nodded. "He's the best option, so far."

Shadri: The old country. A place that brought to mind visions of thick, primeval mushroom forests and the Arriks' soaring mountainscapes, of vicious storms and fallen ruins.

Shadri: the cradle and grave of the Elders' shining civilization.

Shadri: Lara's homeland, which she had promised to bring Stiva to one day.

That day would never come.

A lump rose in Stiva's throat. She spoke around it, her voice tight. "Mother had mentioned him, once. For me."

Twyla reached into her pouch and pulled out a miniature portrait. Taibon, if the representation was correct, was tall, with dark, wavy hair and eyes. He looked handsome, though it was hard to read anything from his personality from the painting. "He's sent me letters. He seems very intelligent and polite, so far."

"You like him?"

"Aye." Shira continued. "There are others. Moran, of Jara, Marcelle's brother. Jahn's older brother, Karl." She rattled off more names. "They've started sending paintings, and poems." She looked out over the rolling hills. "This time next year, I'll be a bride."

Shira had been talking about her wedding almost as soon as she could talk.

But there was worry in her face and in her eyes. Her voice trembled with the slightest quivering of fear.

Thinking of Lara's and Cronn's arguments, of Kele and Talia shouting at one another, it was easy to see why Shira was so frightened. Stiva turned to study her sister more closely, and found fear in her eyes. Fear that a crown, and all its trappings, could do nothing to ease.

Stiva looked at the flower in her hand, and then held it up to her sister. Shira frowned, not understanding.

"This tiny thorn," Stiva said softly, "has done me some harm. I won't die, but my hand will be sore, swollen, and itchy for days. It cannot think or even move, Shira. Here I am, a hundred times larger and stronger, and look at what damage it did me. Yet to look at it, one sees only beauty and fragility."

She handed the flower to her sister.

"But you won," Shira said quietly, turning the rose over in her hand. She met Stiva's eyes. "You picked it. It will die, and you will live."

Stiva frowned. "That wasn't my point."

Shira looked away. "So what am I, Stiva; the flower or the thorn?"

Stiva sighed, and gave up entirely on the flower analogy. "You are the daughter of a warrior king. You are the child of a Reonih seer and bard. There is strength in you, Shira. You just need to find it."

Shira sighed. "Perhaps."

A roar from the brush ahead of them made them both jump, and Stiva caught a glimpse of something large and white moving through the tall grasses. Sighing, she put down her basket, stood, hitched up her skirts, and started off in that direction.

Shira stood too, alarmed. "Stiva!"

Stiva waved her sister back without turning. "It's only Lhin. He's escaped his kennel again."

A short distance later, Stiva found her cat. Lhin was crouched down, thoroughly mesmerized by a tiny hole in the ground where an ophera had burrowed. The cat meowed plaintively at her as she approached, tail switching.

Stiva crossed her arms, eyeing the ragged ends of the rope that trailed from his jeweled collar. "You need to stop chewing yourself loose, you great fool, or I'll make them use chains."

Lhin, as though sensing that he was in trouble, decided to charm her by rolling over onto his back, great paws kneading the air. "You idiot," she chided him gently, unable to resist squatting beside him to rub the great furry belly. A rumble came from Lhin's throat. His purr sounded like a thunderstorm. Stiva dodged a massive paw as it switched the air. "You don't want ophera anyway. They smell. And you're getting fat."

Predictably, the cat immediately tangled his leash in the brush, and started biting it. Sighing again, Stiva went to extricate him.

Came a step from behind her. Stiva spoke without turning her head, "Shira, can you hand me your clippers? I can't quite get this foolish furball loose."

A discreet masculine cough was her reply. Stiva glanced behind her. It wasn't Shira, but Vane.

"My queen." He bowed as she turned. "There are riders approaching. They aren't bearing standards."

She knew immediately that it was Chandris. For a brief moment, she saw through his eyes, and saw the ground rushing by beneath the paws of his cat, a black and red vota that was much more dignified than Lhin, though not half as much fun.

Stiva stood. "It's Chandris. Tell the servants to prepare."

"Are you sure? I think he would have sent a bird." Vane frowned.

Stiva looked at him grimly. "Birds get shot, Vane, or taken as prey. It's him."

Lhin loosed an annoyed growl, only now realizing that he was caught. Embarrassed, Stiva motioned to the cat. "Vane, would you …"

"Of course." Taking care to avoid stepping on the cat's lashing tail, Vane unsheathed his sword and sliced the rope from the bramble. Freed, Lhin hopped up and shook himself, then peered once more into the ophera burrow. Stiva eyed his fur, which seemed to have sprung a garden of burrs, grass, and dirt. Lhin, deciding that the burrow was no longer worthy of his attention, shoved his head under her hand, wanting his ears scratched.

Jarvor, Keorl, Timthe, Delis, Dallan, and a few more of the Black Boot were approaching by then. "There's an ophera colony up here," Stiva told them. "Tell the staff to have some white snakes released on the grounds." She picked a few burrs off Lhin's coat before vaulting up to his back. "Can you escort Shira back?"

"Of course," Jarvor said, "but what about you?"

Stiva was already riding back towards the manor.

Chandris met her in the yard, his face road-lined but thoughtful.

Stiva dismounted, dropping into a formal curtsy before him as the rest of his party, which included Jahn, Aret, Kele, Cerrow, and several others, fanned out, dismounting and stretching after a long ride.

"Hailte," Stiva said. "You look exhausted."

He nodded. "I'll celebrate Lightfest, but after that I'm riding out again."

Road-dusty, sweaty, and in need of a bath, her brother wiped the sweat from his brow and turned to her. Only a few weeks had passed since he had ridden out, but the man who returned was not the one who had left. Stiva sensed the change in him instantly. A new harshness lined his face, and his eyes seemed colder, harder, than she remembered. He looked almost old, as though the journey had taken decades, rather than weeks. The things he had seen waited in his eyes, haunting his thoughts. This was not the reckless brother she'd grown up with, but a warrior king with rage in his eyes and revenge the foremost of his thoughts.

"My gods," Stiva whispered. "was it really so bad?"

"They killed hundreds." Chandris said. She could almost hear the crackle of flames, the screams of the dying, echoed in his words.

Stiva *saw*, as she did sometimes, his thoughts, his mind, his memories of the things he had seen in his absence.

Her brother's voice floated atop the vision. "Itacha will pay for what the Delorans did to that village. And the village before it, and the ones before that." He looked at her, and she could almost see the flames reflected in his eyes. "This is the last time our people will die in such a manner on Aris' soil, Stiva. This is the last time I ride out to find the corpses of my people in smoldering ruins. I will *not* let it happen again. Mark that. Nor will I accept betrayal such as Huntik's."

"You found evidence against him?"

"Coded letters from Itacha," Chandris said. "Kept in a trunk with a false bottom."

Stiva paled.

"He'll go to the Zhur at the next war moon. The Fireborne will have him. They will take him alive, with that letter stuffed into his eye sockets." He met her eyes, and she flinched at the cold rage in his gaze. "Make no mistake about it. We are at war."

Stiva looked at her twin, and saw only rage in his eyes. "Get some rest," she said, "And try to enjoy the holiday. There will be time for war after Lightfest."

He nodded. "We'll talk later. I need to tell you exactly what I saw. You need to know, Stiva. Things I could not put into words. The things that burn and crawl through my dreams."

Stiva nodded. Chandris went inside, trailed by his entourage.

And though the day and the world around her was filled with sunshine and butterflies and birdsong, Stiva shivered as though it were the dead of winter. As the shadows of the castle took in Chandris and his party, she became aware of a presence behind her.

Talia.

Her aunt too, was watching the castle door where the men had entered. "He has goldlust," she said. "He is as mad as Kele. He will make the land run red with blood."

Stiva looked at her aunt, and felt her temper rise. "See to the feast preparations, Talia," she snapped.

CHAPTER 14

"There!" Stiva pointed to a shimmering patch of thornwall where the air seemed to ripple, dimpling like water flowing over stones, showing movement where there should be none, showing motion where there was nothing—at least nothing visible—to cause it. Not the faintest hint of a breeze stirred the day. The landscape showed nothing moving save themselves … and the place her finger had directed all eyes to.

It happened again as the others looked. The tiny piece of thornwall *shifted*, redefining itself as though it were melting, shimmering and wavering the way the air did sometimes in the heat of high light season. For a split second, the movement confined itself to definition and a vague, blurred shape, draconian, began to appear … but then it stopped altogether and the spot once more became unremarkable. The thornwall, countless mils of entangled bone vines and snake tree branches interwoven with thick, thorny bramble, was an ecosystem in itself, imposing enough to have severely influenced the behavioral traits of several animal species. As grey and wrinkled as the sea on a cloudy day, it divided the deep forest from its outer reaches, a border as strange and mystical as the forbidden realm beyond it.

"By the seven moons," Chandris breathed, shielding his eyes with his hand, "You were right. There *is* a kurra over there."

"Where?" Aret demanded impatiently. "I don't see it."

"There!" Chandris and Stiva answered simultaneously, pointing in perfect synchronicity. "Cerrow was right about taking this direction." He looked back at the rest of the party, flashing a boyish grin. "That's a *kurra*! An actual kurra!"

Aret squinted, his eyes scanning the thornwall, but after a moment, he grew frustrated and looked back at Chandris, protesting. "We're going to lose the vodrik."

"Who cares?" Chandris snorted disdainfully. "They leave trails a child could follow. We've hunted hundreds of vodrik. This could be the first and last hunt of the season for me, and I want that kurra."

"Why?" Aret asked, scoffing. "You can't eat them, you can't train them, and you can't even use the bones or skin for anything. Once the thing dies, the hide stops changing colors and becomes this disgusting vein-shot grey color. Besides, tomorrow's Lightfest Day. We have to hunt a vodrik."

"Says who?" Chandris demanded hotly, suddenly annoyed.

"It's tradition and you know it," Kele told him, in a stern tone that announced his disapproval. "And we wouldn't have any tradition at all if every king disregarded it as carelessly as you do."

Chandris' eyes, grown suddenly icy, snapped to his uncle's. "And if all kings had kin that disregarded respect as much as you do, there would be a much smaller aristocracy in the land."

Kele chose not to respond to that, though his eyes flashed dangerously.

"They do make good soup," Dallan said. "And actually you can use the hides and bones. My uncle used to—"

Lyle shot Dallan an icy look. Dallan shrugged and fell silent.

"I still don't see it," Aret complained.

"Right there." Stiva said, pointing again. "Under that huge shard tree, halfway up the thornwall. "Hold, Lhin."

Beneath her, Lhin had tensed, having finally noticed the oddity before them. The great cat's whiskers pointed forward, and his muscles bunched under soft white fur. Stiva felt herself descending as the cat, fully alert, crouched low, preparing to spring.

"Hold him," Chandris warned her. "If he pounces now, we'll lose it for certain."

Aret was still scanning the terrain, frowning.

Kele exploded, discharging his rising temper in a safe direction: his son. "Are you blind? It's dead in front of you, idiot!" He gestured angrily. "Look, there it goes!"

Chandris sounded his horn, and the hunting party turned as one to follow him as his cat, a magnificent black and red striped male, leapt forward.

"I still can't see it." Aret muttered again as the rest of the party charged past him, after Chandris. Stiva opened her mouth to reply, but then Lhin sprang ahead and Aret, temporarily left behind, was suddenly out of earshot.

The kurra briefly became visible as it scaled the thornwall, only to vanish into camouflage once more. The terrain offered ample cover. The shard trees turned the landscape into a palette of pastel colors, gold and green overlaid with undertones ranging from violet to pale pinks and oranges. The oldest of them were nearly transparent, and looked as though they had been carved out of colored glass.

As a child, Stiva had believed that the shard trees were magical and special, a living link between the gods and the earth. Though Ghodrik had taught her long ago that their beautiful rainbow hues and crystalline texture was the result of parasitic shard-worms, they hadn't lost their appeal.

Chandris lifted an arm, signaling quietly. The cats dropped to stealth formation, diving for whatever cover was available and then creeping forward noiselessly, banded tails switching in anticipation. Completely focused on prey that shifted in and out of visibility, the felines were both fascinated and perplexed by the kurra. Forty cats slunk forward in synchronicity, inch by inch, yet not even a twig snapped. The rest of the party remained in place, though some were obviously confused as to why they had suddenly been ordered into stealth formation, as the vodrik had clearly gone the other way.

Chandris pointed forward, giving another silent order, which moved them up to the thornwall. Stiva felt more than saw the hesitation in the others.

That pause was more than fear of the law that named the thornwall as a border. The thornwalls—especially the ones at the outer forest— were a boundary that was often broken. There likely was not, Stiva reckoned, one person in the hunting party who had not violated that border at some point in their lives, herself included. But the interlaced border of brambles and vines was much more than a physical barrier. The thornwalls held power, trapping something elemental and primal behind and within their bony vines. Strange magics, some said, had been woven into the bracken and briar, magics that kept in far more than they kept out. The woods behind the thornwall were wild and mostly untouched, much more dangerous and unpredictable than the forest outside of it. The trees grew thick and dark, and the maze of trails and lesser thornwalls within were complex enough to confuse even the best trackers. In the deep forest, the magics of earth, sea, sky, and fire ran wild, unleashed and untamed, tapped only by the Reonih. Shapeshifters, illusions, strange and savage beasts, and, it was said, even the Zhur, lurked in the deep wood. Numerous accounts of mysterious disappearances and strange phenomena beyond the thornwall were enough to ingrain, at the least, a sense of respect for the divider. It was common knowledge that many who crossed the thornwalls never returned.

In most places, there were dozens—if not hundreds—of mils between the edge of the forest and the outer thornwall, which was more than enough lands to provide adequate game and wood for the surrounding population. Beyond, days' and even weeks' journeys away, the thornwalls grew thicker and higher closer to the Sijhani lands. Massive thornwalls formed the border between the edge of Aursa and the lands held by the Sijhani to the west and the Djaki to the east.

"Now he has us charging the wall." A mutter floated downwind to Stiva. She knew without looking who spoke; Ehodris, lord of Fahrin. Talia's father had an unmistakable lisp. "What next?"

Chandris signaled again. The entire hunting party stopped short.

They waited there for several minutes, frozen in place, staring at the terrain in the hopes that the kurra would reappear.

Nothing in the landscape moved.

"We made too much noise," Chandris said finally, clearly disappointed.

"Most likely it's already gone," Kele grumbled. "We could stay here 'til seventh moonrise staring at this patch of forest like idiots, and go back empty-handed for the Lightfest feast, or we can go kill our supper. I don't know about the rest of you, but I'd like baked vodrik to go with my mushroom sauce, instead of stale bread and a tongue-lashing."

Stiva could have sworn she heard stomachs growling in unison.

Chandris was not about to give up. He turned in his saddle, craning his neck to reassess the numbers in the hunting party. "Khren, Jahn, go get us the vodrik. Take everyone on horseback with you."

"Sire." Lyle spoke up immediately. "That takes over two thirds of the party away. The Grey Bull, White Horn, and most of the Black Boot and Gold Braid. I had rather not leave you inadequately defended."

"Against what?" Chandris snorted in contempt. "A kurra? I don't need eighty men to hunt with me. Besides, the horses will have to circle around to get past the thornwall."

"What of the rest of us?" Ehodris asked, adding belatedly, "Mi'lord."

Chandris turned his gaze into the wood. "We're going after the kurra."

The lord of Fahrin blinked in disbelief. "Surely you don't mean for us to go over the wall?"

Chandris leveled a cold stare at his cousin. "Surely you don't mean to question my orders."

Ehodris turned a pasty white color, stammering, "But … but, sire … it's against the law."

Chandris looked amused. "Are you afraid someone's going to tell the king?"

The srih laughed a little too loudly, and several exchanged nervous glances.

Ehodris tried again. "It is only that we fear for your safety, sire."

"Kind of you." Chandris commented, a dangerous glint in his eyes contrasting with his flat tone. He jerked his head towards the deep forest. "Over the wall, Ehodris."

Ehodris hesitated.

"I gave you an order," Chandris growled. "You can follow it, or you can go back to Aris under arrest."

Kele chose to intervene on behalf of his father-by-law, nudging his cat over the wall, grumbling. "I'll take point."

"You will *take* the vodrik," Chandris snapped. "You wanted it so badly. Go get it."

Chandris expected his men to keep up with him, to push as hard as he did. When they were children, he would grow angry at her if she fell behind, or got tired while they were playing. He despised sluggishness and carelessness. She understood that. She also understood their hesitation.

The party separated. The men assigned to the vodrik looked a bit more cheerful than those ordered over the wall. Those who remained with Chandris looked, as a whole, uneasy.

"There is nothing to fear," Chandris told them, surveying uneasy expressions with a look of disdain. "There is nothing dangerous in the forest by day, and we'll be back long before sunfall. *With* the kurra." He pointed to a nearby area, where the thornwall grew thick. "The cats can cross there. Some clear the thorns from that spot."

Stiva watched her twin with a mixture of admiration and uneasiness as one of the Gold Braid stepped forward, slicing the heavier thorns away.

"There's no trail," Aret objected, scanning the forest floor. "Not so much as a bent twig."

"That's odd." Lyle frowned. "They're supposed to be heavy."

"They are," Vane said. "My uncle got one once. Took six of us to carry the damned thing."

"There!" Chandris pointed suddenly to a spot straight in front of him. Stiva followed his gaze, looking just in time to see another ripple.

As they watched, Chandris sent his cat up and over the thornwall.

Lhin spotted the kurra again, and leapt forward. The cat's long, curved claws found an easy grip on thick branches, and Stiva was jolted suddenly off balance as the cat scaled the thornwall. Once atop it, Lhin stopped, balancing easily on the thicker branches. The kurra disappeared again, and Lhin looked back at her with an accusing expression, as though it were her doing. The great cat loosed a chirrup of annoyance before returning his attention to the elusive creature.

Chandris' cat had jumped onto a thick log. Now it bounded back down, earthbound again in one great leap … but hesitated briefly once his paws had again touched ground. Stiva, upon realizing why, frowned, puzzled. The cat had not caught the scent, though the kurra was close. Chandris, cursing in annoyance, had to point the cat after it.

Vota cats were excellent trackers.

She opened her mouth to say as much to Chandris, but he was already spurring his cat on.

Sighing, Stiva went after him. Lhin crouched low and launched himself with one great leap. As the cat shot forward, Stiva felt herself borne along as though weightless. Behind her, she could hear the crash of branches snapping and brush rustling as the remainder of the party rode after them. They could not all cross the thornwall at once, and thus were delayed.

Chandris would not wait for them.

Nor did Stiva.

She let Lhin go, and the cat bounded forward as though fired from a bow. Within moments, the thornwall was far behind, and the forest had enveloped her in thick, perfumed wilderness; rust and gold leaves dappled with dusky light, shadow and sunlight dancing together, entwined beneath a bright sun. Only the sound of her own breath and the faint rustle of brush disturbed by Lhin's soft steps broke the silence. The air hung thick and heavy, liquid gold and amber.

The rest of the party was soon left behind, along with the sound of their voices, their worries calling her name and Chandris', telling her to wait. Stiva ignored them and nudged Lhin to greater speed. The voices faded into silence, and Stiva felt a fierce exultation.

The taste of freedom was like nectar to her soul. It felt amazing to be released from the ever-present throng of maids and courtiers, the sinuous serpentine comments, the fortress of protocol and policy the crown imprisoned her with. Unseen shackles broke, and Stiva felt a huge weight lift from her shoulders. Liberation was rapture. She threw her head back and drank in the dusky wild air, savoring the feel of the wind through her hair, the wild power of the cat below her, the savage glory of the hunt. Aris ceased to exist, at least for a moment. There was only the pumping of Lhin's muscles and the blurred colors of the foliage rushing past, the taste of the wind in her lungs.

Lhin's powerful strides ate up the distance, bringing her deeper and deeper into the wood.

As it always had, the forest fed her soul.

They went deeper and deeper into the forest. The kurra appeared more or less regularly, showing itself in intervals, somehow always the same distance ahead. Though they had not come more than a few mils from the thornwall, Stiva noticed a slackening in Lhin's pace as weariness set in.

She came upon Chandris quite suddenly. He had paused in a small valley nestled between two hills, looking around with intent, puzzled expression that melted into a sweaty grin as she approached. The twins exchanged a silent look of understanding and a knowing smile. Stiva knew he had felt the same elation that she had, that same blissful, invigorating release. It was exactly the sort of thing they had done when they were children and inseparable; running away from Ghodrik, their tutor, and a gaggle of guards and nurses to frolic around, free for a brief, blissful time. A time long past slipped fingers into the present. The dance went on, the dance of predator and prey, life and death, darkness and light.

Stiva saw the shift again, some distance ahead of them.

Their prey was still ahead of them.

Kurra weren't supposed to move that fast, or have the type of endurance a vota cat did.

A shadow crossed the sun.

"Did you lose them?" Chandris asked.

"I think so." Stiva looked back. "They can't keep up with Lhin. Elin fell back some distance ago, and his cat was the fastest of theirs. They'll fuss later," she added.

"Let them." Chandris shrugged. "They can't send us to bed without supper anymore. Although it might be very satisfying for us to do it to them."

"Chandris!" But Stiva was giggling. "Where's the kurra?"

"I'm not sure," he admitted. "I saw it clearly just a moment ago."

"Did your cat scent it?"

He did not have to answer; she had that from the cat's manner. The beast was intent on the scents nearby, sure enough, but not in a manner that suggested it was tracking any particular prey. Rather, the animal sniffed the wind in each direction, ears flat. Lhin did not seem to have its scent either. They went where they were directed. Though they were glad enough to be running, there was no focus in their manner, no purpose to their gazes or movements as there usually was when they were hunting. Their whiskers drooped, instead of pointing forward the way they did when they focused on prey.

The soft ground of the forest floor remained unmarked, but for their tracks.

The forest seemed to press in around them. Some sixth sense—whatever trace of the Sight she had inherited from Lara—awoke screaming. A cold shiver slipped down Stiva's spine, and the joy fell from her face. She looked around, suddenly nervous.

"What's wrong?" Chandris asked, seeing her face change.

"I'm not sure." Stiva shifted uneasily in the saddle, and shook her head. "Something doesn't seem right. Maybe we should go back for the others."

Her twin looked amused. "Now that's a change; you've dragged me over the thornwall more times than I can count, and suddenly *you're* nervous about the forest?"

"Chandris, I'm serious." Stiva frowned at him.

Her twin wasn't listening. He pointed suddenly, turning his cat. "Look: there it is!"

The kurra had stopped, briefly presenting a clearly visible outline.

Chandris drew his cat up and dismounted slowly, his spear poised to strike. The forest went silent around them. The high keening buzz of insects ceased, and the bird and erlit chatter seemed very distant. For a moment, nothing moved. Chandris crept forward slowly, with the silent, tensed deliberation of a predator about to strike. Then, in one fluid burst of motion, he threw the spear directly into the outline of the kurra.

It buried itself in a tree behind the kurra. And it struck nothing else.

There *was* no kurra.

Chandris frowned, breathing a puzzled exclamation. "What in seven moons—"

The forest exploded with movement around them, its peace shattered. Trees and vines and brush around them, which had been still just moments ago, were suddenly bursting with life and motion. It seemed the wood itself had opened a mouth to swallow them with. All around them, men were emerging from behind the trees and brush and large boulders and they were close, the attackers, so close, death in their hands and in their eyes. They wore boiled leather armor and chain mail over loose woolen leggings and leather boots, and they had the look of the forest, rather than that of the battlefield.

Stiva shouted belatedly, screaming at Chandris that it was a trap. She turned Lhin in tight circles in search of an opening. There was none. The twins were completely surrounded.

Chandris barely had time to draw his sword before the first of them were upon him. "Stiva, get out of here!" He screamed it at her, at the top of his lungs. "Go get the others!"

His voice echoed through the grove, urgent and enraged. Desperation colored his words with a tone she had never heard in him before, one that was eerily beautiful in its rage. It was the first time she had ever heard anything of the bard's gift in him. Some cold, detached part of her mind wondered in fascination about that peculiarity.

The rest of her found it terrifying.

Chandris was engaged even before he finished yelling. The clang of ringing steel echoed through the forest with a resounding clash. He blocked the first blow with an overhand, spun his cat around in a tight circle, and caught the blade of another with his own. Stiva saw the flash of sunlight on steel. A moment later, one of them fell to the ground trying to keep his intestines in his gut.

To Stiva, the resonance of that first deathblow felt like thunder. She felt its vibrations in her soul. Steel sang a song into the forest, where steel was forbidden.

That was when she remembered the drinking horn in her belt. She drew it and uncapped it, thanking herself for being thirsty enough to drain it earlier. Raising it to her lips, she blew a long, low note and then two short ones. Someone struck it from her, but she had time to get that much out, and hope that the others heard the distress call.

Chandris spun, and brought his sword down upon a man's head. He fell to the ground, brains spilling onto the forest floor in a pinkish, bubbly glob. The strike did not kill the man immediately. He kept moving his mouth, as though trying to speak. Stiva stared at him, horrified. The gruesome image before her burned its way through her soul, later returning to haunt her in nightmares.

"They aren't fighting to kill," Chandris said. "They want us alive."

Stiva wheeled Lhin. As long as she stayed on his back, the cat was her best advantage. None of them could outrun him, nor could they reach her without braving his teeth and claws. She could tell, by the roar of fury Lhin released, that the cat's bloodlust was aroused. She had not brought a sword with her, only a dagger and hunting spears. She had been trained, to some extent. The arts of war were not really her forte, but no srih princess was ever allowed to grow up ignorant of self-defense. Stiva was no warrior, but nor was she completely helpless.

But war was in her blood.

A hand clutched her thigh, and she drove her spear into the eye that had guided it. An unwanted, but very real, feeling of satisfaction drove through her gut at the scream of rage and pain that followed. Similar roars were coming from nearby, where Chandris' cat slashed out with deadly claws. She glanced in that direction and saw the great black and red beast pounce. The cat's mighty jaws clamped down on someone's throat, and a fountain of blood issued forth. Enraged, the cat shook its prey. The man screamed, and then the crack of breaking bone split the air as the cat snapped his neck.

He went limp, and fell to the ground, his lifeblood seeping out into the forest floor.

Her twin seemed to be holding their enemies at bay. The years of intense training had done him well. Some number of them turned their concentration on her, trying to separate them.

Everyone was always trying to separate them.

One of them came at her and Lhin lunged beneath her. A single swipe of the cat's dagger-like claws opened a man's neck, tearing his flesh into shreds of meat. Blood poured from the wound like roses. The man crumpled and fell.

Death touched the forest. She felt it in the air.

Chandris, bloodied and enraged, was somehow holding them off. Beneath him, the black and red vota cat danced, limping now, but still dangerous. The look on her brother's face frightened her anew. This was not her twin, this madman with the sword in his hand and death in his eyes. This was some crazed warrior caught in the battle madness the Selin sometimes spoke of.

They shot the vota cat with an arrow. The animal fell to the ground, loosing a roar of pain. Chandris leapt clear, only to be immediately surrounded.

Another shape appeared at the edge of the clearing, clad in crimson. Vane, captain of the Black Boot. Relief washed over her at the sight of him. She was certain the others would be right behind him, and she scanned the wood, watching for them.

They did not appear. Vane rode into the battle alone. The relief turned into dread.

Vane did not hesitate, even knowing the rest of the Black Boot was still—she hoped—en route. He started forward alone into the melee.

Stiva had no time to watch her captain. They were closing in on her, nearer now, perhaps growing desperate. She threw another spear, and cursed under her breath when it fell harmlessly to earth.

A moment later, she was surrounded. Weapons rose on all sides of her, seeking her blood, seeking her life. She felt Lhin's muscles bunch as he prepared to go through them. It felt wrong. It looked wrong. But battle instinct had been bred into the cats of Aris generations ago. Lhin faced them, snarling, and lunged.

They cut him down from under her.

Lhin stiffened, his roar reduced to a whimper. In that, one sickening instant, Stiva saw only a bloody sword drawing back from its strike. And then there came the nauseating sensation of falling as the cat collapsed beneath her, landing with a howl of pain. Stiva was thrown clear. The world spun wildly as ground and sky traded places. She landed with a startled cry on a thick root, just beside the man—now a corpse—whose brains had spilled out. The impact stunned her, but she quickly scrambled to her feet. Fear chewed at the base of her spine, forcing her into motion.

In the next moment, she felt herself yanked backwards. That was Chandris, putting her at his back, the only protection he could give her. She snatched a sword from the hand of a dying man, one Chandris had cut down.

Steel touched her skin with a painful jolt. That was the Reonih in her, that could not bear the touch of it. But she was Aris as well, and that part of her took over as she adjusted her grip and her stance. She swung the sword wildly, her half-remembered moves far from precise, but she managed to cut one on the leg, and knew a brief moment of satisfaction as his face puckered in pain.

Vane was trying to get to her, but he, too, was surrounded. As Stiva watched, one of the men threw an axe at him. It buried itself in his chest. Vane staggered backwards, lifting his sword again.

He fell over before he could deliver the blow.

One of the Selin stepped out of the woods, a man Stiva recognized as having gained admission recently through the arena. He bared a sword, and cut a path of death through the fray. One, two, four, six fell beneath him.

"Get her away from him!" Someone shouted. "Get her alone!"

They did just that.

Stiva was never certain how it happened, but one moment she and Chandris were back to back, synchronized, whole, and then yet another impact tore them apart. The blow sent her reeling, and made her vision erratic. The ground and sky switched places. When they returned to their normal positions, she felt a searing pain as her arm was wrenched behind her back, that and the dread caress of cold steel at her throat. She fought, rather than submit; she clamped her teeth down into a hairy arm and heard a satisfactory yelp of pain. And then she loosed one to match as her arm was twisted cruelly behind her. White painfire blossomed in her shoulder.

"Bitch," a voice said into her ear. "You'll pay for that."

Her captor's hand tangled in her hair, and he jerked her head back, hard. When Stiva could breathe again, she cursed him.

"Your Majesty!" Stiva's captor shouted. "If I might have your attention?"

Chandris looked over, his face hardening. "Let her go."

Stiva's captor sounded almost cheerful. "I'm afraid I can't do that, my lord. Drop your weapons."

Chandris hesitated.

The blade pressed Stiva's throat, drawing a well of blood. The voice darkened to a growl. "Drop them, or she dies."

Chandris slowly lowered his sword. As it fell from his outstretched hand, a keening, whirring sound slit the air, originating from the forest at her back.

Stiva felt her captor stiffen suddenly. The grip on her hair became a weight pulling her down. She twisted instinctively, and then, all of a sudden, found herself free. When she turned to see what had happened, her captor lay sprawled out on the ground, eyes bulging. A thin trickle of blood ran from his mouth. She frowned, initially not understanding what had happened.

Then she noticed the tip of an arrow protruding from his chest. It had pierced the leather armor from behind, incredibly, and exited the other side. Stiva blinked. It would take a shot at close range, to do that. But she could not see the archer. Nor could she find any but enemies in the mob.

The attackers looked around, apparently as perplexed as she was. They did not pause for long, though, but regrouped and charged again.

Something passed so close to her ear that she felt the air shiver. A man approaching her with bared and readied steel stiffened and then dropped in his tracks, an arrow in his chest. More buzzes, more whooshes; more men dropped. The air filled and rang with the whiz of more arrows being fired in rapid succession. One by one, their attackers fell. Every direction she looked in, it was the same. Chandris found himself suddenly, inexplicably, out of enemies. He turned to face his next opponent ... only to find there were none left.

Blinking, Chandris stared around, his expression passing from rage to confusion to utter amazement.

Dozens of men lay dead or dying on the ground.

The twins stared at each other, wordless communication passing within their locked green gazes. As one, they looked around, meeting the fact that somehow, incredibly, they still lived. Chandris stepped closer to her, even as she instinctively moved nearer to him. Even in chaos, their thoughts followed the same path.

Blood-splattered and breathing heavily from the exertion, Chandris put a hand on her shoulder. "Are you alright?"

She could not find a voice to answer with, but she nodded, still shaking. She looked again at the fallen, and, seeing a familiar red uniform, gave a little choked sob.

Vane was dead, his pale eyes staring into the sky, his lifeblood spilled into the forest floor.

"Stiva," Chandris said, his voice low.

She turned, and saw what he was looking at. Lhin lay on the ground, blood staining his snowy fur. A choked cry flew from her mouth as she ran to the cat and fell to her knees beside him, stripping him of his gear. She examined the wound only briefly, and her face was pale and stricken when she looked away.

But then Lhin raised his head, and she realized he wasn't lost yet. She ripped off a portion of her skirt to try and stop the bleeding, but there was nothing more she could do. She stroked his cheek, covering his furry white face with kisses as the cat's blood ran into the forest floor.

Chandris turned his eyes back to the woods, searching. His shout rang out like a bell into the stillness that once more surrounded them. "Who's there? Show yourselves!"

Nothing stirred.

"I said show yourselves!" Chandris bellowed. "By the word of the king of Aris, come out from your cover!"

Something moved in the distance. A tree on the far side of the glade seemed to shed a part of itself. The man who stepped out from behind it clothed and colored so perfectly after the wood that at first it was difficult to distinguish him from his surroundings. With his sun-browned skin, dark brown hair, brown eyes, and brown and rust shaded clothes, none of which stood out at all against a brown and red wood, he looked a part of the forest. The bow he carried was massive, longer than any Stiva had ever seen. Elaborately carved and polished to a deep shine, the weapon should have looked out of place in the hand of such a nondescript man. It seemed fit for a giant. Somehow, though, it did not. It seemed a part of him.

Aside from the Selin who had, it seemed, single-handedly killed quite a few of their attackers, Stiva, Chandris, and the archer were the only ones left standing.

"Where are the rest?" Chandris demanded.

The archer's face went blank, as though he were confused. "Pardon?"

"The others," Chandris snapped. A body stirred that was not yet a corpse. Hardly looking, he plunged his sword into it, ignoring the gurgling cough that followed. "Your company."

"There are no others," the brown-clad man said flatly. "I'm alone."

Came a noise through the forest, crashes and shouts, the sound of riders approaching.

"Chandris," Stiva said urgently, fearing more enemies.

He ignored her. His attention was still on the archer. "You mean to tell me that you killed these men by yourself? With nothing but a bow and arrow?"

The archer did not so much as blink. "That is exactly so."

The noises drew nearer.

"Chandris—" Stiva said again, nervously.

"It's the others." Chandris answered without looking at her, still intent upon the archer. His eyes locked onto the stranger's, haughty and cold. "Prove it."

The archer shrugged and pulled another arrow from his quill. Speed and skill blurred his movements. He notched, aimed, and fired the arrow, seemingly in one lightning fast motion. Arrows pierced the sunlight, appearing to multiply in the bodies of the dead. Those who had felled by one projectile seemed to instantaneously grow more.

"Again," Chandris said.

Once more, the keening wail of arrows in flight filled the glade with deadly song. A few of the men groaned or screamed as more arrows punctured their flesh. Most of them did not move at all.

The archer lowered his bow and stood looking expectantly at Chandris, brown eyes defiant. "Now do you believe me?"

The king of Aris was, for the first time Stiva could recall, utterly speechless.

Chandris turned to the archer. "How did you do that? I've never seen one arrow fired with such speed and precision, never mind dozens."

"It's the design of the bow," the archer explained.

"Show me," Chandris said sharply. It was a command, the way he spoke it, an order from a king. But the undertone of excitement in his voice reminded Stiva of the boy he had once been.

The archer stepped closer, letting Chandris see the weapon more closely. "See, it's streamlined here, and notched a certain way here, for more precision, and the size adds both power and precision. My own design. As you can see, it's quite efficient. It can pierce armor."

Lhin licked her hand, and then closed his eyes, his breathing heavy. Stiva felt her heart break, both for Vane and the cat, each of whom had, in their own way, served her loyally for years.

A hand fell on her shoulder: Chandris, comforting her as he could without words. "Get up," her twin said quietly. "The others are coming."

And she must be queen.

The rest of the party pulled up, jaws dropping nearly in unison at the sight of the carnage.

"Hailte," Chandris said darkly, in greeting. "Nice of you to join us."

Lyle was dismounting even as his cat stopped, running towards Chandris. "What happened? Are you two alright?"

"Yes," Chandris snapped. "We're fine … no thanks to you."

Voices and hoofbeats carried through the wood, the sound of more riders approaching. A moment later, the rest of the party rode into the clearing, Aret in the lead. He stopped his mount short, staring around him with an incredulous expression. The rest of them looked similarly shocked. After a moment, Aret turned to Chandris. His voice cracking, he asked the question all the newcomers were wondering. "What under seven moons just happened here?"

"Reonih treachery is what happened." Chandris growled his answer. "There *was* no kurra. It was an illusion. We were tricked into an ambush."

Stiva looked sharply at her brother.

"We saw you," Aret said, clearly shaken. "We saw you, and then you were gone. We went after the kurra, thinking you nearby. When we heard the sound of fighting we were pretty far off. We cut through a section of the thornwall to reach you."

"You followed an illusion," Chandris told him darkly. "As did we."

A cry of rage and grief cut the forest air. Stiva looked up to see Dallan rushing towards Vane's body. Dallan's pale face seemed torn open—the soul beneath exposed, naked and vulnerable—as though the soul beneath was exposed. He did not shed a tear, but Stiva saw him whisper to his fallen brother as he reached for Vane's hand.

Dallan looked up at Stiva, his expression somewhere between anguish and hatred.

"Honor him," Dallan said. He nearly choked on the words.

Stiva stared at him in dismay, both puzzled and shocked. "What?"

"The first to die for your safety," Dallan said. Tears cracked his voice. "My brother deserves your honor."

Dallan's eyes pierced hers. He did not move. He only kept staring at her, his pale blue eyes filled with accusation.

She knew what he was thinking, and had to force herself not to hang her head and beg his forgiveness. The twins had deliberately slipped away from their guards. Vane would have survived, had they not done that.

"He died for you," Dallan said again, nearly growling. "Did you notice? *Did you even notice?*"

"She noticed," another voice said. It was the new Selin, who stood silent and blood-spattered, watching this. Stiva looked at him, and found herself caught by his gaze.

"Dallan, enough," Lyle said sharply, before anyone else could speak.

Dallan said nothing more, though he glowered at his commander.

"Find Cerrow," Chandris said, his voice livid. "Find him and have him brought to me. Alive, if possible, but dead will do just as well."

Lyle spoke a few quiet orders, dispatching Selin to check the area, to find the rest of the party, to run messages back to the castle and to the estate.

"Who is this?" Aret asked, motioning to the archer, who stood there silently. "Was it his band, feathered these men?"

Chandris looked at the archer, leaving it to him to introduce himself.

The archer cleared his throat a bit nervously before introducing himself with an awkward bow. "Ketran, sir. At your service."

"Strange," Kele said, his voice dangerously quiet, "that these men should rise to attack now, when Aris' forces are at the borders. Strange that we were led here, into the trap, by a trick such as only a Reonih could muster."

Chandris looked at his uncle, a dangerous glint in his eye.

"Don't be fool enough to trust just because you have before," Kele said. "My brother knew that from the first."

"Search the bodies," Lyle instructed the Selin. "Check their coin, look for tattoos or brands. Find out who they were, and who sent them."

"There are some alive, yet," Kele said. "Get what you can out of them. This is no ragtag band."

A man near Lyle was groaning on the ground. One of the Selin squatted beside him and began systematically disemboweling him.

"Who sent you?" Lyle asked. "Go to the gods an honest man."

"Cronn," he croaked.

Chandris did not immediately react to this. He caught his breath, and thought. And then his rage burst from him: he took the dagger, and thrust it through the throat of the wounded man.

Stiva looked away.

The next moments were stained with blood and death. Stiva was pale and shaking by the end of it. But only the last spoke the truth.

A single name.

A blade.

Cerrow.

Chandris paled at the name. Rage clouded his eyes. "He knew," Chandris said, "That I'd always wanted to hunt a kurra."

"But …. why?" Aret asked. "He was loyal to Cronn."

Chandris shook his head. Then, in a sudden fit of rage, he whirled, drawing his sword, and hacking one of the attackers' heads off. "He will die for this," Chandris shouted. "I want every Selin out looking for him. He's in these woods, somewhere."

"It could be a ruse," Kele said.

"Do you hear me?" Chandris shouted. "Find him!"

Kele said nothing else. He shouldered past Lyle and went back to his cat. His anger was palpable, almost as though a thundercloud of rage hovered around him. Scowling, he mounted, and rode off. Aret watched him go, uneasy.

It didn't take a Reonih scrying to know that Talia and Kele would be fighting later.

Aret frowned. "What were you doing in the forest? The ground beyond the thornwall is forbidden territory."

Ket said nothing, but only glanced at the dead around them. "I … I don't—"

"Doesn't matter," Chandris said. "I'm happy you were here."

The Reonih chose that moment to arrive, melting out of the stillness of the wood. They took in the scene with the same incredulity and astonishment than the Selin had shown.

Another group of riders approached. Reonih, this time. Mohr was in the lead. He pulled up on a horse the color of mist and stared around, echoing Aret in both word and tone. "What under seven moons happened here?"

It was omen, Stiva recalled, for bloodshed to happen on a sacred day.

Chandris looked at the high priest with an iciness formerly reserved for sworn enemies. "You tell me," he growled. "It's *your* forest."

Mohr, shocked at the manner in which Chandris addressed him, only stared at his king. After a moment, he managed a single word, which emerged colored by rage and incredulity. "What?"

"These men came from your wood, Mohr," Chandris said coldly. "They ambushed us on *your* land."

Looking at Mohr, Stiva saw resignation in his eyes. Pain. The Reonih high priest shook his head slowly. "I know nothing of this."

"Of course not," Chandris said sarcastically. "And what more useful subject have I, than a sage who knows nothing?"

Mohr went white.

Chandris apparently had nothing left to say to the Reonih high priest. He turned his attention to the dark-haired man who that had proved to be so adept at dealing death. "Who are you, and where is your caste?"

Khirin bowed. "Khirin lri Thynan. I won entrance into the arena and am assigned to the Grey Bull."

"Right." Chandris frowned thoughtfully. "I remember seeing you in the arena. Your skills are impressive."

"At your service, *sayo.*"

One of the Reonih approached Stiva. He was a healer, by his green robes. She had seen him before, but had forgotten his name. "If you like," he said, "I can try to help your cat."

"Please," Stiva whispered. "Anything you can do."

The healer nodded, and went to Lhin's side. Stiva watched him nervously. Two other healers, trailing behind the main party, went to help him.

Chandris went to Vane's still form. He knelt down beside the fallen man, and bowed his head, showing respect. "Fair skies, warrior," he said gently. Then he pulled the murdik stone from Vane's uniform, stood, and unceremoniously handed it to Khirin.

Stiva stared at her twin. "Chandris, what are you—"

"He just saved our lives," Chandris told her. "Seeing as you are short a captain, he may as well fill the void. If you don't want him, I'll put him in the Gold Braid."

He looked down at Vane, and made a gesture, speaking to no one in particular: "Take him back. He should have a hero's burial, and a ballad."

Dallan stared hotly at Lyle and Khirin, until Jarvor came and laid a hand on his shoulder. It seemed the fight drained out of Dallan then, for he just nodded, and went to fetch Vane's shield. Jarvor, Delis, Keorl, and Timthe helped him place his brother on the shield, and then the five of them carried Vane away.

Aret offered Chandris his cat. Stiva's twin mounted and gave her a hand up to its back, so that she could ride behind him. But instead of riding off immediately, he looked back at the archer. "The dead are yours to loot. Surely they will pay well, for they themselves have been paid well, and recently."

Mohr went tight-lipped, for what Chandris suggested was a direct insult. By tradition, such loot should be given to the forest or river spirits, in thanks. Chandris, for his part, did not so much as glance at the high priest.

The archer cocked his hip. "Is that the reward for saving the king's life? To be allowed to steal from the dead?"

Chandris looked amused. "That is but a token. I don't generally carry coin on hunting forays." He pointed back towards Starshire, to the west. "Go to the estate, and there you will find more traditional rewards. It is Lightfest, after all. Do not despair, archer. There will be food, wine, and wenches for you tonight, as well as gold. And I want to hear more about this new bow."

That said, Chandris wheeled the cat and rode off.

In the sky, a single raptor screamed in rage.

———————————

No one was much in the mood to celebrate after that, but, with all the preparations already made, it would have been pointless to cancel the holiday festivities. Stiva ordered the bonfires lit at sunset, just as the bards started playing. Colorful tents blazed like jewels in the gardens. Beneath their silken canopies, servants piled heaps of food on long tables: fried jhar in bluefish oil, chiara sausage, vru, trutes' brains ... the list of mouthwatering delicacies went on and on. The fountains in the courtyard ran with dark grape wine, and fire dancers spun brands against the night. Stiva put on the mask she'd had made for the occasion, a blue and green thing made of peacock feathers, sapphire, bronze, and satin, and settled into her seat at the head tent, trying to shake the bloody images of the attack from her mind. She wanted nothing more than to retreat to her rooms and dive into a book, but she had already learned one fact of ruling: she must speak when she wanted to be quiet, and dance when she wanted to sleep.

Along the ridges and distant mountains, signal fires shone like stars against a blood-red sky, spreading warning, spreading word of trouble from the border.

When the birds came in, it was Stiva who read the ribbons and deciphered the message.

"The north," she said. "The east. The west. A concentrated attack." She laid the ribbons down. "The Selin held, thank the gods. They held. But we've taken heavy casualties."

They sat quietly for a moment, letting dark truth sink into their thoughts.

Orlin and Delora had never been allies: truces between them had been brief and uneasy. But they had cause to work together to unseat the twins, and divide their lands between them.

Chandris' face darkened. "The gods," he said, "have nothing to do with it. If we hadn't managed to hold them, if the archer and Khirin hadn't happened to be there ... Aris would have fallen today, Stiva."

"That's why they sent so many," Stiva said. "They would have taken Kele, Aret, and Maren. Shira. Our entire family in one blow."

Lyle was the next to send word. The Selin had found another mercenary force, this one numbering several hundred. The Selin had defeated them, with the aid of the Reonih, by getting ahead of them and ambushing them.

Selin and Reonih alike were combing the woods for Cerrow, but report after report bore the same disappointing news.

Cerrow was gone, fled.

Chandris was sullen, and even the efforts of the girl at his side—a daughter of one of the border lords—could not lift his mood. Stiva was similarly uneasy. The flicker of firelight, the gleam of it against metal, the sound of a lute and drum, these were familiar things, which she should have found relaxing. Instead, she grew more and more uneasy. Though mead, food, music, and fire all took a bit off the edge of the day's events, she could not shake the feeling that more attackers would appear out of the night. The shadows seemed longer and thicker that night, the wind colder, the world more cruel and unforgiving.

Kira and Reide were there, inviting her to sing. She initially hesitated, and then decided to join them. They sang Cerrow's betrayal together. They sang bloodprice for his capture. They sang death into the Lightest celebrations. For a time, she was able to push the day's events away, and relax a bit.

As the sun touched the horizon, the sky dancers took their place in the middle of the garden, at the light pole. A square platform graced the top of the pole. The dancers—lithe, and almost animal-like in their movements—climbed up to the platform tying the ribbon ends to their waists. The Reonih below carefully moved the ladders away.

Kira raised her horn, and blew a long, low note into the air.

The dancers, one by one, launched themselves off the top of the pole.

Four figures spun through the air, graceful as birds, arms outstretched, elaborate feather capes spread out like wings. Four strands of thick rope wound with colorful ribbon anchored each of them to the long, straight post that rose into the sky. It seemed to slice the horizon, like a dagger or a spear. As the sky-dancers launched themselves into the air, jumping off the platform one by one, the ribbon-threaded ropes wrapped tightly around the pole unwound slowly, guiding their flights, keeping them from flying off as they spun out around the pole, descending only as the coils unwound.

Came the slightest sound of motion beside her. Maren had crept to her side. Stiva put an arm around him, ignoring the frosty look of disapproval Talia tossed at her. He had grown a lot in the past few seasons. He reached her shoulder now, and his face had begun to lose the expressionless innocent look of childhood. Cronn's stubbornness showed in the set of his jaw, but he had Lara's contemplative gaze.

"Why do they do that?" Maren asked. His voice was a whisper, as though he was afraid that to speak in a normal tone would destroy the moment.

"To honor the Skyborne," Stiva whispered. "See how they're coming to earth? They're reenacting the orbit and descent of the Elders."

"What of the other Zhur?"

"We will honor the Fireborne later at night, with the fire dances. The Earthborne we honored at Dawn, with the sowing of seeds. The Seaborne we honor at dusk, at the shore."

As the ropes untwisted, and more and more of their lengths were freed, the dancers spun out further and further into the air.

Maren watched, spellbound. "Can I do that?"

"No, Maren. But you can watch."

"Can I go to the fires?"

"No, Maren, you're too young for that."

Maren was still intensely focused on the spectacle before them. The pole-dancers' movements were precise. They remained at an equal distance apart, their speed unchanging, their movements a perfect mix of outward and downward motion.

"You never paid attention before." Stiva smiled at her little brother. "You were too young. You're growing up, Maren."

Maren's eyes darkened. He turned away. "I know," he said sourly. "And soon I'll be sent away too. Like Shira. I'm going to the Selin camps," Maren said. His face darkened. "Chandris told me last night."

Stiva felt as though an icy hand had clutched her heart; she swallowed her uneasiness and tried again. "Maren—"

"I don't want to go," Maren said. Once, he would have screamed it. Now, his voice was low. Sullen. "I want to go with the Reonih."

Stiva felt a lump rise in her throat. "You'll be fine," she said, trying to keep her voice from shaking. "Don't you want to be a general one day? Command the Selin, perhaps?"

He looked up at her. "I guess," he said sullenly. "I'd rather be a bard," he said. "Or a healer, maybe."

"Those are children's fancies," Talia said. "Your path lies with the Selin. It will do you no good to fight it. You need to learn the art of war."

"But there's no art in war," Maren said. "Only death."

"There are tactics," Talia said, before Stiva could answer. "You have to learn to be strong and brave. That is the road to glory."

Maren contemplated this, his brown creased. The dog at his feet sighed deeply and settled down, nose on paws, as though sensing the tension in the air.

"Can I learn to wrestle, like Aret?"

"Yes," Talia said. "You'll learn much more than that."

"Chandris went to the institution, too." Shira said quietly. "You'll be fine, Maren."

Reide and Kira tried to console her, but she had no use for soft words or reassurances.

"Go," she snapped at Reide, when he asked her if she wanted to play dice. "Play, or don't play. Dance, or don't dance. Do what you want,

Reide. There are men out there who want us dead. I've nothing to celebrate."

Reide stared at her, shocked. She had never snapped at him before.

"You become more like Mother every day," Chandris said, when she finally sat down next to him in their tent.

She leaned back, looking at the celebrations before her. To the unknowing eye, there was no sign of the earlier troubles, save perhaps the increased numbers of guards on watch. The bards kept playing, filling the air with song. The courtyard, strung with lanterns that glowed like fallen stars in the night, was filled with laughter and camaraderie. The revelers danced, drank, laughed, and ate with less and less abandon. They tried their hand at small contests, recited poetry, shared tidbits. Drums and strings floated through the air, wrapping the night in invisible energy. It was magic, that music. It reached into Stiva's soul, awakening something primal.

But she was in no mood to dance.

The world sank into darkness. The watchtowers remained lit.

"I've been sent a present," Chandris said. "From the Viore at Akers. A painting, of his ancestor. The man was weak, a cripple. But he had a mind like a steel trap. He could not lift a sword, but he outsmarted every enemy he had, and died an old man, warm and safe in his bead." He popped a citrus fruit into his mouth. "Do you know what his favorite saying was?"

"What?" Stiva asked.

"I have no greater enemy than the one who pretends to be my friend." The dancers spun and whirled before them. Chandris tore a piece off a spice roll and chewed with little appetite. "It was Cerrow, sent me that direction this morning. We could have lost everything today, over a kurra that wasn't real."

"You couldn't have known."

"You did," Chandris said, looking at her. "You tried to warn me. I should have listened."

"You never listen," Stiva said. "But to be fair, though I never trusted him, I never thought he would go that far."

Chandris laughed suddenly.

Stiva cast him a puzzled look. "What's funny?"

"He used silver we gave him," Chandris said, "To hire mercenaries. But instead, he's made us stronger. That bow, Stiva, that bow will help us crush our enemies."

Stiva looked at the fire. "There must be something," Stiva said. "He didn't do this for silver, or power."

"No," Chandris said. "I know why he did it. He doesn't approve of my interests. They don't want me investigating the Relics."

He was calmer than she would have expected. But she realized that major events did not rile him. A trivial matter could send him into a blind rage, but something like this drew him into pensive thought. His voice was cold and calculating when he spoke again.

"They?" Stiva said.

Chandris looked at her, his eyes like green fire. "Cerrow didn't coordinate this alone." He looked at her. "This was Reonih treachery, Stiva."

She shook her head. "Mohr would never—"

"*Never*," Chandris said, interrupting her, "will never come."

"Cerrow betrayed you. That doesn't mean every Reonih is against you. You know better than that."

"I do. But I also know that they protect their own interests. They have too much power over the people." He turned back to the window, taking a yellow apple from a crystal bowl and biting into it. The crunch of his teeth against the crisp fruit sounded like bones breaking. His words hung on the air, along with the scents of incense and wood smoke. "Even after this, I owe Cerrow a debt, for talking Cronn into sending me overseas. I grew, there, Stiva. I changed. I opened my mind to other ways of thinking. Mohr is the one I do not trust. He has entirely too much influence on you."

"I would have said the same about you and Cerrow," Stiva returned coolly. "But I never trusted Cerrow. I trust Mohr."

He lifted his goblet to his lips, meeting her stare with a cold green gaze. "I trust no one," he said.

There was a short moment of stillness. She could almost hear her twin thinking. *Not even you.*

"You almost got me killed today," Stiva said. "And then you saved my life. I never thought that would happen, either."

"Hopefully tomorrow won't be quite as exciting." Chandris sipped his wine. "How's Lhin?"

"Sleeping," Stiva said. "He'll live, but I'll never be able to ride him again. The Reonih have done what they can."

"Good. I'm glad to hear it. Seems like just yesterday he was a kitten, eating my furniture." Chandris smiled, but his eyes remained cold. He turned to Ket, who sat at his left, and was soon engrossed in conversation about the bow.

They sat silently watching the dancers spinning around the bonfire. Many of the people below wore masks, in honor of the holiday, but here and there, Stiva could pick out a familiar form. Twyla was dancing with the archer, Ket. Jahn was teaching Shira a Vrehnian step. Beside her, Marcelle was dancing with Aret, spinning around the bonfire. He looked, in that moment, like Kele, save that Kele rarely smiled. Her uncle was holding court at a smaller table, tossing dice with srih and Selin, already deep in his cups. As Stiva watched, Marcelle took Aret's hand and led him away from the bonfire, laughing. There was no shame, on Lightfest. There was no judgment. No taboos. Stiva could have gone with any of the men at the fire, and known no repercussions.

Freedom: that was what Lightfest signified. There was nothing but the music, the stars, and the realization that she was alive, that she remained on this earth.

There was Trin, and the memory of another Lightfest. The last she had known here, at Starshire, before Mykhal. Memories rose up through her, ripping open an old wound.

Music throbbed in the air Stiva danced, twisting and turning below three full moons. She drank deeply, savoring the taste of Zorish mead against her throat. She ate smoked meat, cheese infused with herbs, gerfruit and apples bathed in honey, and potatoes in thick, golden butter. She had a stuffed egg that she later swore was the best thing she had ever tasted. She danced with srih, with Selin, and with all of the Black Boot. She danced with visiting lords, with Reonih, with Chandris and Aret and even Lyle. She danced alone, mindless of the eyes watching her, mindless of the world watching her. She danced until sweat glistened on her skin and her muscles were warm and loose. She danced until her breath came in gasps and her legs burned. She should have been tired, but the music moved through her like fire. Looking back, she was able to recognize that night as the moment she crossed the line between girl and woman, and left her childhood behind. At the time, such thoughts never entered her mind. She recalled only feeling alive, wild and free, knowing herself young, beautiful, and vital.

And then she had glanced up and seen Trin watching her, smiling.

The world slowed down. Stiva raised her hand, beckoning to him.

She had been fool enough to think no harm would come of it.

A familiar voice interrupted her reverie. "*Sayo.*" Stiva looked up and found Shira standing before them. She greeted Chandris first, and then Stiva. "*Saya.*"

"What is it, Shira?" Chandris sipped his wine.

"I've decided to accept Taibon's hand." Shira said quietly. "I've reread his letters, and find him intelligent, polite, and funny. I think he is a suitable match."

Stiva turned to Chandris to watch his reaction, but there really wasn't one. He nodded, and reached for the silver bowl of rupalier leaves. "Excellent," he said. "The continued alliance with Shadri will make our house stronger. Have one of the Reonih draw up the official agreement."

"Congratulations," Stiva said.

Shira curtsied, and then turned and left quietly, slipping into the shadows of the courtyard. Stiva saw her look back once, briefly, before the darkness within Aris' walls swallowed her. Her face was cold, unreadable.

"That's an excellent choice," Talia said. She turned to the twins. "And what of you?" she asked. "Surely you mean to marry soon. You need an heir."

Chandris nodded. "Yes, it is time for me to have sons. Once Shira is married, I'll start looking." He looked at Stiva sideways. "You should know that Jahn has expressed interest in marrying you."

Stiva read the question in his eyes, and answered before it was spoken. "I'll never marry," she said. "I've already decided that. I will never bind myself to anything other than Aris itself."

"Good," Chandris said. "Thank you. That is wise."

Words hung unspoken between them.

Our children would kill each other. Drench the land in warfare.

My sons and your sons would all have our fire, but not the twinbond that keeps us in check. They would plot against one another.

Stiva looked at her twin, and knew that he would never let her sons live to threaten him.

Chandris looked at her evenly. Ghosts hung in their gazes, and the souls of the dead stood between them. Then the night wind gusted up, and the shades returned again to the clouds.

Stiva excused herself. She went back to her suite, where Lhin was sleeping on a bed of blankets, and spent the night petting him, her tears spilling into his fur.

CHAPTER 15

As the seasons changed again, Chandris called a council meeting. Dozens of srih, Reonih, and Selin assembled in the Council Chamber. Ruddy lamps attempted to beat back the gloom of a cold day. Shadows gathered in thoughts and corners.

Stiva sat beside her brother. Her face was calm, but her thoughts were turbulent, tinged with fear.

Chandris stood, and the room slowly quieted. His shout echoed around the room, loud enough to be heard some distance away from the chamber.

"My lords," Chandris said. "Countrymen and fellow Arisians."

The last sounds fled the room. An erlit cried out, somewhere nearby. All else was silent.

"Selin numbers have dropped since Caro's time," Chandris began. "My grandfather tightened the restrictions on who was allowed into the ranks. His reasons were sound enough. He wanted a more elite force. He got it. But he also left my father a much smaller army than the one he himself inherited. For years, the Selin ranks have been thinning. There are fewer and fewer men coming out of the institutions to replace those lost in battle, and dozens are discharged each year for minor breaches of conduct. Many of the ousted men join the armies of our enemies. As it is, with the raids from Delora, we have had to use the general army more and more. If we continue to press the general army, our crops will suffer. We cannot leave one field untilled to protect another. To put it bluntly, we need to increase our numbers."

They stared at him with glassy eyes.

Chandris pointed in the direction of a plainly clad woodsman who stood nervously at the side of the dais. "I present Ketran e Ducathe, captain of our new archers' division."

There was a moment of silence. Then chaos set in. Voices rose into the air as one in a thunderous tumult. Some shoved their chairs back and jumped to their feet, waving their fists. A cacophony of angry protests filled the room.

"Where are you going to get them?" Barls asked. "Even if they agreed to it, the Selin haven't enough sons to fill the ranks of both the Selin and another division."

Stiva looked around silently, watching the range of reactions.

"I'm going to recruit from both the srih and the commonfolk, including the serfs." Chandris told them flatly. "They are numerous enough."

"Archers? *Archers?* You expect our sons to fight with bows and arrows?" Lavos shouted. "Peasants' weapons?"

"Not at all," Chandris answered coldly. "I expect the archers to use them. Your sons, Lavos, can continue making shoes, if they like."

Laughter rolled around the room, like that. Lavos sat back, scowling. *You've just made an enemy*, Stiva thought.

The uproar devolved into a less violent din, though one just as deadly, as srih spoke to one another, rather than pummeling the air.

Chandris continued speaking over the next surge of protests, which died down again as he spoke. "The Selin are elite, but they are not immortal. Men are lost each cycle and not enough are born to replace them, much less fill the ranks of another army division. The general army is meant to only be called upon in emergencies."

"You intend serfs to fight alongside Selin?" Erad asked, disbelief coloring his tone.

Chandris nodded. "Precisely," he said. "They already do, in the general army. But I'm going to open up the option for them to make careers in the military, if they like, rather than just fight when occasion needs it. I intend to double the size of the army. I must. We haven't enough men to hold, otherwise, much less prosper. The reports about the raids were no lie. The men I sent to guard the border skirmish daily, harrowed by Deloran and outlaw alike. I have seen the burnt fields myself. I have seen the charred ruins of villages that were once productive and peaceful. I have seen the corpses of farmers and herdsman who never raised a hand in violence. And I have seen enough of both to last a lifetime. Those images boil in my blood. They burn in my words, even as I speak to you now. I will not allow my people to suffer like this."

Chandris held the room captivated. The passion in his voice was undeniable.

Stiva kept silent: she could have spoken, but this was Chandris' moment, and, as she saw it, he should be the one to claim it as such.

Her twin continued. "We need to strengthen our defenses. Aris isn't garrisoned as strongly as it should be. But there is no easy solution. I cannot pull the border patrols back now. It would be an open invitation for our enemies to increase aggression. The raids would grow even worse. Nor can I continue to leave Aris itself undefended. The problem is simple. I haven't enough military force. We're spread too thin. The coronation games got us an influx of capable warriors, who have now finished training at the Selin institutions. But it isn't enough. So I've solved a simple problem with an equally simple solution. I've created a new military branch."

The silence that followed was so thick it was almost visible. There were no cries of outrage, this time, no shocked gasps. Some of the men exchanged wary glances, but, for the most part, the audience sat quietly.

"But the general army—" Ehodris started.

Chandris cut the lord of Fahrin off before he could finish, turning a cold stare on Talia's father. "The general army is only an auxiliary. Those men are farmers, fishermen, and craftsmen, not true warriors. They have to tend their herds and crops. They are needed here. Plus, they haven't the time or patience for extended training or long campaigns. We cannot tax them any more without leaving fields untended. Nor will I loosen the Selin regulations. That would either demoralize or infuriate them, or both. So, while I intend to fill some ranks in this new division with the sons of srih, the majority of the force will come from the sons of commoners. Or daughters, if they so choose."

Stiva spoke up for the first time. "The commonfolk tend to large families. There are a lot of younger children out there with nothing much to look forward to in life except poverty."

Chandris nodded, picking up seamlessly where she had left off. "I'm going to recruit them on a voluntary basis."

"But will they fight?"

The voice came from the back edge of the room. Fentar, one of the oldest—and most loyal—of Cronn's men.

"They will fight," Chandris said assuredly. "Oh, they will fight. They are tired of giving and giving, and getting nothing back. The worse things get, the more they grumble. I will open the gates to the commonfolk and serfs, and give them a chance to do something different, to serve their king and country. Far too many of them have joined the outlaw bands these last few seasons. If they're going to take up arms, they may as well fight for me."

"What if they don't want to fight? Many of them are content being farmers."

"Then they can farm. I expect enough will answer the summons to fill the division. We still need men to see to our herds and crops."

"But it will take years to train them," one of the srih protested.

It was Ket who answered this time. "It will take moons."

The silence, once again, was one of shock. It diminished only a fraction as Ket continued. "It takes years to master the sword. While it may take years to truly become a master archer, a man can become formidable with a longbow within a season."

"It's an effective weapon," Jahn said. "It can pierce armor from three hundred paces. And it's fairly cheap, at least when one compares the price of wood to the price of steel."

The dais creaked slightly as Chandris stood.

"This weapon gives us a huge advantage," Chandris said. "One that will be lost if we wait. If one man has this bow now, before long there will be others out there."

The room silenced as the men realized that this plan had the support of the Selin commander. The balance of opinion began to shift.

"Chandris," Ehodris stammered, flabbergasted, "Only a few moons ago you said bows and arrows were useless."

"A few moons ago," Chandris countered coolly, "I had not seen a man killed by an arrow fired three hundred strides from where he stood." He looked at Talia's sire gravely. "A commoner saved Stiva's life and mine. Maybe they can save Aris."

"Or divide it even more. Have you even thought of that?" Mohr had sat silently until that point. When the Reonih high priest spoke, the entire room fell still.

Chandris looked the High Priest in the eye. "We will find out soon enough," he said flatly. "The first batch of recruiters left this morning. Within a few weeks, I expect to have a new army."

One could almost see their minds spinning.

Chandris looked around the room, his eyes fixing upon each of them in turn. "I will be frank with you, lords. Our enemies are roused. They are like hungry wolves scenting blood. Delora's troops are gathering in the mountains. Last week Orlin tried our eastern border. There is trouble coming. What happened at the Lightfest hunt was only the beginning. We cannot defend two borders from two separate armies and stand. Not as we are. They think they can unseat me, and look to divide the lands of Aris between them. I refuse to let that happen."

"And you think this is the answer." Kele spoke flatly.

"Yes, I do." Chandris looked at his uncle seriously. "I've thought this out carefully. This is the answer to our problems. Think about it. Iron and steel are costly. Wood is much cheaper. The training will be fast. It takes a lifetime to master the sword, but a bow and arrow can be learned within a season or two."

"Have you ever seen a Sijhani archer?" Mohr asked. "They take years practicing. They are extremely formidable, and their skills are not gained in moons."

"Yes, but these are not the bows the Sijhani use. This new type of bow is extremely efficient and, as you and I have seen, very deadly."

They all stared at him with the same expression, a mixture of bafflement and complete shock.

"You will incite civil war," Kele said stiffly. "The srih will never stand for it."

The king of Aris turned glittering eyes onto his prime minister. "War?" Chandris echoed. "I don't have to invite it. It's already here, knocking at the door. At least this way I'll have the force to deal with it." He sank back down into his chair. "But if you are talking about the srih rising up and taking arms against me … I think not." He looked around the room. "Remember: this is more men fighting to protect your lands, as well."

"And what of the Selin?" Kele asked.

"The Selin stand behind Chandris," Lyle said flatly. "We do not make his decisions."

"Nothing changes with the Selin," Chandris said. "We may put some of the greybeards to work training and conditioning the new recruits, but that is nothing new."

"You ask them to fight beside commoners and serfs," Kele put in. "They have never done that. And you think archers are the solution? What under seven moons gave you that idea?"

"You have to ask?"

"Because of Starshire? Have you gone mad? That was *one* man."

He laughed. "Mad? Why? Because I'm thinking and acting, instead of simply doing what every king of Aris before me has done, which was to rely solely on tradition and Reonih counsel." Chandris paused, looking his uncle in the eye. "I intend to put a stop to that. The border wars must end, if we are to survive. A man can bleed to death from dozens of shallow wounds, and a kingdom is no different. I'll not have another stalk of wheth destroyed." He looked around the room. "Kingdoms grow stronger, or they fall apart and are vanquished."

"It may never be over." Kele said flatly. "We have been at war for five hundred years. If Aursa could unite under one king, it would have happened already. Chandris, if it were so easy to change Aris, don't you think my brother would have done it? Or my father?"

"Never." Chandris shook his head. "It requires original thinking, and Cronn's only inclination to that line of intellectual pursuit was limited to inane drunken musings and ambush tactics. Don't mistake me; I can hardly deny that the haystack ambush in the Battle of the Pitchforks was highly creative and successful. My—our—father was an excellent warrior, but he had no vision. Caro, on the other hand, was much more cunning, but he ruled through sheer brutality, ensuring that no one dared to defy him. He also stifled original thought. Besides, neither of them was ever forced into a corner the way I have been. Caro had a mercenary army at hand, and Cronn inherited a much stronger state than we have."

"They have never been defeated either, but that doesn't mean it can't happen."

Chandris' eyes blazed suddenly with green fire. "It will be one or the other. I can promise you that."

He looked around at the shocked faces before him.

"Out!" Chandris shouted, tired of the questions. "We are done here for today."

The room cleared, leaving only a handful within.

"They looked absolutely furious." Stiva cast Chandris a wary look. "Are you sure about this?"

"Absolutely." Chandris nodded. "Oh, they may be angry for a time, if some of their men leave their service for mine, but they can hire more. They will rant and rave and sulk, but they see the sense of it soon enough. They will settle. They will see."

They heard the faint roar of Kele's shout from down the hall.

Aret appeared, looking half-wary, half-amused. "My father thinks you've gone mad."

"I imagine he said quite a bit more than that," Chandris said dryly. "I imagine he's probably still talking. He wasn't exactly pleased with my idea. None of the council was. I expected that, though. It's why I had the servants water the mead before they served it." Chandris set his goblet down on a table. "No matter. They'll settle."

Stiva wasn't so sure.

He drank again, deeply, savoring the taste of sun and earth in the wine as though he were consuming the very essence of both. When he looked at her, his eyes were filled with dreams.

She wondered if the Elders had felt the same way when they crossed the abyss.

CHAPTER 16

"*S* *aya.*"

The voice dragged Stiva back from troubled thought. She stood at the window, her cheek resting against the tinted pane. From her vantage point in the Rose Tower, she had a clear view of the Overlook, the Zhrue Gate, the city falling into the harbor … and the smoke rising from the watchtowers outside the city walls. The watchtower signal fires had been lit far too often since the twins' coronation. However, this was the first time that the fires weren't red, signaling an attack. The greenish hue of these flames did not warn of raiders, as the other fires had.

Plague, the flames hissed, dancing in eerie pulses. *Death. Disease.*

Nearly five decades had passed since the last time cow fever had struck Aris, but the terror and tragedy of that year cast a long, dark, shadow, one that now darkened the present day. When that plague had first been discovered, Caro had immediately taken steps to halt its spread, ordering the slaughter of thousands of cattle. The srih had protested, but Caro and the Reonih had both insisted that meat and hide wasted was better than lives lost. The infected villages were essentially cut off. The Reonih had catapulted supplies over the walls, and the healers had put on strange, horned masks to see to the sick. The dead were taken outside their walls to be burned, and the smoke of those fires carried over the land. The ballads told of farmers putting down treasured cattle, tears streaming down their faces. Not even newborn calves had escaped. The acrid smoke from the massive pyres and the stench of death had tainted the winds for weeks, even down to the castle itself, courtesy of a well-placed wind current. Entire herds had been lost, wasted, and the financial toll of that loss had driven once-thriving farmers into poverty.

It wasn't enough.

Caro had ordered grainbidreeps and alebidreeps on a weekly basis to try and keep the poorer citizens fed. Trouble had arisen among the srih. Some took issue with being forced to give away their stored crops. Others had taken chances and eaten the meat from cattle they thought were clean, or—more likely—given them to their serfs. Amidst a spattering of uprisings, old territorial feuds had reawakened, and the srih took up arms against each other.

Once the plague reached the city, it spread like wildfire. The *summer of death*, it was called.

The final death toll stood in the tens of thousands.

Stiva knew every ballad about the plague, every twist and turn that had guided the course of events. The symptoms. The protections. But she had never understood it, really, never truly grasped the horror of such a tragedy, until this season. The fires on the hill struck a cold, black fear into her heart. She could not eat, and when she slept, the nightvisions cast a shadow of dread over her that followed her even into the brightest hours. In her dreams, the streets and fields of Aris were strewn with corpses that stared at her with accusation in their eyes. In her dreams, Chandris looked at her, the buboes on his neck bulging like fruit, the grey pallor of his skin an announcement in and of itself. In her dreams, his cheeks had split open, oozing blood and pus. His eyes had shrunken into his skull as the green fires within them—the same color as the tower fires—had withered and died. She had looked at her hand, and saw the telltale blisters appearing.

It had taken hours for the dream to release her, for the chill in her heart and her soul to ease.

Chandris, too, worried about the plague. He was pale and silent and never slept, but instead rode the border patrols with the Selin, racing from the hall of one march lord to another, insisting on quarantine. He had ordered inspections of the herds, and the destruction of any with symptoms. The srih who had owned the livestock he ordered destroyed were less than happy. Meanwhile, the raids continued. He had done everything he could to combat the raids, but it was too late. By the end of light season, raiders had burned a third of Aris' harvests.

The voice came again, more urgent. "*Saya.*"

Stiva ignored it, staring out the window. She held a bladed fan in her hand, but did not use it; the Tower was too chilly.

She had a thousand things to do, but she found herself instead staring out the window. The weather belonged, this day, to the fair half of the cycle. The sky shone brightly in a dusky gold sky, and the winds that blew in from the Oburion were warm, setting leaves dancing beneath a few wispy clouds. Her gaze slid beyond the city walls, to the surrounding fields, where rainbow-hued spinflowers tumbled, little bright dots moving downhill like colored stars. She knew she could snap her fingers, and half a dozen maids would fill as many baskets as they could carry with the colorful, fragrant blossoms. She could whistle, and Larin, Nels, or one of their apprentices would immediately saddle a cat, horse, or bird for her, and accompany her into the meadows or along the beach. In the city, the citizens were throwing open their windows, planting their gardens, repairing fences and roofs and shutters damaged by winter's screaming winds.

She stood, looking down on the world, feeling very distant from it. She felt like a caged bird.

A growl came from the rug beside the fireplace. Lhin lay there, snoring and twitching, perhaps dreaming of chasing erlits. Though he had recovered from his wounds, he had aged quite a bit in the last few moons. Stiva had begun keeping him in her rooms full time, in part because they were warmer and more comfortable for him, and in part so she could spoil him more easily. The old cat spent his days napping before the fire, quite amicable to having his ears scratched and his tummy rubbed.

The Black Boot, despite her orders, kept feeding him treats. This was the one rebellion she would tolerate.

Stiva rubbed a jeweled hand against her forehead, where the slightest ache was growing. When she spoke, her voice sounded strange to her own ears, flat and mechanical, as though even the faintest echoes of music had left it. "Send word to the Reonih and the srih about the plague. There is to be a quarantine on all cattle. Every herd in the infected region must be slaughtered and burned. Send a regiment of Selin out to oversee the process and make sure that the farmers don't try to use any of the meat."

"As you wish, *saya*." Loris said. His voice was calm, but a trace of sorrow colored his tone. "There are nineteen more cases awaiting your seal. Have you reached a decision on the Chorin situation?"

"Yes." Stiva sighed. "Paine?"

"*Saya?*" The scribe jerked his head up. The look of panic in his eyes belayed the fact that he too, had been daydreaming.

"Record the following correspondence." Stiva paused to sort out her words before continuing. "To the Lord of Chorin, regarding the House of Herith: We hereby notify you that, with the Viore of Herith having departed this life, the estate of Herith is left, as it stands, without proper heir. We will not allow the young daughter of Herith to be united with the line of Chorin in lawful marriage because of her tender age. Therefore it is our decision to render the holdings of Herith, and the duties and obligations of the deceased vassal, into the keeping of Lord Fentar of Mir until the child is of a suitable age, at which time a proper husband shall be selected for her. Herith's serfs, should they choose to remain, shall also be under the care of Fentar in the time being. He is not to change their rent, work hours, food tithes, or any other aspect of their contracts, unless it would be in their favor."

"Very good, my lady," Loris said approvingly. "Though I don't think Chorin will care overmuch for the response."

"Chorin," Stiva said coolly, "is a snake. Have you prepared the next case?"

Loris looked down, shuffling through a small pile of paperwork. A single spectacle lens was perched precariously on the end of his nose. He adjusted it with a practiced thumb before speaking. "Ah, yes, the matter of the border dispute between Borok and Vers."

Stiva frowned. "Again? I thought Chandris had settled that already."

Loris looked at the papers again. "This is a different area. They both received an annex when Reins died."

Stiva nodded dully. Such issues once would have had her sending frantically to the Reonih for advice. Now she rendered decisions quickly, and with growing confidence.

"It seems the new dispute has arisen over a valley, previously thought unremarkable," Loran said, musing over the documents before him. "There must be something of interest within, though neither party mentions what it is."

"Truffles," Stiva said. "Borok sent some to us just a fortnight ago."

"Ah," Loris said. "And the valley?"

"Settled." Stiva glanced at Paine. "The land has been Borok's for generations, but his father clearly sold the valley to Vers three years past. Are the Fenhar documents ready?"

He nodded. "You need only sign and seal them."

Crossing the room in a few strides, Stiva took the proffered quill and scrawled her name over the parchment, then nodded at the scribe, who carefully tipped the candle over the paper. A single drop of blood-red wax landed beside her signature, and Stiva pressed her ring into it.

That is Aris, she thought, staring as the crest of her House set into the crimson liquid, *carving our crest into the blood of this land.*

"Majesty?" A third voice interrupted them. They both turned and found chubby Tirik, one of her heralds, peering cautiously into the room.

"What is it?" Stiva asked.

"There is someone here for you, *saya*. A man named Khirin. He said you would be expecting him. Huran is also waiting."

She had almost forgotten, despite the fact that Chandris and Lyle had both sent her messages to tell her he was coming today. Stiva nodded, giving her permission to grant the newcomer access, already annoyed at the intrusion. In truth, she wasn't particularly concerned with who commanded her guard, even knowing that such was a dangerous perspective. But someone must, and she had no reason to refuse to meet the man Chandris had decided was best. "Send him in," she told Tirik. "Loris, Paine, you are dismissed. We will continue tomorrow."

The herald exited with a bow. Loris gathered up his papers and followed behind him. A moment later, the gleaming doors opened again, allowing Khirin entrance before shutting again behind him.

"*Saya*," he said quietly, bowing his head.

Stiva eyed her new captain curiously. Khirin was tall, though not unusually so. His dark hair was straight and worn long, though most of the Selin kept their short. He wore Selin colors and weapons, but something intangible separated him from them.

"So you've come," Stiva said quietly.

He said nothing.

"I see they have given you an officer's uniform," Stiva observed. "Yet you have no badges. Not even a gem carved with a family crest. No battle honors."

"No." His voice was quiet. She was happy to note that he gave her none of the adoration the srih did. His undertone was steel. "I have not yet fought with the Selin in true battle."

Her brows lifted. "Nor against them, I hope."

"No."

She frowned. "You display no clan colors. Whose bear you?"

A flash of emotion crossed his eyes, but was gone as quickly as it arrived. He looked towards the wall, then back at her. "None."

The crease in her brow deepened. "Are you dishonored, then? Are you outlawed?"

"I am Selin," Khirin said flatly. "I am not from Aris."

"Where, then?"

"Kralin, most recently. Orake, originally." A pause, hesitation, the faintest shadow of uncertainty. "Do you order me to answer the rest?"

She swallowed, turned her back on him to stare once more out the window. "No," she said. "Keep your secrets, if you wish."

"Thank you, *saya*."

She looked out the window. A vlorship had come into the harbor. Jahn's men, she assumed. Beyond, a dark smudge spread across the horizon. Storms came in quickly, in the light season. "Essentially, you've been promoted due to valor on the battlefield, because of your service at Starshire. You've been given a position of rank. A position of high rank, actually. You're to be in command of my private guard. You and Terne have some authority over the city guard and the garrison as well in case of an emergency, but they have their own officers. For the most part, you need only to be sure things are running smoothly. The palace guard commanders will report directly to you and Terne. Your concern is my protection. You'll coordinate duty rosters, oversee things, report to me. I'm assuming you are aware of the duties involved."

"Of course," he said.

"Understand one thing," she said quietly, still looking out the window. "You are here because he chose you. If I send you away, there will only be another sent to replace you, and you are as good as any. I have one shadow already. I do not need another. You are a shade. A ghost. You trail me, like a shadow. You stand in corners and in hallways, and you do not move until I move. You do not hear what is spoken. You do not see."

She turned to face him, and found herself staring at a mystery.

"If you would prefer to go about unprotected," Khirin said, "then tell me now, and I won't waste my time here. I understand there has already been one attempt on your brother's life since Starshire, in which luck or gods intervened."

"Actually," Stiva said, "it was the Gold Braid."

He did not so much as blink. "I have agreed to take control of your personal guard. I have agreed to serve you. Already I have seen a half-dozen ways an assassin could get to you."

"The Black Boot," Stiva said, motioning to the door, "has been my personal guard since I came of age. They have proven themselves, time and time again. Your placement here is unusual, but do not think them soft, or welcoming. You are their commander, promoted because of valor on the battlefield. You have large boots to fill. Vane was an excellent captain, and they respected him. You, however, are an outsider, to them. You've proven yourself on the field. If you hadn't, you wouldn't be standing here. They will die for you, and will expect you to do the same. But they will kill you if you step out of line."

"Where were they, at Starshire?"

"Following an illusion," Stiva said flatly, "as were we. Following Reonih magic. Betrayal." She looked at him, the memory of that day crossing her eyes. "I always wondered, though. How did you find us?"

"I saw the birds start from that direction," he said, "and I crossed tracks where there should be none. I was in the Grey Bull at the time. Baros gave me permission to ride that way. I arrived just as Vane ..."

He trailed off.

Stiva nodded. "Dallan is still mourning his brother. They were close. In fact, they had no family left, aside from each other. He's ... moody, but loyal. Listen to what he tells you."

Khirin nodded. Stiva looked again at the sword at his hip. It was finely wrought, of high enough quality to be a proper clansword. The pommel was plain, with no crest or coat of arms.

Outside, the skies grew darker.

He glanced at Lhin, who was curled up in his bed beside the fire. "I see your cat has pulled through. I'm glad of it."

"He's lazy now, and spends most of his time sleeping," Stiva said. "I would advise befriending him, regardless. He's fond of dits, belly rubs, and erlits, when he can catch them. The Black Boot—especially Jarvor and Delis—give him far too many treats, though they deny it." She looked at the cat. "He saved my life once, and he'll do it again, if need be."

"I don't think he's up to much fighting these days," Khirin said.

"I have other defenses as well," Stiva said after a moment.

"No doubt," Khirin agreed. "If you are like most queens, you have a castle filled with men you do not entirely trust, as well as the cats, and likely some piece of jewelry on your person, a ring, perhaps, endowed with a tiny needle and enough gheos poison to kill ten men."

She stared at him, unable to disguise the astonishment in her face. "How did you know of that? Even my maids do not know that."

"The srih all think alike," Khirin told her calmly. "I may assure you, the ring—it *is* the ring, isn't it?—will not save you if an assassin gets that close. Anyone sent against you would be immune to the poison, as you are."

Stiva was completely stunned. "What?"

"When you were a child—" Khirin interrupted himself to lower his body down onto one of her sofas, neglecting to ask permission. The breach of conduct narrowed Stiva's eyes, but she decided to leave him be. "When you were a child," he continued, "you were very sick once, for more than a week, were you not? You retched and sweated and shook. Your body burned with fever, and it felt that all of the ice in the world could not cool you. Your head felt swollen. And your stomach felt as though you had eaten razor blades."

Stiva froze. "How did you know?"

"Those are the symptoms of gheos poison. Most of the time, death strikes before the symptoms. Gheos is still the poison of choice among the srih. I suppose the fact that the poison comes from Shadrian butterflies has a romantic touch. I wouldn't be surprised if there was a butterfly on the ring. Such ornaments are not exclusive to Aris, believe me. Before whoever it was that gave you that ring did so, they had to be certain you wouldn't accidentally commit suicide. And so they poisoned you, tiny doses at a time. The first bout would have been pure hell. After that, each time they gave you more, but your body had developed a resistance. You withstood it. Other episodes would have been similar, but each would have been progressively shorter and milder. A few days, then a few hours, then a few minutes of pain. After a time, you would have only felt a twitch and slight nausea."

"We were seven." Stiva stared at him incredulously. "They *poisoned* us?"

Khirin nodded. "Chandris too, I would imagine. I'm surprised you didn't know."

We could have died, Stiva thought. Then she realized that Lara, not Cronn, had orchestrated it. The gheos poison only came from the mushroom forests of Shadri. A third thought crossed her mind. Maren and Shira had both been born by then. The twins were no longer the only heirs.

Aris was known for calculated risks.

Honor. Courage. Serenity.

Stiva fought for composure. The battle was easier than it once had been: her face and voice were calm when she spoke. "Speaking of Shadri," she said. "Representatives of Taibon, the crown prince, will be arriving soon, to parlay terms of a marriage with my sister. Part of your duty will consist of making sure they, too, are protected."

Khirin nodded. "Of course, *saya*."

It was then she saw the amulet around his neck. "You are Sijhani," she said quietly, when he said nothing more. "You worship the Mother, rather than the sword."

"I worship the sword," he replied, his voice husky with recent excursion. "I have spent time with the Sijhani. Enough to learn their ways, and respect them. But I live by the sword, in the world the Mother created. "

"This world is not our mother," Stiva said darkly, "and she knows it."

She went back to the window, to stare again at the sea. The skies were darkening quickly, and the leaves bent in a sudden wind, showing silvery undersides. In the distance, the flicker of the green flames dimmed as wind met fire. "The Selin don't take kindly to strangers in their midst. These men grew up together, Khirin. They suffered through years of training. That bond is going to be hard for an outsider to infiltrate. They will never accept you, unless and until you become one of them." She hesitated. "I will let you leave, if you want. If you change your mind, I would understand."

"No." The steel in his tone surprised her, as did the suddenly determined look on his face. "I'm no coward. I don't run from enemies. Why should I flee from men who are supposed to be my allies?"

"If you are familiar with the srih," Stiva told him, "you know how secure their alliances are. I don't think your time will be wasted. Aris is a violent world. Already two poison tasters have died since Chandris and I were crowned. Many of my ancestors were killed by assassins."

My own father was probably poisoned, though the healers said it was his heart.

The words never left her lips as such; they were only a faint breath, sent out into the sea wind.

She gave him a direct look. "I want to be certain you understand this. You are not my jailer. If ever you try to prevent me from coming and going as I please, I myself will have you killed or exiled. Maybe some of the other queens you speak of prefer to be coddled and kept safe, like porcelain dolls. I am not one such."

He looked almost amused. "You are a queen," Khirin said flatly. "I had rather imagined that you would do what you like. I have never yet heard of a queen in chains, nor one who didn't sneak lovers into her chambers in the dark hours."

Stiva could have spent an hour telling him about queens who had very much found themselves in chains, but she wasn't inclined to revisit the old Reonih ballads at the moment. She looked out the window again. "This crown is a chain," she heard herself saying. Bitterness, long oppressed, rose into her words. "And if ever again I should love a man, I would send him away, to save his life."

A few raindrops fell through the sky outside.

"Tell me what you know of the state of things here," Stiva said. "Tell me what you know of the troubles that burden us."

"There is no shortage of them. There is Delora. Itacha is relentless in his raiding. There is the matter of the lords holding the border. There is Barls. There is Trian. There are the mercenaries in the mountains. Plague." He hesitated. "There are rumors of internal trouble."

"Aris loves to talk," Stiva said quietly. "By supper, they will be whispering about you in the taverns. By dawn, they may very well be plotting your death."

He met her gaze, but said nothing.

"I understand you won entrance in the arena."

Khirin nodded, his jaw tight.

"I saw you kill that day in the wood," she said finally. "I've no doubt of your skill. But I am taking a chance on you. You had your opportunity. You could have killed Chandris and me both, had you wanted that. You did not. By that, we trust you. But only Chandris and I saw you. *They* did not. And nor will I sing your praises. That would only insult them. You may well die, proving yourself to them. You may be formidable, but you are, I trust, human. Mortal."

"As far as I know," Khirin said dryly.

"If you need council," she said. "Go to Lyle, Kele, or Aret. They can advise—"

He interrupted her, which made her eyes widen. "If I am to take command," he said, "it must be command. I will take orders, but I refuse to have to run to him—or you—for every decision I make." Khirin looked her square in the eye. "If my job here is to protect you, I answer to you first, and Lyle second."

"As you will." Stiva raised an eyebrow. "Personally, I don't think you can hold the Black Boot in line. These men earned their positions. They will not take kindly to being placed under the command of an outsider. You will be challenged. You may very well be challenged within an inch of your life. When it happens, don't come to me. I will not bend one syllable of one rule for your convenience. And I will not lift a finger to help you. If you can't live up to standard, you're on your own. Neither I nor Chandris will tolerate less than excellence, from you or from any other captain."

The skies opened then, and the rains came down, cloaking the world beyond in a silver veil of water.

She turned away, looking once more out the window. "You are dismissed."

He bowed deeply and left. It was only after he was gone that she realized he had greeted her not as a Selin, but as a srih.

CHAPTER 17

The Hall of Ancestors was dark, even on the brightest days. Oily torches cast shadows on the stone walls, which were hung with the likenesses of the twins' forebears, the kings and queens that had haunted and ruled the ages of the past. The twins' own portraits had been added recently to the collection of paintings that decorated the stone walls.

Hard faces and cold, sharp eyes, captured in oil and dye, stared into the shadows. The ancient weapons that hung on the wall seemed to glow, as though an inner light radiated from them. It took very little imagination to see the shades of their bearers in the shadows, a long line of vanished warriors and dead kings. It took little imagination to picture the souls those weapons had drank, and—if certain myths were to be believed—entrapped within cold steel.

Stiva told Jarvor and Timthe to stay at the end of the hall, where two Gold Braid members stood guard. She continued on alone, but paused beside Cronn's sword, studying it. She had not thought of her father in some time. The pang of sudden grief that coursed through her was unexpected and poignant.

Across the hall, winged Zhur danced on thick canvases, drawn in ochres and violet and greys. Skyborne crossed pale, cloudswept moons. A form danced in fire, commanding flames. A shadowy figure twisted in dark seas, beneath churning froth. A glance at the painting of the Skyborne was all it took for the dreams to surface again in her consciousness, for the damp air to seem suddenly colder, and the whispers and stares of half-imagined ghosts to grow stronger, more insistent. The Zhurlord in the painting seemed to pulse with life. Ink-black eyes stared at her with the rage of a broken god.

Somewhere far off, the trailing sound of a lyre faded into silence.

Chandris stood before the small shrine at the far wall, contemplating either the elaborately carved resin shrine, the oil lamp that burned there, or the portrait of Rtheric that hung above it.

He did not turn at Stiva's approach, no doubt recognizing the sound of her footsteps. His voice was quiet, a calm that set her nerves on edge. "I sent for you nearly an hour ago."

"It takes the pages an hour to reach me, with all these people in the halls."

They were of a height, walking past the likenesses of their ancestors. They were of a gait, matching their steps effortlessly. They had both chosen to wear green that day, both requested stuffed eggs and gerfruit for breakfast. Yet, though they stood side by side and walked side by side, they were worlds apart.

Chandris studied the weapons on the walls, the swords and battleaxes and maces that had brought down warrior kings. "These swords," he asked her quietly, "these weapons. What do they mean to you?"

Black wings against a pale moon.

Stiva's voice was a whisper. "Death."

"Is that all you see in everything? Death?"

Stiva shook her head, banishing the ghosts and dreams away, and continued on. "What do you see?"

She knew the answer even before he spoke it.

"Power."

An erlit dove in front of them, its scales burnished crimson and gold by firelight.

"I can feel them, in here," Chandris said. "In this hall. I feel their blood in our veins, their battlefire, their determination."

When Stiva offered no comment, he moved a few paces, staring intently at one of the paintings.

"He is my favorite, I think." Chandris pointed at the image of a long-dead king. "Thris. I've always admired the way he fought the odds. A younger son, sickly, never expected to survive childhood, much less rule.

But he defied the srih, defied everyone's expectations, and even defeated Hector."

"He went mad, in the end," Stiva said darkly.

An erlit screamed down the hall, as though in agreement.

They passed Cronn and Lara's portraits, and stood there silently a moment, paying respect to their parents. Cronn and Lara seemed to be glaring at their eldest children.

The shared moment ended by unspoken agreement. The twins moved on in unison, their steps perfectly matched.

"Which do you favor?" Chandris asked, still looking at the paintings. "Stoic Karn? The mighty Glen? Or the shrewdly clever Xavier?" He paused, contemplating the face of a dead king. "Perhaps the tragic tale of poor, romantic Niko and his mad wife has a special place in your heart." He paused, then continued thoughtfully. "Then again, knowing you, your favorite probably isn't even on this wall. Yours is probably carved into Shadri's godtree."

"My favorite was Mother," Stiva said darkly. "You know that."

They stopped before a sword that had once belonged to Caro. Stiva looked at her twin, taking in the lines on his face, the sharp angle of his limbs. "You look thin, Chandris. I've hardly seen you lately."

"I've been spending most of my time with the council and the generals." He rubbed his eyes, as though she had reminded him of his weariness. "Making plans."

Something in his tone chilled Stiva. She took a step back involuntarily. Studied him, and found a stranger standing there before her, a stranger whose eyes burned with a cold, hard determination. "Plans for what?"

He ignored the question, pointing instead to a painting of a cave on a sandy beach. "Riders' Point," he said. "Remember when we went there, that summer? With Kele and Talia, Aret and Mykhal? I'm going to visit it again this year, I think."

Stiva found herself quickly growing impatient with the delays. "What do you want, Chandris? Why did you call me here?"

"A few moments of your time," he said. "And your support."

"Support?" Stiva stared at him. "What do you mean?"

He looked her straight in the eye. "I'm ending the Reonih tithes," Chandris said flatly. "I didn't tell you because, frankly, I knew you'd argue. It's done, Stiva. There is nothing you can do to stop it."

At first, she thought he was joking, or that she had heard him wrong. Stiva froze, her heart pounding in her chest. "Ending the … ending the tithes? Chandris, you can't be serious. The Reonih live on those funds."

"I assure you," Chandris said flatly, "I'm quite serious. The Reonih are a drain on resources we need elsewhere. The money we give them needs to be put into the army and roads and the economy in general. The harvest, as you know, was poor this year. The plague is a further strain. We've lost thousands of heads of cattle. We will have to buy and trade for food even to survive the winter. Our coronation wasn't cheap, Stiva. Nor is feeding our new archers' division. Aris' treasury is not drained, but if we continue as we are, it will be. And we've Shira's wedding to plan for."

Stiva felt dizzy.

"It has to come from somewhere else," he continued. "We cannot afford the tithes any longer. So I won't pay them. It's that simple. I refuse to watch my people starve while the Reonih line their pockets. So I'm ending the tithes."

Just like that. Only, Stiva reckoned, he had ended a fair bit more than that. He had ended an ancient tradition, one that stretched back to Aris' first king.

Stiva regarded her twin, eyes narrowed. "Chandris, the Reonih are bound to us by every tradition we hold. Kings have always tithed the Reonih. You speak of casting off a tradition that is as old as Aris itself. Do you think to survive a war with no healers? Do you think to deal yourself with the magics in the forests, with the gods? Do you think to tell the srih yourself when to plant and when to sow, and which herbs to take for what illness? How do you mean to uphold the law when there is no one to speak it? Have you gone insane?"

The rage she had seen in him a moment before cooled somewhat, and he regarded her calmly. That was Chandris, volatile, explosive, erratic in his moods. But he was salient, somehow, in his madness: his voice, when he spoke again, was placid. "Quite the opposite, dear twin. I have gone sane, sane enough and strong enough to see through the web of lies and influence they weave."

Stiva stared at her twin, shocked. "How can you say that? They are our people, Chandris. You've just cast them into poverty."

"Hardly." Chandris shook his head. "The people will pay them out of pocket. They will give what they want to give, what they can afford to give, instead of being forced to hand over more than they can spare. And they've lands they can clear and cultivate. We'll have woodsmen in the forests, soon, chopping down trees. They can plant in the cleared areas, just as our ancestors did."

Stiva just stared at him. "And what if the people side with them?"

"I *hope* the people side with them. As I said, they'll be paying for their services. I told you there would be changes," Chandris said. "We just added several hundred Selin and an entire archers' division. We need to feed them and arm them. Who will pay for that? The commoners? Serfs?" He shook his head. "They give enough. I won't bleed them dry."

Stiva looked up at the wall, at a recent portrait of herself and her twin.

The similarities in their looks were striking. The differences between them threatened to swallow a world.

They stared at each other a moment, only a few feet apart, yet separated by a huge yawning abyss that threatened to swallow their world. "You punish them all for one man's betrayal. Cerrow's betrayal does not speak for all of them."

"Nor did he act alone." Chandris rubbed his eyes. "This isn't about Cerrow, Stiva. It isn't about Kira, or Mohr, or Reide, or Tehran. Aursa is a patchwork of kingdoms steeped in war. I'm trying to make something better." When she opened her mouth to protest, he held up a hand, silencing her. "It's decided. The new dictates will be posted at Lightfest."

An erlit dove from the rafters and flew over the twins, disappearing into the shadows with a raucous shriek. The Hall of Ancestors was hopelessly infested.

"It's not a death sentence," Chandris said. "They are our people too, as you said. I don't deny that. I'm not persecuting them. I'm not making these changes without overseeing the transitions. I'm not exiling them, or throwing them in prison. I simply refuse to give them another drop of wine, or another kernel of grain for free. I'm just changing the way things are done. They just need to earn their keep, like everyone else. They will survive," he said shortly. His voice twisted in sarcasm. "They have the favor of the gods, remember?"

Listen to the whisper, not the roar.

"There will be some appointed posts, which will be paid positions, but the days of free handouts are over. I am tired of seeing Aris' citizens labor for nothing while the Reonih sit on logs and talk about the clouds and the stars all day, yet never have an empty table come sunset or a bare foot come the dark season."

Stiva stared at her twin, hoping beyond hope that he would burst into laughter at any moment and tell her it was only a prank. "You speak as though their knowledge is worthless. They are healers, historians, judges, teachers. What are we without them? Their knowledge alone—"

"Exactly," Chandris said. "*Their* knowledge. That magic is ours by right. They hoard that knowledge. They know the magics of the Elders. Or their science, if you prefer. They *know*. They kept that wisdom, even through the shadow time. And they keep us in the dark."

She did not know, later, looking back on the moment, whether it was his voice or his eyes that warned her, or something more ethereal. "This is about more than the tithes," she said. "You want the Relics."

His eyes went back to the portraits. "Some of them," he said, gesturing at the likenesses of their ancestors, "were buried with Relics."

Stiva paled. "You wouldn't—"

"Enter the House of the Dead?" Her twin tore his gaze from the oiled pictures of ghosts and met her eyes with a gold-green stare. "Respectfully, but yes, I would. While we fought plagues and lost the technology that got us across the stars, the Reonih were secreting our legacy into tombs and caverns. Our people *crossed space*, Stiva. The Reonih no longer get to hold those abilities from us."

It was a long time before Stiva found her voice. "What do you think will happen if you anger the Reonih?"

"What do *you* think will happen?" Chandris turned her words against her, a trace of mockery in his tone. "Do you think everything will burn? Do you think the skies will hold still? Will the seas turn to fire?"

The visions struck her again.

Black wings, rocky cliffs, blood on stone.

"Delora has crossed our borders one time too many," Chandris said calmly. "The outlaws have taken one coach too many. The barbarians have burned one village too many. The people have had to burn one bull too many."

"You can't change a centuries-old tradition on a whim. The people will never stand for it. You ... you just can't do that to them."

He whirled on her in a sudden fury, anger flashing hot in his eyes. "Tell me once more what I can and cannot do, and I will—"

"What?" Stiva answered with a rage to match his own. "What will you do, Chandris? Lock me up, silence me, send me away? There are those who will remember it if you do."

Chandris looked at her coldly. "And there are those who would thank me for it."

He would not mention Barls by name, but it was clear enough who he spoke of.

Stiva stared at him. It was a moment before she found her voice again. "You cannot change the world alone, Chandris," she told him, "however much you want to."

Chandris looked at her, and then away. "And you cannot keep it from changing." He pointed at one of the portraits on the wall. "Xerier. Do you remember the quote he is most famous for?"

Stiva swallowed. "Every season comes from another season's end."

"Their time is past," Chandris continued quietly. "They held that heritage for us, but it is time we took it back. Do not mistake me, Stiva. I wish them no harm, and I have no desire to fight them. I agree that their knowledge and their services are important, and I intend to pay them for those I consider truly necessary. But they wield too far much power and too much influence in court. Kings are meant to rule. Not priests."

"You're wrong," Stiva whispered. "The Reonih are more than just priests. They hold forces at bay. Chandris, there are things out there that do not bow to swords or titles. The Reonih stand between us and them."

"Chandris, listen to me," Stiva said. "You are breaking an alliance that stretches back to the shadow time. The Reonih guard the science carefully; you are right about that. Maybe they don't even have all of it. Maybe each tribe only has a little bit. But they do hold it, and they hold it for a reason. It's deadly. It destroyed our homeworld. Or did you forget why the Elders came here in the first place?"

Chandris tilted his head. "You know more than you should, for one who was never meant to wear the robes."

"Not so much." Stiva shook her head. "I only know the songs. But they know, and they keep that power silent for a reason. That's all I'm saying. And what if they decide to launch their own war? Did you think of that?"

He looked at her, tilting his head slightly. His next words chilled her. "Then we go to war."

"They have the Relics, Chandris," Stiva said quietly. "And they know how to use them. I don't want to watch you goad them into turning on us. Those weapons ruined our ancestors' home world, and nearly destroyed this one. Aris could not survive that. We cannot stand against that power if they unleash it on you. They would destroy us. They do have that capability, even if you refuse to see it."

"I see corruption," Chandris said flatly. "Secrecy. Deception."

"Ah. Here we go; the Zhur. You are as clay in their hands, Stiva." Chandris leveled a critical look at her, as though he were chastising a child. "You dream of them, I know, for I share those dreams. But that is all they are: dreams, memories at best, nothing more than illusions. The Zhur are gone from this world, if ever they were here at all. The Sijhani have taken their gods back."

Stiva looked at him evenly. "Then whose dreams smashed the old cities into ruins?"

Chandris looked at her coldly, then turned and walked away.

CHAPTER 18

The voice would not stop. Neither did the blows; they rained down on the boy's starving flesh like stars falling from the sky, each one donating a fresh burst of blinding hot pain. But, despite the agony they caused, the shocks were not what truly tormented him.

It was the voice, and everything about it—its words, its tone, its owner—that tortured the skinny, ragged boy.

Another strike brought a fresh wave of pain, and his near-skeletal body churned with nausea. Another blow. The world was silent around them, utterly still … except for the voice.

"What are you, a worm or a maggot?"

More blows, each harsher than the last. More pain, a rising wave that brought a flood tide of agony behind it. More insults.

More.

A bird screamed in the sky, the raptor voicing the boy's unsung shrieks for him. He would not cry out, not now, not ever. Even if it killed him, he refused to let them hear him scream. He tried to use the trick his Reonih mother had taught him, the one about inhaling deeply and letting his breath fill with the pain so he could then push it out of his body as he exhaled, but the blows and the insults were coming too hard and too fast for him to be able to concentrate. After a moment, he gave up and retreated deep within himself.

Another blow. The voice continued, aiming insults and curses and embarrassment at him alongside the cane. He allowed himself a single tear.

Starbursts of pain colored his vision.

The voice continued. Blows fell, searing his skin like burning coals.

The boy gritted his teeth.

The world turned red around him.

Still the voices continued.

Another voice joined it, one that echoed from somewhere deep inside his flesh, from his past, from a time and a place and a world he had never been able to forget, no matter how hard he tried. A place where he had never gone hungry or been beaten, never been forced to the point of exhaustion and beyond, never woken blue and shivering from the cold.

He knew at once that this voice had come from, that dream-wrapped, golden world. The second voice called out from within him, from the innermost cells of his very being, where, he realized suddenly, it had always resided. Aye, it had always been with him, hidden and waiting, silent all these years.

Something awoke within him, even as the cane struck his back again. Something stronger than the cane that was battering his back. Something ancient.

The boy refused to hear the other voice any longer. He let the words fall on him like rain, dropping away from his flesh like water. He could bear blows, and still bear honor. Insults. That was a different story. So he refused to accept them.

It was that simple.

Another blow. He gritted his teeth now, welcoming the pain that made him whole. Eventually the beating stopped, as though the whipmaster had realized the blows were no longer having much effect. And still the boy did not look at him, nor at his comrades, who stood in a perfect circle around him, watching silently, the only visible link in the chain that bound him to this wonderful, wretched place. He did not know the whipmaster's name. The voice was enough. He knew every detail of the face attached to it, and that was enough. Somewhere inside himself, he promised the second voice vengeance, though he knew that to give it would be dishonorable.

Silence hung thick in the air.

It took the boy a moment to realize that it was over, that he had survived the punishment. He gave himself a moment of blessed rest, and then struggled to his feet. His limbs shook and throbbed in protest, yet he made himself stand up and straighten his screaming legs into a warrior's stance, forcing his tortured flesh to obey his will.

The world spun and dipped crazily for a moment, and he shut his eyes for a moment, until it settled. Until he had control over his pain-wracked body. Until the second voice drowned out the memory of the first, and stopped it from ringing in his ears.

Honor. Courage. Serenity.

Then he looked his hero, who stood watching silently, in the eyes.

"We will eat vodrik, tonight," he said grimly. "Or the vodrik will eat me."

Lyle said nothing, but his brow creased, and he studied the boy a bit more closely for a moment, contemplative. A faint flash of recognition crossed his eyes. He was seeing the very thing he had served his entire life. A House that had set the world on fire.

Ally, the inner voice said, *but not one to take for granted. He will not serve or save a fool, and he would spare you no pain, but he would die for you.*

Gazes locked, and old warrior and young stared at one another. They were bound by blood, though they were not true kin.

After a moment, Lyle gave a brief nod. "Go, then," he said. "We shall see whether the wolves sing victory or sorrow to the moons tonight. I have to get back to the castle, but I'm expecting a report in the morning."

Maren did not look at any of them, but hunched his shoulders and stuck out his lower lip, then walked with shaky but determined steps away from the circle. Away from the boys he had not been able to feed. That failure would scar more deeply than the wounds bleeding down his back. He was determined to override it. Slow, painful steps led him back towards the forest and the vodrik he had not killed.

The other voice stayed with him, echoing its ancient mantra.

The vodrik met him in its own time. He did not seek it, other than to track it into its territory, marking his presence with urine, as the vodrik had. Normally, this might drive the vodrik away from the scent of humans, but he knew, somehow, that this vodrik would understand his challenge, and rise to it.

He waited, denying himself the warmth and comfort of a fire. The moons rose as the night grew colder and longer, and finally, the chilling, lupine song filled the air.

Maren rose to his feet and howled.

That was when the vodrik came.

It approached him from the front, not troubling itself with stealth. It padded into a shaft of velvet moonlight and paused to exchange a long stare with its rival. While feral yellow eyes met determined green, the air was still and electric around them. Maren felt himself grow dizzy, as though his consciousness was expanding. He heard his ancestors' voices in the wind, and his mind felt the thoughts of the thousand generations that had lived and walked and bled and died on this soil. And the vodrik looked back at him with the eyes of the natives and the Reonih and the animals who had lost their lands to the invaders that had fallen from the sky centuries ago.

The song of the pack, ancient and mystic, filled the air once more.

The vodrik launched himself through the air, closing the distance between them with one huge leap. There was no more world, after that, no forest, no trees, no wind … only silver fur and yellow eyes and fangs and claws that sought to tear his flesh. He had fully intended to stab the vodrik, but instead his blade fell forgotten to the ground. He would fight fair.

A gash opened, that crossed face and neck and shoulder in one swipe. They rolled onto the ground, in a timeless dance of battle. Maren bled onto the vodrik, and felt his mind melt into the animal's. They became one, one mad, determined creature warring with itself.

In the end, he stuck his thumbs into the eyes and burst them, and felt the wisdom within them turn into jelly on his hands. The vodrik wept blood, and stopped moving altogether. It looked up at Maren with sightless eyes, waiting.

He slit its throat, and his arm, letting his blood mingle with the vodrik's as it poured into the ground. He did not weep, though tears rose to his eyes.

There were three castes of Selin were waiting for him when he returned, sent by Stiva to escort him home for the twins' naming day celebration. But the child they had been sent to retrieve never returned to Aris.

What came back was Selin.

CHAPTER 19

"**M**ohr."

Stiva's voice ventured forth hesitantly, her soft, quiet tone the precise antithesis of the sharp, authoritative voice so often driven from her throat as of late. As Aris' crown had settled onto her head, complete with its own set of rules, the authority, pressure, and responsibility it carried had uncovered a previously unknown range of characteristics in both her and her twin. More and more, she found herself harsh, demanding, and suspicious, wary of enemies, wary of friends. More and more, she found herself struggling to keep her thoughts to herself and her emotions hidden, lest she be read too easily, lest she be mistaken. Family traits she had thought herself innocent of were surfacing in her character as of late, brought bubbling to the surface like scum gathering atop a cool, clear pond.

But here, in a quiet, mystical grove, they fell away from her like the skin from a growing serpent.

The sacred groves of the Reonih were known for intimidation.

It was a place well-deserving of reverence, this quiet, rust-shaded glade, beyond the third thornwall, where deep brown shadows clustered beneath the scaly red trees of a thick, tangled wood. A shadowy world, that forest, for the entwined boughs and blood-colored leaves blocked out the sunlight, even in the brightest hours of the light season. The world beneath the canopy lived in a state of everdusk, drenched in eternal twilight. The ancient trees cast shadows that stretched long fingers into the grove, even by day. A place of sacred power, the glade dreamt of magic. An aura of mystic force radiated from the Aorhan glyphs carved into the stone altar at its center. A sense of power and of timeless immortality permeated the perfect circle of towering ancient rupaliers that ringed the clearing. Nearby, a silver stream twisted through the shadows.

Yet for all its mystic beauty, the grove dreamed of death. Souls clung to the cooler shadows. The branches, though naturally red, were the color of dried blood, and they grew twisted, as though tormented by nature. The leaves whispered and danced, even when there was no breeze to stir them. Birds would not rest there, or even fly often overhead. In fact, animals avoided the spot entirely, warned away by intuition or perhaps, more eerily, by knowledge half-recalled from a former life. For though this place witnessed gentle rites, it also housed the darkest, most powerful ritual practiced by the Reonih, and the only one that involved invoking the Zhur.

Sacrifice.

The blood of thousands had fallen to earth here. Though in recent times the practice had waned, it had not entirely ceased.

Trin had died in such a place.

Now, standing once more in the grove, Stiva felt her lover's presence among the trees and the wind. She shut her eyes, and his face immediately formed on her closed lids. Trin: strong, brave, beautiful … damned. He had given his life, that the gods may favor Aris again. Trin had faced his death with serenity, going almost proudly to his demise. He had, in truth, accepted his own death with more composure and less bitterness than those he left behind shared between the lot of them.

I have been dying since my first breath, he had said to her once, *but I will never be truly dead until you have forgotten me.*

Stiva opened her eyes, and there was only the forest and its denizens, the buzz of insects, and the distant sound of birds. The wood was still, as if frozen in time. A butterfly fluttered into the glade, then danced quickly away.

Shades.

But it was daylight still, and the hidden powers lay sleeping.

In the center of the glade, a robed figure raised his face to the sun.

"Mohr," Stiva said again, more sharply than she had meant.

The high priest stiffened, and the little red dog at his feet barked sharply. Stiva realized that she had not disturbed restive contemplation, but meditation. Shame filled her even as Mohr turned coal-black eyes on her and fixed her with a furious glare. The high priest of the Reonih was accustomed to—and deserving of—greater respect and courtesy than she shown him by intruding here, uninvited, in the most sacred place in all of Aris.

Then again, the queen of Aris was also due more respect than a cold stare.

"I disturbed you," Stiva said simply, clearing her throat. Mentally, she reminded herself that queens did not apologize. Acknowledging the discourtesy was as close as she would venture. "It is early, yet," she added quietly. "I had not expected you to be working."

Mohr did not reply immediately. He rose and slowly stood, power radiating from him as heat did from a fire. The dog at his feet watched her quietly, its eyes pools of mystery.

Stiva felt herself reduced to a child before him.

Queen and sorcerer faced each other silently.

"You are no longer an apprentice bard," Mohr told her, his facial expression unchanged. His voice was naturally deep and resonant. Here, in this place, it seemed the voice of the earth itself rumbled forth from his throat.

The worst of Reonih arrogance usually consisted of a glare or some demoralizing insult. The results of truly offending a Reonih were rarely instantaneous. Theirs was a silent, deadly rage that could take seasons to come to fruition.

"Nor am I merely the daughter of one." Stiva replied evenly, looking him straight in the eye. She, too, was learning to play the game. She, too, was Reonih, able to mince words with the best of them.

Mohr did not so much look at her as he looked through her. "You don't belong here anymore, Stiva," he told her flatly. "Your eyes are filled with his ambition, your head with his words. You should not have come."

The remark angered her, and that anger escaped in her voice. "Are you telling me I no longer have the right to walk the forest without your express invitation?" Stiva raised her chin. "These lands lie within our borders, Mohr, and under our protection. We limit our access out of reverence, but that does not give you the right to tell me where I can and cannot tread."

Mohr chose not to rise to such a fiercely baited question. Instead, he only looked at her coolly. "You do not own this place any more than I do. Though it lies within your borders, it belongs to the gods alone. What lies beyond the thornwall is sacred territory. From now on, you come with an offering for the Seaborne that dwell in these rivers and lakes, lest you offend them."

"Why?" she asked sweetly. "Are the gods hungry, this season?"

Mohr looked at her coldly. "You are not exempt from showing reverence, crown or no crown."

"Am I to take that as an order from the gods themselves?" Stiva felt her temper rising, a tide of rage that matched the fury of the golden king whose likeness she bore. "I earned my right to walk this path, Mohr. You cannot take the Reonih blood from my veins without opening one, and I would not suggest that. You cannot erase the time I spent here. You can resent me for being born in hold instead of hollow, for having one king for a father and another for a twin, for the choices I've made, but you cannot do so without losing your greatest advocate."

"Advocate?" Mohr raised one grey brow, seeming to taste the word.

"Yes, advocate." Stiva clenched her fists, raising her eyes to him defiantly. "Go ahead. Tell me to leave. Tell me I no longer have the right to come here without permission, without invoking the anger of the gods. I will listen. I will go, and never return. I'm not inclined to wasting my voice on deaf ears. Or in defense of them."

She hated herself for saying that, hated him for forcing her to it. Since childhood, she had always looked up to Mohr, almost as though he were a god himself. He had been one of her brightest idols, her mentor, her inspiration.

And now, he had the potential to become her deadliest enemy.

Mohr drew himself up straighter. "Nor am I. I plead your case to the Otherworld. I can only advise you against disrupting the harmony of this place."

"I find it despicable that you see fit to charge me a toll. Especially after all the jewels and silver I have thrown into the rivers this year."

His eyes met hers, stricken. For a moment, she saw emotion flicker there, within the mystic shadows of his gaze. Then it was gone.

"You accuse me of something?"

"Wisdom." Stiva answered flatly. "I accuse you of knowing that the lives of your people depend on the beliefs of the commonwealth. So long as they believe they need the Reonih, you have a hold in Aursa that no king can break. If they lose that belief, their power will crumble. It isn't just Chandris that is beginning to question you. They say the towers are now teaching other methods, and dismissing your ways as antiquated. I don't think you want that, Mohr. I don't want that. I think you would do anything to keep the hardship outside the thornwall. Even invoking sickness and famine. But it is Chandris your anger truly seeks. And you cannot reach him that way. You can poison every well, sicken every cow, every hare, every vru in the land, infest every sprig of edible vegetation, send a hundred plagues … he will be the last to feel it."

"I'm not a god, Stiva," Mohr said. "Plagues happen."

"They do. And the last time this particular plague struck Aris, it happened on the heels of a rift between Caro and the Reonih high priest. Ninian, I believe."

"Nivian." Mohr corrected her in a flat tone.

"Nivian, then. The time before that, there were again tensions between the forest and the crown. I know the ballads, Mohr."

Mohr stared at her, as close to shocked as she had ever seen him. The little dog approached Stiva, sniffing at her feet. The child inside her wanted to scooch down and pet it.

The queen ignored it.

"You do," Mohr said, "But you don't know the weather poems. This plague comes when the winds blow in from the sea. When the rains come too early, and the fogs come in thick, when the grain grows a pale yellow mold."

Stiva just looked at him.

"What do you want here, Stiva?" Mohr asked tiredly.

For the first time in her life, Stiva heard more than passing anger in the tone Mohr directed at her. For once, the hostility was real, and possibly permanent. It hurt her, but that pain settled into the midst of a hard ball of logic that stood before him as queen of Aris. She forced herself to swallow her emotions, remembering why she had come. Her voice was a whisper. "Truth, for one."

"Truth." Mohr seemed to savor the word, tasting it.

"He will not stop," Stiva said, her voice low. "You know that. What neither you nor I know is where the Reonih will fit in when this is over. And that is what I came here for."

Mohr studied her coolly. "I thought you at least understood my position here, Stiva. My time, spent easing your conscience, is wasted. If you wanted a runecast, you should have gone to Mehran."

"Aye, aye. He'll throw bones and read entrails, scatter his runesticks and painted stones … then feed me some vague, jumbled prophecy that makes no sense until the event it foretells is done and over with." Stiva gave an ineffectual wave. "My own Aorhan runesticks could accomplish that much."

"Then you should address the council of elders and ask for a more powerful—"

"I'm not after a scrying, Mohr." Stiva cut him off. "I didn't come here to ask advice. I came to give it."

"About what?" Mohr asked. "The new laws Chandris is going to pass regarding the tithes? Save your breath. We saw the portents a long time ago. A blind child would have seen it."

Stiva allowed herself only a second to be surprised. In truth, she had half-expected that the Reonih would, one way or another, have anticipated Chandris' next move. She swallowed and sought Mohr's eyes, earnest grief in her own gaze.

"A blind child," Stiva asked. "Or a spy? I know you've eyes in the castle."

"You have," Mohr said after a moment, "overlooked something."

She frowned. "What?"

"The Relics." Mohr's gaze fastened on hers. "As you said, he wants them for himself. His obsession is no secret. Soon, he will demand that we turn them over to him. And that, we will not do. I do not want the Zhur hunting here."

"Aye," Stiva said. "You are right. He might demand that. But I am the one standing here."

"And what is it you want for Aris?" Mohr inquired, a more gentle tone invading his voice. "For yourself?"

Silence. It was more than a rhetorical question. She was shocked to realize that the only answer that immediately came to mind was escape.

Slowly she raised her eyes to his face. "The same thing he does," she said quietly. "Peace. Prosperity. An end to this eternal warfare, to poverty and disease and the troubles we face. Our visions for Aris are identical. It is the methods we disagree on."

"You respect your Reonih heritage," he said finally. "He disregards it entirely."

Stiva shook her head, frustrated. "It is only that he questions the relationship between the Reonih and the srih. He has raised some valid points, which I cannot easily dismiss."

Mohr raised a thin brow. "Such as?"

Stiva sighed. "We support you entirely. We give you the best of our herds. We give you our wealth, that you may throw it into rivers. Some of our people are starving now. Your torque"—she pointed at his neck—"could feed ten families for a year. The food and riches we give you could save too many lives for us not to question the necessity. You guard our knowledge. I do not question the value of that. Neither does he. But it has become, in the basest terms, a battle between two needs: the need to sustain the Reonih versus the need to sustain the people. Wisdom is valuable. But so are other skills, other gifts. We do not expect our people to toil for free. We do not expect you to, either. But what use is wisdom to the dead?"

She saw resignation in his eyes. Pride. Pain. And a determination that all of her words would slip off like water against stone.

"And yet ignorance," he said, "sometimes serves the living."

"Where is Cerrow?" Stiva asked.

Mohr shook his head. "Fled," he said. "Near or far, I do not know. Your men haven't found him. My men haven't found him. Nor will they. He was a hunter before he became Reonih. He learned the Sijhani ways of evading trackers. He could be five feet from us, and we wouldn't see him unless we wanted him to."

"And if you did?" Stiva asked.

"I cannot pretend he has no allies," Mohr said. "Nevertheless, they, too, remain silent. He is likely gone, by now. But he betrayed us that day, as well as you."

"Likely," Stiva said. Her voice was cold and flat. "And not without help."

Mohr stared at her for a second and then he softened. "Oh, my dear, Stiva, how you have changed." He sighed. "Forgive me. I was struck by the image of you as a child, when you used to shed your clothes and wrap yourself in vines, hoping to catch a glimpse of one of the fey."

"I have seen them, you know," Stiva said quietly. "The Zhur. I dream of the Skyborne every night."

Mohr froze. "What?"

"Does that surprise you?" Stiva tilted her head, squinting against the setting sun. "You forget, Mohr, that half of me is Reonih."

"Half of you," Mohr said seriously. "When you are here, you must fight off the other half. When you are in Aris, you must suppress your Reonih traits. And yet half of you walks around in a man's form. You will never be whole, Stiva. No matter what you decide, you will always be torn. In your position, that will destroy Aris long before any plague."

She felt tears welling, but fought them back. As she must.

"Stiva," Mohr said, more gently. "You cannot stop what is meant to be. Everything ends. Things are changing. The world spins faster and faster through the abyss. There is nothing you can do to stop that, but you can guide things, at least somewhat more than the rest of us."

Stiva looked down at the ground, torn between anger and despair. "Mohr, since Chandris returned, I have never stood against him. On anything. I gave him my word that I would not cause division, and I stand by that vow. I have not always agreed with his decisions, but I have supported them, regardless. He speaks to me of what he wants for Aris, and I believe in that dream. It is his methods that frighten me."

"I have seen men break power, and I have seen power break men," Mohr said. "With women, the boundaries are a bit more fragile. You are much more easily read than Chandris. You show insecurity, when you look to others to guide you. You may either be a servant to your throne, or you can make the throne your servant. It's up to you."

She paused, contemplating his words. The little dog curled into a ball at his feet.

Mohr's voice crossed over her like smoke in the wind. "People are going to die no matter what you do, Stiva." His eyes were intense as he turned towards her. "More will die if you don't make a stand now and make it clear whose side you're on. Every time you and Chandris have an argument, there are heads turning, whispers behind hands and bladed fans. No one is certain of your loyalties on this matter. Not even Chandris. You asked a moment ago what use wisdom is to the dead. How useful is ignorance, to the living?"

"I've seen what you hold. Chandris is right about one thing: you do hoard knowledge. I know you have devices that store knowledge. I've seen the crystals and the boxes. I've heard the songs recorded before the passage."

Mohr stiffened. "You are right, in saying we guard knowledge. More accurately, we preserve it. To let it fall into the wrong hands would be disastrous. And to let it slip away would be an abomination."

"Aye." Stiva nodded. "I agree with that. And perhaps your value as historians alone is worth a thousand times the blood and silver we have given you. Without the bards, the sagas and stories and even the names of our former kings and queens may have been forgotten long ago."

"Precisely. Our worth is clearly visible," Mohr said, "when you look at the ruins of Elder society, the great steel obelisks of their day, or the crumbled foundations of ancient cities. Their tales are silent. Their knowledge faded. Only the soul is eternal. Only ruins and ballads survives such a clash. Only the stars remember what we have been. And only the moons know what we will be."

"I'm not overly concerned about my next life right now, Mohr." Stiva frowned. "It's this one I'm worried about. My decisions are not the simple choices I grew up facing; what dress to wear, what wine to drink, who to dance with. My choices affect thousands of lives. I believe balance must be found on this world, before it can be maintained with the next. How can we achieve equilibrium with the Otherworld, when we cannot even keep our borders stable?"

"You speak of stability," he told her, "and yet you stir dissent."

"I want nothing but peace and prosperity for Aris. So does he."

"Peace," Mohr said, "may not be in human nature, Stiva. It is certainly not in Chandris'."

"The last thing he wants to do is shed Reonih blood," Stiva said.

"But he will not hesitate if he sees it as necessary for what he wants." Mohr finished her sentence for her. "Do you really think he can accomplish that? Can you seriously tell me you've never worried that he will destroy Aris in the attempt to elevate it?"

"Do you think we're in a strong position? Meager harvests, plague, and debilitating raids have taken their toll on our resources. Foreign traders are taking advantage of Aris' needs, and raising their prices. Theft is on the rise. Stolen wares, often as not, turn up in the marketplace at two or three times their original cost. There is talk of dissent among the march lords. There is talk of dissent among the people. And yet the Reonih remain unaffected."

"Stiva—"

She cut him off, angry. "I came here to tell you," Stiva said, "that I will do what I can to make this transition easy and slow. We won't let you starve. We won't let you freeze."

"But you will not tithe us our rightful shares."

"Chandris is right about one thing," Stiva said. "We need the archers. Else we may all burn."

"And what will be left? A soulless society?"

A crow screamed in the sky.

"It isn't my opinion you should worry about, Stiva. Do you think your people will stand for it?"

"They will do as they are commanded," Stiva said coldly.

"The wheel is turning for all of us, Stiva. There is nothing you can do to stop that. But you can guide things, at least somewhat more than the rest of us. The Reonih will stand with you, if you stand with us."

Mohr walked to her and pressed something into her hand. The little red dog followed, underfoot as always, then tugged at his robes, wanting to play.

"I will tell you this," Mohr said. "We do not keep the Relics from you out of selfishness. There are songs you don't know, Stiva. Songs about what happened on Denebola. This technology, it can save lives. But it can cost lives. This world, she is our mother now. Every cell in your body, every thread on your back, every piece of art and furniture you own, comes from her. The methods used to get the materials for these things, they poison planets. Denebola was not the first. At first, there is prosperity and wealth. The sick are healed, the hungry are fed. Diseases are eradicated. Lives are saved. But then, do you know what happens, Stiva? The world becomes overpopulated. It is sucked dry of life. It becomes a toxic desert, incapable of supporting life. And in the end, clear rivers and bountiful lands become a poisoned, lifeless waste. Millions die. Everyone and everything will die. Men become cannibals. The carrion eaters are the only survivors of such a world. That is what happened on Denebola, and on the world before it, and the world before that. That is we guard against. That is why the Zhur fought. What Chandris thinks is the key to prosperity is only a pretty road to oblivion. It may take one generation, or twenty. It matters not. The endgame is the same."

"You can stop this, Stiva." Mohr whispered. "You can save Aris from throwing away its heritage." Mohr tilted his head, studying her. "Certainly it has at least crossed your mind that if you chose to usurp him, you would have the support of the Reonih, and that of a good number of the srih."

His eyes bored into hers, asking a silent question.

A soul-ripping choice.

"I know what you are asking, Mohr," Stiva said quietly. "You want me to stand against him."

"Rivers of blood," Mohr said, "Fire raging over the land. Death in the fields. And still, he looks to divide us, when we should be unified. He sows discord, not strength."

"And you tell me you do not want war? That would divide Aris far more quickly than a change in tithes."

"Perhaps." Mohr said. "Perhaps it would bring unity."

Stiva looked around the grove. Golden sunlight, crimson leaves.

Sedition, slipping through the shadows.

"Lightfest is some moons off. There is still time," Mohr said. "Time to think. Time to convince him." His pale eyes met hers. "Time to choose."

Stiva turned to him, sunlight glittering in her eyes. "Your way through this is simple and clear. Stop throwing silver into rivers, and buy some food instead."

Mohr looked at her calmly, his eyes seeming to hold the secrets of sun and stars. He bowed deeply. "My queen."

Stiva turned to leave. Passing by the stream, she hesitated, staring into the clear rushing waters.

And she pulled a silver button from her dress, and tossed it into the waters before leaving.

CHAPTER 20

Khirin moved silently through the castle complex, gliding expertly through the currents of servants, Selin, and srih that flowed like a river through Aris' halls. The srih and servants slid duteously out of his way more often than not. Selin were not so courteous; they moved aside only grudgingly, their eyes cold and hard upon him as he passed. A few even went so far as to purposely collide with him. More than once, he heard his name in the air as he passed. He stayed his hand, letting the whispers drift unchallenged, even though the taunts reawakened the black, consuming rage two grueling hours of vigorous exercise had only partially tamed.

Many of the snickers subsided into silence when he looked at those causing them. Most thought twice about carelessly toying with him. It was no secret where their hesitation came from. It was reverence for the badge he wore over his heart. The twins' insignia.

Not that it had done him much good the night before.

A few hours past, he had slept, falling exhausted onto a thin pallet at the midnight of a long, trying day of training and duty. He did not mind exhaustion. It warded away the dreams that otherwise burrowed into his mind, the nightvisions that haunted his sleep, often leaving a bitter aftertaste on his waking thoughts. Once, he had dreamt of a cold, shadowy keep in Kralin, or a marbled ruin in Orake. Cassandra, laughing and golden, a bloody knife in her hand. His dreams had lately taken on a different aspect, of wings and mists and cloud-wrapped moons.

Somewhere between the numbing touch of sleep's oblivion and the first pale wisps of dawn, he had stirred, either restless in his sleep or warned by instinct that did not sleep, ever. He had opened his eyes just in time to catch the flash of moonlight dancing along the edge of a blade. A silent shadowy figure drew near as he slumbered, hoping to slit his throat. Sheer reflex had saved him; his body had reacted even as his mind still fought to shake off the fogginess of slumber.

The Black Boot numbered one fewer this morning. That was exactly what they had intended, but the one missing from their ranks was not the one they had meant.

Dawn had seen a small but solemn procession headed out the Crimson Gate, bearing west. Twenty Selin in full dress headed for the forest, half of them sharing the weight of a single object. A shield, matching their own. The shrouded figure that lay motionless atop it should have been burned, his ashes buried in the Selin crypts surrounding the House of the Dead. But it was northward they went, to Reonih land. It was they who must deal with Keorl now.

Keorl had not died on patrol or even on duty. An officer had killed one of his men. This was not an everyday occurrence, even—especially— among the Selin. Word had spread with the change of the guard, and as yawning grooms swept aisles and the bakers and laundresses set to work, a strange silence settled over Aris. Not the calm, everyday quiet of peace.

The calm before the storm.

Dawn had watched a silent figure slipping out to a forgotten garden tucked within the maze of walls and towers, and then working through the exhausting forms of the ancient martial art of Yu'Thurina. The garden, forlorn as it was, was private and secluded, overgrown enough to feel wild, as though the forest had reclaimed this one tiny spot in the castle. The garden did not judge. He had tried to purge his body of emotion with sweat and deadly precision, until his muscles and bones throbbed in protest and his flesh screamed with the strain. But the calmness he sought did not come. And now, as he strode through the complex, with its labyrinthine halls and labyrinthine intrigues, he wondered if he had been a fool after all, to think he could ever be Selin.

His skills, he did not doubt. The bitterness, the ache he refused to acknowledge, was simple envy, for the brotherhood he knew he would never share. The thing that kept him going, the memory seared into his thoughts: his father's corpse, bloody and defiled.

Dawn had watched a sleepless queen staring at the sky as color pervaded it, her eyes filled with the restless dreams of the Zhur.

Tension filled the winds that day. Aris seethed with anger. There were skirmishes here and there along the borders. The fields smoldered with the last of the great bonfires as thousands of heads of cattle were destroyed. As if that weren't enough, heavy rains had drowned many of the year's crops in the field. Then, rumors that Itacha was gathering forces in Delora, preparing to march. Patrols flowed from one march lord to another, guarding against raiders and rebels, and harrying bandits. But none of these things provided any sense of lasting peace. The srih quietly armed themselves, stirring in their castles to reckon the chances of siege and battle, scrutinizing their own defenses, building and breaking alliances. The patriarchs of the great Houses watched Chandris carefully from behind thick walls, alarmed and uneasy at the unpredictability of their king. The forests crawled with mercenaries come sniffing around after the scent of war like carrion birds to a corpse. In Aris, Selin, soldier, and archer eyed one another warily.

The silence from the direction of the forest—Reonih lands—was deafening.

In the towers, a bell tolled, signaling the turn of the watch.

———————

"I understand there was an incident last night."

The voice, musical, feminine, Stiva's, crept along an ancient wall bricked with large brownish-grey stones, into the intricate twining of the branches and tiny razor-sharp leaves of the ivy that half-covered it, to the center of the small rose garden, which was taken up by one massive tree, through which dappled sunlight fell. The fountain around it was silent today, its waters still and quiet.

The plants had died with Lara.

"I handled it," Khirin said quietly.

"Handled it?" A trace of rage flashed through the royal voice. "You should have come to me."

"I am here now." His voice was barely a whisper, but there was steel in the tone.

"Yes." Stiva looked at him coolly. "To tell me now what I should have known by dawn."

"There was no danger to you."

"Questions were asked of me at breakfast. I had no idea what to say. I am a queen. Uncertainty itself is danger. Ignorance is danger. Do not put me in that position again, Khirin."

Sudden temper hardened his voice. "Would you prefer I let such men stand at your back? He came at me in my sleep, *saya*."

Stiva eyed him coolly. "You did not have to kill him. You would have made a better example by stripping him of rank. To the Selin that is a fate worse than death."

Neither of them was sure if Khirin held that view. The thought went unspoken.

Khirin's gaze met her eyes. "That would have meant loosing someone who once guarded you very closely into the underworld, where your enemies will hold out their hands to him. Men might pay very well for the sort of information he could give."

Stiva's eyes narrowed.

"That is where they go when their honor is taken." Khirin continued. "They become assassins. Mercenaries. None of these men will turn on me and walk away from your guard alive while I command it, Stiva. Be assured of that."

Dallan and Jalen were guarding her, and both of them were glaring at Khirin from the arched open doorway. They were not within earshot, but that hardly mattered. Neither bothered to conceal their hatred. Dallan's eyes burned with animosity, pale blue orbs of ice that reflected the sun like daggers.

Stiva turned on him angrily, green eyes narrowed in rage. "There is enough tension here without adding discourse within the ranks. This isn't the first incident, either. I heard of another episode last week. Something that happened in training. You broke a man's arm. His *sword* arm."

Khirin did not so much as blink. "I apologized," he said casually, without a trace of remorse.

The apology, as she had heard, had been a cold, distracted mutter, emotionless. It had shocked even the Selin. She wondered if the Black Boot would take his orders, in the heat of battle, or follow their own judgment. If they would try again, to kill him.

His tone was ambivalent. "He may thank me for it. His close guard was horrible. He will correct that now, I think. It may save his life one day."

"And it could cost you yours." Stiva hissed. She turned on him. "These are not children you can toy with, Khirin. They are warriors. If you push them too far, they will kill you."

Khirin leaned forward. "These men—"

"Three of them have come to me today, asking for your heart," Stiva said tersely, cutting him off. Her tone lightened, deceptively casual. She tilted her head. "Shall I give it?"

A shadow crossed the sun.

A bird cried in a golden sky.

He remained silent.

When she spoke again, her voice was softer. "Jarvor spoke well for you. And he also worries that there will be another attempt on your life. He is right on that. Likely they will try again. And again. And they will continue until they either respect you or manage to kill you."

Khirin said nothing. His face was blank, his eyes unreadable. Stiva shut her lids against him, opening them a moment later to the dappled play of shadow and sunlight on the walls of the enclosed garden.

Across the garden, a half wall looked over into the larger patio terrace. Down there, amidst benches and fountains and potted citrus trees, the srih and Selin and Reonih moved back forth over faded stones. Someone successfully told a joke. Laughter streamed like ribbons through the air.

It seemed alien, as though it had no place here.

He said nothing.

"Humanity tends to forge itself into small communities," she said softly. "Tribalism is our nature, and it has both benefits and drawbacks. We came from Denebola as one people. It took less than a generation for factions to form. No matter what happens to Aursa, even if we all take the same gods, look the same, dress the same, talk the same … we will find ways to divide ourselves, to hate each other. That is human nature.

The Selin is a tighter circle than most, for theirs is a bond drawn in childhood, forged of sweat and pain and blood. You match them in skills. For that, you have earned some respect. Now you must earn their trust." She hesitated before continuing. "You do not have time to win them slowly."

Khirin frowned. "What do you mean?"

War. That was the gist of the message Mohr had sent her that night, the fortune the black dove carried to her window. *He will drown the land in blood, and it is left to you to check him. The lords are restless, and the cattle continue to sicken. Your brother angers the gods, and the peasants begin to rage as well.*

The bards told a dozen variations of the same thing. *War*, they said. *Everyone wants to know what side Stiva will take.*

Stiva closed her eyes.

"There is war coming," Stiva told him darkly. "You know that as well as I do."

His eyes pierced hers, but he said nothing.

Time paused. Stiva watched a tiny pink and violet butterfly flitting about in the breeze. From below them, soprano giggles, alto chuckles, and serpentine whispers screamed into one ambient hiss. An erlit shrieked from amber skies.

Far below, in the harbor, a bell clanged, its ring resounding against the crash of the Oburion.

She heard the beating of vast wings. She felt the air move, as though a massive bird flew just above her. She saw nothing, though the beast moved the air around her. A sudden wind blew her hair and dress back.

Time resumed, and life moved forward a step.

"Do not," she said then, "kill again. Not Selin. Punish them as you see fit, but do not kill another of them." She paused, toying with the velvet cuff of her sleeve. There was fear in her eyes, and her voice, despite her attempts to hide it. "Bring them to heel, Khirin. Soon. There will be trouble this season. These are not children you can toy with. They are warriors. If you push them too far, they will kill you. Selin do not fear death anywhere near as much as they fear the loss of honor."

Khirin turned right outside the barracks, a path that took him to a covered archway that led between the orchards and gardens outside the third, entering a long, arched breezeway that was marked by intricately carved statues. His thoughts were still swirling, chaotic.

Came a sudden movement in the corner of his eyes. A hand grabbed his arm.

Khirin was in no mood tolerate unwanted contact.

He did not even pause to see who had stopped him, but lashed out even as he turned. His fist hit the bone of someone's jaw with a satisfactory crunch. The body the jaw was attached to staggered backwards under the force of the impact, crashing into what appeared to be a moving stack of greased torches, at the bottom of which two hairy, sandaled legs could be seen, source and method of transportation. The impact toppled both the men and the torches, which ended up strewn over a rather impressive length of hall. A girl carrying a silver tray of pastries and chara tripped and fell as one of the brands rolled under her feet. Her platter went off on its own, scattering its contents all over the floor, which was being mopped by another servant.

"Watch where you're going," came the belated protest from the man formerly carrying the torches. "If you had been carrying a brand we'd all be black and shriveled by now."

Four sets of eyes fixed angrily on Khirin, who ignored three of them and honed in on the fourth, which belonged to a fairly nondescript man, of average height and build.

Khirin blinked. "Rueth?"

"Khirin." Rubbing his jaw, the man Khirin had struck rose, straightening his uniform. "As cheerful as ever, I see."

"The world grows smaller after all." Khirin mused, narrowing his eyes.

"Too small for you, eh?" Rueth cracked a wicked gleam in his eyes.

"They say Aris is the land of echoes, the land of illusions, and the land of longing," Rueth said cheerfully. "They say its art and history are truly the marvel of Aursa. Very enriching. Are you feeling enriched? That bruise looks like it was very enriching. That's a shiner."

Khirin started walking away.

The man hurried to catch up. "I heard the Black Boot had a little incident recently."

Behind them, a young man passing by stopped to help the serving girl pick up the pastries.

"What are you doing here?" Khirin said.

"Nothing that will interfere with you," Rueth said. "But you know, I just may decide to stay."

Khirin shrugged. "Chandris is a good king to stand behind. There's money to be made following his banner."

There was money to be made riding against Chandris as well. Everyone knew it.

Rueth's eyes were bright, almost gleeful. "I've found a park I'm fond of. They call it Mirror Pond. The name is fairly unimaginative. Especially for Aris. You'd think it would be called Silver Moon Under A Purple Wind Pond. But Mirror Pond, as it turns out, is accurate. The third bench offers a wonderful view of the water and the swans and lizards. It's especially beautiful when the war moon is full. The moonlight on the water, the reflections of the torches … stunning. Made better with a horn of Zorish mead or a flask of wine."

Rueth's voice was friendly, but his eyes were cold. "Our mutual friend and benefactor wishes to remind you of your duties. He also wants to warn you against the food at Three Cups. It's been terrible lately."

"Be on with you," Khirin told him, his voice a low growl.

Rueth nodded and went on his way without another word.

As Khirin passed the spot where the young man was helping the servant pick up the platter's spilled contents, a slender white hand met a tanned, calloused one. The murdik stone Khirin tossed down in reparation for the spilled goods settled to the floor unnoticed. Following the hands' lead, eyes also met.

"You don't have the hands of a servant," Ket observed. "I dare say it's been some time since you did dishes."

Twyla cocked her head, unable to prevent her own smile. "You have the hands of a forester."

Ket blinked. "Archer, actually. My name is Ket."

"I know who you are," Twyla said, the smile fading. "I've seen you at court. I hear you are training the new recruits."

"We came in from the institute at Yorns yesterday." Ket took a closer look, noting the quality of her clothes, the set of her hair, the simple but tasteful jewelry. His voice dropped a notch. "You're one of *her* maids, aren't you?"

"Aye."

"I wouldn't have expected a court flower to be saddled with such trivial tasks as serving food."

"The kitchens are a bit short-handed today," she said. "I'm not yet so soft I can't carry a platter."

"Your hands are soft enough," he said. "It's only your eyes that are hard."

To escape his gaze, she turned her attention to the spilled food. "You needn't bother with the food. It will be given to the poor. The others will clean up the mess. It's only the dishes I need."

"In that case," Ket snatched up a pastry that had stayed on the platter, "one more won't matter, right?"

Twyla raised a pale brow, caught between amusement and offense. "Your manners are atrocious."

"Thank you," Ket said brightly. "That's precisely why I stopped to help a servant with servants of her own." He chewed slowly, savoring the taste of the pastry. "This is good. You make it?"

"Gods, no." Twyla shook her head. "I'm a terrible cook. I can make yrehn, and bread, and that's about it."

"Too bad," Ket pretended dismay. "I was about to propose."

She giggled, despite herself, and looked at him more closely. "I do know you, archer," she said, then added, "We danced at Starshire, after the Lightfest hunt."

"So we did," Ket said quietly, sobering at the thought of that bloody day. "And then you left me to dance with one of the Selin. I looked for you later, but never found you again. I've never had my heart broken quite so quickly."

She smiled. "Too much wine," she said. "Too much worry. I went to bed early. That was a hard day."

His eyes sobered. "That it was."

"You seem to have done well by that turn of fate," Twyla observed.

"Chandris seems to find me useful. So far, at least."

Twyla's tone darkened. "Then I would advise you to maintain that opinion. Chandris is a man of changing whims and deadly moods. He is not above reversing your change of fortune over something trivial. Last week he banished a man from court for laughing wrong."

"Ayorl," Ket said. "I was there. And the man's laugh is hideous. It sounds like a drunken chicken falling off a cliff onto a cow with bloat."

She giggled, despite herself. "That's terrible. Hilarious, but terrible."

"I'm not wrong."

Twyla stood up slowly. "I should go."

His gaze bored into hers. "You're more than a maid," he said. "You're her eyes. I bet you know about every letter that comes in these gates, and every false bottom trunk, every hollow picture frame. You're quiet, but you see everything."

Twyla wasn't sure what to say to that, but her cheeks flushed slightly. "You're presumptuous," she said. "And outspoken. Those can be dangerous traits around here."

"You know," Ket said. "I usually am more reserved. You seem easy to talk to."

She absorbed that with a slow nod. During the brief conversation, their gazes had become firmly locked. "I would have your name," he said finally. "If you please."

She hesitated only a moment. "I'm Twyla."

"You're beautiful," Ket told her bluntly. "One of the court roses."

"You're a charmer." Twyla gave him a slow smile.

At which he took her hand kissed it. "Only when I've been charmed."

Their eyes met and locked. In that gaze were born the embers of a fire that would one day drown the land in blood and fire. But at the moment, there was only sunlight above them, and, far away, the call of sea birds screaming madness into the wind.

Four days later, as the moons Vhrohos and Calista—the moons of wisdom and love, respectively—danced in the sky, Khirin slipped to the bench at Mirror Pond. The chalk marks on the bench were easy to spot. The scrawlings looked like a pair of initials to the unknowing eye, but

Khirin quickly spotted the telltale twist of the lettering. It took him only a moment to find the spot where the note had been cleverly stashed in a fake rock. Once he got back to the castle, he went to one of the gardens, where he would have a spot of privacy decoding it.

He deciphered the name written on the tiny piece of paper inside it, and then swallowed it, his eyes turning to the shellscale castle above him, which had a vaguely menacing feel. The swallowing was in part to get rid of evidence, but part of it was more nuanced than that. He absorbed the name, as his weapons would later absorb the life force of its bearer.

The code, once deciphered, revealed a single name.

Barls.

He looked up, and found himself staring into a pair of familiar blue eyes.

CHAPTER 21

A wide tower room, with tall windows that looked out over the Oburion.

A cluster of srih ladies assembled, as they often did, a jeweled, silk-clad circle of musical voices and high-pitched giggles. The fading tapestries hanging on the tower's stone walls depicted scenes from the past: battles and births, weddings and deaths, wars and romances and tragedies. Wild animals watched these events with eyes of carnathian and emerald and amber. Wolves, vodriks, drossen, vianths, aurochs, and erlits danced with birds, fish, horses, and cats. Other tapestries depicted historical scenes, not only from Aris' past, but also of Elders' society, Reonih circles, the terror of the Zhur, and the shadow time, the dark years that had followed the fall of the Elders. The wall hangings offered a furtive, often brutal glimpse into the songs and history the Reonih bards kept alive. Against the richly colored intricacies of tapestries and carpets, candlelight gleamed on polished thi-wood, holding back the greyness of the day outside. A fire crackled brightly in the large stone fireplace, not quite necessary, but comfortable.

Like the flames, the ladies' voices whispered and danced and hissed as they worked. Near each of them lay a new basket, woven from stripped wheth stalks of the year's last harvest and decorated with bits of shell, ribbons, beads, and tiny splinters of shard-wood. The harvest circle was an ancient thing, both practical and traditional. The tradition of making sewing baskets at the beginning of the dark season stretched back to time forgotten. Such circles had inhabited this tower room every winter since the castle had been built. The ladies were embroidering the linings now, the final step. Sharp needles pierced colorful pieces of silk or soft linen, decorating them with lucky charms, family sigils, or fanciful borders. Sharp eyes and sharp tongues pierced the air and atmosphere.

Neither baskets, linings, nor gossip were truly the center of attention today.

Near the middle of the room stood a girl with a basket of her own, which was much larger and plainer than the rest. She was calm, though she cast frequent nervous glances at Lhin, who was curled up near the hearth, purring.

Shira, Stiva, Twyla, Talia, Mina, Adele, and Marcelle sat on low sofas, drinking hot yrehn and nibbling on hutberry spice rolls and scones. Trays were set out before them with fruits and cheeses, hot buns, candied petals, and Shira's favorite, arithyn eyeballs. Reide, Carin, and Fiurn sat in a corner, playing softly. A Reonih scribe sat at a table, taking notes.

The girl reached into the basket and pulled out a swatch of material, which she presented first to Stiva, and then to Shira. "This is a mixture of Shadrian silk and Yolyneian satin. It works very well as a double layer matched with Jaran lace, or embroidered with gold or silver thread. If you tilt it, there is a slight hint of iridescence. This is one of the finest materials available. The Queen of Vrehn used it on the bodice of her wedding dress, and the gown was breathtaking. My father is one of the only merchants in Aursa who can obtain this silk."

Oohs and *aahs* accompanied the swatch, as they had several previous examples.

Shira's voice floated over it, quiet. "And the price?"

Talia clucked her tongue with disapproval at Shira's inquiry. Stiva cast a puzzled look at her sister. It was at least the fourth time Shira had asked after price, though she knew full well there was no need for her to conserve. Chandris and Stiva had both told her that, though things were tight this year, budget was not an issue where her wedding was concerned. She was marrying the crown prince of Shadri; it would not be honorable to stint on such an occasion. Yet Shira had asked after price again and again ... and invariably chose the most expensive option. She seemed determined to spend every coin in the treasury, which was entirely unlike her. Stiva shook her head, puzzled.

The merchant's daughter managed to quote a ridiculously high amount with a perfectly straight face.

Talia sniffed. Twyla gave a little murmur. Even Marcelle blinked.

"I'll take it," Shira decided. Brows lifted almost simultaneously around the room, though none dared too blatant a reaction.

The girl, to her credit, did not allow her expression to change. She only nodded. "An excellent choice, my lady."

Shira addressed the merchant's daughter once more. "That is the material I want. How long does shipment take?"

The girl did not hesitate. "My father has a small supply at home, more than enough for a dress. It could be delivered within a few days."

Shira nodded. "Very well."

Stiva turned her gaze back to the courtyard. From her vantage, she could see the Overlook and, beyond, the Second, where a Black Boot training session was rapidly degenerating into a brawl. The Black Boot had endured the rest of Khirin's unusual drills, which included things like smashing their shins against logs and bashing their heads into walls. These methods were meant to build pain tolerance. Khirin had also been instructing them in different breathing techniques, strikes, and weapons. The Black Boot had borne this well enough, understanding that it was to their own benefit. But they had drawn the line at deliberately hitting their own balls with sticks.

Khirin had issued a challenge to decide the issue. Though the daily sparring was often brutal, it was rarely as heated and sincere as what was going on below. Khirin was holding his own against a steady stream of opponents, but the Black Boot was attacking full force, and with bare steel. As Stiva and Talia watched, a blade sliced through the air where Khirin's neck had been a moment ago.

They were trying to kill him.

In a moment, Stiva guessed, they would succeed.

The fact that Khirin himself had—-apparently—challenged them would absolve them all of any dishonor or criminal charges should he die during the spar. Dallan, in particular, seemed intent on sheathing his sword in his new captain's flesh.

Khirin blazed among them like a dark star, proving his mettle. Not one of them was able to get him with their blade. He was holding them off. Which was no small feat, considering the fact that it was the cream of Aris' elite he was up against. The Black Boot were no slackards. A man would have to be immortal, to hold them off for long.

Which Khirin was not.

A slash opened across his chest as Stiva watched. She waited for him to call a halt to the spar, but he did not. Would not.

Fool, she thought.

She was not certain why she intervened. Not at that moment—as she opened the window and called out to halt the spar—and not in later ones.

The combatants paused, panting. They turned their faces up to her, squinting in the sun, breathing heavily. Stiva raised her forefinger in silent gesture, ordering single combat.

The Black Boot regrouped and obliged, obviously disappointed.

"I'm not so certain that was wise, Stiva," Talia observed. "If he can't control them, he's certainly of no use to you."

"Perhaps." Stiva was unconcerned. "But if he dies today, he is also useless."

The merchant's daughter started showing purple materials.

Marcelle spoke out, her voice musical, yet cold. "I've heard Shadri is full of poison," she said. "Poison flowers, poison fish. Even the butterflies are venomous. Do you know what they did to Adron's sister? They fed her a poison that made her skin bubble up. She threw herself from the Arriks, they say, because they murdered her lover. And the storms are sheer madness. I hear that when the Surges come down, one cannot see the bladed fan you are holding before you. Entire villages are sometimes washed away without a trace. And the—"

"Marcelle," Stiva said, in warning.

"In my homeland," Marcelle continued, "A young bride spends seven days in the Tower of Love before her wedding. She is bathed in rosewater and anointed with sacred oils. The elders tell her the secrets of the flesh, and young girls bring her flowers and write their wishes on colored silk scarves. In Shadri, I hear they give you a bird that has been tortured."

"Marcelle!" Stiva snapped. "Have done with this."

She heard then, for the first time, the echo of her twin's rage in her tone.

Twyla had gone white. The room fell into silence.

Marcelle met Stiva's eyes, and Stiva found a sudden, unexpected coldness in her friend's face. It stung. Marcelle and Reide had long been her closest friends, and the thought of Marcelle turning on her chilled her, even through the warmth of the sun.

"I should have ordered more," Shira mused. "Add another three yards of the silk."

Stiva looked at her sister. "Are you determined to have the most expensive wedding in history?"

It was meant lightly. But there was no laughter on Shira's face, and her tone was sullen. "Chandris, no doubt, will outdo me when he gets married."

The amusement fell from Stiva's eyes. She turned her head, briefly inspecting her sister. The vision was mildly disturbing. Shira had changed, somehow, transformed right before her eyes, and yet Stiva had not noticed the difference.

It was not the changes themselves that upset her. Children grew, even younger siblings. There was nothing extraordinary about that. What was unsettling was that Stiva herself had failed to notice the changes. This Shira, the one who stood before her, at the brink of maturity, had grown somehow into her own beauty. Stiva reached into memory and found an image of a gentler, more familiar Shira. Stiva and Chandris took their looks mostly from Lara. Maren was the spitting image of Cronn. Shira, alone of them all, bore little resemblance to either parent, but instead bore the unmistakable stamp of Cronn's mother, Zran. With her mahogany hair, oval face, and clear grey eyes, Shira grew into a closer image of Zran's portraits every day.

Stiva bit her lip, debating whether or not to broach the issue of Aris' failing treasury, glanced at her aunt.

Her voice carried over the room, a prism shard. "I think we're done, as we've all picked our materials. Mina, Adele, see her out."

A slight ghost of a breeze stirred the air, swept with the fragrance of several fine perfumes mixing as they left.

As though on cue, Talia looked sharply at her younger niece. "You're being reckless and selfish."

Talia was nothing if not blunt.

"I was told to spare no expense," Shira said coolly.

The room fell silent.

Stiva studied her sister's face closely. She did not like what she saw in her sibling's grey eyes. There was a harshness to the set of Shira's face and shoulders that she had never seen before.

"She's being sold off like a prize cat to bear sons for Shadri," Marcelle said. "She's a pawn, just like the rest of us. No wonder she tried to jump from her balcony last night."

The room fell silent. Even Talia blanched.

Marcelle was srih, nobility through and through. Her voice did not rise in volume, nor change in tone, but there was ice in her eyes when she spoke, and an animosity Stiva had never heard in her before; arrogance, entwined with her quiet, graceful poise, arrogance and the warlike nature that had put her father on the throne of Jara.

Shira stared at Marcelle, shocked. Beside her, Twyla had gone white.

Marcelle's face registered no emotion. She was, Stiva noted, wearing Jara's colors, and had her hair up in the particular knot the Jaran nobles favored.

Echoes of a long-ago summer day, when four of them had released doves from the tower and mused dreamily about flying away. They had been caged, all of them, caged by the decorums and the demands of being srih, of being perfect. And as they had grown, the prison itself had changed, made its traps and dangers more pronounced, more visible.

I wish we could fly away.

Stiva swallowed. Her voice emerged ice cold. "You tell me this now, as though it were some petty thing. Why didn't you come to me when it happened?"

Marcelle ran a slender finger around the rim of her goblet. "You were too busy at court, being surrounded by worshippers and basking in the glow of adoration."

Stiva stared at Marcelle. "*What?*"

"You surprise me, Stiva. I hadn't thought you so vain. However, that's all that matters to you now, isn't it? Pleasing Chandris, pleasing the srih. To the point of stabbing the Reonih in the back—"

"Marcelle." Reide broke his silence, his voice harsher than usual. "That's enough."

Jarvor shifted at the door, turning to face the table.

Marcelle opened her mouth to retort, but apparently thought better of it. Her lips closed. She narrowed kohl-rimmed eyes, looked at Stiva coldly, and then stood. "If you'll excuse me," she said coolly, "I'll need some air. I've probably said more than is *proper* for a hostage to say."

Stiva felt rage course through her like lava flowing through a volcano, but she held it in, giving a curt nod and an icy stare. Marcelle curtsied and left the room, the satin of her dress shimmering in the morning sun.

"Aret asked for her hand," Reide said quietly. "Chandris refused, on grounds of having known her carnally."

Stiva went pale.

"Out," Stiva said quietly. "Shira, you stay."

The sewing room emptied in a flurry of rustling silks and laces, the tinkle of jewelry. The evacuation was immediate, more rushed than was necessary, yet Stiva gave it only a moment's attention.

"Is it true?" Stiva asked.

"If I was going to jump," Shira said calmly, "you'd be planning a funeral today, rather than a wedding."

Uncharacteristically moody, Shira picked up the sleeve she was embroidering and looked down at her half-finished work, unhappiness painted across her delicate features like poison misted over a rose. Jealousy was not in Shira's nature, any more than it was in Stiva's. Chandris had enough for the whole family. But bitterness was another thing entirely. Now, for the first time, Stiva saw resentment in Shira's clear grey eyes: acrimony created by the realization of the staggering differences birth order could bring.

"What is going on with you?" Stiva asked finally. "She's right, you know. You've chosen the most expensive material, the most expensive food, invited every srih in Aursa, ordered extravagant gifts, summoned more bards and actors than I can count and announced four days of games and tournaments. This just isn't like you." She rubbed her forehead, where the faintest headache was growing. "Shira, have you any idea what state Aris is in? What state our treasury is in?"

Shira raised her chin and looked away. "I was told the wedding should be fit for a king."

"You were not told to go beyond all measures of sanity." Stiva, for once siding with Talia, took up where her aunt had left off. "Nor were you told to drain us entirely. You know the state of things, Shira. Royal weddings are never cheap, which is only proper, but this is beyond extravagant. The caviar is reasonable, and the Jaran wine, and the white feathered masks. Your decision to give Taibon twelve vota cats—with jeweled tack—as a present is within bounds, if barely tasteful. But to import cocoa from Zors for all the guests, and have the silverware specially made and set with Grecan diamonds, and then not only commission a vlorship to take you to Shadri, but to fill it with imported oils and spices … this is getting ridiculous, Shira. What has gotten into you?"

A deep bell tone sounded the changing of the guard.

Stiva waited for the tolls to stop before continuing. "Chandris has been in council for days, trapped by the complaints of vassals grown increasingly—and understandably—infuriated by the losses inflicted on them by bandits and raiders. The royal treasury is depleted, and now we need to rely on imports to make up for the goods we lost to bandits and plague. The new archers' division has depleted it even further. There simply isn't enough money. People will go hungry this year, Shira."

"But of course, one wouldn't know that by looking in the castle pantry," Shira said coolly.

Stiva stared at her sister.

"He wants me married," Shira said quietly. "I'm not blind, Stiva. I know what I am to him. A bargaining chip, the price of an alliance, nothing more. I simply want to increase my value. It ups my chances of survival. Yours, I can't vouch for, if ever you marry."

Stiva's eyes narrowed. "What is that supposed to mean?"

"I heard Frethin of Trian asked for your hand. And Jahn."

"I said no."

"As you've said no to the others. He won't let you, even if you agree," Shira said. "Not until he has an heir. He won't risk the crown going to your sons, or chance war if you both have boys. I heard him say as much, the other day."

Had Stiva not already known this, had she not already had several discussions with her twin on the subject, had she not, in truth, completely agreed with Chandris on the matter, Shira's words would have undoubtedly sparked another battle between the twins. What was unsettling about it was that Shira was obviously aware of this. It stunned Stiva to find her little sister, who had always done everything in her power to keep peace between the twins, suddenly doing the opposite.

Stiva spoke quietly. "I thought you were happy with Taibon. Just a few weeks ago, you spoke of nothing else. What changed your mind?"

"It isn't that there's anything wrong with Taibon, Stiva," Shira explained finally, looking miserable. "He's handsome, funny, polite, and smart. He's been very kind to me so far. He's sent me entire caravans of presents, and been thoughtful enough to ask about my favorite colors and materials so that my rooms will be finished before I even arrive in Shadri. And he has the grace and bearing of a … of a …"

"Prince?" Stiva supplied the word with a smile.

"Or warlord. Is there a difference?" She turned back to her reflection.

"What is it?" Even as the words crossed Stiva's lips, another thought crossed her mind, and Stiva tilted her head. "Are you in love with someone else?"

"No." Shira twisted one of her rings around, a nervous habit she'd had since childhood. "No," she said again. "I'm just not in love with him. I don't think I am, at least. I mean, there isn't anything wrong with him. Compared to the others I had to choose from, he's a dream."

"We all thought you were very fond of Taibon," Stiva said gently. "Chandris and I want you be happy. We were both thrilled when you seemed to like Taibon so much. You and Taibon will make a striking pair. You seemed to get along so well when you met." Stiva continued more quietly. "What is this?"

"Don't worry, Stiva." Shira picked up a small hand mirror and looked at her reflection. "I'm entirely grateful for being sold off like a piece of cattle, if not entirely free of bitterness." Shira sighed. "I was thinking the other day about Mother and Father, and how one could see their love, even when they fought. I don't think I'll ever feel that way about Taibon."

"You two couldn't stop smiling the whole time he was here." Stiva put a hand to her forehead, where a dull ache was beginning to grow. "That's a good start."

"Dancing and playing through-the-gate with someone isn't the same as being married to them. Don't try to give me the speech about how arranged marriages often work out wonderfully. I've heard it more times than I can count. And I only need to speak two names to discredit that argument: Kele and Talia." Shira gave Stiva a direct look. "Is that what I have to look forward to? A lifetime of interspersed periods of argument and separation? Is that what you consider fine? A violent drunkard for a husband? A son who will barely acknowledge me?" Shira's voice broke. "I would rather die alone."

"Shira—" Stiva reached a hand out. "You chose him."

She sighed. "What's the use of talking to you? You always defend him."

Stiva frowned. "Shira, Taibon was your choice. You're going to be queen of Shadri. You're acting as though Chandris is sending you to some prison island. What more could you ask for?"

"The freedom to love who I want, though I know better. I saw how that worked for you."

Stiva winced. "Shira—"

Shira looked at her coldly. "If you tell me that it's a sacrifice I have to make for Aris, or point out that nearly all the srih are married into such arrangements, I will walk away."

Stiva's eyes flashed. "Don't talk to me about sacrifice."

"Why?" Shira said. "Because of Trin? You got a crown for his death."

Stiva slapped her. The blow sounded a harsh *crack* into the stillness of the room.

Shira touched her cheek, which was slightly red, but did not lose her composure. "You're just like Chandris," she said.

Stiva stared at her sister, marveling. Steel colored Shira's voice, where before there had been silk and satin. Shira had always been the fragile one, the gentle one.

Then again, Shira was of Aris.

It stung bitterly to think that beneath that beloved equanimity might lurk the monster that raged in Aris' blood.

Thick silence fell over the room.

"You're right," Stiva said coldly. "I am just like Chandris. We want you to be happy. But if you're determined to become like Talia, then you will become like Talia. And that will be your doing, not ours."

"If you're trying to comfort me, Stiva, it isn't working. Yes, Taibon is a great warrior, and he is handsome and jovial. And he may one day be a drunkard, a shadow of his former self. I think you are right. I may one day be like Talia. Bitter and vicious and razor-tongued."

"You're better than that," Stiva said.

"Am I?"

The sisters stared at one another.

"It wasn't always like that with them," Stiva said quietly. "They didn't argue very much before Mykhal died. You were too young to remember, but Kele wasn't always the belligerent drunkard he is now. He was one of Cronn's best warriors in his youth. When he was younger, Kele was actually a lot like Aret. He laughed a lot. He used to chase off the nurses and Ghodrik and take Mykhal, Aret, Chandris, Marcelle, and me for long picnics on the hillsides, or swimming at the beach. Cronn and Lara would be furious with him, but they always forgave him. Even Talia couldn't stay mad at him for long."

"I remember," Shira said quietly. "And I remember Mykhal. Do you?"

Words brought back ghosts, the shades of so many that were gone now; Cronn and Lara, Mykhal.

Trin.

Stiva bit her lip as memories welled up with a strength and a pain untouched by time. Hearing his name spoken was like an arrow through the heart. She turned on her sister in cold fury, eyes dark. "Do not," Stiva hissed, "ever try to use his name or his memory against me. I haven't forgotten him. I forgave Chandris, because I chose Aris over rage. I won't forgive you for playing my emotions."

Shira turned away, staring through the window at the restless sea. She twisted her ring nervously, then caught herself and put her hand down. The fire snapped. The wind gusted. But the air inside the tower room was utterly still.

"I don't have the strength that you and Mother have," she said, after a moment. "I know the sorts of choices you have to make. I've seen you step into Chandris' shoes when he is away, and make those decisions with such conviction, such assurance. I see respect in the srih and the Reonih when they look at you. I don't think I can do it, Stiva. I haven't that strength, to determine military matters. To see through the twists and turns of political issues and the men behind them, and see the truth behind them. I've never understood the nuances of politics the way you and Chandris do. All my life, wars have only frightened and confused me. I am not the judge of people you and Chandris are."

"Shira." Stiva looked at her sister through a veil of sympathy. "You do have that strength. I saw it a moment ago, in the way you spoke to me. Ruling is like riding. It comes naturally after a while. Believe me, when Chandris crowned me, I was more terrified than I have ever been in my entire life. But I grew into it. I'm still growing into it. You don't have to command a garrison, or move forces, or hear civil cases. Mother never did any of that. She simply gathered information. Cronn asked her advice because he trusted her judgment."

"Mother was Reonih. It was different for her. She had resources he did not. Resources I will not." Shira sighed, and then shook her head, the fear in her eyes making her look somehow younger, almost childlike. "She had power, Stiva. You could see it in her eyes, even when she was daydreaming. You could see it in her garden, the way she touched a plant and made it grow. You have that power. I don't."

"My plants die, Shira," Stiva said gently. "I killed a lotus just last week." She sighed. "Power or not, Caro never would have let them marry if she hadn't been a princess. They were a love match. We know those aren't common among royalty. But nor would Chandris force you to marry against your wishes, Shira. You know that. You chose Taibon, and I have never seen you more sure than the night you did so. You can still change your mind. But I don't think you want to. Taibon seems wonderful. And you'll have Pahnryn."

"He's sent no word of the wedding," Shira said.

"Pahnryn will be fine, I'm sure. Mother said he was cantankerous."

"He never bothered to acknowledge her death." Shira's voice was steely. "I will have no ally in him. I doubt I'll even hear from him unless he wants something."

"See," Stiva said sweetly, "you're already learning."

Shira's eyes widened.

She left without a word, without curtsying.

CHAPTER 22

The approaching wedding brought another unexpected visitor to Stiva's suite, this one entirely welcome. Aret sought Stiva out on her patio, where she had gone after a somewhat heated meeting with Chandris to ponder the darkness in her twin's eyes and his words.

"*Saya.*" Aret bowed deeply. "There is a huge white beast in your parlor. It has stolen several dits from my bag. I must beg you for compensation."

"Aret!" Stiva slapped his arm playfully. "I've told you to stop spoiling that cat."

But she was laughing, and so did he. The laughter brought them both back to familiarity. They were blood, and despite all that had passed over the cycles, they were still close.

Stiva waved him to a seat. "Wine? Fruit?"

"Please." Aret nodded. "I hear there has been a bit of an uproar this morning."

Stiva filled a glass herself and offered him one. "Barls was found dead, his neck broken. He appears to have fallen from his balcony. But he was in debt, so the rumor mill is working overtime."

Barls—like anything to do with Trin or Aret—was a touchy subject. But Aret only sighed. "You cannot underestimate the sharpness of srih tongues, Stiva," he told her soberly. "They spill blood too easily, and while they prefer weapons to words, it is the words that move them first."

The watch turned. Aris roused itself as the guards were relieved. Dusk was falling. Somewhere on the grounds, one of the bards sang sunset magic, calling darkness to a blood-red sky. Cairn, Stiva thought, though she wasn't sure. They sat quietly a moment.

A maid approached them, refilling the decanter of greenberry wine on a nearby table. Her hair, which was worn long and loose, nearly obscured her face. It took Stiva a moment to recognize the servant Chandris had burned at his coronation. The Reonih healers had done an excellent job with her. Though her cheek, neck, and hands were scarred, the traces of the injury were much more subtle than Stiva would have expected.

A lump rose in Stiva's throat. The memory of that episode still sickened her when she thought of it.

The girl cast Stiva a shy, furtive look. Her lips moved, and Stiva saw her bow her head. When she looked up, tears shone in her eyes. She knelt, kissed Stiva's hand, and then slipped off, her steps light and cautious, like that of a cat.

It was only as she turned that Stiva noticed the bulge in her belly.

"That's the one who got burned," Aris said, looking after her. "She looks well."

"Yes," Stiva said. "She seems to be doing well."

"I've heard rumors," Aret said. "They say there is tension building, between Chandris and the Reonih. Is it true?"

Stiva nodded. "He is changing the tithing system, in part to support the new archers' division." She thought about mentioning the Relics, and decided not to. "Have you seen your mother?" she asked instead, changing the subject.

"No." Aret shook his head. "I've managed to avoid both of my parents so far, though I don't imagine my luck in that area will hold out for long."

Stiva studied him, taking note of the faint creases on his forehead, the hardened, haunted look of his eyes. "You and Kele still haven't worked things out."

"No." Aret sighed. "Nor will we, I fear, until he realizes that I'm not going to sacrifice my career for the duchy." He looked at her sideways. "How is he?"

Stiva shrugged. "Drinking heavily. More than usual."

"I hadn't thought that was possible." Aret's expression darkened.

Stiva looked down. Aret's boots were still wet from the fountain near the Zhrue Gate, where according to custom, all washed their feet before entering the castle.

"Just passing by," Stiva said slowly, her eyes narrowing. "You haven't seen your parents yet. Your boots are still wet from the fountain bath in the First. You haven't seen Chandris—he's been in meetings—but Talia is only sewing, working on a tapestry for Shira, and Kele is probably somewhere about. It's early. He probably isn't even drunk yet. But you came straight to me. Why?"

Aret looked away.

"You want something," Stiva said flatly, her tone cooling considerably.

Her cousin kept silent.

"What is it?" Stiva continued. "A promotion? Land? Gold? The hand of some lord's daughter?" She turned away. "Talk to Chandris."

"I cannot," Aret said quietly. "Not about this."

Stiva turned to look at him again, startled by the seriousness of his tone. Seeing the misery etched into his face softened her. Her anger fell away, replaced by worry. "What is it?"

Aret hesitated. After a moment he spoke, his tone uncertain. "Stiva, I have never asked you for anything." He her eyes with a troubled gaze. "I never would, unless it was urgent."

And there it was, unsaid, unspoken—not even so much as whispered at—but there, nevertheless. Not even her own cousin could look at her now and see her as anything but a source of power and wealth.

Honor bound her to his wish, to a debt he had never claimed of her. He had lost a brother, and that ultimately had been her doing, though certainly never her intention. Aret had never even so much as hinted that he blamed her for Mykhal's death, nor had he ever looked at her with anything but genuine affection. It mattered not. One way or another, Stiva had started the chain of events that had taken Mykhal's life. She was ultimately responsible, and they all knew it. But no one had denied that she had been as devastated by Mykhal's death and the events surrounding it as the rest of them, if not more so. Mykhal had been dear to them all, but Trin had been hers alone to mourn. The guilt of both deaths was hers to carry. That truth, however, made nothing easier for the rest of them. It was a parasite, that pain, always gnawing within her;

Mykhal's memory entwined with Trin's, the loss of two lives held so dear.

That pain hung over her now, like a cloud, the price she had never paid.

Blood debt.

"What is it?" Stiva asked sharply, more harshly than she meant.

Aret hesitated. "I ask confidence, before I speak, Stiva, before I say more. I ask that this remain between us, and trouble no one else."

Stiva blinked. "Aret, I—"

He held up a hand, cutting her off. "It isn't on my own behalf. I ask nothing for myself. But what I ask—and you can refuse it, Stiva, knowing full well I hold nothing against you—what I ask is not going to be easy. There are lives at stake, and there is honor at stake."

"Very well." Stiva nodded. "I will keep my silence, so long as that does not endanger Aris."

"No." He shook his head. "Not at all."

He did not speak immediately. He went to the window and looked out over the city and harbor, a silhouette against the falling sun. "I have a problem."

"So I surmised," Stiva said dryly.

He drew a deep breath. "You remember my friend Khren. He's been in my caste since we were children."

"The redhead? Of course. He sat with us at the coronation." Stiva nodded. "What of him?"

Aret took a deep breath. "He's had a child, very recently. Or rather, his wife has."

"Wasn't she pregnant at the coronation?"

"Yes, but that child was stillborn. This one lived. Lives."

"He wants to be released from the Selin to raise it," Stiva guessed. "Is that it?"

Aret looked shocked. "No. Of course not. Khren is fourth-generation Selin. He would never desert his caste."

"Then what is the problem?" Stiva frowned, puzzled.

"The child itself."

"Recently born and already causing problems?"

"It isn't that the child is causing problems," Aret explained, "it's rather that he has one."

Stiva waited.

"The child is deformed," Aret explained. "His hands are twisted. He will never hold a sword. He will never be a warrior, and so he will never inherit. The council will reject him, beyond a doubt. That isn't a probability. It is a given."

Stiva sobered. "I see."

Explanation was not necessary, beyond that point. By law, the infant sons of Selin were presented shortly after birth to a Selin council of greybeards, whereupon they were carefully inspected for deformities or visible weaknesses. If they passed the inspection, they were guaranteed entrance into the Selin training institutions at the age of seven. Then, if they survived the long hard years of training, they became Selin. Admission to the ranks of the Selin guaranteed them citizenship, land, a salary, and, perhaps most importantly, honor.

Those were the lucky ones.

Stiva knew full well what happened to children the greybeards rejected. The infant would be left outside somewhere, exposed to the elements. Most likely, weather and predators would make short work of him. If he was extremely unfortunate, outlaws would find him, and sell him into a life of misery across the seas. Or, if he was more fortunate, someone would find him and either raise him themselves, or bring him to a Reonih theorica, where he would spend his days, under their care, in the company of others like himself.

Either way, he would never be who had he been born to be. He would never be Selin. It was to the benefit of the Selin, that weakness was not allowed into their ranks.

The benefit of the child was another matter entirely.

The sons of Selin grew up to be Selin. Or they did not grow up at all.

Stiva toyed with a crystal goblet. The taste of the wine seemed to have gone rancid in her mouth.

Aret spoke quietly. "The child will be presented for inspection at the next full war moon. Khren's wife is the daughter of a Selin. She is heartbroken already. She knows what will happen. And the child will never have a sibling that might soothe her. She nearly died giving birth. She is barren now."

"Aret," Stiva sighed. "I understand what you're asking. But even if I could persuade the council to make an exception, he probably wouldn't survive the training."

"No, that's not it." Aret shook his head, filtered sunlight gleaming bright in his gold hair. "That's not what I'm asking. It's out of the question. The Selin would be furious. It would be unfair to anyone else who has ever had a child rejected. There are other Selin who have had sons turned down. And this is not something the boy can hide or grow out of. He can never be Selin. He will not even be able to hold a sword or a spear, much less wield one with any efficiency. The general army wouldn't even take him, except maybe as a cook. And the child's deformity is no secret. When the baby was born, our entire caste rushed to see him. It cannot be done that way, Stiva. Too many already know."

Stiva frowned. "What, then?"

"Can you get him into a theorica?" Aret asked. "Possibly outside of Aris?"

Contrary to the Selin, the Reonih considered such children blessed. If they survived, they were seen as special to the gods. Seers observed them closely, and their apprentices cared for them as part of their training.

"If he is accepted," Stiva said, "he will be fed and clothed and carefully tended to. He will live in the forest, surrounded by seers and others like him. He may be set to gardening or some other simple chore. If he is lucid enough, he may even learn a craft or become Reonih himself." Stiva's eyes met his. "He may someday be put to death, if and when a situation warrants a special sacrifice."

That was a little too close to home. She saw pain flash in his eyes.

But Aret shook his head bravely. "That is an honor," he said quietly, his voice husky. "At least this way, he has a chance." Aret looked down at the floor, then back up at her. "If he spends his days showered in love and sunlight and laughter, and then one day walks through fire to meet a god … that is a far kinder life—and death—than the battlefield would ever give him."

Trin danced through her memory. Mykhal.

She hadn't been able to save either of them.

Aret was asking more than a favor. He was asking her to deceive Chandris, to act without his knowledge, to make a choice he never would have agreed to.

Honor. Courage. Serenity.

Aret's eyes met hers. "Stiva, I'm asking you to save the child's life. If he is rejected, he will be left in Gherot Canyon to die. That is the law. Khren came to me bawling on the night he was born. I have never seen him cry. Not when his father died. Not when his brother was killed before his eyes on the battlefield. Not when his first two sons died. For this child to suffer … that would be worse than death, for him. I fear he would fall on his sword before he suffered that sort of pain and indignity." Aret paused. "He saved my life once. I owe him."

Stiva blinked. "I didn't know you were in danger."

He gave her a faintly exasperated look. "I am Selin, Stiva. A warrior. My life is in danger more often than not. We are not immortal. We die. Frequently, sometimes, as in the Battle of the Golden Star, or the Battle of Greyson's Point."

"Delora," Stiva said.

Aret nodded. "They've gone ahead and given it a name and official status. There were enough dead Delorans afterwards to warrant it. I think Carin's writing the song."

"Isn't that the one you got promoted for?"

"Yes. And so did Khren. My own promotion would not have occurred if not for him. He killed a man who had his sword at my throat. I won't bore you with the details of every escapade. Suffice it to say that we have drank, fought, trained, ridden, laughed, starved, and grown together. He was with me when Mykhal died."

Stiva sat back, thinking. "Does Khren understand that he would never see the child again? Would he agree?"

"Aye." Aret nodded again. "He knows he must give the child up, no matter what. He needs only know the boy will be taken care of. He would at least have a chance with the Reonih."

A moment passed, then another. Aret waited silently, tension evident in the set of his face and his shoulders. She made her decision, had made it, she realized, as soon as he had asked.

But she made him wait, because, kin or no, she couldn't afford for him to think her easily turned.

Stiva was not wearing a crown at the moment, but it sank into her thoughts and into her soul.

There was only one choice she could live with.

"All right," Stiva said finally. "I'll arrange it. But, cruel as it sounds, it may be best if you two say nothing to Khren's wife until it is done. Her reaction must be real, or people will ask questions."

"Of course." Aret was visibly relieved. The gratitude in his eyes and in his voice was earnest; she did not doubt that in the least. "Stiva, I cannot thank you enough."

"Go find your mother," Stiva told him.

They clasped hands fondly, a quiet sound that echoed for seasons and cycles, until eventually it grew into a thundering crash that shook Aris to its core.

CHAPTER 23

The Red Scorpion tavern was busy for a weekday, its scarred wooden tables crowded to overflowing with a widely varied assortment of patrons. People were already beginning to arrive in Aris for the wedding, though it was still several days off. Srih and merchant, Selin and Sijhani, serf and servant, farmer and fisherman, craftsman, artisan, and woodsman, commoner and foreigner: all blended together into a lively crowd that spilled out from the large main room into the back chamber, which was more commonly known as the game room. The sidewalk tables and patio were packed as well, and a line had formed at the door. On the other side, the back of the tavern opened into a small courtyard, where more tables had been set out around fishponds and arbors. This was also full. Fat silver fish dreamt beneath the maribels, below the clouded roar of voices, cups, and laughter. Barmaids slipped back and forth through the crowd, carrying huge platters of food, ale, and spirits, cheerfully tossing raunchy comments at one another and customers alike. The Red Scorpion was known for good food, good mead, and cheerfully bad manners. It was one of the more popular taverns in the soukh.

For a traveling bard, it was a lucrative venue, and an easy one. The Red Scorpion was particularly generous when it dealt with the blue robes, and therefore was a landmark stop for any bard touring Aris. There had been fewer of those lately though, and fewer still of renown. Stiva had made every effort to continue Lara's policy of maintaining a standing open invitation for any traveling minstrels to visit the castle, but the growing tension between Chandris and the Reonih had negated that. The bards did not come to Stiva as often as they had to Lara, whom they had known for one of their own. Whether it was fear or resentment of Chandris that stopped them mattered little, and apparently the fact that by long-standing law all Reonih were guaranteed protection and safe passage did not reassure them overmuch.

The halls of Aris no longer rang with song, but with the voices of an army at war.

So the minstrels came to the city instead. They came frequently to the Red Scorpion, for no more particular reason other than that the Red, as it was called, had an excellent selection of mead and ale, and roasted vhar that was to die for.

Reide sat in the murky depths of the tavern's shadows, ensconced in a corner niche with a pitcher of mead and a trencher of bread stuffed with mushrooms, olives, dits, and cheese. Beneath the midnight blue of his robes, a faint frown marred his features. The two figures at his side were quiet also, tense, though they sat close together and sometimes held hands or whispered private musings into one another's ears. He did not notice that, any more than he noticed the giggles of a serving girl some traveler had pulled onto his lap two tables over, or the scowls and curses decorating a table nearer the door, where it seemed a drunken brawl was about to erupt.

A robed figure stepped gracefully onto the platform against the northern wall.

The room fell silent. Or nearly so. A small crowd that had gathered around a high-stakes dice game at the back continued to provide occasional bursts of loud, raucous laughter, boos, and cheers, despite the annoyed glares of other patrons. A group of students sat inebriated and giggling around a keg of Zorish mead, happily oblivious to the rest of the world. A screeching fishwife who was in the midst of giving her husband a tongue-lashing continued her tirade, much to the amusements of the students, who began to mimic her as her husband tried unsuccessfully to sink through his seat.

The bard's first note chased the last bit of noise from the room.

The song wound its way through the air, words borne on silvery notes of sound, quietly speaking of things that should not be happening.

War, was its whisper, to those few who could hear it. Though the song spoke of the past, the bard sang of the present.

Reide listened carefully, taking silent account of the latest word of kings and queens and distant lands. He had come early in order to secure this table, which was his favorite. Tucked into a tiny alcove, it was secure from the pickpockets and game sharks that hunted the crowd on the main floor. The window beside the table offered a view of the courtyard and, beyond, the harbor. He enjoyed the view, but liked the window more because it provided a means for escape, should he need one. He often came here with Kira, Carin, and Fiurn, but this night he had other company.

Settled and secure, Reide left it to Ket and Twyla to watch the crowd, letting the song command his full attention.

"He *is* good," Twyla commented, between songs. "You were right, Reide. I remember him now. From Shadri, isn't he?"

"I'm always right." Reide answered without looking at her. The music started again: a saltarella, this time. He ignored the fried clam Twyla threw at him, too absorbed in the play of notes dancing across the pungent air to reciprocate.

"Do you know him?" Ket asked.

Reide nodded briefly, still not taking his eyes off the bard. "Eloris. He's from Shadri. Here for the wedding. He used to visit Lara, but he hasn't been in Aris for years."

The minstrel sang of death and war, and the fading of ages.

Silence owned the air as the first song ended. A smattering of applause and a few hungry shouts grew quickly back into the tavern's usual raucous din as the bard paused to drink from the tankard of mead a tavern maid had set at the table beside him.

Reide stretched the cramps from his legs and blinked as though waking.

"Is he coming back to the castle with us?" Twyla asked, as the next song started.

Reide shrugged, and then shook his head doubtfully. "Not tonight. I think he is going to see Kira first, and then come back to visit the castle."

If he doesn't run.

Reide left the afterthought unsaid. He felt Twyla's eyes on him—deny it as she would, she, like Chandris, had inherited Cronn's piercing gaze—but he refused to answer the silent questions in her stare. Eloris' cautious approach to the castle would have been unheard of in Lara's time. Reide knew without a doubt that Stiva would fight her twin tooth and nail before she let a bard suffer even the slightest injustice within the castle walls. But he also knew that Chandris acted when and how he chose, and that Stiva's influence on him only went so far.

The Reonih had not survived by initiating fools.

The bards were not about to blunder heedlessly into the keep of one who may be an enemy. Not a single blue robe there would ignore the song, or its implications. Omens and war and warning signs danced in silvery notes in the tavern's thick air, a warning straight from the heart of the forest.

The songs continued, each bleeding seamlessly into the next.

Sedition, the bard sang. He breathed rebellion into the tavern's smoky air, and the tavern swallowed it, unknowingly. When songs stopped, arguments arose: some were in favor of the reforms, others against. One table devolved into a brawl in the pause between the sixth and seventh songs.

Tension hung thick in the air.

Reide's frown deepened.

The mead had grown warm and the bread cold by the time Reide found the appetite to test them. He found the flavor strangely improved by time spent in the bar's thick air.

The bard played for more than a full watch. The sun had touched the horizon before he finally bowed and then bent to collect the bowl that sat on the ground before him. Within, the gleam of copper, silver, and even gold belied the appreciation of a lively crowd. His second performance, later in the evening, would probably prove even more lucrative.

The crowd blinked and stirred, the patrons sighing and stretching as though released from a spell. The buzz of conversation filled the air once more as song fled it.

Reide rose abruptly and stalked out of the tavern without a single word to his companions, leaving them no choice but to follow suit. His frown deepened as he stepped out of the Red Scorpion and into the dying red-gold light of day. He stopped on the street outside the tavern, blinking as his eyes slowly adjusted to the fading daylight.

Twyla was the first to join him. Ket emerged a moment later, looking mildly annoyed.

"Why do I always get stuck paying?" Ket demanded sourly. "Everything we do, everywhere we go, somehow *I* always end up footing the bill."

Reide scanned the crowd gathering outside the tavern. He answered Ket without looking at him. "The owner here never charges me. He knows I bring business when I play."

"Why didn't you tell me?" Ket demanded.

"I never interfere with business transactions," he said calmly. "It's unethical."

"Tell me again why I keep your company," Ket grumbled.

"Because I make you look good."

"No, that wasn't it."

"Because I am unfailingly intelligent and witty."

"Definitely not."

"Because I let you."

"No, I think it's the other way around."

Though Reide was quick with his banter, his face remained drawn. Ket took Twyla's hand, and they walked away from the tavern, navigating a steady stream of pedestrian traffic.

Aris' great soukh was packed, filled near to bursting. The soukh was enormous, consisting of four stories above ground and two below. It contained a veritable maze of booths, cafes, shops, and taverns. And the soukh was nothing if not confusing. According to local lore, one could follow one's nose to any item imaginable. One could find Sijhani leather work and crafts, Kralinic jewelry and Jaran clothing, Trianic woodwork and Vrehnian weapons, Shadrian silk rugs and Reonih wicker goods, oils and spices and perfumes from a dozen ports, some as far as the Yeverad Sea, or even further. Deloran wool, vaianth hides and oils, Zorish spices, the bones of behemoths from Turrel, Orlinian leather … the list of available goods was endless. A person could walk the soukh in an hour, or spend a day within its twists and turns and still not see it all. Laid out end to end, the soukh was seven mils long, or seventy, or seventeen, depending on who one asked.

Spring—the season of water—was always a busy time in Aris' market. The Lightfest holiday celebrations, which coincided with the season's first harvest, always brought a wave of traders. The first faires of the season inevitably drew crowds from near and far. This year, with the royal wedding approaching, the city was packed with visitors. Every inn and tavern was filled to capacity, and many homeowners had taken advantage of the sudden influx of visitors to rent out extra rooms at outrageous prices. Tents and caravans dotted the fields outside the city walls.

The soukh, which was busy even in the dead of winter, was chaotic. Merchants sniffed the wind, smelled money, and dreamt of better times to come, of wealth and opportunity. Vendors shouted and vied for the attention of the throngs of shoppers, trying to entice them into narrow booths crammed with goods. Here and there, Reonih walked the streets, settling the disputes that arose from the exchange of different currencies. Beggars, vendors, and prostitutes wandered the maze, competing for the attentions and coin of the passerby.

Stone-faced, Reide navigated the crowd, guiding them through the labyrinthine twists and turns of the market. At times, they had to walk single-file to avoid being separated. They could see the castle above them, its shellscale a cone of bloody gold in the fading sunlight, casting its shadow across the world.

He walked silently, aware that there were others missing that might once have come along. Shira, Stiva, Mykhal, Marcelle, Aret, even Chandris would once have been with them. Those days were long past. Yet he could feel them around him, ghosts of the living, like phantom limbs.

Ket broke the silence, turning to Reide with a casual look. "So what news do the bards carry today?"

Reide stopped in his tracks and turned to stare at the archer, his face darkening. "What?"

"I asked you," Ket said calmly, "what word the bard brings."

Reide's voice and eyes were suddenly ice-cold. "I get the same news everyone else does."

Ket met the challenge in Reide's eyes coolly. "Not quite."

Reide did not answer. Instead, he grabbed Ket's collar and slammed him hard against the wall of an alley they were passing, ignoring Twyla's startled cry of protest. A few passers-by turned to look at them, but quickly decided not to get involved and hurried past.

"You fool," Reide hissed. "Don't you understand that there is protocol, in everything the Reonih do? You don't just ask a question like that unless you're either an idiot or suicidal. You do not ask about Reonih affairs."

Despite the fact that Reide was practically choking him, Ket kept his cool, though a dangerous glint flashed through his eyes. "Maybe I just want to know what I'm in for if I stick around."

"Ask a seer," Reide snapped. "In case you hadn't noticed, I'm not one."

"Take your hands off me, bard," Ket growled. Steel flashed in his hand. "Now."

Reide didn't move.

"Let him go, Reide." Twyla protested. Her plea went ignored.

"I know about the code," Ket said. "I just don't know it myself. You got news today. I can see it in your face. And I don't think it is particularly cheerful word. Something is happening. I can see it. I can feel it. Yet you will not say a word to us or warn us. And I have to wonder if I should still call you *friend*."

"There is a reason for silence," Reide growled. "What we want Chandris to know, we tell him ourselves. The same goes for you."

Ket met the bard's rage with anger of his own. "I'm not stupid, Reide, and I'm not entirely uninformed myself. Lie to me, if you like. It only means I can base my decisions on less than accurate information. I have men to worry about now. And I'm not here because he sent me. I came on my own."

Reide adjusted his hand, tightening the pressure on Ket's throat. "If you're up to some game with me, archer, be warned. You could get yourself killed. Or you could get me killed." He jerked his head in Twyla's direction as Ket began to choke. "Or *her*."

"Reide, stop," Twyla pleaded, distraught. "Let him go."

Reide stared back at Ket, his eyes boring into the archer's with an intensity that belonged more to a warrior than a minstrel. Then, suddenly, he let go. Ket gasped deeply, filling his lungs with air that smelled of the sea as Reide watched coolly. Twyla was at his side instantly, her arms around him as though by instinct.

"So could you." Ket shot Reide's words back at him. "And you know damn well you could summon these same bards with a whisper into Stiva's ear, and have them perform the same songs in her garden." He hesitated, gasping for air as Reide squeezed harder. "But they won't speak to her now, will they? They do not trust her any more than they trust her twin."

The bard eyed him quietly, debating, weighting the odds of one move against another. Suddenly he turned to Twyla, asking her a silent question. Communication flowed between them, wordless. Reide's eyes bore a haunted look, while Twyla's were simply stricken and miserable.

She knew what he was asking. Trust.

So many things came down to trust, when there was precious little to go around.

Twyla nodded once in affirmation, attesting to Ket's character. "I will vouch for him," she said.

Reide paced a tight circle, then turned to face the archer once more. "They've moved the Relics," he said suddenly, in a low, tense voice. "Hidden them. That is their reaction to Chandris' interest in those artifacts. Do you know what that means?"

Ket frowned. "I thought all of Aris' Relics were already in one place."

Reide shook his head. "I'm not talking about just Aris. The High Priests of all the Reonih tribes held a secret meeting, and agreed that it was too dangerous to continue to keep them in various, known locations. They moved them all to secret places, and left only baubles behind."

Ket's frown deepened. "Why?"

Reide took a deep breath. "Chandris has been asking a lot of questions about Elders' technology. It looks like he is going to try and resurrect it. That makes the guardians of that science kind of … nervous."

The archer's expression grew grim. "That is a lot of power sitting in one place," Ket said. "Or even a handful of places. Too much, if a single person ever takes it."

Reide nodded. "Precisely. And sooner or later, someone will. Someone will try for it, and try to find out how to use it. Those are the weapons stockpiles of a fleet of starships, Ket. Weapons that drove back the Elders' enemies. Weapons that nearly obliterated the entire planet. Weapons that roused the Zhur, and cast us into the shadow time."

Ket did not change his expression, but they saw the shadow cross his eyes.

"Needless to say," Reide said darkly, "only the High Priests know where they are. They either killed the men who moved them all, or used mutes or idiots."

"I presume," Ket said slowly, "that Chandris does not know of this."

"I presume," Reide echoed, "that you are not going to tell him."

"Sooner or later," Twyla said, "Chandris will find out. He has enough Relics already to know a bauble from a tool. He'll know he's been deceived."

Ket looked around. They were in public, in a crowded square, but one couldn't be too careful.

"There is one more thing," Reide said then. "Something you both should know."

They both looked at him expectantly, waiting.

"What is it?" Twyla asked, when he offered nothing more.

There was anguish in his eyes when he answered, a worry that did not belong on his face. "The Zhur are hunting again," he told them, his voice low. "That means Relics have been used."

Twyla huddled closer to Ket, as though suddenly chilled. "Are you sure?"

Reide nodded. "A dozen girls the last few weeks. The way the Zhur kill … it cannot be mistaken for anything else. Be careful in the forests, if you must cross the thornwall."

Ket's face was serious. "Aye," he said. "Thank you."

"Do not breathe a word of this," he said.

By the time he looked at them again, Ket and Twyla stood close together, Twyla held protectively in the crook of Ket's arm. "You two," Reide said, "are disgustingly cute. Try not to get killed."

"Likewise," Ket said. "Except for the cute part."

They watched him dubiously, their faces and eyes both holding the same look, a mixture of reproach and worry. Looking from one to the other, Reide both envied and pitied them for having fallen so quickly and deeply in love.

"I'm headed back to the forest for a few days," Reide said, finally. "I trust you can make your way back."

With that, he turned and left them.

Twyla and Ket stayed where they were, soaking up the last moments of freedom before returning to the castle above. "Will you tell Chandris?" Twyla asked.

"Will you tell Stiva?"

Twyla bit her lip. "This isn't mine to share."

Ket kissed her forehead, and then they started walking back towards the castle. "Don't worry your pretty head about such things. If there is a war, I'll get rich, and buy you that." He pointed to a nearby vendor's stall, the centerpiece of which was a rug that someone with horrible taste had woven into a cacophony of loud colors.

"That? It's hideous!"

Ket wandered over to the next stall, and chose a necklace from the rack of displayed jewelry. The elderly couple immediately started describing the finery of the craftsmanship, but their salesmanship was unnecessary, at least in this case. Ket paid for the necklace quietly, and then turned and hung it around Twyla's neck.

"This is better," he said. "It's the color of your eyes. The jade matches perfectly."

The tolling of the bells sounded the changing of the watch, a jerk of the invisible chain. Twyla and Ket walked silently out of the soukh, holding hands. Once into the maze of Aris' streets, they separated, following separate currents in the flow of traffic.

CHAPTER 24

Stiva waited impatiently for night to claim the land. Only one moon, red Octavian, rose full in the dimming sky. The waning light gained a crimson tint as, somewhere in the descending night, one of the Reonih sang the sun to sleep.

The sound of music and laughter from the court trailed through the air. Taibon had arrived days before, accompanied by his father Adron and several Shadrian nobles. His stay was short: he'd spent a day at Starshire, visited Aris' beaches, and been to court three times. He had sailed back to Shadri that morning, taking advantage of tidal conditions. Stiva had found him pleasant enough, though somewhat hard to read. Chandris, Aret, Kele, and Lyle had taken him hunting, and Shira had accompanied him to several plays. Word of the impending marriage was already spreading like wildfire through Aris.

Stiva only felt dread when she thought of the marriage.

Aris sank into darkness.

A knock sounded on the door, and Stiva heard voices outside. She stood as Twyla entered, carrying a tray of yrehn … and frowned, when no one else followed. "Where's Reide?"

Twyla looked at her, sighed, and set the tray on a low table. Fragrant steam followed her into the room. "There's a problem."

"What is it?" Stiva's frown deepened. "Has something happened?"

"Nothing critical. Carin and Fiurn are both down with the flu. Reide's not going to be able to get away from court." Twyla crossed the room in a few steps, lowering her voice even though there was no one else in the room. The castle was riddled with sound tubes and clever spies, so it was never wise to presume there was no one listening. "Your excursion is going to have to wait."

Stiva breathed a curse and then lifted a painted nail to her teeth, thinking quietly. In a way, the news relieved her, for Reide's sake. The less he knew, the less he had to tell, or to haunt him.

Adele entered, carrying a second tray, of apples, hot buttered bread, and cinnamon. "Chandris has just left his rooms," she said.

Stiva chose an apple, and waved the tray away. Adele put it on a sideboard.

"Where is he going?" Stiva asked.

"The kennels, first," Adele said softly, looking hopefully at the rejected tray. "Then to the mews, to see the new falcons, and then to court."

"My brother," Stiva mused, "has taken quite an interest in the mews as of late. Graig says we shall have to expand it soon."

Stiva wondered—not for the first time—if Chandris' new hobby was somehow connected to her own dreams of wings and smoke. He had the same dreams, she knew, though he rarely spoke of them. She was no longer sure which of them was more haunted. Only that the nightvisions grew stronger every night.

A deep bell rang through the air. The city gates were closing for the night.

Stiva glanced up to find Adele still looking at the tray. "Go on, Adele. Take this with you. I won't be down to court tonight."

Adele took the tray and left. Stiva nibbled the apple thoughtfully. "I'll go alone," she announced, with an air of resolution.

"Don't be ridiculous, Stiva," Twyla scoffed. "You can't go into the city by yourself."

Ignoring this, Stiva went to her wardrobe.

"I'm coming with you." Twyla stood back, her hands on her hips, standing in silhouette against the last fading trace of orange-pink daylight coming in through the open arches of Stiva's sitting room, which led to a private balcony garden.

"No, you're not." Stiva emerged from the wardrobe holding a soft bundle. She shook her head at Twyla's words. "I need you to cover for me here. Help me out of this dress."

"Stiva," Twyla protested, frowning, "this could be dangerous. At least take Jarvor and Delis with you."

"So we can go dicing again?" Stiva asked, sweetly sarcastic. She shook her head, the sugar falling from her voice. "No. This is different. I'm not going to dance or drink in someone's garden."

"Why do you want to go sneaking about in the first place?" Twyla's eyes narrowed, seeing something unusual in Stiva's determination. "What is this all about?"

"It's just something I have to do." Once freed of the formal gown, Stiva put on a simple dress of dark brown wool. Opening the bundle she'd taken from the wardrobe, she unfolded the robe that had once been her mother's. This one was not the blue wool of a bard's robe, but a plain brown color. Lara had worn it in her apprenticeship, spent so long ago in distant Shadri.

Fighting the lump in her throat, Stiva donned the garment quietly, and then switched her silk hose for more durable woolen ones. She tied a leather pouch to the rope belt just behind the sheath of her dagger. Turning, she surveyed herself in the mirror. "I need gloves."

Twyla, shaking her head, disappeared into the closet. By the time she returned, gloves in tow, Stiva had scrubbed her cosmetics away and twisted her hair up into a sloppy bun. It was a younger, more innocent face, slightly smudged and rather unremarkable, that watched Twyla cross the room.

Twyla narrowed her eyes. "You've put a glamour on yourself."

"Hardly." Stiva laughed, then reached into a goblet and spattered a few drops on herself. Wine, they said, was the perfume of the common class. "But I may as well have. No one will recognize me."

"That's what I'm afraid of. If no one knows who you are, you've no protection at all." Twyla sighed, and then tried another tactic. "Chandris will have me killed if he learns of this."

"He would do no such thing," Stiva said, wrestling with the clasp of a jeweled bracelet, "and you know it. If anyone ever laid a hand on you, including him, they would be the rest of their life regretting it, believe me. Illegitimate or not, you are Cronn's daughter, and that makes you kin. Chandris may not consider you a sister, the way Shira and I do, but he would protect you just the same. And he would never have you hurt, much less killed."

Something like pain crossed Twyla's face. "I'm not so sure of that," Twyla said quietly. She reached out and unsnapped the bracelet, and then put it in a jewelry chest. "He's changed, Stiva."

To which Stiva replied coolly: "So have I."

Twyla did not seem to know what to say to that. She stood quietly, her features traced with worry. "Please don't do this," she said finally, her voice quiet. "The city is tense. There have been fights and even protests. If anyone sees you …"

"Twyla," Stiva said firmly, "I'm going."

Twyla sighed, still skeptical. "It—whatever *it* is—can't wait until tomorrow."

"No, it can't." Stiva shook her head again. "It has to be tonight."

"What is so special about tonight?" Twyla demanded.

She looked at Stiva, and, in doing so, saw beyond her, out the window. In the night sky, the blood moon appeared to be perfectly balanced atop one of the castle's spires.

Crimson Octavian governed war, first and foremost.

Twyla narrowed her eyes. "The red moon is full." She looked at Stiva. "It's something to do with the Reonih, isn't it? Something you don't want Chandris to know about. That's why you won't take the Selin. You don't trust them to keep silent."

Stiva began pulling on soft leather and fur boots. "Stop worrying. I'll be fine. We used to do this all the time, remember?"

"We used to climb the walls and taunt the cats, and I don't see you doing either of those things now."

Stiva said nothing, but sat down and bent forward to adjust the boots.

Twyla shouted for Khirin.

Stiva's head shot up. She glared at Twyla, who casually leaned back against the wall, smiling innocently as the door opened and Khirin entered.

"You called for …" Khirin trailed off, taking in Stiva's drastically changed appearance. His brows lifted. "Going somewhere?"

The captain of her guard was as much of a mystery now as he had been when he'd arrived. Silent, serious, Khirin was unobtrusive, asking nothing of her, offering no information about himself. When they spoke, words came easily between them, his thoughts often following her own, or vice versa, but much went unsaid. On occasion, he would offer some insight or suggestion, all of which were both accurate and intelligent, to his credit. For the most part, he remained detached, efficient, and cold.

As a Selin should.

"Go back to your post." Stiva pulled the boot off and shook a pebble out of it, then put it on again. "I don't need you."

"You don't."

Where Twyla had protested with words and logic, Khirin argued with a cool stare and silent warning. In a way, his very presence there in a way proved his point; had Aris been safe, he would not be there at all.

Feeling his eyes on her, Stiva was suddenly self-conscious and painfully aware of his presence. He emanated calm, but it was the sort of calm that masked rage. It unnerved her.

Stiva hated being unnerved.

"No, I don't," she repeated brusquely, and concentrated furiously on the boot. It stuck, going back on. Stiva frowned, pulling harder. "I said 'Here in'; she thought I said 'Khirin.'"

Khirin looked at Twyla, who smiled innocently.

"Here in." Khirin scratched at the faint shadow of stubble on his chin. "As in 'Here in Aris, kings hire elite bodyguards so the royal bed can be well-protected while the queen goes out alone into a night teeming with cutthroats and thieves?'"

Twyla caught most of her giggle in time, but a trickle slipped out. Stiva shot her a furious look and then turned the same icy gaze on him.

Khirin looked back calmly. "You are not going out alone."

Stiva sat up, meeting his gaze with narrowed eyes. "I do as I please, Khirin."

He ignored that. "What are you up to? Lover's tryst?"

"No!" Stiva turned her attention back to the boot, which was stuck. "It isn't your business. Go back to your post. If I wanted an escort, I would have called for one."

"She intends," Twyla informed him, "to go alone into the city, with only a dagger."

He actually dared to look amused at that. "And what happens tomorrow? Are you going to dive into the sea and play *Chase* with the sharks?"

"Twyla!" Stiva snapped. The boot finally came on, and she sat up, glaring at Twyla, who stared back innocently.

"I'm going with you." Khirin said.

Even Twyla blinked. Stiva stared at Khirin, more astonished than angry. "What did you say?"

"You heard me," Khirin said calmly. "You either go with me, or you go with the entire Black Boot. Your choice. But you are not going alone."

"What gives you the right to tell me what I can and cannot do?"

"To tell you?" Khirin shook his head. "I cannot. I can merely insist. You can, of course, override any decision I make, or send me away. And I can resign; *after* I send the Black Boot up here. And then you can explain to Chandris why I did so."

"You wouldn't." Stiva's eyes narrowed, met his: two black pools of shadow.

"Watch me," came the reply. "My job is to protect you. I cannot do that if you refuse to listen to common sense."

They stared at each other a moment, gazes locked in a battle of will.

"You're going to have to trust me someday, Stiva," Khirin said quietly. "Or send me away. I am useless here, without that."

Stiva glared at him. "Fine. But disguise yourself. I don't wish to attract attention."

At which he merely took off his armor and the tunic and cloak that marked him Selin. His clothing underneath was dark and rather plain. Twyla went to the wardrobe, pulled out a black cloak, and handed it to him. He put it on wordlessly.

"The sword." Stiva motioned to the blade that never left his side. "That is a srih weapon. We are not going among the srih. Leave it off. Take something less remarkable."

"The sword stays." But he fastened the cloak partially, concealing the blade beneath folds of cloth.

Stiva eyed him sourly. "You're very arrogant. And you have not once used the proper honorific." Turning away, she added irritably: "I could have you killed for that."

He bowed his head, but offered no apologies.

Stiva stood up. "You will say nothing of this to anyone."

A raised eyebrow, followed by the briefest nod, was her only answer.

"What shall we, *saya*?" Khirin asked formally, gesturing to a carved thi-wood wall panel, "The hallway or the secret passage behind the wardrobe over there?"

Stiva stared at him. "How did … how did you know that?" She shot an accusing look at Twyla, who shook her head, clearly as startled as Stiva.

"Every castle has them," Khirin said. "Shadri, Vrehn, Jara, any keep you name. It was easy enough to figure out where yours was. I studied this area carefully on the other floors. Are you ready?"

Pity, Stiva thought, *I can't punish him for thinking.*

He raised an eyebrow. "You weren't going to walk out the Zhrue Gate like that, were you?"

Twyla crossed the room and went to the panel. Her tone was almost cheerful, though her eyes were sharp. "Allow me."

She pressed a hidden lever, and the panel slid back.

Icy blackness waited before them.

Aris had not survived by making foolish presumptions about safety. Like most castles, Aris was—as Khirin had discerned—safeguarded by a secret network of tunnels. The tunnels had been built to provide escape in a desperate situation, but were more often used as a means of moving about covertly. It was hard to say which use they had been put to more. Forced to choose, Stiva would probably guess the latter.

Khirin stepped back and bowed formally. "After you."

"No, you go first," Stiva said sourly. "That way you eat the spiderwebs."

Khirin pulled a brand from the wall and stepped into the waiting darkness. The shadows swallowed him without a stir. A moment later, all she could see was the light of his torch moving into the blackness.

Stiva found herself suddenly rooted to the floor. She stood there, staring into darkness, her mind racing ahead of her through the dark winding passages. The bloodcurdling tales Kele had reveled in telling them when they were children all flooded into her mind at once. Legends of the tunnels' undead occupants flashed through her thoughts: a crazed cannibal that had escaped from the dungeons, the ghost of a murdered servant, elves, Reonih shapeshifters with a taste for human blood. Zhur. Though Stiva had traversed the tunnels many times and seen no such things, those tales still came unbidden to mind every time she entered the damp, dark labyrinth. The nightmarish images were interposed with jumbled memories of forbidden childhood escapades and hasty late-night scrambles through the tunnels. *Rats, erlits, snakes, spiders,* Trin had whispered to her once. *They, too, fear the ghosts.* Fear, leaving a coppery taste in her mouth. Chandris holding her hand, whispering to her that there was no need to worry, because he would protect her. A youthful Aret, dangling a fat purple spider before her, his laughter quelled as Mykhal slapped him for scaring her. Caro, long ago, white-bearded and paled by age, showing the twins, Aret, and Mykhal the barely noticeable glyphs that would help them find their way around.

Darkness waited, thick and oppressive. The torchlight paused ahead of her as Khirin stopped and turned, waiting.

She was Aris. Cowardice was a worse crime than trespass. The ghosts would forgive her tread on their shadowed domain once more.

"You look nervous," Twyla said sweetly. Leaning forward, she whispered into Stiva's ear. "I don't think it's because of the tunnel."

"Hush," Stiva said irritably, and walked forward into pitch blackness.

When she reached Khirin, he said nothing, but turned and moved on. The brand he held did little against the oppressive darkness. Shadows pushed at them from all sides. At the edges of the feeble circle of light appeared rough, moisture-slicked walls, icy puddles of muck, little shiny spots of motion belying insect life.

"Watch the tenth step." Stiva called ahead as they descended the first stairwell. "The ceiling there is—"

Mid-sentence, she hit her forehead soundly on the spot in question. Colors danced before her eyes. Stiva swayed, dizzy, as color spots dotted her vision, and put her hand to the wall to support herself. She heard more then saw Khirin pause and turn.

He had missed the overhang. Of course.

"Maybe it was the sixth," Stiva muttered, rubbing the sore spot on her forehead.

"Are you alright?" Khirin crossed the short distance between them in a few steps, and then adjusted his torch for a better look at her face.

"It's just a scratch." Stiva stepped back from him, still shivering. She rubbed her arms vigorously, hoping that he might think her trembling was from the cold.

"Aye," Khirin agreed. "But it's going to bruise. And I think you broke the overhang."

Stiva glared at him. "You weren't hired to make jokes."

"I wasn't joking." Khirin pointed behind her.

Stiva turned. The wall was pocked and pitted with age. But there was a fresh hole, a crumbled pocket of plaster in the space she had hit. A fresh pile of stone on the ground lay beneath it.

"Just go," Stiva snapped.

They continued on, through a labyrinth of narrow, damp walls, navigating a series of twists and turns. The rough stone walls gave way to smooth, flat substance, veined with cracks and dark with mold, but still impressive.

Khirin paused to take a closer look at the material.

"These tunnels were made by the Elders, before the shadow time," Stiva said, her voice echoing eerily in the passageway. "Aris was built on the ruins of one of their cities."

"Someone has been here recently." Khirin pointed to a spot where a fresh handprint had swiped some of the dirt away from the walls.

Stiva shrugged. "The tunnels are crawling with moles," she said. "Eyes in the dark, eyes in the heart." At his questioning look, she explained: "An old saying."

They walked on, finally exiting the tunnel via a trapdoor that let into a townhouse she and Chandris owned. It had sat empty for as long as Stiva could remember. Two horses were waiting in the stable. Reide had procured a bay mare for her, and a black gelding for himself. Stiva would have preferred a cat, but Lhin had never regained his full strength, and Stiva feared that such a taxing ride would be too much for him. Nor was she yet comfortable enough riding his son to take him on such a journey. And so it was horseback. Fortunately, they wouldn't have to cross any thornwalls. These two seemed well-trained, at least. Unlike cats, horses could be exchanged between riders without seeming to care much. But a horse offered little in the way of protection in a close fight, except those trained for battle.

Khirin tacked up both horses, gave her a hand up onto the bay, and then mounted the black. "Where are we going?"

Stiva's reply was short. "Outside the city."

He persisted, giving her a direct look. "Why?"

Stiva didn't answer him, but took a key from her pocket and unlocked a small side gate that led into a narrow alleyway. They rode out, and she locked the gate again behind them.

They ventured into the city as the night fell. The streets took them in silently beneath rising stars. It had been a long time since Stiva had ventured into the city incognito, especially after dark. The world she looked down upon every day from her window seemed different now, up close. Darker, and more dangerous. Streets she thought she knew seemed unfamiliar, and the people who walked them, her people, looked at her coldly. One man in particular stared at her, and something about his gaze gave her the chills. Khirin turned and stared him down, and he retreated into the shadows.

Suddenly Twyla's warnings about tension in the city became much more real.

Somewhere in the darkness, a child cried.

Eventually she had to say where they were going, if not why, for in truth she wasn't entirely certain of the best route. Aris' lower streets were twisted and mazelike, and she had planned for Reide to guide her. Khirin gave no comment, but led her down this street and that, navigating the warren of roads and alleys easily, as sure of his way as anyone born there.

Hoofbeats rang out on the cobbled stones of dark quiet alleys and streets strewn with trash.

They moved through the underbelly of the city, and Aris met her with a face she had never seen, a face that was cold and dark and dirty, a face that stared at her with eyes of hunger and pain. Cramped, rundown apartment houses greeted them with barred doors and closed shutters. There were no torches here. Only the occasional light of feeble candles flickering behind grimy windows illuminated the darkness. Dogs growled and snapped in the shadows, fighting over bits of trash that littered the alleys. Pale, thin people stumbled around, glassy-eyed and unsteady.

Stiva stared into Aris' darkest alleys, and found the slithering evils of things she had never faced. Hunger. Fear. Filth. Disease. The faces staring back at her were often pale and gaunt, with eyes utterly drained of hope. A child, dirty and thin, cried out for hunger. Nearby, a pregnant woman dug in a gutter for food. A few steps away, a thin, dirty man was lying feverish and delirious in an alley, ignored by passerby. In the shadows beyond him, a young girl with eyes four times her age took a murdik stone from a fat man and then disappeared with him into the night. Four men were roasting a rat on a fire fed by dried seaweed.

A mother, crying over her dead child.

A man, beating his wife.

The ugliness of the world she ruled struck her like a hammer, and the blow sent a sick feeling through her soul.

She did not realize that she was crying until the tears blurred her vision.

"You've never seen this side of life before, have you?" A quiet voice reached her through the shadows. "It doesn't exist in your world. Not in this form."

Stiva tried to keep her voice steady. "I knew the plague hit people hard, but I didn't ... I didn't. I mean, I knew there were poor ... somehow I thought we were doing enough." She had never felt directly responsible, before. The weight of that accountability sunk like lead through her soul.

In her mind's eye, she saw the Stiva of a few hours past, waving away a tray of food some of her subjects probably would have killed for. Guilt stabbed her like a knife. She felt nauseous.

"Rebellion," Khirin said quietly, as though reading her thoughts, "often starts in poverty. Sedition as a seed is often only a wish made by somebody cold and hungry. It has been going on for an eternity, Stiva, and it will probably never change. The srih benefit. The poor suffer. The cycle never ends. Aris, like all states, stands on the backs of those who labor in its shadow."

"Do you think I'm like that?"

He surveyed her carefully. "No," he said finally. "But if you had asked me before tonight, I may have given a different answer."

The pouch felt heavy, of a sudden. She reached in and tossed a silver coin to the next child she saw. And the one after that, and the one after that.

The silver had been meant for the gods that dwelt in the Gherot River.

The children needed it more.

"It won't do any good," Khirin said, after the fifth child. "They'll give the money to their parents, and it will be in some barkeep's pocket by this time tomorrow. Or it may buy a few meals, a pair of shoes, but they'll be hungry again next week. Moreover, if you continue, we'll be robbed shortly."

Stiva looked at him, stricken, but realized he was probably right.

"Besides, you are in a position to change more than a few coins ever could." He looked at the sky "Let's go," he said, nudging the gelding forward. "We have a ways to travel yet before we're outside the walls."

The horses' hooves rang out on a half-empty street. Though the main gates closed at dusk, two small side gates went manned through the night. Stiva went to one she knew to be manned by a friend of Reide's, who would let her out quietly and keep it to himself.

The city released them into the surrounding lands by way of a small gate. They emerged into the night air as the voices of nocturnal birds rose up to the sky. They crossed the moonlit fields outside the city gates, passing the cottages of serfs and, further back, the castles of their srih landlords. An hour later, they had reached the edge of the forest. The trees seemed silver and red, shivering in the breeze, and the wind carried the perfumes of mosses and leaves, along with the promise and memory of ice.

Khirin broke the silence. "Who was Trin?"

The question took Stiva by surprise, but she gave no reaction of this. Nor did she look at him as she answered his question. "Trin was the one man foolish enough to make me love him. He died for it. That death is the reason why Barls hates us so. He was one of theirs. Remember that if you like, but do not speak of it again." She hesitated, glanced at the night-drenched world ahead. "Why?"

"You call for him, sometimes, in your nightmares."

More than once, he—like the rest of her guard—had run into her bedchamber, sword drawn, only to find her screams caused by nightvisions, and the things that walked her nightworld. The rest of the Black Boot did not mention it, *ever*, though it had been going on for years. Nor did they speak of the fact that Chandris' nightmares often occurred simultaneously with Stiva's.

"My dreams," Stiva snapped, "are of barbarian gods, when they are my own. When they are my brother's, they are of empire: war and chaos, gold and glory and darker things."

"Aris fears his dreams," Khirin told her. "And yours."

"They fear change," Stiva said suddenly. "Aris never changes quietly. Even the seasons here pass in violence. Aris is changing. Chandris is forcing it to. They know it. They feel it."

"They are uncertain of your loyalties." He looked at her directly. "You're going to have to choose one day, Stiva. You cannot straddle the wall that is forming between Chandris and the Reonih forever. Once it served you to act as the liaison between them. Once. No longer."

"I know," she said softly. He only nodded slightly, but she read the question in his eyes.

"They want you to usurp him," he said. "Don't they?"

She looked at him, eyes narrowing. "You want to know, don't you? Why should I trust you? If I say the wrong thing, will you put a knife in my heart?"

"If I wanted that, it would have been done long ago." Khirin's voice tightened. "Or a moment ago. But I am not the only one wondering where your loyalties lie."

Nearby, a jewel-scaled serpent slithered into the night.

"I think they're going to try to overthrow us anyway," she said, "regardless of my position on the matter."

"Probably," Khirin said.

She looked at him, taking in his profile. "I do trust you," she said. "I don't know why. I don't think I should, really. But I do."

She kicked the horse on, leaving the words hanging behind them in the air.

They reached Gherot River, and then turned at the fork where it met a tributary, riding a long a wide, shallow riverbank that was lined with rocks. Moonrise found them turning into Gherot Canyon, a place where the river had carved its way through stone, leaving behind a surreal, desert-like landscape. Grey stone cliffs rose, lifeless and barren, around and above pockets of rich vegetation. The moonlight shone even redder in the night sky than it had. Octavian seemed a drop of burning blood in the darkened sky. The canyon walls reached up on either side of them, barren and imposing, drained of color in the night.

Stiva scanned the ground intently as they rode forward.

"What are you looking for? Tracks?" Khirin asked her.

Nodding, Stiva looked up at the war moon, a crimson drop of blood in the sky, judging the time. "They should have been here by now."

"Who?" Khirin pointed. "Them?"

Behind them, lights bobbed in the distance.

Stiva cursed. "We need cover."

"There." Khirin pointed to a nearby copse of vegetation and trees. When she nodded, he dismounted, leading both horses into the tangle of thick brush.

Presently a party rode into view: a group of greybeards, red-robed and armed. White-bearded, all of them, yet they rode easily, their eyes keen and sharp. Stiva knew every one of them by name. They all visited the court with varied frequency, serving as advisors. These men were the sages of warfare, who served as advisors to both Chandris and Lyle in matters of warfare. Some were old enough to recall not just Cronn's battles, but Caro's.

Selin.

Elders.

Judges.

Stiva felt Khirin's eyes on her as they rode past.

Slowly, the night quieted. The sound of hoofbeats died out in the distance. A little while later, the party returned, riding the other way. Stiva held her breath as they passed, certain that they would see her.

Eventually, the chorus of nocturnal birds and insects resumed, and they knew themselves alone.

"Come on." Stiva was mounting even as she finished, and left the ravine at a full gallop. They tore down the shoreline, the rocky ground flying past beneath their horses' hooves.

It took them only a few minutes to reach the grotto, which was tucked into another ravine, within a circle of stones. A red bundle lay on the bare ground in the middle of it, surrounded by flowers and herbs.

Howls cut the air.

Stiva jumped down before the horse had completely stopped.

Khirin's mount reared suddenly, scenting wolves. She heard him shout something at her, but could not make out the words.

A grey shape slid through the shadows before her as she ran. Out of instinct, Stiva flapped her arms wildly, the cloak making her appear much larger than she was.

The wolf turned and crouched, snarling. Then, seeming to change its mind, it slunk off, having tasted the despised scent of humans in the air.

Stiva raced across the clearing, then skidded to a stop before the bundle and fell to her knees.

The child lay naked and helpless on a shield he had been born to carry but would never lift. He raised a tiny, misshapen fist up to an angry red moon, his voice a piteous mewl. As Stiva reached out for it, a sickening feeling of guilt cast a cold black shadow over her soul, that her own House condoned such a thing.

The child raised a twisted hand and howled weakly.

A shadow fell across her, blocking the moonlight.

Stiva spoke without looking at him. "The shield was made for him at birth." She reached forward and plucked the infant from the shield's center, cradling him gently. "You should know that. If you ever have a son, he will be given a new-made ceremonial shield. At first, it will be plain, but decorations will be added on his first full moon, his naming day, his totem day. His first battle, and his last. And all in between."

Khirin crouched, reaching out to gently take one of the child's tiny, malformed hands into his own. He said nothing, but his eyes when he looked at her spoke volumes.

Stiva looked down at the child. "They gave him a warrior's burial rites," she said quietly. "Though he never was initiated, nor will he be, he died Selin, and he died fighting. That he died fighting life itself does not reduce that honor."

"He isn't dead," Khirin said quietly, stating the obvious.

Stiva looked up at him. "To them he is," she whispered.

The child whimpered weakly. Stiva pushed back the hood that covered him, revealing a thick mass of red hair.

"Leave me," Stiva told him. "Take the child and wait."

He retreated into the shadows, a piece of shadow leaning against a tree, casual but alert, the child in his arms contrasting oddly with his warlike appearance.

It was up to her, to placate the gods for theft of a promised sacrifice. That was the Reonih way. Initiate or no, something in her balked at the thought of walking away without some sort of remedial act.

Stiva began the ritual, drawing a circle around her and calling the four directions. She lit a candle on the ground, and surrounded it with objects that held the essences of the elements. The shield went into the Gherot. The last of the silver coins she had brought followed it. It was solstice, a key night for rituals. And the fact that Octavian alone was full made the night particularly special to war and warriors. She beseeched the gods of war, with a song and a prayer, a silver coin and a few drops of blood, to favor Aris.

Stiva was almost through the ritual when it happened.

She sensed the disturbance before she saw it. A heavy, palpable tension filled the air. The woods suddenly grew quiet around her, the nightbirds and crickets falling silent. A flock of birds took flight, crossing the third moon, tiny Calizar, moon of hunters, in a storm of wings and screeches.

Stiva's skin prickled. As she looked up, her eyes scanning the skies, a harsh blast of icy wind gusted up, seemingly out of nowhere, whipping her hair and clothes around.

Everything happened so fast it became a blur. A piece of the night sky broke apart and moved, riding the wind that swept between worlds. Something moved through the air on black wings … something too large to be a bird.

Zhur.

There was a flash of steel as Khirin moved, standing protectively before her. He passed her the child as the winged figure dove down again. Stiva caught a glimpse of its face as it sped past. The visage of a middle-aged man stared down at her from the sky, bearded and gruff, his black eyes expressionless, his skin grey-blue with the pallor of death. It wore armor, but the pieces were alien to Aris, looking more like the carapace of a deadly insect than anything the Selin wore.

A hiss. A shadow. A whisper.

A voice from a realm beyond death called her name.

A shadow swept down soundlessly across the night sky, bearing down on her out of nowhere, so fast she only saw it coming out of the corner of her eye. The Zhur was impossibly fast. One moment the sky was empty. In the next, black wings and steel filled her sight. A frighteningly cold human face stared down at her from the air above the circle. Instinctively—foolishly—she threw her arm up in front of her face, still holding the child close.

As though hiding her eyes could protect her.

Words and runes filled her ears as it spoke to her, using a language no human had ever spoken. The sound of its voice pierced her soul. She forced herself to stand up and open her eyes.

This time, the face was that of a youth, darker skinned, his teeth flashing white.

Steel flashed again, reflecting blood-colored moonlight. Khirin met the thing on its next pass, his movements fluid and fast. The weapon danced in his hand. It seemed alive, no cold thing of steel but a living creature. The Zhurlord dodged the sword, and rose once more into the air, and then turned and dove for her again.

This time it came to rest on the ground, facing her directly from across the stone circle.

Its face changed, even as she watched, its features shifting and morphing. It was still human, but this was a different face, again, older and paler. Then it changed again, and she found herself staring into the eyes of a god.

A thousand visions struck her brain at once: memories, visions, dreams. She stood frozen in place, her mind blanketed by a mist of magic and power. She saw eternity, in the gaze of the Zhur. She saw the blinding, brilliant heart of the universe, and heard the screaming of distant stars.

The Zhurlord stood there in the moonlight, its edges shifting, as though obscured by mist.

It raised a leather-clad hand, beckoning to her.

Stiva took a step forward, holding out the child involuntarily.

"*Saya?*" Khirin's voice hissed through the night.

She took another step forward, her words and thoughts lost in the gaze of a god.

A bolt of lightning split the air, originating from the shadows at the edge of the grove. It narrowly missed the Zhur.

The thing fled, taking to the sky on velvet wings. A moment later, it fled through the clouds.

As its presence faded from the air, the fog lifted from Stiva's mind. The child in her arms mewled weakly.

Kira stepped out of the shadows, her face hooded and harsh beneath the light of a blood-red moon. She said nothing, but her eyes echoed her thoughts. *You should not have come here. You toy with forces you have no business dealing with, and you have roused the Zhur with your carelessness.*

"Kira," Stiva said quietly. "Thank you for coming. I wasn't sure you would."

Kira glanced up at the sky, and then slipped the Relic back into the pouch at her side. "We've read the portents," Kira said. "The babe has a role to play in the world. Our laws are the laws of the universe, Stiva, not just those of Aris."

"And had he been unimportant," Stiva said. "Would you still have come?"

"Of course." Kira stepped back and surveyed her thoughtfully. "Your brother does not know of this, does he?"

"He will dream of it tomorrow," Stiva said quietly.

Kira looked to the sky again. "How many were there?"

"Just the one," Stiva said.

"You called it," Kira said. "You summoned a Zhurlord. Someone will die for that tonight."

Stiva shook her head. "The child is near death. That is what drew it."

Kira's eyes glittered in the night. "Children die every day, but the Zhur do not often frequent our skies." She reached out her hands. "Give me the child." When Stiva hesitated, Kira tilted her head. "Isn't that what you came here to do?"

Stiva hesitated only a moment before handing him over. "Take him away from here," Stiva whispered. "Out of Aris."

Kira nodded, took the child gingerly, and turned away. Stiva caught a glimpse of a tiny, claw-like hand beating the air, then becoming firmly entrenched in Kira's hair.

Deformed or no, the babe certainly had a grip.

Stiva called out after her. "Kira!"

Kira stopped and turned.

A hundred words rose through Stiva's throat: thanks, sorrow, anger. There were a million things she wanted to say. She wanted to talk about the Zhur. She wanted to forget about the Zhur. She barely stopped herself from apologizing for her absence from the forest. But she felt the turning of the wheel, as she stood in the forest, watching Kira holding the child, her face and voice calm, her thoughts harsh. Instinct—or reverence—stopped her from speaking her true thoughts. This was not the time or place for discussion of other matters, not here, in the sacred grove.

"Thank you," Stiva said. "Come to the castle, when you can."

Kira nodded and curtsied, and then slipped off into the night.

A black shape twisted in the skies. Khirin sheathed his sword, his dark eyes shining in the night.

"We should get back," he said.

Turning, she looked back, and sensed unseen eyes watching her. Something broke the surface of the river. In the distance, the wolf pack sang to the crimson moon. And that made her wonder which gods had been denied.

That night the Zhur killed. The body of a farmer's daughter who looked, it was whispered, very much like Stiva was found in the forest, mutilated nearly beyond recognition.

CHAPTER 25

The matriarch's garden; a hidden escape tucked between the king and queen's chambers, a green respite from the castle's endless shadowy stone corridors.

Sun and stone surrounded a tangle of overgrown vegetation. What had once bloomed under the loving care of a queen's delicate hands now fought weeds and bracken for a beggar's existence. The flagstone paving was shot with emerald veins of weed. Vines hung over the latticed trellises like drapes, a tangle of bramble had overtaken the herb garden, the potted trees were grey and untrimmed, and moss and lichens covered the statues. Wildflowers, seeded by the wind and the droppings of birds and erlits, had taken the place of their pampered counterparts. Maribels and lady's kisses, windsong and goldenrod thrived amidst a tangle of weeds and the thorny bramble that crept towards untended fishponds. The koi and the water-dragons had survived on insects and lily pads, having long ago stopped expecting Lara to come and feed them bread crumbs and iridescent beetles. They would not eat from Stiva's hand, and so she had stopped feeding them.

In the sky, an erlit screamed a song of rage.

She stopped short, stunned by the speed of the garden's decay. It seemed too rapid. Lara had been dead only three cycles, only—

forever

—and yet there remained only traces, here and there, of the seasons she had spent cultivating this place.

For a moment, she saw it as it had been, and colors and sweet fragrances filled her senses.

For a moment, she saw Lara, moving among the roses.

Stiva shut her eyes against a sudden prickling of tears, then opened them, taking time to really look at what lay before her.

Lara's garden was overgrown and neglected, having long been abandoned to the erlits and the kirit lizards. But it was alive, despite the abuse, changed, but alive. It was a spot of silence in a screaming world, the eye of the eternal storm that raged in Aris. It was the one place that had always offered seclusion and a serenity one did not often find within castle walls. She remembered sunny afternoons spent here, when Shira had just been a toddler and Maren not yet a gleam in Cronn's eye, how she and Chandris had played and chased each other around the fountains, wrapped in sunlight and the sweet fragrances of Lara's roses, spellbound by the musical sound of their mother's voice. She remembered her mother's fury when Lhin had decimated the fish pond that one time, how Lara had actually shouted and Stiva had wept and Cronn had just stood there and laughed and laughed and laughed until tears rolled down his cheeks, though he had bought the fish from Jara, and paid a good sum to have them shipped alive.

Days past; they haunted this place like ghosts, images and shadows and trailing wispy voices, phantoms, dead things that would not rest.

Stiva blinked and they faded away, replaced by the harsh ring of steel meeting steel. Echoes from the Second … the Selin were training, below. But it was not the sounds of violence and strain that she sought to escape.

Deep in thought, she moved around the fountain. Its waters had been still too long; a greenish scum had formed atop them.

There came a change in the sunlit garden. The srih and servants fell silent, and hush fell over the garden. The Selin at the door of the garden came to attention as Chandris entered, flanked by the Gold Braid.

It was more than rank which turned all eyes onto Chandris and kept them there. Even Stiva was acutely aware of his presence. Gold glinted in his hair as he crossed the room to Stiva's side. Power clung to him like perfume.

He paused to fix a cold emerald stare into Khirin's eyes. "You live," Chandris said quietly, icily, "because you kept her alive, that day in the wood. There will be no more second chances. Get your men under control."

Khirin stepped back and saluted. Stiva nodded, dismissing him.

"Walk with me, Stiva," Chandris said, still looking at Khirin as he held an arm out to her.

Without a word, Stiva joined him. They moved off, leaving Khirin behind as they passed through an arched doorway onto the open terrace which wound its way around the outside of the palace.

The Black Boot and Gold Braid fell into step behind them, keeping a respectful distance.

The sun touched mid-sky. Somewhere a bell clanged in recognition of this.

They moved as one, their steps evenly matched. Eventually, they reached another vantage point and stopped there, two identical green gazes staring out over the world they had inherited.

The Second was astir with commotion. The Selin were training even more furiously than usual. Beyond the Second, beyond the castle walls, beyond the city walls, moving figures could be seen, massed in three fields. One could not see the arrows from that distance, but the targets were visible, and one could make out individual groups set to different tasks. Some were wrestling, some doing calisthenics, running, or practicing drills. Bits of crimson could be seen here and there, wandering around them. These were Selin, set to getting their new comrades into shape. They were setting their new charges up against a brutal regiment, forging an army out of untempered flesh and sheer willpower.

Stiva could tell even from a distance that the recruits were exhausted. Here and there, one lay prone on the ground. These went basically ignored. They would, by Selin reasoning, either recover, if they were strong enough, or sicken and die if not. Either was fine. The Selin wanted no weaklings in the army.

The twins stood silently for a time, watching the movements below them. "Training is going well?" Stiva asked.

Chandris nodded quietly. "No one has ever seen an army like this," he said, after a moment. "Ket's new method of making bows has completely changed the effectiveness of an arrow as a weapon. They can pierce armor as though it were butter, and it can be mastered in a few moons."

Chandris glanced at her. "There has been some trouble in the north. Faulner drove another Deloran war party off his lands, and had a hard time of it. And an Orlin raiding party struck us on the eastern border. The garrison pushed them back."

"I heard of it last night." Stiva said.

He moved on, and she went with him. They went through his suite, navigating a series of terraces, until they stood again outdoors. Stone walls left behind, the twins moved into the open air, into the sea wind and sunlight. Above them, the echoing cries of gulls rang through a pale sky. From their vantage, Chandris and Stiva could see the city and harbor. The Oburion lay mirror calm, a rare state for the usually rocky waters.

In the field outside the city, makeshift barracks had sprung up, beyond the fairground, which was at the moment covered in tents and wagons. The practicing archers were dots on the field, barely visible.

He looked down at the field again. "They're growing restless, hungering for the battlefield now. And they will have it soon enough."

Stiva frowned.

"I suppose you've heard that the road along Aris' border is completed. It's paved, and already in use."

"Yes," Stiva said. "I've been getting updates from the overseers. But you didn't come here to tell me that."

"No," Chandris said. "I didn't. I came to find out why you ordered five granaries to be opened."

The smile fell from Stiva's face. She stopped short, taken aback by the anger in his voice. "The people were starving. I fed them."

"Was that Mohr's advice? Reide's?" Chandris voice twisted sarcastically. "Or did you cast the runesticks yourself on this one?"

"No one advised me." Stiva told him. "No one needed to. I went into the city and saw our people starving. I had to help."

"Help." His jaw twitched slightly. "What do you think I'm trying to do?"

She had expected rage, open hostility, when he learned what she had done. Instead, she found his anger calm and cold, and it unnerved her anew. It was usually heat, with him, shouting and stomping and a rage that echoed through the halls. This was a new Chandris: composed, arctic, collected.

"You haven't helped anyone," Chandris told her grimly. "There are still crops in the field. There was no need to use those stores. You could have called a grainbidreep. A day's harvest would have been easier to lose. Now we've hardly anything left, and most of what we do have is going to the army. With the food we've ordered for the wedding, we've *nothing* to fall back on if another harvest fails. People may starve this year for your sympathy, Stiva. But it will not be my warriors who go hungry."

Stiva looked at him, and found a stranger before her, one with haunted, ice-cold eyes. "Your men will not fight better if they see their families starving," she told him flatly. "And I've already sent hunting parties north, after the valianth herds, and commissioned three more fishing ships. The Reonih predict a decent summer. It was a calculated risk."

"It was a reckless move."

"You may watch your vassals so closely you could probably tell me what color socks they're all wearing, but you haven't a clue as to how the rest of your subjects are faring."

He frowned. "What are you talking about?"

"The commoners. They till the fields, they reap the harvest, and tend your livestock. They keep us alive."

His eyes flashed. "All I do, I do for our people. If you do not know that, you know nothing."

"This is what I know, Chandris: Aris stands on the backs of those who labor in its shadow. They've starving in the streets out there, and they look to us for help. You spoke to me of the devastation the raiders caused in the north," Stiva said. "You sent letters telling of the devastation. But have you ever gone into the city, and seen the poor that live in the shadow of the castle?"

"Do you think they'll do better if Delorans sack the city? If every field is but a charred mess? What do you suggest, Stiva? That I let them dictate my decisions?"

"That you don't make the mistake of every overthrown king before you," Stiva said. "*All* our people need food, Chandris, not just soldiers."

"Including Delora and Orlin, and they will take ours if I cannot defend it." Chandris looked at her coldly. "The stores that are left will go to the army. You'd best hope your hunters and fishermen come back with holds and wagons loaded. The Reonih will have none of what is left in our granaries, save they earn it."

Stiva felt herself shaking. She curtsied and turned to leave.

"I didn't dismiss you, Stiva."

Stiva froze. He had the authority, technically, to keep her there. But he had never used it against her before.

She looked up and found her twin staring back at her, his eyes cold and glittering.

"There is one more thing," Chandris said. "I'm commandeering the Relics."

The day went dark around her.

Black wings

Blood on stone

Rocky cliffs

Chandris held something out. A scroll. "The new dictates," he said. "I expect your full support."

Stiva took the scroll, her hands shaking.

The twins stared at one another, unspoken words dancing between them.

"We've inherited a land of soil and stone," Stiva said. "I fear your dreams will leave it in ashes. I fear your peace will drown the land in blood."

Before she could react, Chandris had seized her by the upper arms, twisted her, and slammed her against the wall. Khirin, Jarvor, and Delis immediately moved forward … only to find themselves blocked by the Gold Braid.

Tension hung thick in the air. The two Gold Braid guards at the door immediately stepped forward. Khirin and Dallan met them, drawing weapons.

Black Boot and Gold Braid found themselves facing one another, not as allies, but as possible foes.

Fear drove adrenaline through Stiva's blood. She felt her heart pounding in her chest. Looking into her twin's eyes, she saw only emerald rage, and the dreams of a mad king.

Chandris' voice was livid with fury. "Don't think me a fool. The land is full of whispers and speculation. What will Stiva do? What will you do, Stiva? I know the Reonih are plying you, wanting you to try to usurp me. If you take one step towards insurrection, it will end in death: yours and theirs, and it will cost the Reonih my good faith."

"Let me go," Stiva tried to twist out of his grip, but he was stronger, and held her as though in a vise.

"Tell your men to stand down," Chandris said. He drew her closer. She could smell the sickly-sweet tinge of rupalier leaves on his breath.

"*Saya,*" Khirin said. "He will not touch you and walk away."

"Stand down," Stiva said. She tried to keep her voice calm, but she was trembling.

Khirin stepped back, but stood ready, his eyes burning into Chandris'.

"Stand down!" Stiva said again.

Khirin gestured. The Black Boot sheathed their weapons, but stood uneasy, ready for the situation to escalate again.

Chandris let her go, by shoving her away from him.

"Stand by the Reonih," he hissed, "and hope that the gods put food on their table. Or stand with me, stand *with* me, and I will *see* that they are fed. You will make yourself clear at the wedding, Stiva. I told you when I returned that I would not tolerate sedition."

Chandris' eyes flashed. "I will tell you this once. Do not fight me on this. I will not bend, and I will not back down. Your place in this is to mend relations."

"You really think you can do this, don't you?" Stiva whispered.

"Yes." There was no hesitation in his voice, only steely determination. "Yes. Aris will shine like a star."

Stiva felt her voice shaking. "Aris will burn."

Chandris surveyed her coldly. "I expect a declaration of your support shortly."

He turned and walked away.

In the valley below, the roar of the army filled the air like thunder.

CHAPTER 26

Shira's wedding day dawned clear and warm, a perfect day crowned by perfect weather, which was a good omen for the impending marriage. The hills around the city brightened with color, and the first hints of light season rode a gentle breeze that rang with birdsong as flocks of waterbirds returned from warmer lands. Bells rang out across the city, tolling bright tones through the air; flutes and lyres trailed cheerful voices after them. The Reonih met the new season with the Lightfest Ballad, as was traditional. Stiva laid in bed until the song had faded out, then rose and went to the window, which she opened to lukewarm air that smelled of salt and musk and earth.

A darker sound twisted through the air beneath them. That was the Selin, chanting. They met the day in full uniform, murdik stones glimmering in the sun. They, too, were in jovial spirits, laughing and joking, but theirs was a dangerous vigor.

Stiva shut her eyes, listening to the chant. It seemed to have soaked into the very stones of the castle around her.

It seemed impossible that Shira was getting married.

It seemed impossible that Lara would not be there to see it.

It was the first time since childhood Stiva hadn't participated in the Lightfest Hunt. A year to the day, and she could still smell the forest glade, the scent of rich, loamy earth and freshly budded leaves tainted by the coppery smell of blood and the stench of death. Every time she looked at Dallan, who had grown increasingly sullen and angry in the year following his brother's death, she knew that the memories of that holiday would haunt them all for years to come.

Stiva looked at the Reonih in the sunlit yard below, and found herself struck by the sense of timelessness they exuded. For each bard, sage, or healer that passed before her, she saw thousands of robed figures, the Reonih of generations past, who had walked this land and whispered its secrets for centuries. They did not inhabit Aris; they were a part of it, as though the very land itself breathed through their lungs. Her throat tightened.

Stiva turned her eyes to the north, to the rolling hills outside the city. Tucked in among them, far out of sight, Starshire waited. *Sanctuary.* That was what Starshire had always been to her, a place where the sun seemed brighter and warmer, a place where she could relax and shed the layers of negativity that clouded around her in the castle. Her childhood memories of the summer estate were painted warmly in feelings of safety and laughter. Anger and war and rage belonged in the city.

A darker recollection stained those images now. Stiva shook the images from her head, and continued on her path.

She was masked, as all Aris was. The city below was mobbed with people. Most of Aris had come to witness the wedding. Every street corner was packed with traveling bards, actors' troupes, fire dancers, buskers, and seers. The soukh, always bustling, was even more packed than usual. There were games in the arena and on the beaches, and in the harbor, a parade of brightly lit ships would be the main event. Music and laughter raced through the sunlight.

Stiva felt dead.

Shira's rooms were a chaotic frenzy. Stiva picked her way past a tangle of dresses, ribbons, and shoes and made her way into Shira's dressing room, which was, as she had expected, mobbed.

Shira sat at a dressing table in the morning sun, with no fewer than four maids fussing over her, moths to a flame.

When Shira turned, Stiva found a lump forming in her throat. "You look like Mother," she said softly.

Twyla carefully inserted a hairpin into Shira's intricately braided coiffure. "She does," she said. "I've told her as much."

Taibon had arrived, accompanied by his father, Adron, and several Shadrian nobles, just days before the ceremony. Stiva, kept busy overseeing the preparations for the festivities, had seen them mostly at court, where the entertainment Talia had arranged left little space for conversation. The Shadrian royals were somewhat reclusive and a bit reserved. They were polite enough, but their demeanor remained rigidly formal. Stiva had not yet decided whether she truly liked them or not. It was hard to listen to them speak. Their accents reminded her so strongly of Lara that it hurt to hear them.

Shira looked at her sister from beneath a flawless application of makeup. Twyla stood back, surveying her handiwork. "I think that will do."

Shira looked at Stiva. She said nothing, and her eyes barely changed, yet Stiva recognized the silent plea for approval. "You look beautiful, Shira," she said. "Perfect."

It was the truth. Shira's face was flawlessly made up. Her hair shone, and Twyla had put it up perfectly in a style that highlighted her eyes and oval face, and set off her slender neck perfectly. Diamonds sparkled at her ears, neck, and wrists. The dress she had chosen had turned out to be even more breathtaking than Stiva had expected; the material, at least, had proved to be well worth its outrageous cost. It shone with the slightest hint of iridescence. Stiva noted it in a glance, thinking back to the day Shira had chosen it.

I'm entirely grateful for being sold off like a piece of cattle, if not entirely free of bitterness.

"Thank you," Shira said. Her voice was soft, as it always was. It trembled slightly, as did its owner. "How long do I have?"

"An hour or two." Stiva gave her sister a soft smile. "Don't worry, they won't start without you."

"No," Shira said, not reacting to the joke. "I don't suppose they would."

Stiva looked around the room. The maids were fussing over each other, talking about the upcoming festivities. One couldn't wait to watch the arena games. Another was excited for the night fair. They gossiped, as always, about who was in favor, and who had lost esteem. Their giggles warmed the room, but they were grating on Stiva's nerves.

"Leave us," she commanded. The chatter moved into the antechamber. Twyla was the last to leave. She shut the door behind her, giving Stiva a meaningful look before she left.

Silence rang through the room. Shira looked out the bay window, saying nothing. Ships of all types bobbed on the harbor's amethyst waves. The ships' parade was a longstanding Lightfest tradition, and one of Aris' more reckless means of celebrating things. As the day went on, the vessels tended to zigzag a bit as the captains sank into their cups. Brightly colored flags hung off the masts and the buoys in the harbor. The sailors spent the day sailing around the harbor, engaging in mock battles, and tossing trinkets overboard to the Zhur. Inevitably, some would end up paying more attention to their cups than to the steering, which was a bit hazardous in Aris' port. Occasionally the sound of a scream was followed by the barely audible echoes of the sailors' drunken cheers.

Stiva sighed, hoping that none of them cracked their hulls on the reefs. One of the vessels caught her eye and she pointed, forcing cheer into her voice. "Look," she said. "The one with the purple and black flags? Isn't that the Shadrian vlorship Taibon commissioned for you? The *Shira Belle*?"

Shira seemed unimpressed. "I've seen it," she said, twisting her ring. "I went aboard yesterday to approve the bedchamber furnishings. It seems alien, somehow: it's filled with Shadrian silks and Shadrian colors, and strange scents." She looked back at the sea, lost in thought. The sky was clear, but the Oburion was choppy that day, and breaking waves turned the harbor into a moving scape of whitecaps. Calista was visible in the sky, a pale sliver, and Vhrohos, a turquoise eye in the night sky.

Stiva watched her sister thoughtfully. "It's the forest for me," she said quietly.

Shira cast her a puzzled look. "What?"

"You look at the sea when you're troubled, when you need to think," Stiva explained. "I look at the forest."

Shira turned her attention to the bay again. "Oh."

Stiva took off her mask, then reached into the small satin purse she carried and pulled out a small package. Shira looked at her questioningly as Stiva pressed it into her hands. Surprise chased apprehension across Shira's face. Both melted into something much more profound as she opened the package. A velvet sack lay within.

"It was Mother's," Stiva said quietly, watching as Shira held up the bracelet. Caught in the sunlight, the diamonds shone like tiny stars. Shira took it and put it on. Stiva moved beside her sister to fasten the clasp. "She wore it to Maren's naming day."

Shira's shoulders were shaking. "I wish she were here," she said quietly.

"Me too." Stiva moved around to face her sister again. The lump rose once more in her throat. She had to force words out around it. "I can't believe you're leaving."

"They're going to hate me," Shira whispered.

"No, they won't."

"They already do," Shira cut her sister off. "It's no secret what Chandris is planning. He's unraveling everything Aris is built on." She stood up and went to a small chest of drawers, pulling out a small packet. She handed it to Stiva without saying a word, but her eyes searched Stiva's face for the slightest reaction as she read it.

It was a letter from Pahnryn, Lara's father, their grandfather. The message was brief and simple, just a few short lines offering a stiff and formal congratulations to Shira for the wedding. There was nothing warm about it, no hint of the kinship or fondness Pahnryn should have shown.

"Hardly a warm welcome," Shira said, echoing Stiva's thoughts.

Stiva sighed. "Mother always said he was cranky. I'm sure you'll find him much more endearing in person."

Shira gave a short, twisted laugh. "Of course he's going to welcome me, Stiva. Just because our brother is trying to dismantle Reonih culture is no reason for him to bear *me* any ill will."

"Shira," she said quietly. "None of us can make Pahnryn into the grandfather he has never been. If you want to soothe relations with him, take the initiative. Contact him, when you get there. You are a member of this House, just as much as Chandris and Maren and I."

Shira gave her elder sister a cold stare. "I know that. So, I fear, does Shadri."

Stiva sat down on a shardwood bench. The jewel tones of the thi-wood gleamed in the sunshine.

"You're frightened," Stiva said. "That's understandable. But there is strength in you. You will find it. You do not need to know everything about wars and politics, but you need to appear confidant and wise. Be silent, if you do not know what to say. Ask questions, and get your answers from more than one source. But do not pretend for a moment that you can afford to ignore people you dislike. Keep a close circle of advisors, those you know you can trust. Do not let them dictate your decisions."

Shira tilted her head, a harsh glint invading her eyes. "The way Chandris dictates yours?"

Stiva stopped short at that.

"I chose Taibon," Shira admitted. "I chose Shadri, and its rulers. They will hate me, Stiva. Because I am of Aris. And I am terrified of that. Taibon's parents still rule Shadri. They already see me as a tool. A walking womb. I fear he does, too."

"You're scared," Stiva said bluntly. "You fear that your life will be filled with misery and anger. You look at Kele and Talia and shiver, because you aren't strong enough for that relationship. You fear that you would crack like an egg beneath such a burden."

Shira opened her mouth as though to deny it, then shut it slowly, and nodded instead. "Aye," she whispered. "I am afraid. I am a coward, Stiva. Even Maren has more courage than I do."

"Shira," Stiva said quietly, "if something goes wrong, the bards can send me word."

"Use the Reonih," Shira said, sarcasm heavy in her voice. "As you do."

Stiva stepped back, stung by the rejection. A knock on the door preceded Twyla's entrance.

Any of the other maids would have waited for a reply before entering, but Twyla had always been unofficially exempt from such restrictions, at least where Stiva and Shira were concerned. She simply walked in, holding a golden cage. Within it, a Shadrian songbird of the purest white sat silently, flapping its wings a bit to retain its balance against the motion of the cage as Twyla walked.

Twyla set the cage down carefully on a table. "From Taibon," she said, by way of explanation. "Where do you want it?"

Shira looked at the cage, and at the fragile creature within. "Open the window," she said tonelessly. "Please."

Twyla cast Shira an odd look, but she did as asked. Shira went to the cage, surveying the little animal within. Songbirds were not rare things, but a pure white one was quite unusual. It was easy to see why. The creature was beautiful, almost like something from a dream. Its form recalled something of the swan and something of the dove, but it held a grace all its own. Its movements were delicate, its eyes a deep, liquid gold, painted in sorrow.

Shira opened the cage and took the creature onto her finger. It trembled visibly for a moment, made a mournful, nervous sound, and then settled onto its perch without a struggle.

"It's tame," she said. "Do you know how they tame these? With the screams of dying pigeons. The bird begins to sing only when it cannot bear to listen anymore. So they torture bird after bird, until finally the bird begins to sing to drown the sounds out. And by doing so, it makes the sounds stop. That is why the command for them to sing is the same as the command to begin the torture. Otherwise, they won't sing a single note. Likely a hundred pigeons were tortured so this bird would sing on command." She stroked the soft down on the bird's head gently, speaking a single word. "Begin."

The bird released a long, pure note, a silver drop of sorrow and vitality that seemed to echo into Stiva's soul.

"It's like you," Shira said. "It only sings when someone tells it to."

Shira crossed to the window. With one motion, she released the songbird into the air. Stiva's heart sank as she watched it fly into the sun. The bird would die. The creature had been caged too long to bear freedom. It had never learned to hunt, to fend for itself, but been coddled and hand fed, forced to witness endless days of death and pain.

A moment later, an erlit rushed past, and a shriek of pain announced the songbird's fate.

Twyla entered. "Stiva, Mohr is waiting for you."

She put her mask back on, so that neither Shira nor Twyla could see the tears welling up in her eyes.

———————

Khirin leaned against the alley wall, staring at the piece of paper in his hand.

The emblem of the Dralek seemed to leer at him from the parchment. It was drawn in black, meaning there was to be no hesitation.

And on the other side, a single name.

If I say the wrong thing, will you put a knife in my heart?

"Get your people out of the city." Stiva's eyes fastened on Mohr's, proud and pleading at once. "Tensions are building fast, and there will be trouble soon, when the laws are posted."

Mohr gave her an even look. "I cannot do that. It's Lightfest. If you want the Reonih out of the city, order them to leave."

"You know as well as I do there would be riots if we ordered that."

"The people are here to celebrate the change of seasons. They're here to marry, and see a princess marry."

Stiva balled her hands into a fist, but retained control of herself; her voice was steady when she spoke. "Those who stand behind you are ready to stand against Chandris, and vice versa. They are likely to protest the new dictates with violence. You know as well as I do that means Selin, and that can only lead to civil war, bloodshed. I do not want that, Mohr. I don't ever want to see a war cross the thornwall. I do not want a drop of Reonih blood spilled. But I can't stop it alone. I need your help." She met his eyes. "Pull them out. You are the High Priest. It is your place to guide the Reonih, not mine."

"There has always been war," Mohr said. "We have earned our rights in this society. We earn our keep."

"This is different." Stiva said. "Chandris has raised the stakes. Whether you realize it or not, you are standing in a place between change and annihilation. And tradition alone will not keep you safe."

"From your brother? Breaking it may not keep him safe, either."

"Listen to me, Mohr. You've got to pull them back."

Mohr whirled on her, eyes flashing. "We will not retreat. You tell me to listen, but it is you who haven't listened. I've heard everything you said."

"The dictates have already been stamped, rolled, and sealed. They will be posted after Shira's wedding. The tithes are ending entirely. The Reonih will receive a large portion of your funds on a strictly voluntary basis from now on. You are to charge for services you provide. You will have but a token share of what is left in our stores this season. There will be other changes as well, but likely those are the ones that will affect you most directly. I cannot and will not override the new laws, and I do not think you can expect a reversal."

"Then," Mohr said coldly, "I do not think you will see us working for an improvement in the state of your herds and crops."

"Then you will starve to death with the rest of us!" Stiva snapped.

Mohr looked at Stiva, condescension and something akin to sorrowed sympathy brewing in a coal gaze. "I thought we had taught you better, child. All those years of schooling, and still one basic fact of life escapes you. The will of the gods—"

"It is the will of the people that should concern you now, Mohr." Stiva cut him off harshly. "And the will of your king."

Mohr drew back, studying her carefully. "What are you trying to tell me, Stiva?"

She held out the scroll.

He took the scroll, handling it gingerly, as though it could burn him. "Are these official?"

"They will be posted tomorrow."

"This is your support?" Mohr said. "This is why we gave you the chance to learn our ways. You are Reonih by blood, Stiva."

"Stop baiting me, Mohr," Stiva snapped. "I no longer have the luxury of being fickle. And you no longer have the luxury of being able to easily shoo me away. I am your queen. If you think another would serve you better, then leave my lands."

"My duty," Mohr said, "is until death. I will leave your lands when the Zhur take me."

Hearing those words, Stiva could have sworn she felt her heart break in two. Yet she managed to swallow the lump in her throat and looked up at him, forcing back tears, forcing herself back into composure. "Chandris has told me more than once that he is open to my ideas regarding changes, things that could be done to improve the lives of our people. That includes the Reonih. I've convinced him to continue funding the theoricas, and to pay the healers for their work. I'd also like to start a college, perhaps something like the one in Vrehn. I would very much like for you to be a part of the process. If you cannot preserve every tradition, you can at least help us guide the path the future will take."

Mohr tilted his head. "Is that all you offer me for complacence? The chance to give advice?"

"I offer you the option," Stiva said. "I cannot be responsible for further division between robe and crown if you refuse to take it."

Mohr stared at her.

"And the Relics?"

Stiva was silent.

"You betray," Mohr told her. "And you will be betrayed."

Stiva opened her mouth to reply, but was interrupted by a knock at the door. Mina entered, curtsying before Stiva. "They are ready now, *saya*." Mina said. "Chandris is on his way."

Stiva nodded and waved Mina away.

Mohr bowed deeply, and then produced something from his robes. "For you."

Stiva reached out her hand, puzzled.

It was a Relic. It fit neatly in the palm of her hand. Her fingers curled around it instinctively.

"It's light," Mohr said. "But it carries the weight of a dozen dead worlds."

The high priest bowed, and then turned away.

The peal of huge bells split the air, summoning the wedding guests to the ceremonial hall.

———————

Stiva once more walked the Hall of Masks. The ceremonial hall was once more filled with srih, Selin, and Reonih, but for the first time a section had been set aside for the archers' division. Ketran stood in the front row, looking decidedly uncomfortable in formal wear.

The Ceremonial Hall had been completely transformed.

A circle of greenery had been prepared, and vines and ghiti flowers had been carefully arranged, turning the hall into an indoor grove. Candles and lanterns shone like stars in the dusky shadows. Incense filled the room with thick smoke.

The dais had been moved aside: Shira and Taibon were the center of attention, and occupied the raised platform. Chandris and Stiva sat in the audience, in the first row, with Taibon's parents.

Mohr performed the ceremony. If he was upset or angry with Chandris, he did not let it show. He called the corners, and spoke to the Zhur, asking the blessing of elements. He tied the belt around Shira's waist, and bound the couple's wrists together.

Shira stood proud and straight, her voice clear as she exchanged vows with Taibon.

Mohr bound their arms together with silken cords, and put garlands of ivy and roses on their heads. He cut their wrists, so that their blood mingled together.

And with that, Shira married the crown prince of Shadri.

Her eyes, when she met Stiva's, were cold, not the soft grey of summer clouds, but the steel of a flashing sword.

Kira sang the bond-song in accompaniment. Her voice was silver, now, growing sweeter with age, holding the crowd enthralled.

Across the city, as the fires were lit, the music began. The Reonih started their rituals, welcoming the turning of the cycle, the moment where the dark half of the year met the light. The sky dancers leapt from massive poles, twisting and turning mid-air. The music rose, the rhythms throbbing and pounding into the night. Aris reverberated with drums and lyres. And as dusk fell, the people of Aris lit great fires on the hillsides, in the city square, along the shore.

Buskers, musicians, bards, and dancers had staked their spots throughout the city, setting up on sidewalks and corners, in courtyards and taverns. Every park had grown a faire or farmers' market. The srih jostled for prestige by inviting actors' troupes and bard to perform in their yards and gardens.

Marcelle approached, curtsying. "You sent for me."

Stiva nodded. "I wanted to let you know you'll be going home in autumn. You seem … unhappy here. Your father has agreed to send your younger sister here as a hostage. He's also agreed to give your hand to Jahn. Assuming you accept."

Marcelle's face did not change. "That is for the best."

Talia spoke up. "The alliance with Vrehn and Jara pleases us very much," she said.

Marcelle glared at Talia. Her gaze was a dagger, surrounded by velvet. "I'm sure you are very happy about the matter."

Stiva looked out over the floor. Chandris was dancing with one of Adan's daughters.

A serving girl dropped a note into Maren's lap, and then moved to drop another dit into the pot of boiling oil. Kele lifted his cup, draining it in one long swallow, and then turned to glower at his wife. "Leave the politics to us," he growled. "Or is it impossible not for you to stick your nose in everything?"

Talia glared at her husband, and then abruptly stood and left the table.

Twyla leaned forward to whisper in Stiva's ear. "Two of the poison tasters have died. The ceremonial bread was poisoned. The bakers are whipping up another batch."

Stiva felt herself starting to shake. "That bread was only for Shira and Taibon," she said, her voice shaking.

Before them, dancers spun around the room, masked and free.

Stiva turned her attention back to the bard. This one was from Shadri: his robes were the same color that Lara's had been.

He sang a song she did not recognize. A Shadrian ballad, one to do with the Elders.

She glanced around, and saw Kira's face, intent on the bard. Reide, Carin, and Fiurn were similarly captivated. She did not notice Maren slipping away from the table.

She went cold as realization struck her.

They hadn't taught her all the songs.

Stiva frowned, trying to pick up anything she could from the unfamiliar song.

The clue came in the final chorus.

They were calling for war.

In the north, Itacha moved his cat—a great red male—to the top of a hill. Below him, the manor of Adan spread out across the valley below. He raised his hand, and a hundred shapes moved forward.

The Deloran king looked down over the land, at the fires in the fields. Lightfest was the perfect time for an ambush. Bonfires glittered in the fields, and the faint traces of music and laughter hung in the chilly air.

One of his generals rode up on a black horse. "We are ready now," he said.

"Glory!" he screamed.

The sound of hoofbeats filled the air like thunder as the raiders swept down into the valley. The cats, running before the horses, were silent, but even more deadly.

The sound of revelry turned to screams.

Maren peered into the darkness ahead, squinting into the shadows. He looked back over his shoulder, debating once more whether he should or should not bring his castemates. But the note the serving girl had dropped into his hand specified that Chandris wanted him to come alone.

He hadn't been in the tunnels for some time. He had a fair idea of which ones led where, but memory grew clouded.

He wanted to return to the hall, to have another fried dit. He hadn't minded the dancers' performance as much as he once had. The young women were, he had to admit, captivating to watch.

Suddenly an arm caught him around his neck. Maren struck out with an elbow, and stomped his heel down where he assumed his attackers foot would be, then spun around, baring his blade.

Four of his castemates stood there grinning at him.

"What are you doing?"

"What are you doing?" One of them echoed.

"I have to meet my brother," Maren said. "You shouldn't be here."

"We're supposed to be watchful," Paras said. His dark skin was barely visible in shadow: his eyes and teeth flashed white in contrast, the color of bone against midnight. "I saw you sneaking out of the hall."

"I'm supposed to go alone," Maren said.

"What if we just explore on our own?"

Maren considered this. "I ... I guess that would be ok. Just don't get lost! These tunnels are huge."

The four boys looked around at one another.

Maren looked in the direction he had been headed. "I have to go this way," he said. "Just don't let anyone see you."

Taber held his hand out in a fist. "Triple Fire!"

They echoed the words back to him. "Triple Fire!" They cried, bumping their fists together.

"Let's meet back here in two hours," Maren said. They nodded agreement, and he slipped back into the shadows.

The boys ventured forth together, excitement and fear rushing their words, their steps.

They slipped past a cistern, looked out through grates at various scenes, eventually finding themselves at a vantage point to look down into the great hall.

"Wait," Cael said. "Chandris is still in the hall. Who's Maren going to meet?"

———————————

Stiva waited until her twin returned. They had not spoken since the incident at the garden, save for formalities. He looked surprised when she turned to him.

"You will have my support," she said. "But I want to have a hand in these reforms. We need to ensure that the systems that benefit our people stay intact."

Chandris leaned back. "Such as."

"Funding for the theoricas," she said. "Tutelage for the children of serfs, not just the srih. Tolls on the roads. Yearly grainbidreeps and alebidreeps."

He nodded. "Very well," he said.

She held out a scroll to him. "These are my ideas. Funding for the healers and theoricas remains intact. We will set aside land for you to cultivate. Should the srih want private tutors, they will pay themselves. The law-readers will be paid by tithe, as always. We're also making provisions to build a true college, one staffed by both Reonih sages and foreign intellectuals."

Chandris frowned. "This could have waited another day."

"Do not post the dictates," she said, "until after the wedding. There are too many people in the city."

He looked up at her, and she saw herself reflected in his eyes. Silent understanding filled his eyes. He nodded.

She stood, and the hall fell silent.

"My loving people," she started. "I want to offer my congratulations to my sister, Shira, on her wedding day."

Stiva looked at Shira, beautiful, glittering, calm. Shira nodded. Beside her, Taibon inclined his head politely.

"I also want to assure you all, for those who have heard rumors, that Chandris and I stand united before you. We are prepared to do anything, to sacrifice anything, to endure anything, for the sake of you all, our people. We celebrate a strong new alliance with Shadri, and welcome the new branch of our military."

She hesitated, looking around.

"There are those of you who are wary and concerned about changes that are coming. Let those who speak against Aris speak their fears openly and truly, for we all know that fear dies in the light of day." She lifted her goblet. "To Aris! Honor. Courage. Serenity."

The crowed echoed the words back to her.

Stiva waited for the room to fall quiet again before continuing.

"As some of you may know, I used to enjoy singing quite a bit. I haven't done so much recently, but this is certainly a special occasion."

She moved to the bard's platform, and looked at Reide, Carin, and Fiurn. "Play 'The Ballad of Arctina," Stiva told him. "And 'The Song of Solara,' and then 'The Carrion Queen.'"

Reide nodded, his face unreadable.

She was nervous, suddenly, which seemed odd, as she had grown so accustomed to being in the public eye. Reide, Carin and Fiurn started playing, and the room fell quiet. She hadn't practiced much, but her voice was there, loosened a bit by honeyed wine, and as the song started, she felt the music move her soul, swelling and coursing through her on a wave of emotion.

Stiva kept herself focused on intent, on energy. Protection, she sang to them. Prosperity. Peace.

She was halfway through the second song when realized suddenly that she had forgotten the codes. She knew the song itself well enough, but the second verse, which spoke of the nature of the threat, stumped her.

Panic coursed through her. There was no time to check. She made a guess.

The faces of the Reonih watching her grew suddenly perplexed, and then resumed their intent look.

Only a handful of bards in the crowd knew what she was doing. She watched their faces, and dug into herself, finding, somewhere in her center, both the steel of Aris and the wood of the Reonih.

That she would protect her people. That she would die for them, if necessary.

That Aris must unite to stand.

And it was only at that moment that she felt whole: Aris and Reonih, queen and bard.

When the song ended, the cheers and applause were deafening. Stiva curtsied, her heart pounding, and turned to walk off the stage.

Kira and Reide turned to her.

"Did I do that right?" Stiva asked.

"You said that there were whales coming to invade," Reide said. "But other than that, I think you made your point. You said you were here to protect them, and see them through these changes."

"I cannot stop these changes," she said. "But I can guide them. I will make sure you are treated fairly."

Kira's eyes shone with tears. She knelt before Stiva, and kissed her hand. "Your mother would be proud," she said. "I'll make sure the correct message goes out as the bards move on and tell of the wedding."

From across the room, she caught Chandris' eye. Her twin was staring at her, his face unreadable.

Maren approached the intersection carefully, walking as he had been taught, by placing the balls of his feet down first. It was something of a game to him, to see how quietly he could walk.

He reached the meeting place quickly. From above, he could hear the muted din of the celebrations in the great hall. Snippets of a voice. He thought for a moment it sounded like Lara, and then he realized it was Stiva.

Something moved in the shadows behind him. Maren spun, and then froze, staring at the figure before him.

"Kind of you to accept the invitation, my prince." Cerrow stepped forward, cloaked in black robes.

Maren opened his mouth to scream, but Cerrow moved forward, pressing something against his mouth, and the world went black.

Stiva and Shira stood facing one another. Stiva, on the dais, was a step above her sister.

Shira stepped forward gracefully, curtsying before her sister. At her side, Taibon bowed deeply.

"Fair voyage," Stiva said. "I trust you'll send word regularly."

Shira nodded. There was much she could have said, but there was only silence in that moment.

The hall stood at attention as Taibon led his bride away.

In a tall, stone keep in the forests of Kralin, a woman lay on a birthing bed. Sweat glistened on her skin, plastering her hair to her face. She threw her head back and screamed.

A moment later, a tiny, weak scream echoed her own.

"A son," the midwife said.

Cassandra held her arms out.

"Lri Thynan," the mother whispered to the child's ear. "That is your name. You may not be allowed to carry it, but it is in your blood."

Maren tried repeatedly to free himself, but the shackles would not give. The stone altar was unforgiving beneath his limbs.

Selin don't cry, he told himself. The tears slipped out, regardless.

Something above him moved in the clouds.

And then another noise, closer, the crack of branches snapping underfoot. Maren's head snapped sideways. First one form, and then another, revealed themselves, separating from the shadows. When he recognized them, relief washed over him in waves.

It was his castemates.

They did not speak, did not greet him, but slipped silently to his side. The smallest of them—Perry, his name was—was the quickest at picking locks. He started worrying at the first one: a moment later, it snapped open, and Maren's right wrist was freed.

The sound of wings overhead made them look up. A black shape dove from the clouds, dancing around a pale sliver of a moon.

Calizar, the hunters' moon.

Steel flashed in the starlight.

"There's something out there," one of the boys hissed.

"Hurry!"

In the fields, laughter turned to screams.

The watchtowers blazed to life over the carnage.

The sound of hoofbeats in the night.

The whiz of arrows split the air.

"It's stuck!" Falor hissed. "I can't get this one."

Great wings blacked out the moonlight.

"What the hells was that?"

"Just hurry!" Maren hissed.

A new voice called from across the darkness. "Hey!"

The boys jumped. Derk let out a little shriek of surprise.

They turned as one to find Mehran striding across the clearing. "What the hell are you all doing?" he hissed. "I've heard of Selin pranks, but this, this is going way too far. Do you have any idea how dangerous this is?"

The boys fell silent.

Falor tried to speak. "Please, ma'am, we didn't—"

"Be quiet! Lyle is going to hear about this!"

Mehran strode up to the altar and started fussing with the broken lock. It took her a moment to pry it open. Maren rolled off the alter, pale and shaking. "Thank you, Mehran. They didn't—"

He never finished what he was going to say. Something dove down from the sky.

Steel flashed.

Blood on stone.

Black wings beat the air.

Mehran let out a sickening gurgle and crumpled forward onto the altar.

The Zhurlord rose again to the heavens, leaving the Reonih's bloody, mangled body below.

The boys backed away, trembling and pale. Then, almost as one, they turned and fled through the wood.

The halls of Aris lived that night; deep into the dark hours. Long past the time when most of the city's citizens should have taken to their beds, the great hall yet rang with music and laughter.

Stiva tore through torch-lit halls. Painted faces spun in laughter; she felt disoriented, drunken almost, as though knowledge had literally sent her reeling. It seemed the world was melting, the edges blurring together into a mad collage; couples pressed together into shadow, entwining, voices and sounds and scents and scenes fled into one another at a dizzying speed as she fled the shaded halls of the main castle for the smaller buildings that surrounded it.

Keorl and Timthe trailed her, slipping through the crowds like a ghost.

Darkness covered Aris like a blanket, thick and unmoving. Four moons were visible, each shedding dim beams of a different shade of pastel: Ayala, pink-orange; Vhoros, blue-green; Ahura pale yellow. Barely visible, Cindhur, a trapped satellite of some unreflective material, emanated only a faintly reddish darkness. Below the painted beams, the sleeping city wore a hazy gold aura, caused by the reflection of torches and lanterns upon the stone. Windows glittered like tiny golden stars, beacons of warmth and safety against the blackness of sky and ocean, a thousand shining points of light which represented people's homes, represented families, the names and faces and souls of Aris.

Stiva returned to her chambers to find the entire Grey Bull, and several of the Black Boot at the door. She paused, frowning. "What is this?"

Jarvor looked at her, his face grim. "You may not want to go in yet, *saya*."

"Why? What is it?" Stiva pushed past him, only to stop short at the door.

There was a dead man in her parlor. There was no mystery to how he had died: blood stained the marble and quarkstone floor, pooling in a sticky mess that had already congealed.

Stiva went white. Behind her, Twyla gasped, and her hand flew to her mouth.

Jarvor nodded his head towards Delis. "Delis and Dallan were guarding your door. Lhin growled, or we never would have heard him."

"Where's Chandris? Have his rooms been searched?"

Dallan nodded. "We've sent word to the Gold Braid."

Stiva started forward. "I have to get my—"

She took a few steps and stopped short again.

A white shape lay near the fire, unmoving, his coat stained with blood.

Lhin.

Lhin, whom she had raised from a kitten, when he was nothing but a spoiled bundle of white fur and tiny claws that fit into her lap. Lhin, who had borne her—literally—from childhood into sovereignty, who had been her comfort in Chandris' absence and when Trin died. Lhin, who had never wanted anything but the occasional fish and the chance to stretch out in the sun while she scratched his stomach. Lhin, who had never, would never, could never plot or whisper or spin lies behind her back, who ate her furniture sometimes and unraveled her tapestries, kept her awake at night with his snores, was gone.

It was the last straw. She knew she was breaking. She felt emotion rise in her, a combined maelstrom of fury, pain, and rage, so strong that it felt her flesh could not contain it. She felt herself begin to tremble violently, as she backed away from the body of the only living being who had never betrayed her, never left her.

She felt madness breathing over her shoulder, willing her to break down into hysterics, to rant and rave and tear out her hair, until they locked her in a tower somewhere and spoke her name with sadly shaken heads.

Voices echoed down the hallway, carrying into her suite.

Honor. Courage. Serenity.

Khirin slipped back into the tunnels, the smell of blood heavy in his nostrils, salty and sweet, life and death. He moved quickly, tucking the black mask into his boots. Though he was unaware of this, he crossed Cerrow's footsteps.

He emerged in a closet down the hall from Stiva's room, joining the crowd outside Stiva's door as his men carried Rueth's stiffening corpse away.

Far out in the harbor, the lights of the *Shira Belle* slipped into darkness and vanished from view.

In a nearby suite, Marcelle lit a Jaran lamp. Reddish light spilled over fine blankets. Pools of shadow and light gathered in the carved thi-wood bed.

Color and light spilled into the room as she turned.

Aret lay on her bed, reclining against silken pillows, his head propped up on one arm. He watched appreciatively as Marcelle disrobed slowly, and then crawled atop him.

"Put a son in me," she whispered. "A son with the blood of kings."

Stiva stood on her balcony, her vision eclipsed with black wings. The butterfly ring on her hand caught the last light of Calizar, the hunters' moon, and reflected it back out to sea.

A pulse of vivid rainbow color flashed in the waters of the Oburion, marking the strike of a lightfish hunting in the depths. Other than that, nothing stirred.

Stiva shut her eyes, listening to the silence.

Something shivered in the night, unseen. Something made her freeze, of a sudden. Something made her look up into the silence of the sky.

Within that quiet, she heard again the flutter of large wings.

Stiva stiffened, her breath caught in her chest. Heart pounding, she turned and searched the night sky, staring into the darkness, her eyes fighting to distinguish form in the shadows. Nothing moved. Nothing stirred, but the fright refused to diminish more than a fraction.

The weight of Lhin's death hung over her heart, a leaden blanket of sorrow.

A shadow swept down soundlessly across the night sky, bearing down on her out of nowhere, so fast she only saw it coming out of the corner of her eye. The Zhur was impossibly fast. One moment the sky was empty. In the next, her sight was filled with black wings and steel, and a frighteningly cold human face. Instinctively—foolishly—she threw her arm up in front of her face, hiding her eyes, as though that could protect her.

A hiss. A shadow. A whisper. A voice from a realm beyond death called her name, then spoke to her in a language that seemed somehow as though she should understand it; words without meaning pierced her brain.

Stiva stared at the sky, shaking uncontrollably. Frustration bubbled up in the place of the dead, emotionless state she had known that day, frustration that brought tears to her eyes and drew her fingers into fists. It was enough; she had been haunted by him for years, and her sanity was wearing thin.

Her shout, her rage, filled the silence of the night. *"What do you want?"*

The figure descended from the sky, until it stood just steps away from her.

It had Mehran's face.

Stiva's blood ran cold at that. She stumbled backwards, knocking a vase off a pedestal.

The thing moved forward. She remembered, then, the weight in her pocket, the weapon Mohr had given her.

She had seen the images in his box, but some of her grip was instinctive. She lifted it, and saw a tiny green light spark to life. The device fit easily into the palm of her hand. There was a button where her index finger fit. She pushed this, partly by instinct, partly out of curiosity. Lightning shot out of her hand, cutting the night.

She hit the Zhurlord in the chest. It broke apart, disintegrating into a hundred ravens. The birds took to the sky, a moving swarm of darkness that flew into the moon on gossamer black wings, and then slid, once more, into one form.

Along the hillsides, the watchtowers flared into light. The fires were red.

Aris was under attack.

Far below, in the city, Twyla and Ket were among the revelers of a night fair. Bonfires and lanterns hung like stars in the night, and the sound of music and laughter carried over smoky air. They were masked, and thus freed, to hold hands, to dance, to steal kisses on a stone bridge, beside Mirror Pond, in a square filled with fire dancers.

"Twyla," Ket said. "Next year, I want to dance the fire with you."

Twyla paled. "Chandris will never allow it."

"I think we can bend him," Ket said. "He's built an army on my design. He owes me a favor, I would think."

Twyla threw her arms around him.

Ket's next words were miscarried.

Came a distant rumble, like a faint thunder, but the sky was clear and cloudless. No, this was a different noise, multi-toned. Like the sound of the ocean crashing against a rocky shore.

Or the sound of many voices raised in anger.

Disturbance fluttered through the soukh. People fell silent, listening. The very sound of the market changed, dropping to a low, intense buzz. Others noticed it and looked around uneasily, searching the source of the sudden tension. The noise became identifiable. It was the sound of voices, twisting into a single angry chant.

A figure passed them at a run. Then another, and another. Nervous tension shifted through the crowd. The chanting grew louder, and chased all the other sounds away.

"What's happening?" Twyla asked, as if they could read it in the air.

Ket caught the arm of a random person running past. "What's going on?"

The runner, a thin man whose mask was pushed back over his hair, turned to Ket with wide eyes.

He pointed. "The towers are lit," he said. "There's been an attack."

The sound of hoofbeats preceded the arrival of the city guard. "Return to your homes!" They shouted.

Chaos followed the guards. First one angry voice cut through the air, and then another. Someone screamed. They watched in horror as one of the city guards toppled from his cat suddenly, a dagger embedded in his chest. All of a sudden the crowds were moving, roiling like a turbulent sea, shoppers and merchants alike forming a stampede that was as unstoppable as a tide.

They both saw the watchtower light up. "We have to get back," Twyla said nervously. Fear tinted her voice. "Lyle will close the Zhrue the moment he hears of any discord."

Ket nodded grimly. "Come on. We have to go through the market."

The crowds pressed close, shoving and jostling as thousands suddenly sought to flee the market. The entrances jammed quickly as a horde of people all rushed at once for the exits. Tables were upended, their contents spilled onto the ground. Booths collapsed and racks and shelves of wares were overturned in the chaos. Above the crash of glass breaking and cases being overturned, angry merchants added their shouting to the madness.

Behind them, the sounds of trouble grew louder; the air rang with violence. Over the rising clamor of tumult, one could hear the sound of blows being struck, of glass shattering, and people screaming.

The sounds of violence.

The sounds of their world falling apart.

Outside the market square, things were somewhat calmer. The streets were emptying rapidly. Shops and liveries were closing, and many had shuttered their windows.

She looked back at the soukh. "I wonder what started—"

Outside the castle walls, blue lightning split the sky.

In the city, revelers stopped what they were doing, turning to stare at the display of light at the castle. The crowd gasped as one, and then screamed and ran for cover.

"Relics!"

"They're using the Relics! The Zhur are attacking!"

Black wings dove from the sky.

There was no time or need for words then. The streets erupted into chaos. They ran, racing through twisted narrow alleys barely wide enough to let them pass, and fleeing towards the fragile safety the castle offered. They ran, as the city erupted into violence behind them.

She stopped mid-sentence, interrupted by the peal of a bell as the castle itself added its own voice to the madness. Her eyes widened; Ket's narrowed.

They both recognized that bell, and what it meant.

Selin, called to arms.

When they were some distance up the hill the castle sat on, they turned and looked back at the madness they had left behind. Ket surveyed the scene below with a grim expression.

"Come on," he told Twyla, as he turned away from the view. "She will be looking for you both. And Chandris will be looking for me."

Behind them, the crackle of flames filled the air with smoke. Heralds ran through the streets, ordering everyone to return home.

On the dark, silvery sea, another young queen too, stood watching the night. She stared into the waves, where dark shapes slipped through the waters beneath the ship that bore her name, occasionally turning pale faces to her.

Deep in the forests, beyond the thornwall, the man once known as Cerrow stepped outside, leaving the warm glow of firelight behind in favor of the cold night air. He walked for some distance, yet he had no sooner reached the stone circle than he heard the flutter of wings above him.

The Zhur floated gracefully to earth, cloaked in shadow.

Cerrow stared at the being before him, watching its face shifting in the moonlight. He moved forward cautiously, putting something down on the ground. "For you," he said, by way of greeting.

Dark wings rose, blotting out the moonlight. "We don't want such trinkets," he said. "Our kind have no need for such things."

"My gift was acceptable?"

The Zhurlord said nothing. Its face shifted again in the moonlight.

"You know what is coming," Cerrow said. "They've broken the treaty."

"Yes." The Zhurlord's voice was velvet and shadow. "We knew they would. Kings never keep their treaties, beyond a generation or two. I'm surprised it lasted this long."

"Fear," Cerrow said, "has a great effect on people. Once, my people were terrified of the ghosts and gods this world holds sacred. Now they are more cynical, more arrogant."

"Humans have always been arrogant." The creature's face shifted in the moonlight. "And do they know the power such things hold? Do they understand that these things not only heal the sick and allow the poor to live in comfort, but will poison the earth and the water? There is a price to pay for such magics, and we will not stand to see this world drained as others have been. We will destroy every single human being on this world before we allow such atrocities."

"Our treaty," Cerrow said, "Stands valid. We are prepared to stand against them with whatever it takes to hold these lands."

"Power," said the Zhur, "is poison. We will allow retaliation, but if you think to hold these things yourself, then you will meet the same fate as your ancestors."

There was a moment of silence.

"When you hunt," Cerrow said, "when you take your fill of human blood and souls … does it sustain you? Pleasure you?"

"It is our nature," the Zhur said. "Emotions are not involved. You will see for yourself, one day."

Cerrow looked up at the sky. "I am not ready yet," he said. "My work here is not done."

"There are others," it said. "Time does not constrain us."

"How many are you?" Cerrow asked.

"We are many. We are one."

"And the others?"

"They are waiting. They will wait." The Zhurlord's face shifted as it spoke, changing from youth to age. "Future and past are the same to us. Time has no control over us. But there are things we read in the clouds, in blood and fire. Moments we are drawn to. Like you, we know how to listen when we must."

Cerrow bowed deeply.

With a flash of steel and starlight the Zhur retreated to the skies. Silken words fell from his lips, to land in the renegade's ears. "Protect the boy. Beware the king's greed. And do not think yourself above our justice."

The dark form was gone. Cerrow looked up at the sky, and wondered if he ever remembered that his name—one of them, at least—had once been Trin.

⸻

Dawn came slowly to Aris.

The streets were quiet, though not entirely empty: some of the revelers had passed out on sidewalks and in alleys. Reonih moved through the streets, checking for corpses. There were a few, but it turned out that most of the bodies lying prone in the street were merely drunk. Two businesses had burned, and their owners were picking through the smoldering remains.

Chandris found Stiva in the matriarch's garden, staring over the sea. Message ribbons filled her hands.

"Delora tried us again last night," Stiva said, without turning.

"Yes," Chandris said. "The archers obliterated them."

"You haven't posted the dictates yet."

"I'm doing away with the tradition of only posting laws on Lightfest. It's pointless."

She looked out over the sea. The amethyst waves were mirror calm. Barely a ripple broke their surfaces.

He paused, and then looked at her, the anger in his voice replaced by cool determination. "I'll be sending the army out within the season. We're marching on Delora. I've had enough of Itacha's games. I intend to take Delora. And I intend to hold it."

Stiva closed her eyes.

"After Delora," Chandris said, "Orlin. After Orlin, Trian. Kralin. Aursa is a pack of mad dogs, tearing one another apart. I intend to put a stop to it. These wars are bleeding us dry." He looked at her, and she saw the dream, burning gold and bright in his eyes. His voice softened somewhat. "Comes a time, Stiva, that everything must change, when warriors must live in peace, and peaceful men must go to war. You are right. We have known five bloody centuries of war. King against king, clan against clan, House against House. This land is sown with bones and blood and tears. I have seen enough of it. Five hundred years' worth of kings seeking to outdo one another, and never a higher power to balance their bloodlust. Fighting this one and that, shedding lives like tears. There must be one king, over everything. That is the only way Aursa will ever know peace."

Stiva looked her twin in the eye. "Peace," she said, "may not be a natural thing."

She turned and walked away. "I'm going hunting," she said.

Khirin trailed her, darkness in the sunshine. Chandris caught his arm.

"You received a message," he said. "Ignore it."

Khirin looked Chandris in the eye. The king's eyes were bloodshot, and he could smell the sweet stench of rupalier leaves on his breath.

"No *message*," he said, "is ever sent to just one person. I intercepted the other. I will *intercept* further ones as well."

Chandris narrowed his eyes. "Excellent," he said. "Dismissed, captain."

Khirin bowed and straightened. He watched Chandris walk away, and then turned to follow Stiva, his thoughts turning over themselves.

Below, one of the Reonih began to sing.

CHAPTER 27

Reide scowled as he walked. Several angry thoughts crossed his mind, but he could not easily voice any of them. His feet hurt, his stomach rumbled, his entire body shivered and shook. It would have taken him only a few moments to prepare himself for this journey, but he had been refused that tiny courtesy. Moreover, he could hardly protest the inconvenience. One did not whine to the Reonih First Bard about a blister or a certain, insistent longing for a fat chunk of yellow cheese and a flagon of chilled greenberry wine. Kira often did things without explaining herself, a habit which annoyed all of them on occasion.

Reide sourly noted, however, that Kira wore her thickest shoes. A leather sack hung at her side, beside a drinking horn. No, one did not question a First Bard, any more than they would a High Priest or a First Healer. One simply did as they said, without protest.

Kira chose an erratic route, no doubt to ensure that they would not be followed or tracked. They walked in circles and spirals, doubling back twice. Time dragged on.

One did not ask them to share their lunch, even if one's stomach was growling loudly.

Kira led them deeper and deeper into the forest, guiding them down an animal track that twisted and turned through the forest like a snake, threading though the rupaliers and shard trees and finally into the thickest wood. They came in time to a rocky ravine, where a cairn of stones marked a tomb.

Reide looked around, puzzled. "What is this place?"

Kira did not answer. Instead, she looked around and up at the sky, as though confirming that they were alone. Then, to Reide's shock and horror, she began dismantling the cairn.

Reide simply watched for a moment, speechless. This was blasphemy, to defile a place of the dead. Tombs were gates to Otherworlds. They were more than sacred. They were dangerous.

Kira, already red-faced, paused long enough to grunt up at Reide. "Are you going to help, or just stand there?"

Reide stared at the First Bard in shock. His tongue felt suddenly thick in his mouth, and he had the distinct feeling that Kira saw him as a lumbering oaf. After a moment, rather than try to find a sensible reply, he simply moved forward and help, despite his distaste for the chore.

The cairn, it turned out, was not a pile of stones, but a single layer of stones, blocking a wooden half door. Kira cleared the last of the stones away, and then opened the gate.

Blackness waited within.

Reide peered into gloom, noting the stone steps descending into a passage that was blacker than any night.

Kira straightened, brushing the dirt from her hands. "You did, I presume," she said casually, "mark the way."

The bard managed a whispered reply. "Aye."

"Good," Kira said curtly. She tossed something silver into the darkness, then reached inside it and pulled out a torch.

"I don't quite understand," Reide said nervously, "what I am doing here. What is this place? An initiation cavern? A godtree?"

"No." Kira's refused to answer the question. "Seriously, Reide. Do you even see any rogan trees? Come," she said, turning into the darkness. "This way."

The earth took her in without a hint of disturbance.

Reide had no choice but to follow.

There was darkness within. His eyes adjusted slowly, taking in the gleam of moisture collecting on damp stone, a smell of dirt and minerals and rust. They moved further into the passage. A light flared up ahead of him as Kira lit her torch, and Reide threw his hands up to shield his eyes, which had already grown accustomed to the darkness.

Kira turned to him, her eyes cold and fierce in the firelight. "Step where I step. Step *only* where I step."

Reide sighed and followed Kira into blackness.

The stone walls, damp as they were, were covered in markings. Some he recognized as the work of the Sijhani: curling, intricate depictions of vodriks and erlits, vaianths and mastodons, dragons and cats and other beasts. Recreations of hunts and celebrations. Images of the Elders, descending from the skies. These were hundreds of years old, these etchings. Long before the Elders had crossed the abyss, the Sijhani had carved their dreams and nightmares into the rock with intricate, breathtakingly beautiful designs wrought from charcoal and ochre.

But not all of the paintings had been done by Sijhani. Some were more recent, and more familiar. Aorhan runes, the work of the Reonih, decorated the top of the tunnel. He recognized immediately what they were.

Wards.

They walked for hours, moving deeper and deeper into the bowels of the earth. Kira navigated the veins of the cave confidently, taking her directions, Reide suspected, either from the runes on the walls or from memory. Reide walked uneasily, despising the stifling feeling of so much earth above him. Being underground felt like he was being stifled. The crushing weight of earth hovered just over his head, intensifying the sense that unseen eyes were watching him. They passed the blackened circles of fire pits, and the midden heaps of tribes whose very names had faded to dust. He felt as though he were treading unwelcome on sacred ground. Ghosts glared at his back, and shiny black insects scuttled out of his path, gods of this underworld realm.

This was the realm of the Zhur.

At once, the cave opened up before them. Reide stopped and stared around him in astonishment. They were in a vast cavern, by the shore of an underground lake. A small wooden rowboat sat on the rocky landing.

Kira stepped into the boat, then turned and looked at Reide expectantly. Reide got in behind him, eyeing the wood skeptically. "Is this thing going to hold?"

"It isn't far," came Kira's nonchalant reply.

"I can't swim."

"Learn," Kira told him flatly. "It isn't hard. Just kick and flap your arms and float."

The rock walls widened, stretching off into blackness. Reide could not tell how large the underground lake was, but the echoes gave him the impression that it wasn't tiny. The boat rocked gently as they crossed open water. Squinting, Reide tried to spot the other shore, but there was only murky shadow before him. Then the walls drew in again, and vague shapes became visible in the stone as the torch slowly illuminated the darkness as they approached land once more.

He made out steps, and then doors. Not roughly hewn stone, but smooth metal.

The boat landed gracefully at a makeshift dock. Kira, without comment or ceremony, stepped out of the boat, then turned and waited for Reide to follow suit. The boat rocked as he exited, and he ended up planting one foot solidly in the water. Kira raised an eyebrow at this, but made no comment. She turned, walked up to the door, opened it, and went inside.

Reide followed, trying to shake the feeling that he didn't belong here. The spaces below the earth were not for him, nor for his kind. He wasn't sure if he imagined the distant rumble, or the fact that it sounded like a roar.

Inside, Kira touched something on the wall. The room was suddenly filled with light, blinding white. Reide had to blink several times before he could see. When his eyes adjusted again, he found that he was in a vast room. Rows and rows of shelves stretched out into the distance before him. Everywhere the gleam of metal shone, dully reflecting the lights. This was not Aursan metal. This metal was like nothing he had seen. It was smoother, stronger, paler. The material was untouched by rust, seamlessly molded into various shapes, some plain, some complex. Their style and manner left no doubt as to what they were.

Relics.

Kira's voice echoed off the walls. "I am not long for this world. I have seen the white raven in my dream. I will be dead soon. You will be master bard of Aris after I am gone."

Reide looked at Kira, not even trying to disguise his chagrin. "Why me? I don't want that, Kira. I've never wanted that."

"It doesn't matter what you want. You can refuse, of course, but you won't. You're the best bard we have," Kira said flatly. "I will see only a few more seasons. My mind can hold no more secrets."

She looked at the floor then, at dust marked by recent feet. "The shrine at Gochoree has grown too vulnerable." Kira said. "We left enough there to fool some, but these things ... were brought here." She looked back at Reide, her eyes bright and piercing. "Do you know what they are?"

Reide was spellbound, but he knew, of a sudden, what they were. He managed a cracked whisper. "Relics," he croaked. "Weapons."

"Some," Kira nodded. "This, Reide, is Reonih history. And Elders' history. As you may have guessed already, we each have our own stores. But these are more than weapons. They are tools of science."

"I still don't—"

"There are codes in the ancient songs," Kira said. "Directions, if you will. Translations, to the language these books were written in."

Reide stared at Kira.

"There are songs that are not sung. There are songs that are only taught to a few in any generation." Kira's eyes locked onto his, intense and burning with the power that raged in him. "These things will see daylight before you die. I have a few more songs to teach you. The most enigmatic of them all."

A chill went down his spine. He knew, without asking, what the song entailed.

The use of the Relics.

Reide scanned the room's contents, and turned to Kira. "I never knew there were so many."

"Aris has no idea how many of these Relics the Reonih have." Kira nodded. "The tribes have all agreed this was best. The known places are not safe from Chandris. There are several other places like this, but this one, this shrine, is in our care now. You will, in time, pass the knowledge on to your successor." She looked Reide in the eye. "I charge you with the knowledge of this place. You must guard it with your very life."

"But the pact," Reide said. "We made a pact with the Zhur."

Kira's eyes were hard. "We did," she said. "It still stands. They will hunt again."

Reide absorbed this quietly. "But the new announcements ... do they not help?"

Kira looked him in the eye. "Stiva has made her choice. She will do what she can to mediate and support us, but ultimately she stands with

Chandris. We had hoped her support would stay him, but it seems she is even more worthless as a queen than she was as a princess. Send word through the bards. We are preparing for rebellion. Chandris cannot stay in power."

Somewhere in the forest, a baby with twisted hands cried. A Reonih sage picked it up and consoled it, unaware of the face watching from his hearth fire.

To be continued in:

THE BLOODGOLD QUEEN
The Aris Empire: Book II

ABOUT THE AUTHOR

Morgan Sylvia is a metalhead, an Aquarius, a coffee addict, an award-nominated horror and fantasy author, and a work in progress. A former obituarist, she is now a full-time freelance writer. Her publishing credits include three novels, four poetry collections, several novellas, and dozens of short stories. Her first novel, *Abode*, was recommended by the Library Journal, and her second poetry collection, *As The Seas Turn Red*, was nominated for an Elgin Award twice. She was one of the writers for Realm.fm's award-winning audio drama *Undertow: Blood Forest*, as well as its follow-up *Undertow: The Pulse*. Sylvia belongs to several writers' groups: the HWA, the SFWA, the New England Horror Writers, Horror Writers of Maine, and Tuesday Mayhem Society. Her most recent releases are a short story collection, *The Withering Hours: Dark Folk Horror* and an audio adaptation of her novella *Carrion Harvest*. Find her at morgansylvia.net

Bibliography

Novels
Abode
The Aris Empire, Book I: Dawn
The Aris Empire, Book II: The Bloodgold Queen (forthcoming)
The Aris Empire, Book III: The Zhur Lord (forthcoming)

Novellas
Carrion Harvest
The Art Of Devastation

Story Collections
The Withering Hours: Dark Folk Horror

Poetry Collections
As The Seas Turn Red
Hemlock And Hellfire

The Serpents Of Twilight
Whispers From The Apocalypse

Chapbooks
Nocturnes
Of Static And Nightmare

Audio Dramas
Undertow: Blood Forest (contributing writer)
Undertow: The Pulse (contributing writer)

Audio Adaptations
Abode
Agony Chamber
Carrion Harvest
Of Marrow And Abomination

Curious about other Crossroad Press books? Stop by our website:
http://crossroadpress.com
We offer quality writing
in digital, audio, and print formats.

Subscribe to our newsletter on the website homepage and receive a free
eBook.